# Caresco, Superman

André Couvreur

# Caresco, Superman
# or, A Voyage to Eucrasia

translated, annotated and introduced by
**Brian Stableford**

A Black Coat Press Book

Visit our website at www.blackcoatpress.com

ISBN 978-1-61227-254-2. First Printing. April 2014. Published by Black Coat Press, an imprint of Hollywood Comics.com, LLC, P.O. Box 17270, Encino, CA 91416.

# *Introduction*

*Caresco, surhomme, ou le voyage en Eucrasie: Conte humain* by André Couvreur (1865-1944), here translated as *Caresco, Superman; or, A Voyage to Eucrasia*, was originally published by Plon, Nourrit et Cie in 1904. It is a sequel to *Le Mal nécessaire* (1899)[1], and is a rare example of a boldly speculative sequel to a grimly naturalistic work, all the more exceptional because the author had previously published two naturalistic sequels to *Le Mal nécessaire* in *Les Mancenilles* [a noun improvised from the specific name of *Hippomane mancenilla*, a highly toxic shrub] (1900) and *La Source fatale* [The Fatal Source] (1901), which make up a trilogy collectively entitled *Les Dangers sociaux* [Social Dangers].

When he published *Caresco, surhomme*, Couvreur was interrupting a second naturalistic trilogy collectively entitled *La Famille* [The Family], which he had begun with *La Force du sang* [The Strength of the Blood] (1902) and *La Graine* [The Seed] (1903), and was due to complete with *La Fruit* [The Fruit] (1906). The last title is advertized in *Caresco, surhomme* as *en préparation* [forthcoming], but the belated publication date suggests that the author was struggling with it, and might have set out to write a utopian fantasy in the hope that a change might be as good as a rest.

As things turned out, the move established a signpost to things to come; Couvreur went on after publishing *Le Fruit* to produce many more works of satirical speculative fiction, most of them featuring a protagonist markedly akin to the superhuman version of Armand Caresco, in his ambition to take practical biology to new experimental extremes. When Couvreur eventually returned to naturalistic fiction, late in life, it was not to the earnest naturalistic didacticism of *Le Mal*

---

[1] translated as *The Necessary Evil*, Black Coat Press, ISBN 978-1-61227-253-5.

*nécessaire* and its immediate sequels, but to social comedy with a light satiric edge in "Hymen & Co." (1928).

*Caresco, surhomme* therefore represents a crucial watershed in the evolution of Couvreur's literary method, if not his deeply skeptical and ironic outlook on the problems of human biology and their potential solution or possible intensification. It is, in one sense, a straightforward extrapolation of the "moral" to which *Le Mal nécessaire* appears to point, emphasizing that kinship by concluding with a last line that is a virtual repetition of the last line of its predecessor. In its substance and narrative strategy, however, it is a very different book, and there is a sense in which it is not a sequel at all, in that the matters deliberately left unclarified by the refusal to provide the first novel with any kind of explanatory epilogue are also left without the slightest comment here. Apart from Caresco himself, there is no mention of any character featured in the earlier novel, and no explanation is offered for the fact that the nature of the erotic obsession that caused the surgeon so much trouble in *Le Mal nécessaire* has somehow been replaced by a very different but equally damning perverse obsession.

Although only five years separated the publication of *Le Mal nécessaire* from that of *Caresco, surhomme*, a good deal had happened in the interim, including the publication of several works whose ideative content and narrative methods probably had a considerable influence on the decision to write the further text, and on the form it took. The boom in medical fantasies to which the first novel had made a significant contribution had continued in some profusion, but one fictional surgeon who must surely have attracted Couvreur's special attention was the anti-hero of H. G. Wells' *The Island of Doctor Moreau*, which he had presumably not read in English when it first appeared in 1896 but must have come to his attention when an abridged version was serialized as *L'Île du docteur Moreau* in the *Mercure de France* in 1901.

Wells was by then beginning to have a considerable influence on a number of French writers, including Alfred Jarry, one of the forefathers of surrealism, who published *Le*

*Surmâle: Conte moderne* (tr. as *The Supermale*) in 1902. If Caresco can be seen as stepping into Dr. Moreau's shoes in developing godlike ambitions and a similarly symbolic role, he also takes aboard some of the surreally comedic aspects of Jarry's protagonist.

The inspiring possibilities in those two novels might seem a trifle at odds with the Naturalistic allegiance of Couvreur's early works, in that the *Mercure* was still firmly associated in 1901 with the Symbolist movement, and Jarry was very obviously in the vanguard of that movement. However, the dedication of *Caresco, surhomme* to Paul Adam, who made a deliberate attempt to synthesize Naturalism and Symbolism, which included taking aboard futuristic and utopian themes, proves that Couvreur was not the kind of Naturalist who defined himself in opposition to Symbolism; as a well-read man, he was undoubtedly familiar with contemporary works in the Decadent and Symbolist vein.

The content of *Caresco, surhomme* suggests that another novel that Couvreur probably read in the interim between the two Caresco novels was *Les Aventures du roi Pausole* (1901; tr. as *The Adventures of King Pausole*) by Pierre Louÿs, which carried forward an intense erotic sensibility initially put forward in the best-selling *Aphrodite* (1896), offering a sympathetic portrait of a libertine utopia. Although Couvreur reacts sarcastically against that notion of utopia in *Caresco, surhomme* he was obviously intrigued by it, and perhaps fascinated by it. Although less explicit than contemporary pornography, which was undergoing something of a boom (to which many Symbolist writers contributed pseudonymously), *Caresco, surhomme* nevertheless employs a license unseen in utopian fiction since Rabelais, and hitherto unknown in *roman scientifique*. In that respect, the novel might well have been influential, being rapidly followed by Maurice Renard's *Le docteur Lerne, sous-dieu* (1908)[2], which has some graphically

---

[2] translated as *Dr. Lerne, Sub-God*, Black Coat Press, ISBN 978-1-935558-15-6.

perverse sex-scenes, and Fernand Kolney's extravagant exploration of *L'Amour dans cinq mille ans* (undated but probably 1908)[3].

As well as translations of H. G. Wells, the press associated with the *Mercure de France* also published the first full translations of Friedrich Nietzsche's *Also Sprach Zarathustra*, as *Ainsi parla Zarathustra*, initially in 1898 and then in a revised version in 1903. Although the German original had been published in the 1880s, and excerpts had been published in French translation in 1892, it was until the two *Mercure* editions appeared that the book's extravagant advocacy of the *übermensch*—rendered into French, of course, as *surhomme*—began to excite fervent controversy. Although Nietzsche is not mentioned in the text of Couvreur's novel, the use of the term *surhomme* is clearly intended to refer to that controversy, and Caresco obviously considers himself to be an "overman," reproducing many of the features that Nietszche (albeit rather inconsistently) attributed to such hypothetical individuals.

The main thrust of Nietzsche's philosophy was the attempt to move beyond the traditional concepts of good and evil—which, according to him, defined good in a purely negative sense as the absence of evil—and to formulate a positive notion of good as creativity, so that his evolved "overmen" would be innovative artists committed to the improvement of life, having abandoned the infantile imagination of a posthumous paradise in which the evils of this world might receive recompense. Caresco is a different kind of Superman, with megalomaniac ambitions that a Nietszchean *übermensch* would have thought puerile, but his creation of Eucrasia is a deliberate extrapolation of the "ethics of the herd" that Nietzsche so despised, in which a supposed state of ideal happiness is achieved by the elimination of evils and the substitution of a more psychologically satisfying notion of posthumous recompense than the judgmental Christian model. The

---

[3] translated as *Love in Five Thousand Years*, Black Coat Press, ISBN 978-1-61227-155-2.

objections posed to that ideal by Couvreur's philosophical critic, Zéphirin Choumaque, are very different from Nietzsche's, but the playing field on which the contest takes place is very similar to the one marked out by Nietzsche, licensing the somewhat-unsympathetic adoption of one of his key terms.

Given the recent publication or translation of these various other works, *Caresco, surhomme* can be seen very much as a product of its time, taking up themes that were on the contemporary table of literary discussion in Paris—especially in the pages of the *Mercure de France*, one of the capital's principal literary magazines and the one that seemed most conspicuously to be in the forefront of literary evolution. In reacting against all of them, Couvreur can be seen as a conservative—as he certainly was, philosophically and politically—but in his adoption of a new literary method, he was arguably as *avant garde* as any of his contemporaries, and ahead of his time in certain significant respects.

Even in Paris, *Caresco, surhomme* must have seemed to many readers to be an exceedingly *risqué* text. Kolney was not the only author to follow in its wake by considering the question of erotic relationships in futuristic utopian settings, but the others waited for the more relaxed social atmosphere of the post-war decade, when Marcel Rouff produced *Voyage au monde à l'envers* (1920)[4] for the *Mercure* and Victor Margueritte wrote *Le Couple* [The Couple] (1924), and none of those successors is quite as shocking in the lubricity of its inventions, or anywhere near as flamboyantly scathing in its satirization, as *Caresco, surhomme*. Couvreur's novel is deliberately old-fashioned in its explicit citations as well as its choice of models, taking its ostensible philosophical stance from Seneca, its basic literary template from classic utopian fiction and its rhetorical method from Voltaire, but it is a thoroughly modern work in terms of its imagery and unashamed

---

[4] translated as *Journey to the Inverted World*, Black Coat Press, ISBN 978-1-61227-039-5.

melodrama, and in the flamboyant absurdist excess of its sym-bolic climax—which would surely have made Sigmund Freud laugh, had he ever had the opportunity to read it.

It is possible that the extent and manner of the novel's dealings with eroticism did not do much for Couvreur's repu-tation, and that its risqué nature is largely responsible for the fact that it is now an exceedingly rare text. It might be signifi-cant in that regard that although Couvreur, like Rouff and Margueritte, took advantage of the post-war relaxation to write two more erotically-charged texts in *L'Androgyne* (1922; tr. as "The Androgyne" in the first volume of *The Exploits of Pro-fessor Tornada*) and "Le Valseur phosphorescent" (1923; tr. as "The Phosphorescent Waltzer" in the second volume of *The Exploits of Professor Tornada*), all his subsequent works were subjected to a relatively rigorous self-censorship, answering to a much sterner sense of literary decency. At any rate, the fla-grant eroticism of *Caresco, surhomme* is a significant compo-nent of its ground-breaking originality, as well as going a long way to making its flawed utopia seem a great deal more attrac-tive than many earnestly uptight models.

Choumaque, the philosopher provided by the author as a viewpoint for the evaluation of the utopia cannot regard its erotic component as a mere distraction, and finds it very diffi-cult indeed to abstract himself from its temptations in order to maintain his conscientious Stoicism. It would be wrong to say any more at this point about the manner in which that intellec-tual contest develops, because it would function as a spoiler, but I will add a brief afterword to the text commenting on the nature and value of Choumaque's specific opposition to the Eucrasian utopia, and his own solution to the supposed prob-lem of "the necessity of evil."

It is possible that contemporary readers who had found the conclusion of *Le Mal nécessaire* direly uncomfortable might have found the conclusion of *Caresco, surhomme* more satisfactory, and it might well be that Couvreur orchestrated his conclusion with exactly that possibility in mind. The fact that the book is now exceedingly difficult to find, however, implies that if the move was an attempt to curry favor, it failed. The novel is, nevertheless, one of the evident classics of French *roman scientifique*, and one of the most interesting works of the brief boom in "scientific marvel fiction" assisted by the translation of H. G. Wells' works into French.

In spite of its more conventional story-arc, many readers might still find it a slightly discomfiting and rather irritating story, as well as a highly improbable one, but it is as well to remember, in this case as in the case of *Le Mal nécessaire*, that Couvreur was always far more interested in raising interesting questions than providing definitive answers, and was exceedingly well aware that cavalier sarcasm can be a very useful strategy, in philosophy and literature alike, when the intention is to prompt thought rather than close it down.

The present translation will be followed by three volumes collecting a sequence of stories written by Couvreur between 1910 and 1939, featuring an anti-hero who took over several of the projects initiated by Caresco, and eventually began to term himself "the Superman" when he acquired control of his own mini-utopia; the three volumes are collectively entitled *The Exploits of Professor Tornada*. Together with *The Necessary Evil*, and the present translation, the five volumes make up a very unusual and intriguing set, in the context of which *Caresco, Superman* becomes even more interesting and thought-provoking than it is in isolation.

This translation has been made from a photocopy of the Plon, Nourrit edition kindly made by Marc Madouraud from the copy in his collection. I am very grateful to him for his generosity in supplying it, and to Jean-Marc Lofficier for acting as intermediary in securing it.

Brian Stableford

# CARESCO, SUPERMAN
## or, A VOYAGE TO EUCRASIA

*Letter to Paul Adam*[5]

*This is a tale for the grown-up children that we all are, and if I have thought of dedicating it to you, it is because I would have liked you to write it. Accept it nevertheless as it is—which is to say, as a canvas that will lack the rare and sparkling ornamentation of your style, the magnifying fantasy of your imagery and the prodigious resources of your deductive mind: all qualities that would doubtless have transformed a modest philosophical story into a solid work of art.*

---

[5] Paul Adam (1862-1920) is nowadays best remembered for his historical novels set during the Napoleonic wars, but he was more celebrated in his own day for attempting to fuse the concerns and methods of the Naturalist and Symbolist Movement, which we often considered to be opposed. He only wrote one futuristic fantasy, the novella *Le Conte futur* (1893; tr. as "A Tale of the Future"), but he routinely introduced passages of utopian and futuristic speculation into his naturalistic works, and in his essays—notably the introduction to a collection by Fédéric Boutet published in 1903—he appealed for the development of a new literary school dedicated to examining the possible ways in which the evolution of science and technology might transform social life. (The introduction in question is translated in the Boutet collection *The Antisocial Man and Other Strange Stories*). *Caresco, surhomme* can be seen one response to that appeal.

Do not reproach me, however, for having risked this fable. I have the excuse of having amused myself in inventing it, even if my invention does not interest others. To take the principal character of Le Mal nécessaire, *the surgeon Caresco, from brutal modern reality, in order to transport him into a pure fiction, had the attraction for me that all dreams have, when one gives them wings and lets them take flight toward the infinity of hypotheses. Who among us has not demolished Society completely in order to construct another, marvelous one, endowed with all the attributes of happiness? Everyone, if he has not striven to do so, has certainly thought about thus employing the best choice of its philosophical elements, whether they are humanitarian, political or religious.*

*I have, therefore, attempted to edify an Eldorado on the foundations of Science, and more particularly the science of Life, putting science in the service of pleasure. After having undermined so much and built so much, it has not seemed to me that the new community ought to be better portioned, from the point of view of a definitive result, in the coin of Happiness, than the one in which we are agitating so painfully. Perhaps I will be criticized for arriving at that conclusion. I pray, however, those who will look further than the décor in which I have set my tale, will not cry paradox, and will not doubt my gratitude for the innovations and ameliorations due to human genius. No one has more respect for them than I do.*

*Although I put on trial existences that are too soft and felicities that are too easy, I concede that they are the indispensable salary of* Effort. *But it is also necessary that the beneficent Effort in question does not find itself canceled out by the results that follow in its wake, and our mores do tend to reduce it singularly. That is what I have tried to prove in this little parabolic tale. Forgive me, my dear Paul Adam, if I have not succeeded as well as you would have done.*

# CHAPTER I

The negro orchestra—they were all the rage in the great restaurants of Paris in 1950—was concluding the frenzied andante rhythm of the first act of *Yolulu*, a Chinese opera that was said to surpass the most beautiful French works, and which, in any case, manifested for alert minds the long-foreseen realization of the yellow peril. One of the musicians—the one who had been blowing an ophicleide with the greatest force—detached himself from the group of black contortionists and slipped between the tables to pick up the gold coins earned by the noise with which he had just stunned the customers.

He was a superb fellow, who might have been thought to be made of bronze. His primitive legs, clad in narrow bright red trousers and his orangutan back, espoused by his tight green waistcoat, excited the covetousness of all the bejeweled young female diners. What amused them the most, however, was his skill in catching the coins that they threw in his mouth. He collected them with such a flash of his white teeth that the generosity of the women, spurred by a competitive ostentation, went beyond measure. Fifty louis were engulfed in that natural alms-box.

At one of the tables at the back, two men indifferent to the banal spectacle were smoking and chatting. One of them, the older, looked slight out of place in the elegant milieu. Dressed, as was his companion, in a heliotrope suit with a square-cut shirt-front, according to the latest fashion, he appeared to be about fifty years of age, of medium height, with a protruding abdomen and massive short and slightly twisted legs. His face, lustrous with acne, was hidden behind a bushy gray beard, so abundant that the luminosity of his large nose was scarcely visible, while a bald spot, encircled by a crown of hair that was still black, seemed astonishing, like a desert succeeding the vegetation of a fecund plain. In spite of that hirsute appearance, however, one immediately experienced a sympathy for his physiognomy, simultaneously wild and humorous, his rubicund complexion, the delicacy of his cloudy and weary blue eyes and the more accentuated brown bushiness of his eyebrows.

The other diner contrasted with him by virtue of the powerful and harmonious beauty of his twenty-eight years and the distinction of his bearing. Although a temporary infirmity forced him to keep one of his arms in a sling, he revealed vigorous muscles, broad shoulders and a slim build. Nothing affirmed his grace and strength as much as the charming and energetic contours of his face, where one might have thought that the pale brown beard, vaporous over the lips, stiff and pointed at the chin, reflected its ardent color in the delicate profile of the nose, the clear and lively expression of the green eyes and the abundance of his naturally curly hair, darker brown in color. Sometimes his gaze strove to pierce the blue spirals of the smoke, and then filled with a mirage particular to those whose heart is supporting the offense of a chagrin; immediately returning it to the door to the room, however, he kept watch on every entrance and exit. Such an evident preoccupation attracted the reproaches of his companion.

"Come on, my dear Marcel, will you give up looking outside now?"

"What if Hélène were to appear, though? Tell me, Choumaque, what should I do?"

Choumaque slid his hands toward his belt to hitch up his trousers, although they had no reason to fall. It was a tic that instinctively accompanied every anxiety of his thought. Then, chewing his almost-extinct cigar, which was yellowing his beard, he said: "My friend, I'm a Stoic philosopher, a disciple of the great Seneca. In addition, I have, as you know, created a doctrine of equilibria—and those combined principles permit me to face up to all the insults of life. Nevertheless, I can't bear much longer hearing you talk any longer about the woman who has caused you such great annoyance. I've already made a great many sacrifices.

"Let's recapitulate. When you were ten years old, and your parents Monsieur and Madame Girard, sugar wholesalers—now departed, alas—confided you to me, I was able, for a sum of three thousand francs a year, to master my irritation at having to correct the solecisms and barbarities pullulating in your exercise books. It was hard. However, I had the courage to guide you to the completion of your studies and enable you to triumph in examinations until you joined the navy.

"When, subsequently, as lieutenant of a vessel, you threw your resignation at the anarchist government's head and exchanged your naval saber for a boulevardier's swagger-stick, again I had the virtue—no less heroic, believe me—of striving to contain your passions, as the great Seneca did for his pupil, Nero. I accompanied you in the civil broadsides that you fired, and warned you against the parasites who were sinking their claws into your rich inheritance.

"Then came your love for Hélène, the noble whore with the innocent air, who cost you very dear, at the same time as she was deceiving you with all your friends except me. I was then teaching philosophy at a baccalaureate-factory with Père Frontispice, who flirted with his kitchen staff, had his way with them and then sacked them for immorality, changing them every fortnight.

"It was necessary for me to stand up to both of you, to throw myself into the whirlwind of parties, go with you to racecourses, listen to stupid plays every evening, sup champagne in late-night restaurants, stuff myself with Chinese music, run after you through bars and dens of vice, ingurgitate many fiery liqueurs in the company of pimps and prostitutes, and finally to occupy the banquette of the carriage that you took when you went home to bed, witnessing the preliminary manifestations of your tenderness.

"I never got to bed before three o'clock in the morning. I let go of my dear philosophers, Descartes, Spinoza, Leibniz, Kant, Spencer and Hegel. I moved on, and worse. I no longer knew the joy of rediscovering them, those precious friends, of disputing their ideas and proving to them—with my feet in slippers, slumped in an armchair by the fireside, my pipe in my mouth—that my doctrine of equilibria, influenced though it was by the stoicism of Seneca, my great ancestor, was a thousand times better than their theories for explaining the world.

"Oh, the exhaustion of the following days! My appearances before the dunces at school! My hours of teaching, spent struggling to find another drop of saliva on my arid palate! You'll never know how much I cursed the two of you, my lad! Hélène especially, the whore, who made a complete fool of you! In vain I strove to render her more faithful to you. In vain I swore, every time I discovered the thread of a new intrigue, to show you where it led, to separate you from her. But every time, too, a sentiment retained me, the dread of tearing the rag that then replaced your heart.

"Finally, when the happy moment arrived when the treachery of your mistress became too evident, when you caught her swooning in the arms of your best coachman; when, enraged by seeing you stopping the compensation for her…displacements, she tried to have you murdered by hired thugs—an attack whose effects still force you to wear your arm in a sling—I renounced my position as a schoolmaster, abandoned my dear Latin quarter, my dunces, my books of philosophy, and my games of chess in smoky taverns in front of foaming beer-tankards, in order to come and install myself at your bedside and look after you as a Sister of Charity would have done.

"That, I esteem, is the very weight of devotion. It required, in order for me to be capable of it, all the affection that I have for your twenty-eight years, and the irresistible sympathy I have for your delightful naivety…

"Well, I tell you this: if you mention one more time that Hélène, whom you'd have been wiser to have locked up—indeed, if I even read her memory one more time in your desolate eyes—I swear to you, as truly as my name is Zéphirin Choumaque, aged fifty, born in Périnchies in the département of the Nord, independent professor of philosophy, dry fruit of university courses and sworn enemy of the untranscendental University…as truly as I am all of that, I'll drop you where you stand, for I'm determined not to run around Paris any longer"—Choumaque pronounced it Pah-ris—"in order to enable you to fall back into the claws of that Hélène."

In spite of the violence of his speech, the philosopher, in concluding with an absurdity, had imprinted a contented smile on his bushy lips—which had not cheered up his pupil. On the contrary, the latter squeezed the philosopher's arm in a surge of despair. "Don't do that, Master. What would become of me without you? I'm suffering so much!"

"Don't complain about it, damn it! For only those who suffer know the value of happiness. Is not suffering the preparation for joy? Why, alas, aren't we able to suffer any more?"

Already, Choumaque was rounding out his gesture to support a scholarly argument with which his pupil was very familiar, when the latter stopped him and directed his attention to the entrance of an individual who had just sat down a few tables away and was asking for a menu urgently.

"Look! That's the man who was looking at us so insistently the other day."

The newcomer did not look seem very remarkable. Had it not been for the memory that the two conversationalists attached to his person, they might not have paid any attention to his exaggerated nose, the enormous cabochons that flashed on his shirt-front or the indefinable expression of antiquity emitted by his seemingly young silhouette. As he set about eating, with a hearty appetite, he took a small round box from his waistcoat pocket, reminiscent of the earpiece of a telephone, and put it to his large ear at intervals.

"Let's leave the flashy foreigner—doubtless some merchant enriched in the pork business—and rise up toward the heavens of the wings of ethics," Choumaque continued, spreading his arms again. "So, I was saying that we're no longer able to suffer, and that, in consequence, we're no longer able to enjoy ourselves. Life envelops us with such a succession of sensations, such a whirlwind of hastily-realized necessities, that the self no longer has the leisure to collect itself in order to desire then, or to appreciate their satisfaction.

"The result is that, in that overexcitement, we traverse the oases of existence at a run, and scarcely have time to palpitate at the falls we make into gulfs. *Nobis vivere non licet*…we no longer have time to live, says Seneca, who foresaw this state of affairs clearly, when he treated the brevity of life—and yet, in his epoch, people were still able to breathe.

"Nowadays, science, whose benefits are acclaimed, the comforts with which it helps us, the genius with which it suppresses our difficulties, no longer leaves us the possibility of drawing breath and savoring things. An example: we go into a dark place; immediately, we flick a switch, the electric light comes on. From then on, what can darkness matter to us? Can we appreciate the *fiat lux*, when it is so easy to procure light? In Seneca's time, it was necessary to strike a flint, and the first spark delighted the heart as well as the eyes.

"Well, that simple example might stand for everything that is desirable. In our day, a woman's caprice leads to a furnished hotel in ten minutes. Good restaurants are crowded, and no longer have any unknown tastes. Electric trains and balloons allow the healthy fatigue of traveling on foot to remain unknown. Doctors anesthetize suffering. Frantic publicity opposes our meditation. It's a perpetual tension of our nerves, at the end of which society is exacerbated, to fall into senility.

"I'm not speaking for myself, a sage who knows better than to consume my life in the delirium of passions or a series of frivolous occupations. But take this place where we're easting now, this environment of yours. Look at that depraved woman, lit up by the thighs of the negro into whose mouth she's throwing gold coins. Tomorrow, she'll offer herself to that musculature, in between two social visits. A brief epilepsy, if she experiences any. What will she get out of it, in regard to happiness?

"Observe, next, the haste with which that gross socialist orator, fresh from preaching and talking about fraternity, the love of the poor and disdain for the rich, is devouring his food, slobbering over his collar. He ought to dwell upon those enjoyments stolen from the rich, which his lies have earned him, but he hardly has time to moisten his lips!

"It's a whirlwind, I tell you—a whirlwind in which the individual is lifted up, spun and then hurled to the ground, bewildered, uncomprehending, unknowing, unfeeling, only to be carried off again. What's the result? It's that mad gyration, man falling victim to man. Scarcely has a discovery been made, scarcely has a fashion caught on, than others surge forth, more ingenious and more tormented than the last, to which it's necessary to submit. It's a perpetual motion, which leaves no respite, retreat or pardon. Everything creaks, grinds and seethes—and in wanting to engage with it, people exhaust themselves. They work themselves to death in order to submit to the slavery of incessant sensuality, to run after the lure of a happiness they can't grasp. They have to pay dearly for this life of steam and electricity. Women impose skimpy sensualities upon them, leadenly. The palate can't taste that which is too rapidly swallowed. Anesthetized nerves end up no longer being able to vibrate. Publicity vulgarizes marvels.

"We swim in wellbeing, commodities, pleasures—but alas, we aren't aware of them, and are no longer able to appreciate them."

"Where are you going with this, Master?"

"To tell you this: that it's necessary to give thanks to the god of torments who is breaking your heart. You'll have the chance to suffer and to sense the price of deliverance, while you're cured of your love for Hélène. What bliss it will be to disdain her then! She's done you a favor, the whore who had you stabbed!

"Thus, every dolor has its compensation in benefits. I know, it's true, that in the final analysis, as my doctrine of equilibria determines that you won't get a bigger share than a road-sweeper, and that in the hour of your death, the same proportionality of joys and dolors will level out your passage through this base world as for anyone else—but what does it matter? You'll have lived more intensely than the road-sweeper and all the people who surround us, for you'll have appreciated better than them the rewards than beneficent suffering yields!"

"A glass of liqueur, Master? Another cigar?"

The Stoic, after a gesture of supreme indifference, nevertheless accepted the alcohol and the tobacco. The avidity with which he savored them, and the contentment resplendent in his mischievous blue eyes, testified that his rigor could not stand up to proof, for the moment.

They were about to leave. Marcel was already tapping the rim of his plate to request the bill when a movement by the diner they had noticed before stopped them, astonishing them. The individual in question got up and casually came to sit down at their table, after having picked up his plate. Then, while continuing eating, he said, in a distinct German accent: "I overheard your conversation, Messieurs. It amused me greatly."

"You overheard?"

"Yes, thanks to the microphone I carry with me." He showed them the little round box similar to the earpiece of a telephone, with he replaced in his waistcoat pocket. Then, absorbing the contents of a large glass of champagne, into which his curved nose plunged, he went on: "If I've understood correctly, Monsieur Girard is suffering from lovesickness and has lost his appetite for life, while Monsieur Choumaque is complaining that the world is no longer able to appreciate felicity accurately. Is that correct?"

"That is, indeed, correct."

"Well then, I simply propose that Monsieur Girard come to live in a marvelous country where he will forget his suffering, and in which every citizen enjoys a complete eternal and supreme happiness. But first, permit me to introduce myself, for I imagine that what I'm doing might seem unusual to you."

He rummaged in a pocket in which gold coins linked, and pulled a card out of a wad of banknotes, which he held out. The two friends read:

## ZADOCHBACH
*Chief Representative of Caresco*
*Juvisy          Eucrasia*

Choumaque and Marcel could not tear their surprise-dilated eyes away from the card.

Armand Caresco! What a formidable name! Thirty years ago, that surgeon, the master of a world—of *the* world—had retired to the new land that had emerged from the sea following a cataclysm, and had built a new humankind!

There was no story more improbable, no fairy tale more extraordinary than the adventurous existence of that man, once a bandit of the scalpel, who had made a colossal fortune with the point of his blade, which his business acumen had increased even further, and had suddenly become—no one knew by virtue of what remorse of conscience or generous folly—a benevolent philanthropist, a kind of merciful creator, having understood all the miseries and dolors of life, and wanting to spare a chosen people therefrom.

In truth, very little was known about the new realm and its protagonist. The day when the legendary surgeon had quit France thirty years before, followed by the desperate regrets of some and the ferocious hatred of others, a press campaign had aroused the anxiety of nations regarding that new autocrat who was so easily taking possession of a country already coveted by all.

It was no more than a morsel of lava, with no apparent possibility of cultivation and no incentive for immediate colonization, but it was as large as Scotland, commanding the Atlantic, and England had already planted her flag there. A little gunfire and dynamite would, therefore, have sufficed to reduce the philanthropic usurper to impotence and reckon with him, had Caresco not taken a precaution before his disappearance that immediately assured him of the respect of civilized peoples.

Convening, in England itself, a committee of scientists and military men of all nations, he had, before their very eyes, devastated and ravaged an entire region ten kilometers square, killing everyone. Should one not leave in peace the inventor of an explosive that, simultaneously with its blast, expanded a profusion of deleterious gases sufficient to poison an entire population?

A single experiment had sufficed to convince governments, although Caresco had offered them a second, so scornful was he of the work of destruction. As a possessor of such force, he held war and peace in the palm of his hand; it would have been possible for him to install himself as he pleased on the old thrones of kings or the young armchairs of republican presidents and enslave the world. He preferred his morsel of lava, that absolutely new platform, sterilized by fire, where he could build his empire in accordance with his will.

Since then, diplomats had decided to ignore him, and he, leaving the nations to continue their paltry conflicts, had contented himself with reigning over his rock, enigmatic, redoubtable and formidable, the only master, the only god. And when, one day, a secret emissary of the British Foreign Office had come to poison him, it was that emissary who swallowed the toxic dose. Some time afterwards, moreover, a bomb had annihilated an entire district of London in a terrible fashion, and as it had been recognized as a device similar to the one employed in Caresco's experiments, Albion remained tranquil thereafter, enclosed in her wounded vanity.

Since then, an airplane had arrived every month at Juvisy, in the vicinity of Paris, where an immense hangar encircled by walls had been reserved for it. It always arrived by night and departed the same way. Nothing was seen of its phantom but the two luminous disks of its beacon lights, like the eyes of a gigantic bird. Neither its gilded wings nor the red color of its fuel tank, dotted with golden vibrions,[6] was visible.

---

[6] The term vibrion is nowadays attributed, even by dictionaries that admit its obsolescence, to bacteria, but at the beginning of the twentieth century it was a common euphemism for a sperm-cell, as viewed through a microscope. That is its mean-

For some time, it was thought to be the whim of a hobbyist aeronaut or a scientist's experiment.

From its initial voyages on, the airplane collected and returned the engineers, workmen, artists and inventors who collaborated in the edification of the new empire: an entire host of laborers who departed poor and came back enriched by the money earned in that mysterious toil. The police and reporters interrogated them, but they did not reply, terrorized as they were by a threat made before their return.

Then, when the Customs, the General Company of Aerial Transport, and various State administrations, ever ready to complicate international trade, learned that goods were being stored, that travelers were being displaced and that there were no papers regulating these transactions, they had become excited and cried fraud, but the scandal they had attempted to kick up was suddenly aborted when the name of Caresco was pronounced. A decree from the French Head of State legitimized the illegalities, and the airplane was able to continue its embarkations in complete tranquility.

The agency at Juvisy, although everything was still invisible, became a center of attention. Innumerable supplications were deposited in the letter-box of the only door opening into the warehouses. They solicited Caresco's favor; they expressed the desire to seek refuge on his island. All the madmen, all the desperate individuals and all the adventurers in the world placed their petitions therein, and never received any reply. Sometimes, however, when the applicants were young and handsome, or capable by virtue of their knowledge or their genius of assisting the impetus of the new fatherland, after discreet enquiries had been made, they disappeared. Their families mourned them in vain; no material trace was ever found of their bodies, nor of their fortunes, if they were wealthy.

---

ing throughout the present work, although ovules are occasionally gathered under the same heading.

That was all that was known for sure about Caresco and his realm. Everything else that was said: the legend of the curious social organization built in his name; the marvels that the most powerful telescopes scarcely allowed to be discerned from far out at sea—for the potentate had forbidden any approach to his island for forty leagues around—was only rumor, sensational false news put out in order to raise the circulation of one-centime newspapers or to interest the readers of papers distributed gratuitously, which had become the custom of almost all dailies half way through the twentieth century.

So, Marcel Girard and Zéphirin Choumaque were equally ignorant of the land of ideal pretention of which Zadochbach's card had so abruptly evoked the suggestion.

The latter did not seem to be rejoining in the effect that he had just produced, and continued eating.

"Yes, Monsieur Girard, if you consent, I shall take you to Eucrasia. My master's genius has edified society there in such a way that happiness is absolute, whatever Monsieur Choumaque might say in denying the possibility; and other amours—and what amours, Messieurs!—will soon have banished the memory of the beautiful Hélène."

"Oh, Master, Master, not to suffer any longer!" said Marcel, suddenly possessed by that mirage.

"It would be the most unfortunate thing that could happen to you, my friend!"

"Stupid!" muttered Zadochbach, addressing himself to Choumaque—and then, more insistently, to Marcel: "Not to suffer any longer! To forget! To enjoy, perpetually and uniformly. Say the word..."

"What do you think, Master? Will you go with me? You know what a lamentable state my heart is in! Hélène, after all her treasons, would like to get me back, and I'll succumb again, I know it! Think about the mire she's dragged me through! Think about what she might drag me through yet! Departure, forgetfulness, is the cure!" Marcel, hypnotized by the hope, was carried away.

But at the condition imposed by the young man, desirous of bringing his friend, the Representative frowned.

"Choumaque, coming with you? Pooh! What do you expect us to do with that old windbag in Eucrasia? Anyway, I'll have to refer the matter to Caresco. Send me a written request at Juvisy, and we'll see. Perhaps you'll receive instructions..."

"You'll accept, Master?" the pupil insisted. "I beg you, don't abandon me—accept!"

"I'm a Stoic. I'm stoical enough to consent not to suffer any longer, if that's possible, although it's inconceivable. And then, to see Eucrasia...that's truly tempting..."

"It would be necessary," Zadochbach observed, "for you to abandon your entire fortune."

"A sage can lose everything without suffering any damage, because all the wealth he has is internal," said Choumaque sententiously. Then he added: "It's true that I have nothing to lose, having no luggage but my wardrobe...and even that is in dire need of renewal."

The Representative had finished eating. They stood up in order to put on their overcoats—but while their backs were turned, Zadochbach disappeared, forgetting to pay for his meal, for which Marcel scrupulously settled the bill.

# CHAPTER II

A magisterial flap of wings lifted the airplane toward the superior spheres. Now they were soaring through the azure, so high, so distant from the world, so far beyond terrestrial phenomena that, looking over the bulwark, from which it was still visible, the little Haitian continent seemed a derisory patch in the uniformly green expanse of the Atlantic. Soon it was not even that; the balloon entered into the most intimate communion with space.

Everything expanded in the infinitely calm purity, in the splendidly blue serenity of celestial space; there would have been an enormous silence if the muted rhythm of the propellers and the maneuvers of the crew, obedient to the shrill voice of an invisible captain, had not disturbed the gravity of the voyage.

"Damn! The cold's beginning to bite, don't you think, Choumaque?"

"Indeed, the sun is no longer having much effect. I feel as if needles were digging into my flesh."

"Let's go back to your cabin, Master. It's warm there..."

"No, my boy, I experience some pleasure in suffering, Besides which, this spectacle is truly too new, and that immensity gives us, for once, too exact a notion of the infinitesimality of our human being, if I might put it thus, for me not to prefer to let myself be stabbed by the temperature for a few more minutes. Tighten your overcoat, and let's stay."

And Choumaque, leaning his elbow on the sandalwood rail, allowed the interrogation of his fatigued gaze to flee into the void.

As for Marcel, he raised his head boldly, gazing at the enormous ovoid fabric that contained the ascensional gas. It was painted red and dotted with little golden vibrions—the color and the symbolic insignia of the realm for which they were heading: spermatozoids and ovules, against a back-

28

ground of blood. In addition, the carapace was enveloped by a network of aluminum wires, almost invisible, joining together at their lower extremity and then separating again to attach to the nacelle.

The latter, in the same elongated form adopted by the balloon, was as big as a settlement, three hundred meters long and fifty broad. Its bow and stern were ornamented with the same sculptural image: a naked woman extending her arms to support two searchlights, which set the immensity ablaze on dark nights, and competed with the light of the stars on clear ones.

The metallic hull was divided into two parts. One, more modest although still luxurious, was reserved for the crew, the engines and the cargo; the other, more sumptuous, offered an extraordinary comfort to the passengers: profound alcoves; a library full of rare books; a theater in which the best orchestras gave concerts; steam baths; richly served tables; and enigmatically closed boudoirs decorated with magnificent fabrics, in which lovely courtesans lying on soft divans awaited the pleasure of the male and female passengers. Refined satisfactions of the senses, intellectual pleasures, intoxications of impressions—all were united there, within those light metal walls; everything offered an exquisite augury of the land of Eucrasia toward which the airplane was headed, and to which it belonged.

At that moment, however, Marcel was scarcely thinking about such things, or of the three days of travel that he had just undertaken without savoring them, absorbed as he was by his amorous memories, His curiosity would have lingered all the more willingly in the study of the invisible machinery of the engine-room, access to which was strictly forbidden to strangers.

He admired the power of the two immense gilded wings attached to the sides of the nacelle, reflecting in their movements the enigmatic force that animated them. Collecting the harsh rays of sunlight, which subsequently spread out in the atmosphere, they fluttered like the wing-feathers of a gigantic

29

bird, rising and falling in aerial strides, or where sometimes content to deploy, without apparent effort, to follow the fluid stream that bore them along.

Beneath the shiny mahogany deck, the dull rhythm of the engines was audible, the beat of the mechanical heart that powered the wings. To maneuver, the slim, handsome crewmen whose muscles bulged harmoniously went back and forth, almost naked, obedient to the orders of a reedy voice emitted by an unseen individual. One of them, a gracious youth as pretty as a girl, provoked the laughter of his comrades by performing a masterly somersault.

Marcel gazed at all that admiringly He thought about the genius that had so marvelously perfected the aerial locomotion, and who, down below, reigned as master in the Isle of the Blessed. At the idea that he was about to get close to him, perhaps to see him, he felt a grave emotion, further increased by the legend that the journalists of the entire world had surrounded the extraordinary man for so many years, and by the mysterious contract that he had made with the potentate through the intermediary of Zadochbach.

The engagement they had made to become his subjects and separate themselves irrevocably from the rest of the world had seemed so strange that he had not been able to believe it until the last moment. Their preparations, the liquidation of their fortunes that had been demanded of them by the Representative, and the farewells to their friends, had been accomplished as so many implausible actions of suggestion. It was not until they found themselves at the appointed rendezvous at Juvisy that they had remarked the avidity with which Zadochbach had taken possession of their money, and the disdain with which he had rejected their luggage—Marcel's weapons and trinkets, Choumaque's books and pipes. It had been necessary, finally, for them to see the hangar and board the airplane to convince themselves that they were not obedient to a fiction.

Then, the departure had taken place, in a mysterious and magnificent take-off by the aircraft, so different in its mechanism from the balloons currently employed that Marcel had forgotten the initial sadness of exile and the unknown. The large gilded wings had emerged from their aluminum elytra, the mechanical heart had begun its muted regular palpitation, and the beacons had lit up splendidly. They had passed through the clouds, soaring through space at a fearful and immeasurable velocity.

They were the only passengers.

For three days, the captain, of whom nothing was heard but his shrill orders, had remained invisible. At the end of the third day—the previous day—they had landed in an unknown country, on a solitary beach, to pick up a third person who was also being expatriated, a woman this time.

As it was dark, the two friends had only seen her elegant silhouette, quickly eclipsed by a private cabin. The graceful image of the unknown woman, her undulating gait, her rather tall stature, marvelously sheathed in a long traveling coat—an entire ensemble of noble grace and harmonious strength—had lulled Marcel to sleep. He remembered, however, the charming gleam of her dark eyes, which, struck by the artificial light, had seemed to him to be full of a mirage of energy and youth. He had compared them with the depraved eyes of the other, the woman for whom regret was still engraved by acid in the silvering of his memory and branded by an iron on his arm.

The parallel had immediately turned to the disadvantage of the former mistress, and in the morning, on awakening, Marcel was no longer thinking about anything but making the acquaintance of the mysterious stranger and discovering whether the reality conformed to all the suppositions, and even unadmitted hopes, that his imagination had engendered.

The cold had become less sharp. A splendid sun set the zenith ablaze, so close that the two friends felt its proximity—although it seemed to retreat again when they looked down at the ground. They breathed in large lungfuls of the gilded air, rarefied at this height, which the oxygen vents opening in the deck charged with the element essential to life.

The airplane's wings, after rapid movements of descent, when they were deployed vertically, rowed without their speed diminishing. The apparatus combined the effects of lighter-than-air and heavier-than-air flight; Marcel admired the effect without understanding the technicalities. He was about to share his astonishment with his companion when a small high-pitched voice coming from behind them, without them having heard anyone approaching, surprised them and caused them to turn round.

"Glory to the Superman! May he favor you with an operation, Messieurs!"

One might have wondered whether the person who had just addressed those words to them was really human, or whether he might be the clever result of some prestidigitation, presenting by the play of mirrors an individual deprived of part of his body. But no: the light was too harsh, the glare of daylight too sincere, for a phantasmagorical apparition to be able to manifest itself. After a moment's attention, Marcel and Choumaque were obliged to recognize the positive verity of the phenomenon before them.

It was a legless man, posed on a silently-wheeled pedestal equipped with a deflector reminiscent of a locomotive's cow-catcher, the sight of whom was at least as extraordinary by virtue of the indescribable complication of his physiognomy as the contours of his anatomy. His torso was swathed in a kind of green leather sheath bolted to the pedestal, and that armature, hermetically sealed, only opening on the right side, to give passage to a single arm, and at the neck, to let through the head.

The latter, covered with abundant black hair, exposed two large appendages whose splayed funnels stretched and pricked up at every sound, in perpetual movement, like the ears of dogs, which bristle at the most imperceptible events. The eyes were invisible, hidden by a cage fixed at the base to the nose, reminiscent of a pair of binoculars. But what secured the originality of the face most of all was the complete absence of a lower jaw. The curve of the jaw and the chin were, in fact, replaced by clean-shaven skin, a kind a glabrous membrane forming a plane that extended to the lower lip, partly opening an entirely toothless mouth.

That disposition must have succeeded a surgical operation, for two semicircular seams circumscribing the cheeks, persisted, designing on that improbable mask a smile that a perpetually-satisfied fish might have traced.

The individual in question, therefore, presented aspects of the human, the animal and the mechanical, and his appearance would certainly have provoked fear if it had not been hilariously ludicrous.

On remarking the impression that he had made on the two passengers, he became even more cheerful, accentuating the pleat of his two seams, and his piercing voice became audible again.

"I astonish you, Messieurs…I can divine your surprise. Permit me, first of all, to introduce myself; I'm the captain of the airplane, and you see in me the happiest man in the world."

A little bell ringing inside his support structure immediately interrupted him, however. In spite of a keen desire not to cut short the surge of his confidences, he put his only hand to the receiver of a telephone hooked on to his stand and applied it to his upraised ear. He appeared to be following a distant conversation, replying to it in words incomprehensible to the two passengers.

Then, replacing the acoustic device on its hook, he said: "Isn't wireless telegraphy marvelous, Messieurs? I announce, two hours in advance, at a distance of six hundred leagues, your arrival in Eucrasia. In that regard, I mustn't forget to give you some information about the country where you're going to live. But what was I saying…?

"I remember: I was making my profession of faith and declaring to you that I'm the most contented man in the world. No, not man—for, thanks to the Superman, I have the joy of being more than a man. Let's say that I'm the happiest soul! My soul remains to me in its entirety, although I'm ready to

33

give it to the Superman if he ever has the whim of asking me for it and has the means to take it, in order to put it in a sealed box."

"Pardon me," said Choumaque, but who do you mean by the Superman?"

"You haven't guessed? Super, *above*—the man who is above humanity: that's Caresco, almost God."

Paying no heed to the astonishment of his passengers, the captain seized an ivory back-scratcher suspended beneath his torso and plunged it into his sheath through the opening at the neck. One might have thought that he was calming the misdeeds of some insect.

"Excuse me," he said, "my scars are itching. Let's go on, Messieurs. I've known the Superman for nearly fifty years, but I dare say that he knows me much better, since there's no fold, no secret corner of my organism, to which he hasn't acceded in order to modify it for the better.

"In 1900 or hereabouts my mother brought me into the world with four legs. We weren't rich; I might have been able to exhibit myself in fairgrounds and earn my living honorably. It was then, fortunately for me and the family, that the surgeon Caresco appeared at my cradle and laid out twenty thousand francs on my swaddling-clothes, in order to have the right to remove my superfluous limbs.

"The operation took place before a select audience, made up of scientists, artists, royal highnesses and even a few great courtesans. It caused a great sensation…I was already famous, and I didn't die. The following year, however, a tumor appeared in my left knee. My family hoped at first that it was one of the excised limbs growing back. At ten thousand francs a leg, you see…

"But no, it was only a tumor. It quickly became so large that my surgeon decided to extract it, and in order for it not to recur, he cut off the leg with it. That was the second operation.

"At about the age of ten, when I was beginning to reason a little, I found the flagrant inequality between the two sides of my body shocking. I was then suffering from a bad corn on the sole of the foot that remained to me, which became inflamed when I walked, and I begged my benefactor to rid me of that painful affliction. To my great joy, he consented to cut off my last leg. That was the third operation.

"From then on, I was totally committed to him, and entrusted a few more things to him for extraction. Then came the era in which Caresco decided to emigrate to the Isle of the Blessed and found a State there. The idea that he was going to leave me drove me crazy. I expressed my despair to him. Behold his generosity, Messieurs! He took me in his luggage—me, a poor, useless thing, devoid of legs!

"He'd always imposed the condition on me of not procreating, to which I willingly agreed, delivering my genital organs to him, which he removed with a flick of the wrist. That was both the most helpful of his actions, and the sanest of my determinations—because, Messieurs, one doesn't suspect how useless, wasteful and sometimes painful those organs are.

"I was burning with the desire to be useful to him—but what, alas, could I actually do? I was intelligent, though—he knew that, since he had opened up my skull in order to destroy there, by fire, the initial lesions of a bout of meningitis, so he was familiar with my brain; he had had it beneath his fingers. He decided, in his infallible wisdom, that I would be the captain of this airplane. Devoid of limbs and sex organs, I would have my intelligence entirely at my command.

"That new situation necessitated, as you can imagine, other modifications in my anatomy, other adaptations of my senses. Sight first: he improved it by means of an apparatus of his invention, which is now an integral part of my nose, sealed on to its bridge, and which I can open, by means of a little window, in order to rub my eyes.

"Then he lengthened my ears, grafting on to them the funnels of a young Siberian wolf, which ensured that I had no need of acoustic aids to perceive the most distant sounds. You can imagine that, from then on, one of my arms because unnecessary—I had, in any case, a chronic rheumatism in my left elbow that gave me stabbing pains during aerial fogs. The Superman was generous enough to cut off that arm.

"Then, as it was necessary for me to issue commands intelligibly—I had a weak voice, alas—the Master had the idea of endowing my mouth with an apparatus that served as a resonator. He composed it ingeniously, and you can still see on my cheeks the two seams that resulted from the grafting operation. Unfortunately, the apparatus didn't work very well, and I had great difficulty swallowing the little balls of the complete aliment of which my nourishment consists. In consequence, Caresco preferred not to employ his instrument. He removed it, and at the same time, opened my throat, scraped my vocal cords and retuned them in such a way that the waves of my voice are now perceptible over a radius of two kilometers.

"In the meantime, he made the acquaintance of my abdomen several times; he removed a poorly-functioning kidney, the appendix and the stomach—which were unnecessary and sometimes dangerous—and a section of the intestines that was dilated. Then he suspected the ulterior possibility of calculi in the liver, and resected a part of it thanks to an operation known as hepatovesiculocholedotomy. That was admirable!

"I emerged from each of these interventions lighter, and nearer to the beautiful simplicity of the cell—which is, as you know, the primal organic element. I blessed his smile when, on bringing me out of the sleep provoked by a hilarant fluid, which gave me joyful ideas, he said to me: 'Captain, you're my masterpiece! You're approaching the perfection that is the human monad!' He addresses me in the familiar manner, the divine Superman—yes, Messieurs, he deigns to address me as *tu*!

"But that's not all. One evening, by an inexplicable negligence on my part, one of the iron cords that support the hull of the airplane broke, and, suddenly released, like a broken violin-string, struck me in the middle of the chest and also the back. That fortunate event put an end to one of my troubles. I was transported, breathless to the Palace of Surgery—you'll be able to see the palace in due course, Messieurs, and tell me what you think of it.

"The Superman examined me. I had five broken ribs, a perforated lung and a crushed coccyx. I was dying. He took out my five ribs, made me a brand new immutable lung with only one lobe, and leveled the bones of my pelvis, with the result that I was not longer just legless but hipless. Look—this is his masterpiece!"

"It's admirable," said Choumaque, who was experiencing the anxiety of talking to an ironist—an opinion corroborated by the captain's perpetual smile—"but it seems to me that you no longer possess a jaw?"

"Indeed, Monsieur Neophyte. Mastication not being necessary to my mode of nutrition, and on, the other hand, my teeth starting to ache one day, Caresco removed my lower jaw—which gives my face, as you can see an acanthopteran appearance of which I'm very proud."[7]

"You're proud of resembling a fish?"

"I'm proud of it, Monsieur, and I wonder what structure my descendants might have had if I'd been able to reproduce..."

"Yes, but you can't, any more," said Choumaque addressing a wink to Marcel.

The half-man had noticed that mockery, but did not manifest any anger. On the contrary; the pleats of his smile became more emphatic. He was radiant. "Well, Messieurs, you see me delighted by it. Hasn't one of you suffered bitterly from amour? And perhaps even you, Monsieur Choumaque, if you interrogate your memory carefully..."

"You know about my past life, then?"

"We know everything!" the strange individual affirmed, calmly. "As for me, I repeat to you, and I shall proclaim it

---

[7] The improvisation *acanthoptère* [acanthopteran] is derived from the name of an order of fish—but not, perhaps mistakenly, that of the order *Agnatha*, the "jawless fishes" that the captain seems to resemble in this regard.

loudly forever, I'm perfectly happy, firstly because I'm Caresco's masterpiece, and secondly because, no longer possessing many of my organs—no legs, no left arm, no right kidney, no stomach, no cecum, no colon, no inferior part of the liver, no right lung, no maxilla and no reproductive organs—I've greatly diminished the chances of physical suffering and the mental disappointments inevitably attached to their functioning or their desires."

"Would it not have been more complete, in that case, to suppress your existence totally?" said Choumaque, with a malice that made his mischievous little eyes sparkle in the tangle of his hair.

"When the Superman wishes to take me!" affirmed the half-man, with pious respect.

"To what marvelous being do I have the honor of speaking? Will you tell me your name?" the professor asked, taking off his hat.

He was surprised to hear the reply, delivered with equal politeness: "I have no name, Monsieur. That too has been removed; I am called 'the captain.'"

At the same time, the captain, reaching down to his pedestal, opened a tab fitted to a rubber tube. A little stream of lemon-yellow liquid ran out and snaked across the deck, proving that not all his functions had been suppressed. He uttered an inarticulate cry, and the pretty cabin boy who had been pirouetting in front of his comrades a little while before came to mop up the digestive excess, laughing.

That simple act of relief was about to inspire further repartee on the part of the philosopher, when an emotion suddenly manifested by his pupil caused him to look in the direction of the object that had produced it. He then perceived a woman of remarkable beauty advancing toward them.

Above average height, holding up her head boldly, she had the appearance of strength and serene grace that is the prerogative of races not yet touched by an over-refined civilization. Everything about her was supremely harmonious, and beneath the long garment that covered her entirely, one could divine the fullness of a flesh that was both powerful and delicate. What was most seductive of all was the majestic rhythm of her stride, and her natural manner of thrusting her bosom proudly forward.

On seeing her appear, Marcel, thought about antique statues, scorning the artificial forms of Parisiennes by the same token. When she came closer, the two friends were able to admire her more completely, and to observe that the perfection of her face entirely corroborated the promise of her silhouette. Her complexion was pale pink; the somber enamel of her large eyes, brilliant with youth, contrasted with the blonde reflections in her abundant sunlit hair; the ridge of her nose was delicate and straight; the moist softness of the lips was constructed on the design of four precise arcs, which one might have thought enlivened by fresh blood. Finally, two ears, delicately terminating the sinewy line of the neck, with the two most delightful lobes that one cold ever hold in a kiss combined with everything else to give the stranger the face of a noble, more refined, Amazon: a striking example of strength and human purity, inspiring at first glance the presentiment that love was about to be born from her radiance.

Marcel could not repress an exclamation of surprise, such as he might have uttered on seeing a splendid work of art. He recognized her as the woman he had glimpsed fleetingly the previous evening, by the indirect light of the beacons, who had made such an impression on his night.

"Tee hee!" murmured the half-man. "Here's our new recruit. She's truly delightful, and I wouldn't have judged her as superb yesterday evening. It's only honest to admit the Africa is still the land of election for beautiful humans. Our realm possesses many such creatures, and Caresco, concerned for the race, has made fecund mothers of them."

The unknown woman having reached them, he introduced her. "Miss Mary Hardisson, the sister of General Hardisson, who fought so valiantly for the independence of his country."

The heroic history of the woman in question, whose adventures had been celebrated in twenty books and twenty novels in the last year, returned to Marcel's memory, and he was astonished to find her above her reputation, even more regally beautiful than the newspapers had proclaimed.

England, faithful to its politics of invasion, had fortified her navy fifty years before and bluffed diplomatically to the point of absorbing all the regions of South Africa. It had only encountered resistance, as it once had in the Transvaal, in one other corner of land, located to the south of Mozambique, where a new people, recently created by emigrants of French, German and, especially, American origin, had wanted, after buying the land from Portugal, to conserve their autonomy and fight to defend their new homeland, which they called the Red Land.

The ogress nation initially threw against the coveted region a few hundred thousand men, who were rapidly defeated by the bravery of the Redlanders and the natural defenses of the country. In order not to succumb to the ridicule of her abortive attempt, and also not to allow the weakness of her army to be deduced, England had sent in motion an entire diplomatic machine, involved in the threads of that political intrigue a number of other nations interested in the enterprise, to which she promised a slice of the cake. Ferocious Turkey, valiant Ethiopia, Japan, rich in soldiers indifferent to death, and Portugal—which, since being anglicized had acquired a veritable folly of domination—easily found humanitarian pretexts for launching themselves against the little nation, to which they wanted to sell the right to exist.

The Red Land, decimated by three years of conflict, greeted the new invasion with savage resistance. Two events marked the new phase of the struggle. Firstly, the court of arbitration at The Hague protested, and Europe took no notice—but when Miss Mary Hardisson stood up in her turn, there was a delirium of enthusiasm. She was admired, for arranging field hospitals and food supplies; even, it was claimed, braving fire like a common soldier and caring for the wounded.

Then, one day, her homeland being at the end of its tether, she has escaped, by means of a perilous flight, in order to move the indifference of the old countries of Europe, to preach the defense of her soil there and to beg various governments to intervene, to put a stop to the abominable invasion of the coalition. Her father's renown had served that cause no less that her great beauty. In Paris the boulevards had welcomed her with splendid fêtes and songs; in Berlin, the students emptied tankards to her; in St. Petersburg, a Grand Duke wanted to marry her; in New York, a showman had offered her a contract to perform in Music Halls, which would have given her ten per cent of the receipts.

She had been at that time, the pretext for the greatest success of the publishing industry. One novel written by an attaché at the War Office in London, which slandered her, was translated into all languages and sold millions of copies. A French lyrical drama, played on all the operatic stages then in existence and transmitted to the remotest corners of every country by all the improved phonographs of the epoch, provided a counterblast to the English masterpiece.

Miss Mary's success was, however, limited to these manifestations of art and publicity. Energy no longer existed, except in her. The bastardized races remained, in sum, indifferent, after being briefly amused by the legend, of which they soon wearied, which became old in a matter of months. Governments had not received her. She had collected just enough to pay for her voyage, and had gone home, with distress in her heart.

Since then, for two months, nothing more had been heard of her. The British press had spread the rumor that she had died, an alcoholic, a morphine addict and an etheromaniac. in a Chicago brothel, but everyone knew what those affirmations were worth.

And now, Marcel Girard and Zépherin Choumaque had found her on their airplane, so haloed with glory, so divinely

41

proud, that they could not retain an exclamation of admiration. She was not astonished by that; she came toward them, cordially holding out her hand, as soon as the captain had made the introductions from the height of his pedestal.

"I knew that I would be traveling with you, Messieurs," she said, in a voice in which a thousand harmonious hints of a slight exotic accent sang, "and I rejoiced in advance, for certainly, of all the nations through which I traveled inefficaciously, France is still the one that remains most faithful to the old traditions of chivalric generosity. Know that, in addition, I am of French origin, since my ancestors were expatriated in consequence of the revocation of the Edict of Nantes. Their name, which was then Hardi, became Hardisson in America, and was conserved as such in the Red Land."

"I disowned my country on the day when I found that it remained deaf to your appeal," said Choumaque, gallantly, hitching up his trousers, the leather belt of which was not maintaining them sufficiently.

"Thank you, Monsieur, but hearts are not extinct in my homeland. They still beat there; they are unable to die. Yesterday, did not the cinematograph show me the most recent battle? Have I not seen the heroism of the peasants, led by my brother, launching a terrible attack on the coalition front? Have I not heard, thanks to the phonograph, the cries of vengeance uttered by those who rendered their souls? There are great resources in our national energy."

"Very great resources, to be sure," affirmed the philosopher, who was thinking about something else and wondering why, after so many protests, Miss Hardisson now seemed resolved to allow herself to be taken to a country from which no one returned. He made his observations silently, however, as much out of sympathy for the beautiful young woman as surprise on seeing Marcel's increasing disturbance.

The latter was unable to detach his dazzled eyes from the stranger. He was obedient to an immediate seduction. He was immediately engaged in tender protestations; he was determined on the slavery of his entire life. The image of Hélène,

42

his former mistress, had vanished at a stroke, in a new light, and he remained stunned by it.

And as if the accord of their sadnesses had been produced instantaneously, both of them looked toward the unknown at which the airplane's prow was pointing. The island could not be far away, for the balloon, although still flying very high, had just traversed a layer of light clouds, the friction of which had allowed them to feel, beneath the thickness of their garments, an impression of muffled humidity.

Yes, toward what enigmatic solutions were their two sufferings heading, so different in origin but so concordant in their denouement? Life finished there, at the curtain of the clouds, but it was about to recommence down below, on the almost invisible patch of land that was gradually becoming less confused, and enlarging in the sunlight.

# CHAPTER III

The captain's voice emitted a strident clamor. Crewmen, with the pretty young cabin boy at their head, ran in response to his command. They were seen, remarkably agile and athletic, racing through the aluminum rigging toward the carapace of red fabric strewn with golden vibrions, and accomplishing a maneuver there necessitated by the loss of gas, escaping through huge valve.

On a forward-set bridge, a silk-clad helmsman was gazing into space with the aid of a huge telescope. It sufficed for him to adjust a control lever for the balloon to modify its direction. At the same time, in an unknown language composed entirely of vowels, he transmitted the half-man's orders through a megaphone.

The latter, on his support, went back and forth and around, stimulating the efforts of his crew. His machine, activated by a fluid force, moved with all the ease in the world, under the direction of a lever similar to the helmsman's, protected from shocks by a shiny metal frame. The voltameter indicated that the supply of energy was almost exhausted, and the half-man was obliged to go and procure more from a contact emerging from the deck. He came back to the passengers, satisfied and happy, the smiling pleat of his cheeks even more emphatic, as if he had been gorging on beneficent life himself.

The airplane, supported by denser air, was flapping its wings more broadly, at greater intervals. As the cold eased, Miss Mary took off her long garment, which had become too warm. The splendor of her bust, held by a tight-fitting corsage, became evident.

Choumaque began to take off his fur, under which he was beginning to sweat, but scarcely had he opened it than he closed it again abruptly, in order to hide his worn jacket and the section of his undershirt that his poorly-attached trousers left visible at the waist.

Marcel had also taken off his heliotrope-colored overcoat, and the elegance of his vestment, close-fitting at the waist and falling in fine pleats over his beige trousers, was revealed. At the same time, the breadth of his shoulders and the grace of his stature attracted the eyes of the young woman, who secretly reproached him for not having the warrior appearance of the children of the Red Land, and disdained the caresses that his eyes had already sent her.

The captain rolled around silently. After a final inspection of his vessel, his voice, half-human and half-mechanical, like his entire being, piped up: "Since the three of you are together, permit me to give you some useful information. In reality, I have no orders to do so, and the agreeable privilege really belongs to the Chief Representative, but Zadochbach is an idler who is late getting up today, and who has a backlog of accounts to put in order—for, as you doubtless know, he's in charge of all the State's financial affairs.

"I suspect him, in addition, of having gone on the spree in Paris, where he has a mistress, and at Juvisy, where he has another. That tires him out, poor fellow. In that double life, he will lose both the remainder of his strength and the confidence of Caresco, who knows everything. Then again, why go to seek over there pleasures that we possess in more refined and complete form at home? He finds a certain spice in it, he says, but I don't understand that reason.

"Anyway, this is what I want to tell you: we're arriving; we'll be landing in less than ten minutes. It's necessary that, from now on, you resolve to lose all personality. That's the best way of not regretting your exile."

"An exile is never regrettable when one returns from it with the cortege of its virtues..." Choumaque quoted.

The captain, having accepted that judgment with a shrug of his shoulder, went on: "You are going become things in the hands of a sole possessor, for the sake of your complete happiness. The slightest whims of resistance or disobedience are punished as crimes.

"Your case is special, Miss Mary; you have come to ask the Superman for assistance, and first among all creatures who have landed on the island since the edification of the realm, you will have the right to return therefrom. That license is a capital infraction of our laws. Let us hope that Caresco will not have cause to regret it. You know that if you do not keep the secret of everything that you are going to see or understand, sentence of death will be immediately pronounced upon you, and carried out within three days. It is probable that another consequence of your loquaciousness would be the rapid extermination of your valiant people. Are you fully decided to submit yourself to all the exigencies of the new life, without recrimination, as a blind and obedient subject?"

"I'm formally resolved to that," said Miss Mary, while the reason determining her presence aboard magnified her further in Choumaque's eyes—who, before that clarification, would willingly have criticized her for renouncing her cause and betraying the admirable work that she had undertaken.

"That's good," said the captain. "Now, Miss, and Messieurs, would you care to lean over the bulwark and look in a southwesterly direction. Perhaps you won't see anything, for we're still a hundred leagues from the realm, but act as if you can see something. In your countries, imagination often replaces reality. In ours, by contrast, imagination is an idle faculty, reality far surpassing what chimeras can engender.

"Lean over, and try to see the morsel of lava that appeared in the wake of the immense cataclysm of 1920, a cataclysm which, as you know, while swallowing up Martinique and Saint-Pierre, provoked a lowering of the waters of the Atlantic and caused our land to surge forth in a volcanic eruption. Caresco took possession of that land, still hot, as a consequence of circumstances with which you are familiar.

"By virtue of a curious predestination, the island has adopted the form of a human body asleep in the sea with its arms and legs extended. I'm not sure whether or not that anatomical disposition influenced the surgeon's choice. Perhaps he was dreaming of some colossal amputation! At any rate, our climate is ideal, and in any case, we have the means of maintaining its constancy thanks to Omnium, which also aids our vegetation powerfully..."

"Omnium?"

"That's true—you don't know about our Caresco's principal discovery. Like me, you'll understand why he omitted to communicate it to the scientific Societies on the day when his genius gave birth to it, in 1918, so much power did it give him!

"Well, Miss and Messieurs, Omnium is the primal element of all matter and force, the essential atomic molecule, whose combination with itself yields, according to the degree of its association, all the substances of chemistry and all the phenomena of physics. Earth, water, heat, light, sound, air, electricity, gas, vapors, metals, animals and human thought are merely Omnium in the infinite varieties of its admixture.

"Your pretty lips, Miss Mary, are Omnium; the fabric of your protruding undergarment, Monsieur Choumaque, is Omnium. Your gaze, Monsieur Girard: Omnium. Also Omnium, the energy that deploys the wings of my vessel; my voice, which commands it, and the leather that protects me! Always and everywhere, Omnium! What a discovery! The world in the palm of one's hand! Life in a crucible! Unfortunately, Caresco has only ever been able to analyze omnial bodies. If he had been able to synthesize it, he would be the creator, he would be God!"

The dwarf wiped away a tear of enthusiasm.

Choumaque began once again to doubt his reason. He was soon obliged to recognize that he was mistaken. "That's understandable, Monsieur," he said. "Omnium gives you useful forces and can, in fact, modify your climate; our scientists have foreseen for a long time that something of the sort ought to be possible. But how is it explicable that vegetation can be born in thirty years on rocky soil? Doesn't humus require centuries to form?"

"That's a question that neophytes of your sort generally ask us, Monsieur Choumaque, because they don't know the

47

practical genius of our master. In fact, the morsel of lava was not covered by the slightest patch of humus; it was new, sterilized by fire; nothing could grow there. Caresco was thus obliged to cover it with earth, and that earth was brought from America."

"From America!"

"Yes, from America, quite simply. That even gave rise to a marvelous bluff, the only story that has ever made the Superman smile, to my knowledge. I was twenty years old then, and I remember it perfectly. I was in command of one of the twenty airplane-barges that brought, from the vicinity of Chicago, the earth moved by a hundred thousand workers aided by a thousand steam-cranes.

"This is the story. When we had loaded enough earth and had abandoned the immense enclosure from which we had extracted it—I was greatly overworked at the time by the numerous trips—the Americans, seeing the place cleared, assumed at first that we were mad, and then, in the second place, decided that there must be a reason for that removal of their soil. Being unable to imagine what it was, for they knew nothing, they imagined that there were deposits of a precious metal that was then called radium. Those people were very stupid, when one thinks about it.

"The opinion of a few licensed chemists accredited the mirage of their cupidity. An enterprise was organized. A great businessman, Koxterbury, the emperor of nickel buttons— you've obviously never had recourse to his products, Monsieur Choumaque, for your trousers are getting away—set up a company with a colossal capital to exploit the mine. It was called the Chicago Radium Company. The five continents got involved in the scheme; gold flowed; the delirium became universal.

"I wouldn't dare say that the affair wasn't powerfully aided by our Zadochbach, who gambled on the rise of all the world's stock markets, with the result that millions of shares he bought at a hundred francs were resold when they reached twenty thousand five hundred…you can see the profit! Part of that terrestrial fortune entered our coffers. But when the crash came, when Koxterbury committed suicide, according to the custom of financiers disappointed in their calculations, the Americans venerated his memory, and were exultant with joy at having been the country with the biggest Trust followed by the biggest Crash. Oh, the fools! We were greatly amused."

"I remember the story," said Choumaque. "Like you, I was twenty years old then, Monsieur Tronc-de-Jatte."[8]

"Call me Captain."

"Yes, Monsieur le Capitaine, I was twenty years old, and I haven't forgotten, the great stir that the collapse caused in our country. My father was ruined at a stroke, and I remember that my concierge hanged herself with her bell-rope. Her tongue was sticking out of her mouth when I saw her, dead, and that spectacle has remained with me, very vividly. Your Caresco caused the ruin and chagrin of a great many humble individuals."

The smile fixed on the cheeks of the man on the pedestal suddenly vanished, or very nearly. Choumaque understood his imprudence in having spoken so freely. Had he not done so, though, the shrill voice would quickly have informed him.

"Pray, Monsieur le Professeur, that I don't report to the Superman the words you've just pronounced, and that he doesn't have his ear to the microphone at this moment listening to what we're saying! I prefer merely to criticize your stupidity and enable you to imagine the magnificent compensation that the Master is offering you in accepting you into his realm. I'll forget your reflection, if you agree in due course that you're as happy as me. For the moment, let me finish what I was saying…or rather, no, here's Zadochbach, who will tell you the rest. Approach, Inexhaustible."

---

[8] This phrase, which I have retained when it is used as a proper noun, is also used as a common noun to refer to the captain, but in those circumstances I have preferred the designation "half-man," because the literal translation of "trunk-in-a-box" sounds so awkward in English.

Then, divining the surprise that the epithet produced in his listeners, he added: "Monsieur Zadochbach is known familiarly as the Inexhaustible, as much by reason of his pecuniary resources, which are unlimited, as his generic virtues, which permit him, at the age of eighty—the same age as the Superman, Messieurs—to warm a woman's bed on a daily basis. Monsieur Zadochbach, the Superman's Chief Representative, is, apart from Caresco, the only Semite in the realm. The plastic Israelite is not suited to our master's esthetic conception. Now, Inexhaustible, speak."

Marcel and Choumaque immediately recognized in the newcomer the person who had approached them in the restaurant and had so casually become their commensal. In the harsh light, his appearance became somewhat paradoxical, his artificial youth stood out so sharply from his old age. The Representative seemed, in any case, to be in a particularly bad mood today; doubtless he was still under the impression of his fatigue, or a disappointing balance-sheet. He spoke hastily, abridging his words as he propelled them toward the extremity of his plunging nose.

"Not much to add, sirs...all calculated, all put in order...anyway, your fortune has now been acquired by the State. You, Girard, three million three hundred thousand...I thought it was more—have you given me everything?"

"I left a million to one of my paternal aunts, who needed it."

"Bad, that...bad!" he repeated, several times. "Caresco certainly won't be pleased..." Then, turning to the professor, he went on: "You, Choumaque, seventy-three francs twenty-five centimes. That's rather meager..."

"I was content with it," Choumaque said, "for I told myself that poverty is merely the absence of the embarrassments attached to wealth..."

"Fortunately," remarked Zadochbach, after having smiled pityingly, "you'll be able to render some service; otherwise..."

He made a frightful slicing gesture, signifying death. He rounded it out almost immediately in order to address himself to Miss Mary.

"You, Miss Hardisson, seven thousand two hundred. But you're a pretty girl, and that's your excuse. I've deposited your money at one percent—given the short duration, a tidy rate of interest. All of it will be returned when you leave. May Caresco operate on you, Miss and Messieurs!"

He withdrew immediately. The captain had also slipped away on his mobile pedestal, silently. The three travelers felt relieved of two disquieting presences. Thus far, the proximity of Caresco's representatives had not augured well for the realm in which they were about to land.

Hitching up his trousers, Choumaque made a gesture that expressed his regret for the past and his perplexity with regard to the future. Marcel, by contrast, engaged himself more deliberately in the adventure. The impressive company of Miss Mary caused him to forget everything else, to the extent of astonishment. He stroked his moustache as he gazed at her.

*Already!* thought the philosopher. *Already that birdbrain is getting a rosy expression. Decidedly, love is as inconsistent as the reservoir of this airplane, whose valve has just been opened. Love is the cube of inconstancy. A little while ago, Marcel was still only dreaming about Hélène, for whom he committed the worst follies. It did no good to rub his nose in the antics of that whore; it didn't ease the bite of his passion. My broad philosophy and my advice, borrowed from the great classics of Stoicism, were as futile as the treasons of his mistress. And yet, a smile from that stranger was sufficient to turn everything upside down, to chase away the memory of Hélène, thus proving more efficacious than the efforts of my intellect. It's enough to put one off either being extremely perverted, like Hélène, or very intelligent, like me.*

He did not have the leisure to extend the discourse any further. Distant harmonies, of youthful voices accompanied by harps, rose up into the azure in gentle waves, reaching their ears perceptibly. At the same time, the temperature became

51

entirely mild. Gusts of sea breeze also rose up and, like the songs, caused them to anticipate the imminence of company. The airplane, obedient to the hidden voice of the captain, gave vast perpendicular wing-beats, like a bird about to alight.

The passengers leaned over toward the void, but were unable to make out anything at first but a confused gray mass surrounded by a blue sinuosity, which was the sea. The oblique four o'clock sun was, however, radiant over that ag-gregation of land and water. Finally, they made out the red and green tongue of the island emerging from the shiny splashing of waves.

In front of them, a little pink dot flying through the air astonished them. Miss Mary aided her sight with a pair of bin-oculars that she wore suspended from her belt. She declared at first that it was a bizarre bird with and elongated form, but when it came closer she announced that it was a human being who was flying.

"A human being who can fly!" Choumaque exclaimed. "That's new, since Icarus of lamentable memory. Pass me the binoculars, if you please, lovely demoiselle..."

He took a few seconds to adjust the glasses to his vision, with the result that, when he searched the air, the phenomenon was no longer there.

At the same time, the delightful naked body of a twelve-year-old boy came, as if falling from the sky, to sit down on the rim of the nacelle alongside them, his legs dangling down into the void. His arms were circled by straps attached to two large emerald wings, presently folded over his back, and hid-ing a small motor. The gracious line of the vertebrae could be seen melting, at their termination, into the pelvic girdle and the prolongation of plump and admirably formed legs. His strongly-developed pectoral muscles were sketched out like the breasts of a pre-pubertal girl. His head was admirably pret-ty, the eyes gleaming with animation, a fine straight nose, cheeks and lips vivid with health, an entire robust youthful-ness bursting forth in fresh tones beneath long curly blond hair, a curl of which hid the forehead.

"I've got here first!" he cried, in an excessively shrill, almost feminine, but nevertheless charming voice. "The others can't fly as quickly as me. I've won!"

"My friend," said Choumaque, swiftly taking off his fur and posing it in such a way as to protect the child's nudity, "I admit all sports, including this one—unknown among us—of imitating the birds, but it's still necessary that your game doesn't offend the modest of a pretty African."

"Modesty? What's that?"

The little devil had thrust away the garment in disgust, which floated in the air momentarily and then disappeared. Choumaque, torn between the desire to teach the scamp a lesson and find out what had become of his cape, remained hesitant. Miss Mary looked away, and Marcel became confused on her behalf—but that embarrassment did not last long. Joyful cries were heard, and a swarm of other little boys and girls, all similarly naked and winged, came to alight on the deck, on the bridge and in the vessel's rigging. They were laughing, chattering, panting and jostling one another, still intoxicated by the distance they had covered, paying no more heed to the travelers than if they had not been there.

It was the real commencement of the marvelous.

The harmonies from below became more distinct. At the same time, sweet floral perfumes rose up, as troubling as the music. They leaned over again and observed the proximity of the ground, covered with a luxurious vegetation. The flash of golden domes mirroring the sunlight, of great multicolored mosaics, an order magnificent in its symmetry, of lines, contours and panoramas, albeit still confused, already revealed the masterly sumptuousness that had presided over the creation of the new city.

They turned their eyes away in order to admire the superb winged women who were flying toward them, singing, covered by light veils, so vaporous that their splendor was transparent therein. Their upraised breasts, their hair floating in the wind, the firm roundness of their abdomen, the simultaneously delicate and vigorous projection of their buttocks, made them as many admirable works of art, which enthused Choumaque's lyricism, causing him to pronounce a few aphorisms on the flesh, which he compared to a divine clay.

All of the women resembled one another, as they resembled the boys and girls. One might have thought that they had been cast from the same mold of beauty. They came closer, forming a cortege for the airplane. They whispered admiring remarks about the couple formed by Marcel and Miss Mary. A hint of lubricity was not unseemly in their bright eyes and the scintillating smiles of their ardent mouths. But Choumaque they mocked; one of them, by way of a joke, brushed his beard with a light caress of her pink foot, shod in a white sandal with mauve laces.

*It's obvious that I'm not producing as good an effect as my companions*, the philosopher thought, breathing in the heady perfume that the touch had deposited in his bushy beard.

The shrill voice of the captain caused the nude figures to scatter. They were about to land. The airplane folded up its wings in its silvery wing-cases. One last glance at the magical spectacle—in which, along a flowery esplanade, to the sound of invisible harmonies, thousands of couples in polychromatic pastel shades, were dancing rhythmically, enlacing and separating with precise and gracious gestures—and then there was a gentle impact.

The airplane came to rest at on the landing-platform; and they found themselves in front of a kind of vast portico supported by two red porphyry columns, elaborately sculpted, with a symbolic allegory on its frontispiece of a naked man and woman lying in front of a sun, and offering new life in the form of a vibrion and an ovule. They hardly had time to admire it, for the captain and the Representative ushered them on to a drawbridge that had just come down and steered them toward a black and silent tunnel, into which they entered, and where, by groping, they found soft banquettes.

"You're now in the tube," explained the shrill voice. "In two minutes, you'll be in our home. You'll begin by getting rid of your dirt."

# CHAPTER IV

When the omnial light emitted by four opaque globes had suddenly illuminated the place where they were, the travelers perceived that they were not alone. Two sleeping near-naked bodies lay on a large divan draped with red velvet, which extended along the whole back wall of the cabin, the paneling of which was gilded and encrusted with capricious black arabesques. One might have thought it a living tableau set up to astonish.

One of the bodies, a female, was lying with her legs folded and her hand posed on the arch of her lower back, parting her mauve silk peplum, in such a way that one could see all the splendor of the torso, with the thrusting breasts, and the abdomen, traversed longitudinally, from the navel to the odorous tuft, by a red stripe heightened by make-up.

Coiffed with a double gathering of brown hair diminishing the forehead, the mat warmth of her muscular face was particularly remarkable, the lips freshly blood-colored, as if the kisses of the sun had been caught therein and sprung forth again over the moist teeth, the velvety cheeks and the transparent orifices of the nostrils, agitated by a tremor that did not quit them during sleep.

All of her ardent musculature was moistened by a slight sweat, which embalmed the cabin with a troubling combination of perfumes by itself. Choumaque had never respired such a floral expansion, simultaneously natural and artificial.

The other body, a boy of about fifteen, draped in a yellow fabric embroidered with gold, was similar to the young flyers that had welcome the airplane a short while before, but was distinguished by the presence of a line, similarly heightened with rouge, escaping from the incomplete sexual organs, which the immodesty of the parted legs permitted the spectators to see.

The attitude of the two sleepers, the position of their gestures surprised by fatigue, left no doubt about the recent exchange of tenderness.

"They're definitely unaware of shame in this country!"
sad Choumaque, shocked.

He was about to take off his frock-coat in order to veil
that new offensive immorality when the indigenes woke up
simultaneously. They embraced one another first, and then,
speaking at the same time, repeating the ritual refrain, greeted
them with the formula with which the travelers had already
been welcomed: "May the Superman favor you with an operation, Miss and Messieurs!"

They were not astonished to receive no response.

The young woman sat up, and threw back the heavy
adornment of her hair with a long shake of her head. She
pulled the peplum over her shoulders, not because decency
invited the gesture, but because she felt the breeze freshening
slightly.

Then, pointing with her finger at the pink line on her abdomen, which was now assuming the importance of a distinctive sign, she said: "I'm the courtesan Carabella. Little Mirror-
of-Smiles and I were at the fête, but we had to come away in
order to come here and welcome you. We're both attached to
your persons. The airplane being late, we caressed. You're
neophytes, and are doubtless unfamiliar with our caresses? In
time, you'll cultivate them.

"For the moment, it will suffice for you to know that
we're very tired, and that we'll have a great deal of difficulty
beginning your initiation today. If you knew how much subtle
experience Mirror-of-Smiles has! For eight years he's been a
giton,[9] as indicated by the red line placed between his legs and

---

[9] This term is derived from the name of Gito, a young homo-
sexual featured in the *Satyricon* of Petronius; it was introduced
into French by Voltaire in his early verse satire *L'Anti-Giton*,
whence it acquired a meaning akin to "catamite." It was taken
up by the Marquis de Sade in *La Nouvelle Justine* (1797),

the hem of his tunic, and he's acquired a great deal of skill. I love the child, and take as much advantage of him as my leisure permits. But haven't we left yet? What is the captain waiting for before launching us? Come on captain, have you forgotten that we're here? Do I have to get up to press the departure button?"

She had raised herself up lazily, and her beautiful body undulated. Her feet, shod in mauve sandals, did not make any noise on the polychromatic carpet. She went to lean over the only door, causing her buttocks to protrude, the silken covering of which was iridescent in the omnial light.

She repeated her question without overmuch impatience, languidly—and it seemed that her desire was immediately executed, for the voyagers saw a partition fall, hermetically sealing the orifice of the cabin. At the same time, they heard the whistling noise of air pressure and felt a slight vertigo, previously experienced when utilizing the elevators of the old world. They were evidently traveling along a tunnel whose walls were in contact with the shell of their cage.

Choumaque felt a slight nausea.

"The journey only lasts a minute," said the courtesan, laughing at the philosopher's expression as his complexion harmonized with the green of his frock-coat. "There! It's done; we've reached our destination." As she went out first she added: "We've just covered thirty kilometers, and we've arrived at the Caravanserai. We'll be going in by way of the Palace of the Head."

The Palace of the Head! The strangers did not understand that at all, dazed as they were by the unexpectedness and rapidity of their journey. They contented themselves with allowing themselves to be guided. They emerged from the tunnel

---

which secured its shady significance. First penned in 1714 or thereabouts, Voltaire's poem was rewritten in 1739, that version acquiring the title; he rewrote it again in 1754, adding the dedication "À Mademoiselle Lecouvreur," which doubtless helped to attract the present author's attention to it.

into which they had stepped two minutes earlier via a gentle slope. Mirror-of-Smiles had taken Marcel's hand, imitating Carabella who had taken Miss Mary's. Choumaque brought up the rear.

After a hundred paces along a path of fine and, bordered by immense verdant plane-trees, they stopped before a bizarre construction resembling in the shades of its colors and its architectural design, an immense human face, smiling and jovial. The open mouth, which displayed sparkling ivory columns ten meters long, reminiscent of teeth, constituted the entrance. They reached it by means of two blue-tinted marble stairways traced in the folds of the smile.

Once through the doorway they found themselves in an immense room, a kind of grotto adapted to the form of the human buccal cavity. The red carpet bristling with stucco papillae represented the tongue. A semicircular gallery, shining like gingival mucus, ran around the location along the dental peristyle. Jets of perfumed water filtering from the exterior walls, were reminiscent of salivary irrigation. The back was constituted by two concave pillars supporting the palatine vault on one side and melting on the other into an enormous red stalactite, which was the uvula.

No lighting apparatus was visible there; the columns, all luminous, radiated a discreet light. No living being animated the silence of the monument, in which the three travelers, following their guides, felt anxious, wondering whether the enormous mouth might be going to close and swallow them. Nevertheless, Choumaque did not lose his critical faculties.

*This is odious*, he thought. *I've venerated Egyptian architecture and its capitals giving the impression of lotus buds. The impeccable harmonies of the centuries of Pericles and Phidias carried me away. The Roman plagiarists, although a trifle heavy-handed, had their value. I've admired the Gothic of the Renaissance, respected the neo-Greek style of the last empire, and even, eclectic as I am, found a certain fancy for this century's art nouveau—but this unexpected conception of architecture, bringing to monumental beauty everything that is frightful and base in our organism, bewilders me. Being unable to protest, I'll content myself with silently lamenting this nasty originality. When I see this Superman Caresco, I'll tell him that he lacks taste.*

These ideas soon evolved, however, for after having passed through that room they found themselves in the open air before a magnificent garden, or rather a park, with patches of woodland, mossy slopes, paths plunging into mysterious shade and lakes framed with rocks, on which the green leaves of nenuphar lilies lay peacefully dormant. To be sure, the simplicity of nature was embellished with a certain excessively pretty artifice, and the graciously-designed flower-beds still recalled certain unnamable details of human structure, but it was soothing to see veritable soil and real flowers.

To the right and the left, far enough away that their gracious caprice could only be glimpsed, charming dwellings ornamented with festoons, perforated balconies, gilded towers and pointed roofs made of shiny nascent metal formed two equally straight parallel lines framing the wild but contrived beauty of the park. There was a mixture of all styles, all lines and all dimensions, deliberately opposed to one another in order that the eye should not be wearied by uniformity.

The background of the scene was constituted by an enormous block of juxtaposed rocks, which one might have thought, from a distance, to represent the lascivious tenderness of a couple. The two horizontal statues were profiled against the setting sun, and a red eruption was glorifying their union at that moment. The spectacle was so unexpected that the travelers uttered a cry of surprise, and suspended their march to admire it.

"We've reached the Caravanserai," said Carabella. "These palaces, now deserted, were inhabited by the first workmen and artists who built the island. You'll live in them during the duration of the first stage."

"Stage? What stage?" asked Choumaque.

"The captain didn't tell you, then, that for some time you'll be subject to a novitiate and that you'll be progressively initiated into the benefits of your new life? The Superman, before whom you'll appear in the near future, will decide, in accordance with your aptitudes, for what employment you'll be reserved. You, Monsieur Marcel, will doubtless be headed for the Palace of Reproduction. Your tall stature, the elegance of your person and the perfection of your form, which I divine to be attractive beneath your frightful garments, will certainly destine you for generative functions. As for you, Miss Mary, it's truly a pity that you'll only be passing through. Your beauty, too imposing to earn you the honored status of courtesan, like mine, would probably designate you to fulfill the no less pleasant office of fecund mother. The Superman seeks out impeccable molds, and you'd furnish him with one. In his wisdom, he'll decide.

"And me?" Choumaque asked.

"You?" Carabella replied, laughing. "As for you, my poor Monsieur, I don't understand your presence in Eucrasia. Go lean over the purity of that lake, which will reflect your person, or better still, contemplate yourself in Mirror-of-Smiles' eyes, which will tell you the truth, and you'll learn that your anatomy is ridiculous and lamentable. I know full well that, two days from now, the master's science will have modified you: that hair will exist where you have none; that teeth will replace the gaps in your mouth; that your bright complexion will be pale; that your regenerated hair will no longer have that bushiness that would frighten ferocious animals; that your dirty jacket of indefinable color and your trousers will be replaced by a more becoming costume restraining the untoward amplitude of your belly—but still, those transformations will only render you a mediocre object of desire in the midst of the beauties that surround us. No, I can't explain why you've been invited to Eucrasia. But the wisdom of the Superman doubtless has something in mind for you."

*After that declaration*, Choumaque thought, *it will be difficult for me to be further mistaken on my account. When in Paris, once a month, I extracted from my wages as a professor the ten francs necessary to be loved by a pretty woman, at least she had the decency to pour me a cup of illusion with her caresses. But here, truly, this courtesan is exceedingly cruel with her verities. It's true that I haven't given her ten francs, nor the equivalent in compliments.*

He ceased these reflections on observing that Carabella's strange prognostications were weighing upon his friends. With his eyes he scanned the admirable décor of flowers, verdure, water and rocks, and the elegantly-aligned villas, and said, approvingly: "So this is where we're going to live. The place isn't unpleasant, although the group in the background might be cruel for the contemplation of a virgin, and for the wisdom of a Stoic as ugly as me. I notice, in fact, that the dwellings seem to be empty. We'll be able to choose two that are adjacent, unless Miss Hardisson consents to lodge under the same roof as us."

"Certainly not!" protested Carabella. "That's absolutely forbidden by the rules. Neophytes cannot live in close proximity. Great God, what would become of strict creation if they were allowed to live side by side, delivered to their instincts? No, Monsieur Choumaque; the men live on the right hand side of the park, the women on the left. They can only meet at determined times, where surveillance is possible. At night, especially, they must remain separated...

"But it's time that we were going our separate ways, Mirror-of-Smiles will take charge of conducting Monsieur Choumaque and Monsieur Girard—with whom he is already, I observe joyfully, on the best of terms. As for me, I'll take care of the lovely Miss Mary. Are you coming, divine one?"

She dragged her away so rapidly that Marcel scarcely had time to address one last glance of farewell to her, which contained the affirmation of a tender fidelity that only his attitude had yet promised.

As for the two men, they followed the boy, who led them obliquely, with the elegant sway of his young body, toward the right hand side of the woods and lawns. They went along charming pathways in which the beauty of the panoramas, as if modified at pleasure, was transformed at every moment, according to whether they turned one way or the other. And yet, they did not walk for more than ten minutes, after which they found themselves in front of a habitation they had scarcely noticed, veiled as it was by the magnificence of giant trees.

It was a veritable monument, the exterior very varied. Only one emblem recalled fidelity to the principles of the land: red flag sewn with golden vibrions and ovules planted at the summit. The rest was quite fantastic in its architecture, an imbroglio of styles, the columns of Greek art mingling with Roman façades and Gothic arched windows; the multiple pointed roofs of the Renaissance face to face with the domes of Arab kasbahs; and, at the corners, the overhanging sections of Chinese pagodas supported by green marble caryatids.

"The Caravanserai of neophyte males," announced Mirror-of-Smiles.

Already, Choumaque and Marcel felt a kind of fatigue at so many implausibilities. Bewildered, they allowed the boy to guide them. In addition, that immense solitude; that absence of human activity around them; that silence, so cruel to their habits; and that contradiction of so much richness without anyone to profit from it, all impressed them in a melancholy fashion. In vain Choumaque repeated to himself that prosperity does not inflate the heart of a sage; his sadness came from another cause.

As soon as they had penetrated into a kind of atrium with vaults sustained by flamboyant sandstone torsades, shining with gilded metal reflections, Mirror-of-Smiles placed his foot on a pedal and the entire atrium, lifted up by a colossal force, began a rapid ascent, passing theory circular landings, all similar, with porticoes painted with allegories that lit up momentarily, giving access to profound and obscure galleries. It was a juxtaposed city that filed past in that fashion, in a vertiginous movement, and in a religious silence untroubled even by the siding of the enormous mechanism lifting them toward the sky.

Having reached the thirtieth floor, the platform came to a gentle halt and they stepped on to a delightfully faded mosaic parquet, which looked as if it had been freshly washed. They felt very close to the firmament, by virtue of the purity and the fluidity of the respirable air. After few more steps, two large doors opened automatically in front of them.

"Here are your apartments Messieurs. You're a hundred and fifty meters from the ground. You'll easily be able to contemplate the view when you've freshened up and before resting from your voyage. Come in..." He smiled with his pretty carmined lips.

Choumaque and Marcel went into the first of the two rooms and were surprised to find themselves in a rectangular space quite simple in appearance, with shiny walls and roses at the rounded corners, and a parquet encrusted with stones that they recognized as fragments of agate, jade and green amber. The furniture was uncomplicated: only one bed, without curtains but profound, soft and inviting; a few chairs, elongated and soft, to permit the entire relaxation of the limbs; and finally, dark onyx tables with feet sculpted in lascivious decorations, with a ratchet that could raise or lower the top at will, tilting the plane or returning it to the horizontal.

Near the bed, a grotto, framed with natural plants, gave birth to a pink marble basin full of warm and perfumed water, probably the bath. A few droplets of water were still dripping from stalactites, indicating that showering was as easy as submersion. On one side wall, however, there was a panel, which captured their attention with the inscription UTILITIES. A hundred small pigeon-holes were arranged therein, each with a label of various designation. Choumaque read a few: *heat, cold, sleep, meal, coiffure, mouth, theater, sensuality...*

The little guide was pleased to observe their astonishment. He explained, as if he were reciting a script: "You have, Messieurs, within arm's reach, the satisfactions of all the necessities of life. Are you too warm? Press the button corresponding to the designation *cold* and the air will refresh you. Are you hungry? Obtain your nourishment by the same procedure. Would you like, before going out, to tidy yourself up, to brush your clothes, clean your teeth, comb your hair? Press the contacts again, and arms will emerge from the wall that will accomplish those functions. Service by means of slaves does not exist here; machines replace domestic servants.

"But sensuality...I don't see...?" Choumaque queried.

"Ah!" said the child laughing loudly. "Try it and you'll see." He smiled equivocally, and took Marcel's hand again, who felt embarrassed by it.

"That's all right," said Choumaque, without noticing his insistence. "I can see that all the commodities of life are assembled within a surface of two square meters, and I'm glad of it, for the fact of having myself served by others has always been painful to my sensibility. It gives me an impression of the unjust division of terrestrial benefits, and when the woman who did my housekeeping in the Rue Monge in the Latin quarter—when that good old woman, lame and prognathous, recompensed monthly by three hundred-sou pieces, brought me my milky coffee in the morning, I remembered the beautiful book *De Beneficiis* by the great Seneca, and I felt a desire to beg the maidservant's pardon. Nevertheless, I liked her company. She had interesting theories regarding love, resulting from her former status as a courtesan fallen into poverty...."

He passed his fingers through the tangle of his beard, pulled up his fugitive trousers, and then shrugged his shoulders. Finally, addressing himself to Marcel, he said: "Well, my dear friend, we have only to let ourselves live and await events. Let our souls be tranquil in the constancy of wisdom. Let's take a bath first. That basin tempts me; I've always regretted only having a cracked tub for my usage, which meant that I could only plunge my body into it in fractions. Afterwards, we'll dine, for it will be time. By the way, child, I don't see a clock. What time is it in your country?"

The child did not seem to understand. The professor was obliged to repeat his question before obtaining a reply.

"The time? Yes, indeed, I know what you mean, Monsieur. The hours of the day don't exist here; only the engineers know and observe them. Even the difference between day and night is often so scarcely evident that it is usually of no interest. Those are superfluous preoccupations, which the Superman has removed from our lives. Let us thank him for taking away all those paltry anxieties, in order to let us think only about amour."

So saying, he accomplished an indecent gesture that caused Choumaque to swell up with holy wrath and take hold of the child by the ear in order to correct him.

"Wretch! Don't you have any respect for me fifty years? Do you know that I'm going to throw you out of the window?"

Mirror-of-Smiles was utterly nonplussed. That reprimand for an act of simple politeness confused him. Was his life not made up of obliging offers to all comers? He was on the point of weeping—and it would have been the first tear that he had ever shed. His beautiful blue eyes, whose gleam was eloquently underlined by dark rings, expressed his astonishment and his sadness.

Choumaque understood the protestation, and suddenly softened.

"I forgot that we're no longer living in a country where morality is dominant in appearance. Go on, child, don't worry! I won't eat you today. Cruelty is a vice contrary to the essence of man; it's unworthy of a soul imprinted with mildness like mine. But I'll slap you if you permit yourself such manifestations again."

"With great pleasure, Monsieur. Believe me, I was not acting with a view to my personal amusement. I was obeying, as it happens, the natural duties of my functions, for I am marked by the finger of Caresco. The red line that I have there on my tunic, and underneath it too, indicates that I'm gelded, and by virtue of that fact, destined to servitude. I began very young, at the age of my puberty, utilizing myself for the pleasure of others. Certainly, I experience some satisfaction therein myself, and it would have been the best time of my present life, since, as soon as my chin is covered with a beard—which is still rare—I shall become entirely a slave. I don't complain, because I know that the future life will compensate me."

"Ah—you believe in a future life?" Choumaque queried.

"Yes, Monsieur; our religion informs us of it. I believe in metempsychosis and ulterior compensations. I'm a giton at present; later, I shall be a slave, but what does it matter, since, after my death, I shall live again and become a complete man. My successive lives will lead me toward perfection."

"That," said Choumaque, "is a reassuring morality, in sum, not far removed from our Christian dogmas, setting aside the question of lubricity—and, I dare say, not far removed from my doctrine of equilibria. This Caresco seems to me not to be devoid of a certain ingenuity. You can retire, little philosopher, and let us take our bath without you."

"In that case, Messieurs good night. I shall go to bed. The pleasures of the fête and the tenderness of my sister Carabella have tired me out. May Caresco favor you, Messieurs!"

He disappeared, after turning a cartwheel, leaving the two voyagers very surprised by his agility and his social role. Their astonishment dissipated, however, before the imminent satisfaction of relaxing their limbs in the warm water, which a delicious unknown perfume rendered even more captivating.

Marcel shut himself in his apartment, similar in all respects to that of his former professor, and Choumaque, left alone, got undressed.

# CHAPTER V

Scarcely had Choumaque stepped into the basin than the rock that constituted its frame sank downwards and narrowed, surrounding him on all sides, to the point that the poor man, his Stoicism being put to a severe proof, thought that he was about to be crushed.

"Alas, I'm going to die here, trapped!"

He was not; the rock circumscribed him just sufficiently to allow him to breathe. At the same time, artificial arms emerged from anfractuosities, equipped with soaped brushes that set about scrubbing the bather energetically in every part of his body, while showers that were successively hot and cold, coming from above, rid his greasy skin of the scoria that fifty years of transpiration had accumulated there.

When the initial panic had passed, Choumaque understood that this new manifestation of mechanical genius had no other effect that replacing human effort. He marveled at it, lending himself obligingly to the cleaning process. When he was finally thoroughly desquamated, the arms were folded back, the rock parted, and resumed its decorative impassivity. The water became pure again, warm, perfumed and transparent. He stayed there for a long time. His pink flesh felt a great wellbeing therein.

"Decidedly," he said, aloud, "thus far, I don't regret the voyage. These almost-supernatural comforts have their charm. But let's wait and see what happens next."

"What happens next will content you even more than the commencement," pronounced a voice behind him.

He turned round, and his first movement was a gesture of frightened modesty, when he observed the presence of a woman who had come in without him suspecting it. She was presently sitting on the bed, looking at him and smiling.

She was tall, rather full-figured, with a fresh complexion, her nose strong and her lips carmined beneath opulent brown hair. Her entire body was swathed in an exceedingly light mauve peplum, secured at the waist by a golden cord. Her age was indefinable, so impressed was she by the curious mixture of youthfulness and age that Choumaque had already observed in the Chief Representative Zadochbach. Two red stripes, embroidered on the silk of her costume at the level of the abdomen gave her a hierarchical importance.

"Don't you recognize me, Zéphirin?" she said, getting up and coming toward him.

"Recognize you? Forgive me, Madame…you must be mistaken…" stammered the philosopher, covering with his hands the part of his person that the morality of sculptors, in his own country, protected with a fig-leaf. Then he added: "But in order to permit me to gather my thoughts, deign to pass me my undershirt.

"Do you stand on ceremony nowadays?" the strange woman asked, still advancing toward the bath. "You weren't so shy thirty years ago, my dear Zéphi."

"You said Zéphi? Only one woman ever charmed me with that abbreviation."

"Well, I am that woman."

"You're making fun of me, Madame, and the joke is particularly cruel at the moment when I only have the transparency of water to defend myself from your gaze. The mistress who called me Zéphi, and who called herself Little Panade[10]—the mistress of whom I conserve the most tender memory, in spite of her perfidies—was thirty years old in 1920. Her habits of drinking and amour, combined with the numerous beatings that she received from her lovers, made her a woman already mature at that age, while you have the appearance of being in your prime. Besides which, she had no teeth, whereas you possess all of yours; and the chestnut color of her sparse hair

---

[10] The nickname is initially given as "môme Panade," the former term implying "kid" or "little girl," but is often extended to "petite môme Panade." The implication is that she began her career as a child prostitute.

showed through at the roots of her badly-dyed red hair. Yours is brown and abundant."

"What does that prove, Zéphi, except that someone has made another woman of me? Let's see—do you require memories? Do you remember the little kitchen the size of a pocket handkerchief, next door to the room you had then, where I fried you garlic in sauces—because you loved garlic. It's a taste you'd acquired from your friend, the painter Marius, who was from Marseilles...

"Do you remember your rivalry and your quarrel with the best of your comrades when he put such an insistence into courting me that I was obliged to give in to him? Do you remember how angry you were when you caught us both in your bed? You had nothing left, at that time...oh, how great our poverty was! And were we not obliged, in order to live, to steal the milk and bread that the suppliers left at the other tenants' door, for two months?

"You had nothing left, I say—not even a chair with which to hit your rival—and you were reduced to taking his clothes, and mine...for under the covers we were as naked as chrysalides—and throwing them out of the window. Our things landed on the head of a policeman on patrol. He came upstairs while you made yourself scarce, was received by us in that simple apparel, and brought us up on a morals charge..."

"Those are details that you might as well have obtained from another, Madame. They don't prove that you're Little Panade."

"You want more precise details? Well, listen. Do you remember...?"

She leaned closer to the philosopher and murmured a few words in his ear that suddenly made him straighten up, with an indescribable emotion.

"Ah! This time, it's no longer permissible for me to doubt! This tends to the marvelous! To quit a woman almost old, and find her again thirty years later, forty years younger! Come on, my girl, now that I look at you carefully in the light, I recognize the once-cherished features! It really is you. That's your charming smile, with more teeth. Those are your eyes, more serious, with fewer crows'-feet, even if that's no longer your hair! Might you be her daughter? But no, Little Panade was incapable of having children, having been dispossessed of her ovaries by the same Caresco that governs us at this moment. How can this be, by Seneca?"

In his emotion he had emerged completely from the water, and was cavorting on the parquet. The crown of his tousled hair, his fat shoulders, his thick torso, his abdomen hanging in numerous creases down to his shirt hairy thighs—his entire anatomy, in sum—was streaming with perfumed water. He had forgotten his nudity.

She enveloped him carefully, in order to dry him, in a thick violet peignoir that had been lying on a chair, and then drew him gently toward the bed, on which they sat down in order to chat.

"How can this be, Zéphi? It is, in reality, incredible. I want to tell you about it, for I have a few moments to devote to you. After the scandal that your rage caused, I spent two months in prison. I left the cell desperate, because I loved you—don't protest, I loved you! You'd never understood that the gifts of the body and those of the heart are two very different things, and that one can share the former while jealously guarding the latter for a dear friend. You'll see how that distinction reigns in this realm.

"I'll go on. So, I found myself on the street, without a sou, wondering whether I ought not to go step over the parapet of the great river that runs through Paris, when I remembered the generosity that Caresco had always shown toward me. Yes, I ought to say that my surgeon had been a benefactor for poor Little Panade. Before I knew you he had fished me off the sidewalk, in the most absolute deprivation, almost dead of the disease that was undermining me. He took me to his clinic to operate on me gratuitously, and when I was better, he even went as far as to give me money to live honestly. I had, in exchange, to come and display myself from time to time, to sing his praises and recount to the numerous acquaintances I made the treasures of pathology that he had found in my abdomen. I was his debtor, and I paid him in moving publicity. Very badly, moreover, for at the end of three months, that honorable life weighed upon me to the extent that I threw my obstetric girdle to the winds, to fall into your arms!

"In brief, I recalled all that before deciding to die, and, wanting to try his generosity, I went to ring the doorbell of his clinic. I found everything in disorder, without a single patient. The surgeon's instruments were being packed up for a great voyage; the operator was going abroad. The sisters in white head-dresses were weeping desperately as they made up the parcels. I understood then that all hope was lost for me.

"I was already going away, heart-broken, along the cold and silent street, thinking about my imminent bath, when I suddenly saw a man coming toward me, who seemed slightly mad and was making wild gestures. *A client!* I thought—but no, it wasn't a client; it was Caresco. On seeing me, he stopped gesticulating and seized me by the arm. 'Is that you, Little Panade? I've been looking for you...'

"I thought at first that he was joking, but the satisfaction that suddenly appeared on his face told me that he wasn't. In any case, the propositions that he immediately made to me explained his contentment. It was thirty years ago, and I remember the whole of that scene as if it were yesterday. Having taken me to a wine-shop and comforted me with a glass of eau-de-vie, to which he added a few drops of a liquid he was carrying on him, he turned me around several times, inspected my teeth, my throat, tested the reflexes of my pupils and the slackness of my breasts.

"'You can still do the job,' he said. 'Your anatomy is suitable; I'll patch it up. Besides which, the science of prostitution and your lubricious tastes are the surest guarantee of perfect service. I'm taking you with me. Is that agreeable to you?'

"'Where do you want to take me?' I asked him, stupefied.

"'It doesn't matter. I've always been good to you, and I want to continue to be, even though you didn't keep your promises to me.'

"He veritably magnetized me with his dominant gaze and voice. Anyway, I didn't hesitate; I accepted immediately."

"Then what?" asked Choumaque, prodigiously interested.

"Then, ballasted by a further sum of money, which permitted me one last imperial blow-out—he gave me just enough to make sure that I'd be poor again the next day—I embarked with him for an unknown destination. It was here that we landed. The land was deserted and chilled my heart, but soon, palaces rose up and five hundred magnificent couples moved into them. A few years later, those couples, aided by a few precious recruits, had founded a beautiful people submissive to the autocratic government of Caresco, who became the Superman. That's it. You know as much as I do."

"But what was your role in that society? This renewal of the flesh—how was it carried out?"

"My role? My new youth?" She got up from the bed, very proudly. Choumaque noticed the definite preeminence of her breasts, once so dejected by lassitude. "I won't say anything about my new youth, Zéphi, because, for one thing, I don't know anything about the methods employed here to return worn-out bodies to their primary vitality. It's up to the engineers and the physicians to explain all that. Me, I simply submit to their practices, to their secrets—and as you can judge, I wear my sixty-two years quite well, without being rejuvenated.

"As for my role, Zéphi, there's none more enviable, nor more highly honored. I'm the High Priestess of the Courtesans. I'm the one who teaches them the science of amour, of which, no doubt, you'll experience the benefits in due course. I employ all my days in that, and sometimes my nights. There's an entire technicality of sensuality that society is wrong to ignore. Marjah and I—Marjah is my colleague, the High Priest of the Gitons—have renovated that art, fallen into

73

desuetude since the fall of Byzantium and the proscription of the *Kama Sutra.* We have recovered the precepts of those remote epochs, combining them with the resources of our imagination and the precautions of scientific hygiene. The Superman is also one of the pioneers, and not the least, of that religion of Pleasure, which he has instituted in parallel with the religion of Life."

"Of Life?"

The High Priestess suddenly became serious. Her face lit up, and directed an almost mystical gaze toward the heavens. Her hands came together in a devotional manner. "Ah! That's where it's necessary to admire the renovating genius of the Superman! Have you, Zéphi, who were, as far as I can remember, a philosopher...?"

"A Stoic. I invent invented the doctrine of equilibria..."

"Have you, who were also an observer, never noticed that all human miseries derive, not from the inherent wickedness of the creature and the social evils that result therefrom, but from the maladroit fashion in which humans are created, arriving in the world charged with a heavy burden of hereditary defects, faults and unhealthy atavisms? No, you've never noticed that?

"Well, Caresco has taken aboard those ideas—and that's why he has perfected life in his realm, by only permitting beings to enter the world provided with perfect health. That's why he has edified, as well as a religion, beneficent creation—and all of us admit and respect his dogmas, with the result that if our people is happy, it's not only because they're rich and abundantly satisfied in all the needs of existence; above all, it's because they're healthy, because they're born... eucrasic!"[11]

---

[11] Eucrasia is an obsolete medical term for physical wellbeing, the hypothetical state of perfect health, derived from the Greek *eu* [good] and *krasis* [combination], derived from the long-maintained hypothesis that illness is caused by a disproportion—a dyscrasia—in admixture of the four bodily humors.

"How admirably you preach, little girl! I no longer recognize you."

"Don't be astonished," said Little Panade, resuming her roguish expression. "I've just been reciting our catechism. But anyway, I can't tell you too much. You'll judge for yourself, in due course. And you'll admire our beautiful civil organization, at the same time as you taste the pleasures of the religion I teach…my Zéphi!"

Choumaque had got up in his turn. The conversation, the comments on amour, the ancient flesh of his one-time mistress, which had become a new flesh, the heady perfume that she was wearing, all combined to inflame him. He drew nearer to the High Priestess, his eyes confessing his desire."

"You teach, little girl," he said, in a voice as harmonious as he could contrive, "but do you also practice?"

"Certainly, on occasion..."

"Well, I believe than an occasion is presenting itself..."

He clutched her to his hairy chest.

She pushed him away violently. "Are you joking, Zéphi? In the state you're in, old and frightful as you are, you dare to ask that of me? I wouldn't obtain any pleasure from it, you know! At least wait until your youth as been restored, like mine. And then, what would Marius say?"

"Marius? What Marius?"

"Your old friend."

"What! He followed you?"

"No, I met him again here, purely by chance."

"That's all right; I'll await events..."

Awaiting events was Choumaque's manner of action. He no longer had those beautiful burning passions of youth that would once have made him throw himself on Little Panade and take by force the sensual pleasure that she was refusing him, and which would also have caused him to set out in search of Marius to demand a reckoning for his past treason. In any case, he was firmly convinced, by virtue of the disillusionments he had experienced in Paris, that women are generally unworthy of the stirrings they provoke. Furthermore, reading philosophy had made him resolute in that attitude of expectant calm. No: he gazed upon the world with amused curiosity; and from those observations he had reasoned and concluded that brief existence passes easily when one is endowed with Stoicism. Did not life always equilibrate, in terms of good and ill fortune?

As his interlocutrice thought she had discovered a hint of resentment in his facile patience, however, she wanted to create a diversion and went on: "Come on, Zéphi, console yourself. Instead, come and looks at the panorama that unfolds beneath us from this height. It's curious, and worth the trouble of being admired."

She drew him to the bay window and opened it wide. The chamber gave access to a circular terrace bordered by a perforated balustrade, on which they leaned. At first Choumaque only saw a luxurious vegetation composed of tall trees of an unknown species, distributed in accordance with a charming discipline. He recognized the back of the fantastic palace into which he had gone a little while before. He was looking down on it, as well as the park, the villas and the stone blocks that one might have thought disposed by Titans to represent an amorous couple. Beyond that, however, to the right and the left, nature extended as far as the eye could see, bathed in the red and gold apotheosis of a setting sun. The perspective was uneven, with mountains and woods, which the star's long streaks touch in places and caused to glitter, in contrast with the shadowed expanses of valleys, like sheets of color and life extended over sleep and repose.

"You can't see very much," said the High Priestess, "but put your eye to this powerful telescope, and follow my explanations. The island, as you doubtless know, has the form of a human body. Direct the telescope toward its contours and you'll be able, in places, to convince yourself of it. The Superman resolved to distribute his palaces in accordance with that disposition of nature. He occupies the location of the Brain. It's from there that he directs the thought and action of his realm. Turn the visual axis of the instrument toward that region, and you'll perceive, confusedly, the mass of brilliant domes beneath which he presides over our destiny. It's fantastic! You'll see that in due course. Come and look backwards now. Don't worry about the telescope; it will follow you of its own accord as soon as we've pressed the omnial switch..."

Indeed, scarcely had they turned their backs on that first face of the view than the telescope, moved by an occult force, came by itself to take up a position within arm's reach. They leaned on the parapet again, the High Priestess having taken the liberty of putting her arm around the philosopher's waist.

"Here in front of us is the natural sequel to the dispositions sketched by the anatomical conformation of the rocky mass. The more you're able to follow the description, the more you'll be able to discern it. There, in front of you—that gorge hollowed out in the rock, is near the place where you disembarked. The shiny little crests that stick up in the form of a lyre are immense halls in which the nation is inspired by musical taste and science. The arms that depart therefrom, seeming to dangle into the water of the sea, belong to the commune, whose habitations are there, very different in their architecture from the one which will shelter you for a while.

"I shall pass over them to arrive at the Thorax, simulated by forests of improbable grandeur, which are presently masked from view. They're called the Woods of Respiration. Know that they're distributed like lungs, with concentric pathways depicting fairly faithfully the curves of the rib. People play and dance there.

"The Heart is that immense red dome, the swelling of which you can perceive. It is, along with the Brain, the most important system in the realm. Immense factories manufacture omnial, sympathetic, telepathic and other fluids there, the services of which we appreciate every day. Telephony, lighting and the various physical energies have their origin there. Also accumulated there is atmospheric electricity, heat from the central fire, the cold of glaciers and the tidal force of the sea, previously unutilized, which our engineers have been able to store. From there, those fluids are redistributed over the entire surface of our soil by a system of channels, which it would be imprudent to touch.

"Lower down, at the level of the Stomach and the Liver, you fall into the domain of subsistence. Chemistry concocts our alimentation there, along with the more delightful culinary dishes that we serve ourselves on days of rejoicing. Heady beverages are also prepared there. Poultry-yards full of birds, the rearing of livestock and the intensive cultivation of cereals and fruits are admirably well-ordered there.

"The systems of water supply and excretion, and waste-disposal succeed those organs, in the location of the Kidneys. Enormous machines distil the clouds, when there are any—which is rare—and valves extract profound and pure water. Nothing is left to the hazard of the elements, which are disciplined to our needs.

"To conclude, separating in the sea, there are the inferior Limbs, populated like the Arms, and the region of the Ankles, where the slaves live."

"But you're not saying anything about the region I can see at the intersection of the legs," said Choumaque.

"You can't see anything of that from here, you rascal," the High Priestess immediately replied, gratifying him with a pat on the backside. "You can't see anything there because we're four hundred kilometers away, and I suspect that your imagination pauses too gladly on matters of generation. You're right, however, and in the place you've just mentioned, where I live, there are indeed very important sections, entirely consecrated to religious necessity: the Palaces of Fecundity and Birth, and also the Palaces of Sterile Sensualities, and the dwellings of the Courtesans and Gitons. The whole is dominated by the Mount of Venus, which soars into the snows and has been smoking for twenty years. But I dare not say too much about that, not knowing whether you'll ever be admitted to it, your carcass being in such a sad state..."

And she stood up, disdainfully, preparing to leave. "I'll run along now, I've already chatted for too long; I need to get back to the Palace of Sterility."

"In that costume?"

"It's the costume of the day. There's a festival of Eucrasia in the gardens of dancing, near the place where you disembarked. The Courtesans, under my direction, and the Gitons, under Marjah's guidance, are meeting with the families..."

"I did, in fact, catch a glimpse of the lovely rhythms of couples who reminded me, by the grace of their movements and the symphony of their colors, of the ballets of the Paris Opéra, which are the best dances in the world."

"Do you think so?" asked the Priestess, with an ironic smile. Then she added: "*Au revoir*, Zéphi. I must go back. Sleep has been ordered for everyone as soon as the sun sets. In consequence, the tube won't be functioning once darkness has fallen. I don't want to miss it, for I'd be obliged to charter an airplane, which would take an hour to make the journey that only takes eight minutes by tube."

"Four hundred kilometers in eight minutes!"

"Yes—that's how we travel here. Adieu! May Caresco favor you."

"Adieu, Little Panade."

"Call me Madame Môme—that's how I'm known."[12]

She moved a flap of the peignoir that was covering Choumaque's nudity and kissed him on the shoulder. Then, after a final recommendation to submit to what was demanded of him, and a last glance at the panel of utilities, several of whose buttons she pressed, she turned a cartwheel, performed the splits that had once caused the crowds at public balls to marvel, and finally left, in a dignified fashion, draped in her mauve peplum circled with gold.

---

[12] I have retained Môme here, because it is used as a proper name rather than a description. Its coupling with "Madame" echoes the fact that those child prostitutes who survived childhood in the early 1900s—many did not—often became procuresses of children, that being their only area of expertise.

"She's fifty years old!" Choumaque said to himself, knowing that she was, in reality, over sixty. Then, in a spirit of emulation, he attempted to execute a somersault himself, while laid him flat on the floor.

It was in that posture that he received the visit of another individual, as unexpected as that of his former mistress. He was still trying to get up when a loudspeaker placed next to the door announced: "Dr. Hymen!"

A little man came in. He was short in the legs, with a stiff abdomen sheathed in a long black frock-coat devoid of a collar, like those clergymen still wore in the middle of the twentieth century. On the front of his waistcoat, open at the front, a dozen minuscule instruments of bizarre form dangled, adding a flourish to the neatness of a sea-green shirt, and clashing with one another. But what constituted his eccentricity even more than the garment was his enormous head, coiffed with an opera hat with a flat brim whose brushed-up felt was so bushy that it matched his tousled hair. Under the hat was a strange clean-shaven face, simultaneously comical and cruel: comical by virtue of the deviation of the long and hairy nose, slanting to the right toward a little turned-up side-whisker; cruel by virtue of the penetrating expression of the glaucous eyes, accentuated by thick eyebrows.

He did not take off his hat, and considered the sprawling philosopher momentarily.

"Ah! Have you gone mad? Have our institutions already turned your head? A bad start, my friend, a very bad start. Get up. I don't have any time to waste. Or, rather, no: stay on the floor, since you're there, and roll over on to your back."

He leaned over Choumaque, parted his bath-robe with disgust, and after having studied him momentarily, said: "*A priori*, you have an ignoble anatomy, and there's not much to be done with you. You've had a bath? So much the better. I'll be able to examine you without getting dirty. Don't move. Let's see..."

He took a measuring-tape out of his pocket, unrolled it and began to take measurements along the torso, the legs, the shoulders and the face. Then he palpated the organs through their walls of fat, delimiting the stomach, the liver and the spleen, and ausculated the heart and lungs with the aid of a stethoscope hanging from the chain of his waistcoat.

At the same time, he murmured: "How has this carrion been admitted? My word, it's revolting! It's bathed in fat, threatened with emphysema and atherosclerosis. The legs are streaked with varicose veins. And he smokes and drinks! You smoke, don't you? You drink, you pig? And you weren't ashamed to apply to come here? And you were let in! Dare to claim that you don't drink!"

"In fact, a few beers, from time to time," Choumaque confessed, nonplussed by this avalanche insults. "But I'll tell you..."

"Don't say anything; you'll have more intelligence."

He had taken hold of the philosopher with an uncommon strength and sat him up. Taking a new instrument from his collection of trinkets, some kind of complex tube that dilated at will, he applied it to his patient's ear, and then set up a screen level with the other ear. Then, connecting the tube by means of a wire to accumulator he was his carrying in his pocket, he passed long sparks of fire through it, which were echoed in an image on the screen. Choumaque felt a thousand tiny shocks, which stunned him.

The other looked coldly at the design produced by the omnial radioscope. "The brain isn't as lamentable," he conceded. "The localizations there are sufficiently equilibrated. I can only see one anomaly, one excessively developed nucleus...my word! It's that of philosophy! You're a philosopher, Monsieur? I'll even say more: you're an optimistic philosopher?"

"My God, Monsieur, if I were less disconcerted by your methods, I'd confess to you that optimism is indeed my doctrine, mitigated nevertheless by Stoicism, which has led me to the theory of equilibrium. For the moment, though, I'd have difficulty putting simple ideas together. Let me collect myself."

"Please do, Monsieur."

Dr. Hymen had suddenly softened, and a certain deference, doubtless provoked by the discovery that he had just made, gave more amenity to the tone of his voice. Choumaque took advantage of the pause to get to his feet, after which a few drops of blood were extracted from him by means of a prick on his thumb. He then perceived that his inquisitor was making notes on a pad attached to the chain of his waistcoat. He was about to demand explanations regarding the purpose of the examination to which he had just been subjected when the little man, having divined his intention, straightened up, making a courteous hand gesture.

"Later, Monsieur. We'll chat later. Today, I'm in a hurry. I still have to identify your friend Girard and your traveling companion, Miss Hardisson. It's been an honor, Monsieur. You can always find me at the Palace of Surgery. May Caresco favor you."

Before reaching the door he raised his arms in the air, and Choumaque thought that he was about to collapse, so full of evident effort were his features and his sparkling little eyes. He did indeed collapse, voluntarily, his body folding in two and his legs taking the place of his head. He was standing on his hands. He maintained himself thus momentarily, swaying; then, with a muscular thrust that caused his bones to crack, he completed his somersault and came upright again. His opera hat had not parted company with his hair; his pendants had accompanied his exercise with a metallic clink.

He disappeared, this time leaving Choumaque utterly astounded.

*That*, thought the philosopher, *was a serious man accomplishing an action that one might consider to be childish. But Mirror-of-Smiles and Madame Môme withdrew in a similar fashion, from which I conclude that it's a simple manifestation of politeness. It's doubtless the demands of good manners that force everyone to leave performing somersaults, and there must be a superior reason for it that I can't imagine. I'm merely astonished by the constant association of the grotesque and the marvelous. Let's await events.*

Having ruminated thus, and having relieved his mind of any other reflection by his customary strategy of expectant inaction, he suddenly felt very hungry. The prospect of an excellent meal, the possibility of which his former mistress had enabled him to glimpse, and, on the other hand, the prospect of Marcel's company, directed him toward the door that connected the two apartments.

He knocked, without receiving any reply. Then, wanting to open it, he searched in vain for the non-existent handle. It was the same with the other door, which opened on to the landing. He was locked in.

As his belly was screaming famine more imperiously, he remembered that satisfaction of all the instincts, all the commodities of life and all the pleasures of sensibility could be demanded from the famous utilities panel that filed one of the room's side-walls. He therefore advanced toward one of the buttons, which he believed to correspond to the word *meal*, and put his finger on it.

A click responded to his gesture, and he was surprised to hear a delightful tune emerging from the floor. He waited for it to end, applauded internally, and then, not seeing any aliment appear, perceived that he had mistaken the switch, and pressed the one for soft music, next to the one for cheerful music and the one for great lyricism. Searching further, he noticed the word *poetry*, and as there was none for philosophy, he rejoiced, promising himself that he would play a great role in Eucrasia.

For the moment, however, more material necessities continued to solicit him. He finally discovered the pigeon-hole of alimentation, and pressed the button. Alas, there was a disappointment as tormenting as his hunger. Instead of steak and potatoes, and *pâté de foie gras* garnished with a tempting salad, he saw two little capsules sprinkled with white powder appear, each about the size of a marble.

"That's how they expect me to furnish the haggis!" he said, aloud. "There's only enough in those two hazelnuts, at the most, to fill the cavity of my third left molar. This joke surpasses the limits of my tolerance, already considerable extended. But, for want of larks..."

He decided to swallow the complete aliment stoically, not without suspicion. Scarcely had he absorbed it, however, than he felt his appetite satisfied and his heart ballasted, as after a good meal. A few agreeable belches demonstrated to him that a fruitful labor of digestion was operating within him. He cheered up.

*In my eatery in Paris,* he said to himself, *I complained about the service, which was slow, and the quality of the nourishment, which, belated in its appearance, was parsimonious. At the most, to help me be patient and console me for my host's avarice, I had the opportunity to contemplate at leisure the pulpy complexion and double chin of the fat idol enthroned at the till. Here, the service is rapid, digestion facile, and I don't have to regret the gift of a tip. It's evident progress, and I ought to rejoice in it. But will it be the same tomorrow...and what will I think of it tomorrow?*

Outside, darkness had just fallen abruptly. A great peace reigned. The walls were illuminated by a kind of phosphorescence, gentle on the eye, and Choumaque understood that omnium, in its luminous manifestation, must be built in to the constitution of the buildings. But what should he do, now that he was alone and the doors would not open?

He wandered around the room briefly. He was tempted to have recourse to the panel, to press all the buttons successively, to listen to verses and music, to see magic shows and ballets, to watch a play at the Athénée-Comique or the Théâtre Français—for the labels promised all those distractions and even more marvels of thought, of voices and of harmony, captured by machines and distributed at will. But a heavy fatigue gripped him, the result of the voyage and so many successive astonishments.

In any case, the anxiety of being separated from Marcel scarcely encouraged him to distract himself. Then again, the profound bed was tempting. He did not even have to undress to lie down on it.

Before going to sleep, he considered insistently a little work of art hanging from a concave wall, just above the level of his horizontal position, in the place where pious individuals in his homeland displayed the lamentations of a Christ, the emblem of their duties, their dolorous dreams and their tormented passage through life. Here, that symbol had been replaced by an entwined naked couple, with genuine flesh tones. He stared at it for some time.

Soon, however, snores echoes by the sonority of the room attested that he was no longer contemplating that attribute of the new religion.

# CHAPTER VI

The next morning, Choumaque woke up late. He had slept solidly for a time that he estimated at twelve hours, and he experienced as a result a very particular sentiment of bliss, a relaxation of his limbs and a clarity of heart such as he had never known.

Although the arched bay window giving access to the terrace was closed, a current of air impregnated with the scent of lilacs was circulating in the room, and it was doubtless that perfumed caress that had extracted him so agreeably from sleep. The savor of those first moments pleased him. He wanted to stay there, lounging lazily in the softness of the delicately feathered bed, his mind completely modified. Charming ideas, memories of the past and hopes for the future, delighted his idleness.

By way of contrast, he remembered the trouble had had experienced, only a fortnight before, in shaking off the gross idleness of the morning, subjecting himself to the contact of cold water and, after having dressed dolorously, quitting his little apartment decorated with engravings and trinkets dear to his contemplation if not his purse, to go and philosophize with the dunces.

Here, nothing was similar. Although the walls were not charged with prints and mock-Tanagra figurines, at least they were garnished with a pale pink paste, in harmonious contrast with the red of the cushions supporting his head, and the violet of the bath-robe he had retained during sleep. The absence of angles in the corners permitted him to breathe without fear of the dust that ferries diseases. He knew that if the whim took him to plunge himself in the basin, the water would be warm and odorous. He did not even have to soap himself or scrub himself, for the machine would take care of that task.

Although the privation of his milky coffee tormented him slightly, he reassured himself with the thought that an aliment less harmful to the occasional palpitations experienced by his heart would replace it. The pipe that he lit every morning had the same unfortunate effect on his organism, and he consoled himself for no longer having it within arm's reach, on the nearby table. The rotundity of his belly described, beneath the covers, a projection whose esthetic faults he deplored.

He was disposed thus, with his eyes turned toward the door, when the same resonator that had announced Dr. Hymen's visit the previous evening informed him of the entry of another unknown individual.

"The High Priest Marjah!"

The door rotated gently on its hinges, and a man appeared, his arms extended in front of him. He was of medium height and his silhouette was harmonious. His yellow costume, admirably becoming, seemed to have been inspired by Byzantine grace and also by respect for the laws of hygiene. A doublet of flexible silk, ornamented by little holes that were as many vents designed to facilitate the circulation of air, while letting out the neck and embracing the torso, fell away from the black velvet belt like the flaps of a Roman tunic, stopping at the knees. His legs described their contours in tights made of the same fabric, stretched at the kneecaps, and covered on the feet by black sandals. Beneath the waist, two embroidered red crosses signified hierarchy.

Abundant brown hair evaporated as far as the shoulders in long contrived undulations, and artifice was similarly detectable in the make-up of the face, with a narrow nose, delicate features, too young and too pretty, contrasting with the antiquity of the gaze.

He was followed by Mirror-of-Smiles, similarly dressed, but with a single red stripe on the front. The child's arms were laden with a vestment.

"May Caresco operate upon you! Here you are, already awake, my dear Choumaque," he said, as if he had known his interlocutor for a long time. And, without paying any attention to his surprise, he added: "I see with pleasure that you're in good form to be subjected to a few modifications."

"I'm ready for anything," the philosopher replied. "Principally, to know what important individual I'm talking to at present."

"I'm not an important individual, my dear Choumaque. I am, on the contrary, one of the humblest servants of the Superman. I'm Marjah, former favorite of the Shah of Persia, presently a eunuch, and until the end of my days, if it pleases Caresco, High Priest of Gitons and Director of Slaves."

"That's an important responsibility," said Choumaque, emphatically.

"It has brought me to you this morning, to discover whether you have been content with Mirror-of-Smiles."

"My God! I haven't had anything much to demand of the child…"

"I regret that, my dear Choumaque, for the little one will not have much longer to allow himself to be cherished. He'll soon be mutating into a slave."

"He told me that yesterday, and I couldn't help feeling sorry for him."

"Feeling sorry for him? Why?" Marjah deposited violet garments at the foot of the bed. "Those will serve you later, my dear Choumaque. For the moment, you're going to follow me to the Palace of Surgery, where you'll spend three hours—the time necessary for your metamorphosis."

"What's going to be done to me? Am I going to undergo an operation?"

"You're going to undergo a dozen."

"But I'm not ready! I wasn't expecting that! You can't surprise people like that when they've just woken up! Has my friend Marcel Girard been informed? And my traveling companion, Miss Mary Hardisson?"

"Don't worry about them. They'll be able to do without you for three hours. Their youth and beauty spare them such annoyances for the time being, but you have to be completely remade."

"Damn! I wasn't expecting that!" Choumaque repeated, shivering in terror, all the more so because, at that moment, he remembered the surgical epic of the airplane captain, and saw once again his little half-body perched on the wheeled pedestal. Was he about to be butchered in a similar fashion, and cut back to the organs deemed to be essential? In vain he told himself that an arm, a leg, a liver, a spleen and so on were very minor matters for a Sage; he could not help trembling.

Marjah looked at him, smiling, seemingly amused by his emotion.

"Truly, my dear Choumaque, you're getting very excited over a little formality. It's unworthy of an intelligence like yours. To judge by Dr. Hymen's report, which I read surreptitiously with the sole aim of reassuring you, at the very most, your abdomen is going to be opened to remove the fat; your breast will be split in order to resect parts of the lung that aren't working well; the varicose veins will be removed from your legs and scrotum; your tibias will be broken in order to straighten then; your teeth will be cleared out in order that new ones can be planted; and the ducts of your liver and bladder that have calculi injurious to their efficient functioning will be cleaned out...trivia, in a word! They'll finish, I think, by scalping you in order to replace your obsolete hair by a more abundant provision. You'll wake up young, almost charming, vivified by the various serums with which your tissues will have been nourished. And you're trembling over so little, my dear Choumaque!"

"Chloroform! I'm afraid of the chloroform."

"Chloroform! What an outdated terror! Chloroform is no longer in use here. It has been replaced by magnetic influences that will cradle you in the sweetest dreams. Let's go! Get up bravely, my dear Choumaque, and follow me."

Confronted by that fine confidence, the philosopher recovered his courage. In any case, he had no relatives on whom to cast the pretext of grief, and the only friend dear to his heart, Marcel, would be unaware of the unpleasant ordeal.

Marjah recommended that he not get dressed, but simply to retain the bath-robe that he had kept on all night, and only to put on a pair of sandals that he handed to him.

They left the room. As they crossed the landing, before setting foot on the elevator, which was awaiting their embarkation, the philosopher scanned the vast gallery with a rapid glance. He was secretly desirous of seeing his pupil—but the corridor was deserted, the doors closed.

The descent was completed in the blink of an eye, the entire mass sinking down silently, causing the same successions of light and darkness to pass before his eyes, so rapidly this time that the images hardly had time to form. At the bottom, Mirror-of-Smiles pirouetted, and then went away.

Choumaque was glad to get out of the caravanserai, to breathe the warm air, gently perfumed with the aroma of lilacs, like that of his room. The sight of the tall trees, the verdure, the lakes, the polychromatic thickets, and even the flower-beds depicting the unmentionable parts of the body, made him feel better. He wanted to see them later, in company with Marcel, and also Madame Môme. Provided, great God, that the surgeon did not dispossess him of that which he could make agreeable to the latter!

He attempted to interrogate his guide, to obtain fuller information, to discover whether Caresco would be modifying his body in person, but Marjah, after so much prolixity, no longer made any reply.

They went through the strange Palace of the Head, where the little salivary cascades were foaming along the red walls, under the irradiation of enormous columns in the form of teeth. Then there was the exit along the path of fine sand and the reintroduction into the tunnel and into the tube, where the two of them took their places.

"A hundred kilometers—two minutes!" Marjah pronounced, pressing a button that lowered the partition and provoked a formidable thrust of atmospheric pressure on the capsule launched into the void.

This time, Choumaque did not experience any nausea, probably because his stomach was empty. He had sat down on the banquette in order to pass the brief interval of the journey, and admired the comfort of the cabin, the caprice of the black arabesques snaking over the gilded wood. He recalled the recent presence of the two charming bodies of Carabella and Mirror-of-Smiles on the soft divan, and their weary attitude. Those curious memories provided a diversion. In any case, the constant tranquility of Marjah reassured him. The eunuch's serious, aged gaze contrasted with the apparent delicacy of his body.

"Are you happy here, High Priest?"

"Certainly, my dear Choumaque."

The expression of the voice belied that affirmation. The philosopher was convinced that, if the man was not unhappy, he did not know absolute happiness either. That opinion had already formed in the wake of a response that Madame Môme had made to a similar interrogation. Happiness! Could they know the price of it, those who knew so many comforts and pleasures? But that was only a passing reflection, quickly interrupted by the stopping of the locomotive engine.

Marjah asked him once again to follow him.

As they came out of the subterranean passage, Choumaque thought that he must be in the region specially reserved to the Superman. He was not mistaken, and the accuracy of his reflection was corroborated by a comment from his guide: "The Brain!"

The monument that was presented to their eyes resembled a vast dome, gray in color, set on the ground. Its ovoid form, the broader extremity directed backwards and the sides flattened, was divided by a large dark fissure separating two hemispheres symmetrically furrowed by numerous juxtaposed meanders, uncovering anfractuosities. The red stripes of a vascular system were the sole decoration of the uniformly dull, severe and disquieting mass, which reminded Choumaque of the nausea once provoked by the menu of his eatery when the latter displayed at the head of a long list of denominations as alluring as they were unfamiliar: *Fried brains in Bechamel sauce.*

That impression soon dissipated, however, when he had passed through the little opening in the median fosse, which gave access to the interior of the palace. The strict order of the vast circular translucent halls of glass, supported by metal lattices, all ablaze with omnial light, gave him the impression that he was penetrating into active Thought, into the cerebral force acquired to the benefit of humankind.

Thanks to the transparency of the walls, he saw people clad in violet smocks working feverishly, agitating in front of machines with complicated components, whose gears were propagating mysterious impulses, lifting enormous levers, crushing and molding metals, always silently, by the simple pressure of contact. Elsewhere, sparking furnaces, licking flames and infinitely varies colors—an entire living alchemy—aureoled the ponderous gestures of grave individuals whose gazes, fixed upon books, calculations, blackboards, test-tubes, microscopes and other complicated instruments, pale silver gleams and golden flames, paid no attention to the passing strangers.

Choumaque noticed once again the antiquity of their souls, belying the usurped youth of their bodies. There were no other sounds than those of toil, the clicking of metals, the muffled rhythm of pistons and the release of valves: a colossal effort produced by the omnial fluid, which a view to giving birth to omnium.

Choumaque and Marjah continued on their way, walking over brightly-colored spongy fabrics that stifled their footfalls. In the meantime, on the frontispieces over the doors, allegories depicted the studies of the people who worked there. In one there was a map of the world, and soils were being analyzed; in another there was a celestial sphere, and the stars were being interrogated. Further on, the ritual burial of microbes advertised the beneficence of serums. Elsewhere, the study was symbolized by a fresco in which the form of a smiling naked woman brandished a torch from which an apotheosis of concentric flashes sprang, and it was deducible that the fluids of Force, unknown energies, light, heat and electricity—all transformations of the unique power—were within.

They continued, Marjah pushing the neophyte, who had a tendency to pause and contemplate. Finally, after turning many more corners, and many astonishments before innumerable halls in which the same labor concentrated the minds of scientists, they emerged, and immediately found themselves in front of another palace even more marvelous than those that had already been presented to Choumaque's admiration.

"The Temple of Surgery—the residence of the Superman!" announced the eunuch, with pious respect, kneeling down.

Choumaque understood that he ought to imitate him, and he prostrated himself. That movement, and the respite of adoration, that followed it permitted him to contemplate the monument, the mass of which astounded him, as much by its bizarrerie as its richness. It would have been difficult to recognize any style or form whatsoever in the incoherence of the projections and reinforcements that constituted the structure. On looking more closely, however, one might have thought it a heap of gigantic surgical instruments hurled on top of one another pell-mell, sealed together by a mortar itself composed of an infinite number of tiny implements enameled with precious stones—rubies, sapphires, diamonds, emeralds, peals and topazes—and arranged like jewels in a mosaic.

In that essential paste, the debris of bones and entire bones—tibias, femurs phalanges and skulls—jutted out in places; maxillas and cheekbones stood out from the wall, designing a rictus; thoracic cavities, fixed in the massif, underwent minuscule inflations proportionate to the enormity of the block.

The sight would have been terrifying if the sunlight striking those slender objects, metals and gems had not dispensed a radiant and savage gaiety. What surprised Choumaque even more, however, was the entrance to that extraordinary construction. It was constituted by the reproduction, scaled up to twenty meters, of an instrument that had been modified at the beginning of the twentieth century to such a point of surgical artistry that all the operators in the world, frightened by the genius of its complication, had refused to employ it, leaving its usage solely to its inventor, Caresco.

By means of its strange mechanism, that implement, once a wound was produced by a scalpel, parted the flesh without wounding it, uncovering and removing almost by itself the organs or tumors that the mission was to extract, ligatured blood vessels, resected limbs, cleaned joints, broke bones and opened the most resistant skulls, and then, when the operation was concluded, reunited the tissues almost without leaving any trace.

The Superman's masterpiece, it had facilitated improbable successes for him. It had been the ideal mechanism to aid his formidable audacity and his scorn for lives. It affected the form of an iron horseshoe capable of widening or contracting at will by means of simple pressure exerted within its rim. According to the caprice of the hand manipulating it, it became simultaneously a crusher, an aspirator, a rectifier, a separator, a speculum, a curette, an osteoclast, scissors, a washer, an amygdalatome, a suturer, a trocar and an enterotome; it sufficed for all the necessities of urgency or slowness; it replaced everything that experience had taken centuries to acquire.

Thanks to that dispositive, Caresco had been able to operate on two hundred patients wounded in a single night after the famous Battle of New York in 1920, which had put an end to the Anglo-American War, in which his thirst for fame had led him to volunteer, and the reportage of the two worlds had obligingly celebrated that feat, unprecedented in the annals of medicine, and lauded the employment of the Carescoclast, a name made up of anagrams of the device's uses.

Still kneeling, Choumaque gazed curiously at the reproduction in solid gold of that legendary instrument, so constellated with diamonds and precious stones that the eye was dazzled. He shivered at the idea that he was doubtless to serve as a further subject for experimentation in a matter of minutes. But the apparition of four brown-skinned women clad in light mauve veils with golden girdles, dotted with jewels, distracted him from his contemplation.

They emerged from the Temple singing a slow chant; they came forward two by two, the couples united by garlands of flowers. The fabric of their costumes was so transparent that the philosopher could perceive the red stripe on their abdomen, the symbol of their status as courtesans. Madame Môme, adorned like them, was leading them, bearing a green onyx amphora on her shoulder in a hieratic gesture, while behind then, a boy was holding up a golden trident whose prongs were diamond-tipped.

The cortege approached two pink pylons erected in front of the entrance. Golden vibrions ran along the steles in question, and their summits were emitting an odorous blue smoke. The High Priestess unrolled her ribbon of women and flowers around her, while the chanting continued, developing and amplifying, following a more rapid rhythm that carried the dancers away. Arms, legs, buttocks, breasts, hair and flowers crossed paths harmoniously; human corollas melted into the luminosity of petals. Then, when the performance was complete, the Priestess held out her amphora, the child plunged his trident into it and brought out a bloody morsel of flesh.

The silence became complete before that action, of incontestable emotion. The quivering shed moved at the end of the pike, describing a semi-circle, was deposited in the scared fire, then sizzled, giving off a gush of brilliant flame, from which a dove took flight amid spirals of smoke. Then dances began again, impelled by a more vibrant harmony.

"What does that signify?" Choumaque asked of his guide, who did not get to his feet.

"Shut up, my dear Choumaque! Marjah replied, in a whisper, with a fearful gesture. "You shouldn't speak here, for your voice might trouble the work of the Superman. However, as your surprise might dispose you unfavorably to the operation, I shall take the liberty of whispering an explanation of what you've just seen.

"You've just witnesses one of the fundamental rites of our religion. The morsel of flesh that the fire has destroyed is a womb that Caresco has just removed. I would have told you that it was a male sex organ if the Holocaust, instead of being offered to the flame by a boy, had been given by a woman. In the latter case, it is gitons who accompany the ceremony, who dance and sing, covered with flowers, while it is a courtesan who sacrifices the organ.

"Now, would you like to know the significance of the rite? Well, this is what our dogmas inform us, which is the truth: the metempsychotic succession never ends. There is in the world a strictly limited quantity of male attributes and female attributes, which evolve in their destination, changing being without changing sex. If one is destroyed, a replacement is immediately engendered elsewhere. This morning, for the harmony of his people, Caresco must have sacrificed one of these organs. Before death can occur in the freshly-extracted tissue, he has it burned, and the dove emerging from the flames represents the essence of the new sexual organ, going to attach itself in another location, in a new-born individual."

Marjah stood up after having spoken. The expression of gravity etched on his face indicated his blind acceptance of what he had just said.

*The man is a believer*, Choumaque thought, *but what I admire most is not his credulity; it's the power of the Superman, who is able to have such nonsense admitted. Caresco is a great joker, unless he's a great madman. I imagine that he's more likely a joker, since he has understood that the religious dream is useful to the submission and happiness of the inferior souls that are the generality. In sum, his doctrine is worth as much as the one my curé taught me—but how I prefer the Stoical conviction of the great Seneca, who wrote an immortal text on the brevity of life!*[13]

---

[13] *De Brevitate Vitae*—his most famous work.

Now Marjah was hurrying his companion toward the entrance. The women moved aside, laughing, to let him pass. The neophyte's silhouette amused them, although the latter attempted to hide from the ridicule beneath the amplitude of his peignoir. Madame Môme's gaze appeared to him to be less cruel than that of her younger and prettier companions, however.

"Courage, Zéphi," she murmured, as he went past her.

That greeting from his former mistress fortified his heart as he penetrated into the Temple. He was able to admire the cold order of the first room that followed the atrium, the white tiling through which wound little streams of blood, the complicated tubing running along the oval jasper walls, and the glass display-cases containing instruments of a purely retrospective interest, since the Superman no longer employed anything but his Carescoclast, and had not done so for thirty-five years.

As he cast his eyes over the display-cases, he noticed that the little implements seemed to be welcoming him amicably and smiling at him with their metallic gaze. A label was attached to each of them, and he read several of them, thus conceived:

*Tracheotomy that saved the life of Prince Arthur of Saxe, son of Kaiser Wilhelm II in 1920.*

*Enterotomy that saved the life of Tsar Alexander IV in 1927.*

*Craniotomy that saved the life of Pope Piux XI in 1919.*

And many others.

All those powerful lives saved, the memory of those surgical events, which the publicity of the epoch had not neglected, were not, however, sufficient to reassure the philosopher, and he was unsteady on his feet as he approached a kind of central altar made of gold, on long legs, covered with a red sheet and disposed like a raised bed. He suspected that it was necessary to lie down on it.

Around the bed, there were no more of those grim displays, nor of the gleaming tools that constituted the wall of the

Temple or filled the museum cases. There was nothing there but a single scalpel in a bowl and the famous Carescoclast, suspended from a long elastic wire fixed to the arch. The great principles of Stoicism did not prevent Choumaque from feeling a chill in the marrow of his bones as he looked at them.

He was about to take his place on the apparatus when the strange physiognomy of Dr. Hymen suddenly surged forth from a trapdoor fitted in the floor. His top hat with the flat rim, tilted slightly backwards, still framed his clean-shaven face, comical and cruel, his oblique hairy nose, his little upturned side-whiskers and his eyes like drills, arched by thick black brows. The rest of his stiff body was, however, surrounded by a long butcher's apron covered with stains, and his hands and bare forearms were soiled with blood.

"Is this the subject?" he said, addressing Marjah. "That's all right; you can go now." Then, giving his lips a gracious expression that was really a grimace, he added, as Marjah drew away, executing a pirouette: "You're going to be patched up, my friend; it won't take long."

"What are you going to do to me?" asked Choumaque, increasingly anguished.

"You'll go to sleep first. For the rest, we'll decide later.

"Shall I see the Superman?"

"He's the one who'll open you up, and it's a great honor that he's doing you, but you won't see him, since you'll be anesthetized."

"I'm hesitant, truly hesitant," the philosopher confessed, raising a trembling hand to an absent belt.

"Let's get on with it! You can see that we have no time to waste!" said the doctor, pointing to other individuals who had just appeared, and who seemed to be awaiting their turn.

Choumaque looked at them, in the direction indicated by his torturer's finger. Through the transparent wall he saw five men and five women, all young and beautiful, built on the same harmonious model that he had already observed several times. Sitting in a circle on the carpet of the atrium, they were playing knucklebones and teasing one another joyfully, but in silence.

"They're certainly more interesting than you," the doctor continued. "In a little while, the Superman is going to attempt on them one of the most extraordinary operations of his long career. Already, in our Fecundities, we create sex at will. Here, in the Temple, we've often transformed women into men and men into women, but the results were always infecund. This time, we want them to be capable of reproduction. The Master will owe to his genius alone the transformation of a woman into a man, and reciprocally, while transplanting the generative organs extracted from the one into the location of the generative organs extracted from the other.[14] That's amusing, ha ha! Then he'll make hermaphrodites! Ha ha! What do you say to that? Then he'll construct his human monad type. That will be the bouquet! You see, therefore, that we have meat on the slab, and that we can't waste any time! Let's go! Hup!"

Choumaque had scarcely understood these last words than the doctor grabbed him by the skin of the belly with the strength of an orangutan, lifted him up in the sir and placed him on the bed. Vainly, he struggled; the two bloody hands held him down. Then his thoughts suddenly reeled. A mobile wire applied to his temples poured a fluid into him that stunned him.

He sucked in air delightedly and felt himself swell up, rising toward the sky. He glimpsed a soft and pleasant landscape. A man he did not know was there, sitting under an oak tree, and he went toward him in order to philosophize. But he tried in vain to construct a seductive controversy; he could not follow the logic, for what he could see was too admirable for him to think about anything else.

---

[14] No more is said about this project in *Caresco, surhomme*, but it is the subject of a subsequent work, *L'Androgyne* (tr. as "The Androgyne" in vol. I of *The Exploits of Professor Tornada*).

In fact, the black eyebrows, the penetrating gaze, the oblique nose, the downy side-whiskers and the furry hat with the flat rim of the stranger sitting under the oak gradually lost their astonishing significance, and were transformed into a ravishing ballerina clad in mauve, exactly similar to Madame Môme. Yes, it really was his former mistress, within the range of his desire, and the color of her costume alone delighted him with a strange ecstasy. She did not prove as rebellious as before; she favored him with unknown caresses, which, successively applied to organs modified in turn by the operation, plunged him into a voluptuousness as long as the practice lasted and as extraordinary as it was curious.

# CHAPTER VII

Almost at the same moment as the philosopher Choumaque was being subjected to the marvelous suggestions of a hilarant fluid, Miss Mary Hardisson extracted herself from a restful sleep.

At first, she had some difficult collecting her thoughts. She experienced astonishment at having woken up in that room, utterly dissimilar to those that the banal luxury of cosmopolitan hotels had offered to her during a year of adventures. Gradually, the disposition of the apartment—the bed-alcove exceptionally decorated with great festoons of white velvet; the neighborhood of the opaline basin in which she had relaxed the previous evening after having purified herself by means of the artificial rock mechanism; and finally, in a corner, the presence of the pigeon-holes of which she had taken advantage to demand a sleeping potion that did not arrive—made the memory of the strange country to which she had come as a last resource more precise.

She remembered again having refused the services of Carabella, offered with a seductive insistence whose intention she had not understood. The courtesan's ardent face, pretty and flavorsome, each expression of which she saw renewed, caused her to compare the woman with the rude wives of her homeland, also beautiful, but of a strong and healthy splendor, as if virilized by sharing the struggles, privations and alarms endured during the war.

She thought about General Hardisson, the organizer of the defense, about the devotion of the farmers collaborating with his audacity, about the cannons that followed his stature.

Harry, her brother! She had loved him more than ever one evening, at the end of a battle, when, while picking up the wounded and the dead, she had found him under a pile of bodies, with blood on his forehead, icy. He had a livid beauty, all of his almost-extinct soul surfacing in his eyes...

Oh, the poor, dear, fraternal head—how she had pressed it against her lips then! How she had shivered with hope on finding that he was still breathing! Then, having cared for him, healed him, she now knew that he had resumed the road of the glorious calvary; she knew that his deeds embodied further bravery. From behind what ambush, at this moment, was his bold gaze scrutinizing the horizon, anticipating the enemy's approach? In what corner of the land had the hero taken refuge with his last tattered flag?

Quickly! She wanted to see Caresco, to obtain the power of his liberating engine!

She got up, and after having plunged into the basin she searched for her clothes. The previous evening, she had put them on the edge of the bed, and was astonished to find them replaced by a pink tunic and a peplum—a kind of long Roman robe fixed at the shoulder by means of a golden clasp studded with jewels, simulating a bird. A long leotard of the same fabric, with translucent mesh, designed to sheath the entire body, accompanied these garments, as well as a green metal girdle in several shades, mounted with diamante roses, and sandals in pink ibis-skin.

The costume resembled, almost exactly, the one worn by the young women who had flown to meet the airplane. The lightness of the fabrics, so favorable to the aeration of the skin, initially prompted a gesture of revolted modesty, and she swore never to disguise herself in that fashion. As she could not remain naked, however, she hoped to find more decent resources via the utilities panel. Alas, the clothing button, when she pressed it, provided her with a host of garments even lighter, more revealing and even more indecent.

Then, rummaging through the pile, she chose the most opaque fabrics, doubled the transparencies, filled in the necklines, and dressed herself in as chaste a fashion as possible, in conformity with her warrior ideals. Then she put on the sandals and the peplum, which appeared to have been tailored specifically to fit her body.

As she turned round her gaze was struck by the flamboyance of a quantity of marvelous items of jewelry displayed in a jade bowl. All kinds of rare stones were set in all kinds of metals, for various usages; they were so curious, so dazzling and so astonishing in their design that it seemed that they could not simple serve for adornment. She was not mistaken, for their alloys emitted bracing effluvia. She looked at them without desire; the only jewels that the daughters of the Red Land wore were stilettos in the hair and daggers in the belt.

Finally, having taken a step toward the exit, she was suddenly surprised by a veritable prodigy. The entire room seemed to expand and become infinitely large. At the same time, she saw the image of a woman dressed in pink, who was none other than herself, appear on the walls, repeated a thousand times. What magic had transported her thus into a palace of immensity? The walls, now covered in mirrors, permitted her to look herself in the face, contemplate herself from behind and from the side, to observe how the broad pleats of the robe, curving regally inwards over the hips, gave her a harmoniously new outline, and how the pallor of the fabric fused gracefully with the blonde flesh of her cleavage.

The sight revolted her, like a sacrilege. Was it, then, for a masquerade that she had left her homeland? To what reproaches would she not have been subjected by her warrior comrades, the she-wolves of the Red Land, if they had seen her thus disguised in iridescence, her waist imprisoned in green metal?

*O my sisters in suffering! You who patch your garments, you whose hands are chafed by washing the bloody linen of our heroes, behold my sacrifice, harsh daughters of my homeland!*

Observing the unruliness of her hair, however, she looked for a comb. Her eyes going to the utilities panel, she pressed the *coiffure* button. Instead of the object she expected, she saw a pigeon-hole open, revealing a machine with complex gears; the latter began to turn with metallic hands that emerged from the box, extended and moved up and down,

103

brandishing hot irons and sketching the gestures of an expert hair-stylist.

She realized that she was supposed to surrender her head to the curious apparatus, but abstained, for fear of something going awry and leading to some complication. She stood there watching the machine cavort until it had finished its service and retreated into the wall, after a click that closed the compartment. Then she remained perplexed, wondering how she was going to discipline her hair, now that the play of mirrors had also attenuated and the walls of her room, having gone pale, had resumed their appearance of uniform pale blue lacquer.

Two women dressed in yellow, with the embroidered cross on slaves at navel-level, arrived at that moment; they greeted her, invoking the name of Caresco.

"You are not coiffed, beautiful neophyte," said the one who appeared to be older, although still young. "Permit us to offer you our aid. We are your servants, by the grace of the Superman.

They made her sit down, and immediately occupied themselves with her. While one of them pushed her head toward the reactivated apparatus and presented her long blonde hair to the machine, the metallic arms combed, it curled it and pinned it up over the temples, with four long curls that snaked over the nape of the neck and fell upon the nacre of her shoulders. The other, took a charming like device from its box, which was applied to Miss Mary's face and set about kneading and massaging it, discreetly accentuating the young woman's complexion and features. It was not make-up; at the most it was a light supplement of health, beauty and charm.

At the same time, the younger of the maidservants went to place her foot on a particular section of the parquet, and the walls, obedient to its pressure, became mirrors again. The neophyte thus understood how she had provoked the astonishing transformation a few minutes earlier, doubtless by walking over that point in the mosaic.

To complete her toilette she was decked with the jewelry that she had disdained. In spite of her resistance, the servants, invoking orders from above, placed on her wrists, ankles, ears and bosom an entire stream of riches—whose value, she thought would have procured many cannons and rifles for the warriors of her homeland. Her face was framed with the light grace of lilacs, which, arranged in a pale bouffant over the blondeness of her hair, seemed to be emerging therefrom to die here, at the place where a large Rembrandt-style hat was positioned. She was obliged to resign herself to it.

It was in that ostentatious accoutrement that she went down a few minutes later into the immense park terminated in the background by the décor of the rocks. A large greyhound with soft eyes and silky fur immediately started following her and became her companion.

The greyhound could talk; it pronounced a few terms of politeness and affection, but so inappropriately that the neophyte, who was too preoccupied in any case, omitted to marvel at them, and the disdained animal ended up falling silent.

Meanwhile, Miss Mary strove to revolt against the suggestion of the radiant morning, the warmth of the atmosphere and the persistence of the perfume of lilacs—which was inexplicable, given that there were none of those flowers among the abundant vegetation that extended before her in a living and languorous harmony, receiving the caress of a spring-like sun. Doubtless it was another surprise of chemistry that embalmed the air in that fashion, for the pleasure of the sense of smell.

She would have liked to feel ill-at-ease among the delightful flower-beds, but she was obliged to submit to their charm. Excessively crowded, their agglomeration, hiding the leaves, gave the impression of fireworks in broad daylight, so many vivid and varied colors were there, from the ardent red of geraniums to the delicate white of hyacinths.

She soon got a grip on herself. She felt sad, and the solitude weighed upon her. To see Caresco, and to see him right away, became her unique objective. But how could she do that? Who could tell her? She was alone; the two maidservants had withdrawn, after kissing her hand.

She advanced, following a little stream that was singing in the moss, toward a verdant arbor with a rustic bench at the center, on which she sat down, in distress. The place was silently restful, impregnated with an enigma of tenderness.

The greyhound, which had followed her, came to place its striped muzzle against her. Insufficient society, alas! Why was she experiencing, for the first time, the new sensation of feeling isolated? She would have liked someone to appear who would talk to her about her homeland, and estimate with her the probability and nature of the help that she might encounter in Eucrasia, and who could tell her how to reach the Superman.

She waited.

Fortuitously, that someone did not take long to appear. Marcel arrived from the direction in which he had drawn away the previous day. She saw his elegant and supple silhouette designed through the foliage, and the ease with which he too was wearing a new costume. It was an orange velvet doublet patterned with black diamond-shapes, terminating half way down vigorous legs clad in tights. The sleeves were short enough to permit the free play of the joints. The widely-separated collar was bordered by dark braid, which, along with the black belt and shoes, broke the uniformity of the costume. The head, coiffed by a large hat designed to provide protection from the sun, stood out energetically, contrasting with the excessive affectation of the outfit. Nevertheless, the foreigner was vexed by judging him so adequate to that banal and mild environment, that artificial nature.

"Miss Mary!" he cried, with a joy that he could not restrain, as soon as he saw her. "I'm profoundly happy to see you again, Miss Mary."

Before obeying her welcoming invitation to sit beside her on the bench he gazed at her, braced in her revealing peplum, the splendor of her shoulders mildly attenuated by the raised hairstyle. He found her delightful, enigmatic and new. He put his hands together.

"How beautiful you are!"

"Oh, let's not talk about my beauty, Monsieur," she immediately objected. "Let's not talk about this stupid accoutrement! There's only one costume becoming to an adversary of the coalition: a suit of armor that stops bullets! I'm furious at having to wear this frippery—can't you see that? I'm furious that these flowers aren't making a bed for our dead, and that I can't make use of those rocks to crush those who are drinking the blood of my brothers! Caresco! Where can I see him? I want to go to the man who can put vengeance into my hands!"

Her two vigorous arms, like those of Bellona, reached out for the individual invoked, and Marcel admired her, quivering with her glorious dream, proclaiming the distress of her native land and gazing into space toward her iron sky. O unexpected woman, avenging Diana! Her peplum had come undone; her bosom was heaving with hope and anger. He desired her, so swollen with the valorous blood of her race.

"Oh, if only I could serve you, Miss Mary!" he said, frantically. "And how sorry I am to know that you're going to flee the oasis where the spring of calm and repose sings!"

"I know those insipidities. I've never be able to listen to them. I need actions, not words!"

Scarcely had Miss Mary stung the young man with that response than Carabella, emerging from a bush, presented herself to them. She had an animated flush, her eyes still brilliant with sensuality. A living corolla among the flower-beds, a flower of desirable flesh emerged from the flowers, her warm and mat-complexioned body was contained, almost entirely visible, in the satin of a recently-crumpled mauve tunic. She gave the impression that she had just been yielding the flavorsome aroma of her firm breasts, while letting down her recently pinned-up jet black hair, to the caprice of an individual who, while passing by, had dragged her into the verdant arbor. The red make-up of her symbolic stripe was still on display, melted in the perspiration of her pleasure.

She put her arms around Miss Mary gently, applying her lips to the nape of her neck with an insistence that the young woman found repugnant. Then, addressing herself to Marcel, she said: "You ought not, Monsieur, to behave so affectionately with Mademoiselle. Can't you see that she's wearing the costume of a virgin? Such as she arrived in this land, so she must leave it. In speaking to her so prettily—for I heard everything—you have committed an infraction of our laws. I alone have the prerogative of giving her, along with beautiful words, a little pleasure, if she so wishes. To you, it's formally forbidden. Let's walk, if you desire, but let me separate you.

She slid between Marcel and Mary, and her two arms, gripping her companions' elbows to the right and the left, indicated her willingness to be as affable with one as the other.

Followed by the greyhound, they traversed a number of charming places. The beauty of the locations unfolded, changing with every fold of the terrain. Only their presence diversified the solitude, and Marcel felt the tranquil and sensual charm of the stroll, languidly. Numerous unfamiliar birds with varied polychromatic plumage were chirping, hardly bothering to move away from their passage. A kind of large leopard, supple and undulating, came to brush Miss Mary's robe in a familiar fashion; she uttered a cry of surprise and disgust, for the beast, which symbolized Albion, had a place in the enemy's blazon.[15]

Misinterpreting that reaction, Marcel thought she was afraid and stepped forward to protect her, but Carabella started laughing.

---

[15] The royal banner of England displays three heraldic "leopards," but the heraldic leopard is a lion in a particular posture, quite distinct from the natural species nowadays called by that name. Given the artificiality of Eucrasia's ecology, however, it is quite possible that the creature mentioned here is similarly emblematic—at any rate, no mention is made of spots, changeable or otherwise.

"Have no fear, divine one! Calm down, handsome Marcel! The animals in our country are not malevolent. They know that we love them; furthermore, we provide them abundantly with an essential nourishment, which they receive every morning, distributed by the Chief Huntsman. Do they not merit our respect, the animals in whom the souls gleam of future beings like us? They evolve, as we do, who are in constant transformation, and who progress through successive stages, always toward improvement..."

Such words in the mouth of a courtesan astonished Marcel, but he remembered that they were the expression of the religion imagined by Caresco. He took advantage of the opportunity to ask: "What will become of you, Carabella, once you have accomplished your present life?"

"I shall doubtless become a mother. I'll have the right to live in a family and have children. We have an entire population of them on the island. You'll see that in due course..."

"The maternal state is, then, the last word in perfection?"

"Yes."

"And afterwards, Carabella?"

"Afterwards? I'll return to the cellular state to become a plant, and then an animal, and then a human being, and so on, accomplishing my role in the eternal cycle of fecundation, unproductive once, capable of reproduction the next time...."

"That's rather well-planned," said Marcel, smiling.

"It's necessary not to mock these holy things," the courtesan observed, gravely. "If the Superman knew that, the earth would tremble."

Marcel dared not dig any deeper into her religious faith, for he sensed that she was sincere. The simple observation already explained, however, why the people were so mild in their treatment of their fellows, animals and nature, why they submitted so tranquilly to the concept of blissful fatalism. Every parcel of living matter, every constituted individual, became, in that fashion, one of the modest cogs of creation, one of the vibrations of harmonious Joy.

They continued their walk.

In the meantime, several airplanes furrowed the air with the muffled rhythmic thrum of their giant wings. They also perceived smaller ones, whose nacelles were occupied by two or three silhouettes. Forming corteges for them, the lovely bodies of children, adolescent boys and girls, were flying and singing. They were clad in pink and green veils, whose long trains floated at the whim of the air.

Carabella named a few of them. One tall man with a curly rutilant red beard threw flowers to her, which she picked up joyfully.

"That man," she said, "is Gilded-Gaze, a sterile spouse. I received his kisses yesterday at the fête. He's married to Veloutine, that fecund mother, dressed in blue like all her fellows, whom you can see sitting next to him in the aeronat. There are three children with them but they aren't his.

"Does that astonish you, Monsieur Marcel? Our laws are formal. Reproduction is not permitted to everyone, and the Superman possesses certain means of preventing it. It's to that law that we owe our happiness. Thus, that husband caressed me yesterday. He's very genteel, and he's called Gilded-Gaze because a golden ingot seems to emerge from beneath his brow eyelids." She suddenly stopped and declared: "But here we are at the Field of Truce."

She pointed to a vast plane surface where, among the flowers and in the shade of tall parasol pines, thousands of mausoleums surged forth. Some of them affected the form of a pink cone; others opened like the calyx of a flower, dividing into two ovoid shells, also pink; yet others were square, simply surmounted with red crosses. All of them contained accessible crypts.

In the middle, a superb Ionian temple loomed up, white and shiny, with golden vibrions and ovules.

Carabella explained: "It's here that the mortal remains of our brothers and sisters are deposited. Their sex is sufficiently indicated by the erection of marble virilities or the gaping of shells of Venus. As for the asexual, courtesans or gitons, the cross on top of their tomb is the distinctive sign. But those are only symbols to which we attach little value, since death does not exist for souls, and at the most, the body, like those which rest here, is subject to a truce before returning to matter...

Having given this information, Carabella wanted to take her companions into the midst of the tombs in order to visit a few crypts. In vain she set out the bait of certain curiosity; she was surprised to observe that Miss Mary recoiled before that incursion into the realm of the dead, and that a teardrop of sadness formed on her blonde eyelashes.

She took them away by a different route.

That fit of sensibility was fortunately dissipated by the arrival of a stranger, the first living person they had been able to approach that morning. He was a man of young appearance and medium height, who tottered slightly as he advanced toward them, as if drunk. As he came closer they distinguished his silhouette, weighed down by intoxication, more clearly.

The costume he wore was violet in its entirety, composed of the same essential components as Marcel's: a doublet tightened at the waist, slender but lacking in elegance, as if secured in a restrictive corset; and tights imprisoning thighs and calves that were too thick in proportion to the thinness of the torso. Of his head, covered in a white cap that even hid the ears, nothing could be seen but the full black beard, frizzy in the moustache an curly toward the point, and the nose reddened by drunkenness, ablaze between two little blue eyes, mobile and astonished.

He was a stranger, and yet it appeared to the strollers that the person was not entirely unknown to them. Indeed, as soon as he perceived them, the man expressed his satisfaction by flapping his two violet arms.

"Finally, I've found you! Oh, my dear friends, how happy I am to be finished with it! What do you think of me? Am I a sufficient mixture of Byzantium and the sixteenth century?"

Having made a complete turn, not without difficulty, in order to show all his faces, the individual has approached and seized the young man's hands warmly, then Miss Mary's.

111

His breath, however, when he could speak again, did not give off the odor particular to drinkers.

"Well, have you nothing to say? You can't place me? Am I so changed, then?"

Marcel was about to go past, pushing the drunkard aside, when suddenly, a gesture that the stranger made—which consisted of hitching up the belt of his tights, although they were solidly maintained by a deerskin strap studded with amethysts—made him recognizable.

"Choumaque! You! My dear old Choumaque!"

"Finally!" the man proclaimed.

"Is it possible?"

The philosopher sat down on the grass. He raised a finger in the air.

"I believe that everything is possible here! Permit me to rest…I'm still stunned by the fluid with which they inundated me before butchering me…they poisoned me with I don't know what. Besides which, my torso, recently thinned out, is rather poorly accommodated to the iron corset in which my organs, scarcely stitched up, are imprisoned. Oh, the sorcerers, the sorcerers!

"Is it truly necessary to calculate, as I have done until now, the slightest manifestations of the human psychosis, when one sees that the raw material can be transformed so simply? Is there no reason to wonder whether they have also made me a different individual, intellectually speaking? Do you think that I still speak like the others? They've scalped me in order to replace my hair—provided, great gods, that they haven't touched my brain, for it's in the head that the principle of health resides. Seneca said so: according to whether the soul is strong or depressed, the rest is vigorous or overcome with languor…"

Then, circumscribing his occiput with both hands and putting pressure on his sensitive temples, he continued: "I have aching hair! Dr. Hymen, when I woke up…for he's the only one I saw, throughout…surrounded my head with a tight bandage and told me that I could safely take it off after ten minutes. It's been at least fifteen. Marcel, would you care to ride me of this instrument of torture?"

The young man lent himself to the task willingly. When he had untied the strings of the skull-cap, his amazement reached its peak on perceiving that the philosopher's new hair was read—mahogany red—while his beard, also newly vibrant, as in his first youth, shone brown. He burst out laughing.

"But my poor Choumaque, what have they done? Although your beard has become dark again, your hair is an ardent russet..."

"Dr. Hymen had doubtless been deceived," Carabella hypothesized. "The poor man is afflicted with a malady of the eyes that causes him to get colors mixed up..."

"He ought to commence by healing himself!" said Choumaque. "But I don't need a cure. I'm simply bi-colored. It's a fact that does not stain my Stoical personality and imparts no prejudice to my doctrine of equilibria—on the contrary. Perhaps women might even find a certain piquancy therein..."

They went back, each of them to their own apartment.

The next day passed without them seeing anyone. They would only make contact with the life of the island after their appearance before Caresco.

# CHAPTER VIII

Marjah pushed them along a dark corridor. They took twenty paces thus. Choumaque had adopted a detached attitude and, in the gloom, he translated his courage into a faint whistling, which the metal walls that he was brushing echoed strangely.

Marcel and Miss Mary felt less valiant. The latter, although she had lost none of the bravery that had once driven her into battle for the defense of her homeland and had made her a heroine, understood nevertheless that she was casting the last throw of the dice, and all her womanly nerves, dominated by the unknown, got the upper hand and tensed. Involuntarily, she gripped Marcel's arm.

"Have no fear, my child...be stoical," said Choumaque, who was shivering with fear, and then added: "Are we not with you? Benefit, on the contrary, from all the philosophy of a rare event, and be thankful for the good fortune that will bring us face to face with the Superman. We're going to see what that extraordinary Demigod has in his bag of tricks, for I'm going to talk to him!"

He did not have time to say any more. They suddenly found themselves in a flood of blinding light that surged forth from they knew not where. They were so dazzled that they had great difficulty, at first, in distinguishing a circular room in which, in front of a long white wood table laden with books and papers, a man of young appearance was sitting, clad in a wretched gray smock covered with bloodstains. His arms, bare to the elbow, bore evidence of recent butchery.

Apparently tall in stature, so far as could be judged by his costume, he was handsome, Semitic in type, with a full brown beard, curly, like his hair, a florid complexion that looked as if it had been reinforced with make-up, a curved nose and a sensual mouth with thick scarlet lips. His vigorous, enormous and hairy right hand, with the thumb folded back

114

into the palm, was resting on the table, next to a fragment of quivering flesh that it had just abandoned.

The newcomers sought his gaze, but did not discover it, for it was turned away, fugitively. And from all that health, all that visible youth, all that beauty, emanated something fatigued, disillusioned, old and horrible: a human paradox that disconcerted the new arrivals and provoked a poignant malaise in them.

It was Caresco.

They had scarcely had time to glimpse him than Marjah threw himself flat in the ground proclaiming: "The Superman! Glory to the Superman!"

The instinct of imitation, the dread of the legendary individual, and, for Miss Mary, the concern of rendering herself favorable, impelled them to follow their guide's example. They prostrated themselves.

Caresco left them confounded by his presence for some time. Finally, encouraging them to get up, his voice took on, in speaking to then, a particular timbre of amenity, even of tender softness when he addressed Miss Mary.

"That's enough. I bid you welcome! Get up, Messieurs…and you too, Mademoiselle, get up."

That benevolent tone immediately put them at their ease. They were then able, their eyes having adapted to the light—which had, in any case, attenuated—to lend attention to the wholly hygienic simplicity of the room, the gleaming tiles, the varnished walls and the individuals who were accompanying the Superman.

Beside the table stood Dr. Hymen, sheathed in his invariable black frock-coat with the green shirt-front. His bushy hair, topped by the inseparable hat with the long nap and the flat rim, was plunged in his stiff hands with apparent phalanges. Seated on a dirty folding canvas chair, like those constructed at the beginning of the twentieth century for seaside holidays, his aspect made him a living antithesis, denouncing the effort of a maniac, incapable, in the midst of so much luxury of beneficent simplicity, of ridding himself of the familiar objects of his former poverty.

Beside him, leaning on the wall, there was another motionless silhouette, of an unidentifiable shape, of which one could not even make out, so rigid and insensible was its stance , whether it was an animate being or a thing. It required long observation to recognize the appearance of a body slid into a long dull sack, from which emerged a small, completely hairless head, without a vestige of hair or beard—or, rather, a round ball of flesh, for the eyes and nose had been replaced there by partitions of pink tissue, while the ears and mouth subsisted normally.

After several seconds of reflection, Choumaque concluded that the silhouette must be a mannequin, unless it was some unfinished automaton containing a precious mechanism in its stomach.

But Caresco's voice rose up. His weary gesture designating Choumaque, he addressed himself to Dr. Hymen.

"Is that the other day's subject? Well, he seems sufficiently successful to me. He's the one, isn't he, who possessed a deplorable vascular system, sclerotized by the imbecilic hygiene practiced in the other world? In truth, a very interesting case! We probably won't encounter another, given that the subjects that arrive in Eucrasia are, in general, young and healthy."

Dr. Hymen, thus addressed, made no more movement than the mannequin fixed to the wall. Caresco, observing the futility of his attempts to engage that rebarbative collaborator, turned to the philosopher.

"Come closer. Do you know that you possessed a very curious carcass? That I was obliged to replace all the arteries corrupted by your bad habits? That I opened your abdomen, resected the varicose veins, purged the lungs, the liver and the bladder and straightened the tibias? You owe me seventy years of existence. Where is the surgeon or biologist who could have rendered you such a service back there, in the country that was once mine? Aren't you going to thank me? Seventy years!"

"The life of a sage is an extent without limits, Super-man," Choumaque risked, with a certain arrogance that made Hymen shiver.

Caresco did not even notice it, however, for he added: "People can say what they like, but there's only ever been once surgical genius in the world, and that's me. I'm the foremost—in that as in everything!"

His dark eyes, as he made that declaration, had lost their fugitive expression. He fixed them on his interlocutor with an insistence as hard and cold as the blade of a scalpel—to the point that Choumaque, simultaneously seized by terror and stirred by a vague admiration, murmured: "Yes, you're the foremost."

"I'm delighted that you recognize the fact. Come closer. What did you do in Paris?"

"I was a teacher of philosophy by profession, a Stoic and disciple of Seneca in intellectual terms.

"I'm not surprised. Hymen, who radioscoped your brain, told me that you had the bump of ethics. But that isn't a recommendation, you know? A philosopher is a windbag, babbling about a heap of theories, each more stupid than the last. The great philosophers, those whose theories are retained, who have created schools and whose names are cited—Kant, Schopenhauer, Herbert Spencer, Karl Marx, Auguste Comte, and that exceptional Emperor of Germany, Wilhelm II, on whom I operated for a cerebral hemorrhage, which resulted from a deplorable arterial system that drove him to the craziest eccentricities, to name but a few—all those brains that imposed themselves on the attention of their contemporaries, were nothing other, mark my words, than diseased brains. They went astray, meekly. There has only ever been one scientific genius to give the exact measure to philosophical truth—no one else but me! What can you say about life, when you don't know the first thing about it? You, with your deplorably-vascularized meninges, have been able to make up some fantastic theory? Come on, confess..."

117

"Certainly," Choumaque conceded, swelling up with pride. "Certainly, I haven't allowed myself to be petrified by the doctrines of old authors. I've created my own theory, the theory of equilibria, purely based on current observation, and based on the certainty that, in all of human existence, the quotient of happiness and unhappiness experienced balances out exactly. Life consists of perpetual oscillations between joy and sadness, in such a way that, in the end, at death, the curve of those oscillations is as pronounced on one side as the other, and that the addition of chagrins produced as sum equal to that of consolations. A dying man cannot, therefore, say to himself: *I have been favored by the good things of the world*, or: *I have been dispossessed of...*"

"That's false!" howled Hymen, suddenly waking up. "What do you make of poverty, stupid orator? What good would it have done, then, for us to create this marvelous island and to have preached compensatory metempsychosis here?"

"Precisely none. I deem that, if misfortune exists, those who are afflicted by it experience, on the other hand, moments of felicity that compensate them amply, setting aside the exaggerations of pity and the staging of nervous states. Are you sure that a poor man suffers as much as he appears to be suffering—as much as you would suffer if, by chance, you were to fall into his situation at a stroke?

"Seneca reports that Apicius, a rich Roman, killed himself because he only had ten million sesterces left; a poor man would have been content to possess a thousand in order to live happily.

"Give a poor man the foodstuffs that a rich man has disdained as being unworthy of his jaded appetites, and that poor man would rejoice a hundredfold, while the rich man would not rejoice at all. Attribute to the poor man a total satisfaction of a hundred, and that will compensate him for the cruelty of a hundred subsequent privations: equilibrium.

"Force an idler to accomplish some effort that a laborer carries out insouciantly, and that idler will feel a hundredfold a vexation that is non-existent for the laborer; attribute to the former a displeasure that will recuperate the value of a hundred other banal satisfactions: equilibrium.

"Without that intelligent idea, society would no longer be possible. It would require, to explain its apparent injustice, the paradisal compensations of religions, or your metempsychosis. Do you see what I mean?"

He had addressed himself specifically to Dr. Hymen, with the result that, having subsequently glanced at Caresco, he observed that he had not been listening. As he concluded, however, the potentate put his head in his hands and said, as if to himself: "The philosophy of a concierge! He's drawn his doctrine from his grocer's scales. Two sous' worth of sugar for two sous' worth of salt! Everyone brutalized! That's what the centuries of civilization have produced, while I, personally, in twenty years, have been able to reformulate a social organization and create a world! The poor fools!"

Nonplussed, Choumaque dared not say any more. Besides which, a strange attraction was forcing him to look at the mannequin. He would have sworn that his thoughts were being drawn off and absorbed by that indefinable object—or, rather, divided between him and a counterblast to his philosophical stance. When Caresco expressed himself again he had to struggle against that influence in order to understand him.

"Let's see! Come closer! Why are you running away from me? I sense that you're fleeing from me. Listen to me: you've arrived in my realm, stuffed with the outdated ideas of the other world, where everything is subjected to old prejudices, constraints on ideas that are, in a way, atavistic. In those circumstances, tell me what you think of my island?"

"I haven't been able to form an idea of it in three days," Choumaque replied, prudently."

"Have you at least formed a first impression?"

"Yes, an impression of admiration."

"Admiration for what?"

"For your cult of beauty."

"Ah! You admit that! The beauty of my people is unrivaled, is it not? And when, by chance, nature deceives me—

when my subjects are born disgraceful; when, like you, they possess a few deformities capable of rendering their appearance painful to others—I correct them; I remake them; I adorn them with a pleasant façade.

"But that's not all. I wanted my people to be extraordinarily happy. I gorge them on pleasures, with no possible weariness; for, in addition to the fact that I know their tendency to wear themselves out, I can, when they begin to flag, charge them with a fluid that restores their appetite—unless I prefer to plunge them in sleep. Here, therefore, is a land of perpetual enjoyment.

"Have you not learned, short as your sojourn among us has been, that I, the first among Pastors, regulate life scientifically, and that everything is admirably ordered in such a way that, in my realm, creation is perfect? Defects and monstrosities cannot grow in our soil. In fact, in order that that should be the case, I'm obliged to create.

"Yes, you'll see my stud-farm, philosopher, you'll observe what beautiful products I engender, in the milieu of my Palace of Reproduction. You'll see how I prepare there for individuals to be born into the best conditions of health and beauty, and how, subsequently, I protect them, step by step, in youth and in maturity, assuring them all the intoxications and sensualities that humans can desire.

"My citizens do not have to think; they do not have to feel tormented by paltry anxieties; they do not have to stir, as you do, philosophical systems that darken the mind; they only have to enjoy, always to enjoy! To enjoy beyond human limits, since I have prolonged their existence by my scientific methods, and have conserved their youth in of age, their strength in decrepitude!

"And when finally, they have to die, they disappear abruptly, without suffering—for no one has ever been seen to suffer in my realm—and without regret, for they know that as soon as they have quit the world, their lives will recommence, improved, more replete with benefits!

"Do you see my genius, philosopher, in having them inculcated, from the earliest age, with the true faith, reassuring for everyone, which explains desirably everything that we all seek to know? The anxious gazes that the dogmatized individuals of the old world cast at the afterlife, my subjects do not cast, for they believe in metempsychosis. Behold, then, the unique religion, that of life, that of enjoyment!

"Tell me, philosopher, am I not an admirable creator? Have I not caused to spring from this rock, by stamping my foot, along with individuals, the mot prodigious institutions? Am I not the greatest of philanthropists?"

As he made his own eulogy, Caresco's voice had taken on such a tone of exaltation that Choumaque, initially disposed to respond with a few objections, dared not utter them, and began to fear that enigmatic man, so powerful that a single gesture of his could doubtless cause death as easily as it organized birth and repaired the errors of nature. He therefore renounced any riposte, and said: "Yes, Superman, you are the foremost of philanthropists."

At that moment, the hirsute object leaning against the wall, and which, given its unchanging position could previously have been taken for a mannequin imprisoned in a sack, suddenly began to shake. The orifice that served as its mouth emitted sounds incomprehensible to the visitors, but of which Dr. Hymen and Caresco seized the significance, for the former uttered an ironic gurgle, while the latter became furious.

"You're lying, vile windbag! You have the impudence to mock me! I have consented to receive you in this privileged land: don't make me repent that, for if I prevent suffering, I can also impart it!"

He thundered as he spoke. With a blow of his hairy fist, he knocked the flesh with which he was toying sideways.

Choumaque's emotion was translated by a tremulous gesture toward his belt.

Do you know what this is?" Caresco went on, pointing at the mannequin-man. "Well, it's my thought-reader...yes, my reader, one of my finest endeavors, for I've modified the encephalum in such a way that all his faculties are either anni-hilated or utilized for incursions into the souls of others. That being has therefore been able to penetrate your brain, while you were talking to me, and to discover your true sentiments there. He's just warned me that you're hiding them from me. That's how I know that you don't believe that I'm the fore-most of philanthropists, although you affirm it. Dare you lie again, now?"

Such noisy laughter concluded that remark that the phi-losopher was offended by it. Knowing now that his slightest impressions were discovered and could be translated to the Superman, he strove to change their direction, by darting a glance at Marcel and Miss Mary. He saw that the latter was very attentive, impatient to make the request that she intended to address to the despot. That spectacle cheered him up.

In any case, Caresco had immediately calmed down. He continued: "So, you don't have faith in my beneficent endeav-or? You'll be convinced in time. In the meantime, would you care to explain to me how you conceive happiness?"

In order to put on a better pretence of listening, the po-tentate put his head in his hands—but peering through the gaps in his fingers, his eyes did not remain inactive. Miss Mary sensed that she was being ardently examined, that the cold gaze was running over her like a jet of icy water that was suffocating her. Dr. Hymen got ready to go to sleep again as soon as the philosopher started speaking.

"Superman, can you conceive of life without death, a point without space, day without night, number without unity, the sea without a drop of water, movement without inertia? No, you can't, for if one did not die, there would be no reason to think that one is alive; if space did not extend, one would not be able to posit a point to limit it; if night did not follow it, day would not commence; and in the same way, plurality ex-ists by courtesy of unity, the sea by courtesy of billions of drops of water, and movement by contrast with immobility. That, you won't deny.

"Well, I affirm that misfortune is necessary to happiness, just as each of the previously cited states is indispensable to the observation of its opposite. In brief, it is necessary to know dolor, not only in others but in oneself, in order to experience joy. Now, your great humanity, aided by your profound science, has succeeded in suppressing effort and suffering among your subjects. You heap them with all the satisfactions of the senses, all the enjoyments of animality—but how do you expect them to appreciate their value, and in consequence, to judge themselves favored, if they never know their price?

"At the most, they will remain in a mixed, neutral state, which will be that of perpetual, inherent, intrinsic felicity—but an unconscious, unconceived, unmeasured felicity. And that's why I say that your subjects are not happy, because ill-being is necessary to well-being. On the few occasions when I have had the opportunity to interrogate one of your indigenes in that regard, they have replied to me: 'Yes, I'm happy,' but they've told me that in the tone of a lesson learned, an article of faith, like a person to whom the question is indifferent, because they've never been given to reflect on it..."

Caresco no longer had any need to address himself to the thought-reader to be persuaded that Choumaque was now expressing himself sincerely. The discussion, although philosophically mediocre, interested him because it turned on his personality. He ceased contemplating Miss Mary through the mesh of his fingers and addressed himself to the philosopher.

"You contend that one has to suffer in order to be happy? Do you realize that with your theory, you devalue the productivity and progress that are the very principles of happiness?"

"On the contrary, I encourage them, but while wanting them to evolve slowly, through successive stages, in order that people might savor the results obtained for their improvement, instead of allowing the ideal to be imposed upon them all at once, as you have done, Superman!"

"So I, alone, obtain the best profit? I am, therefore, an egotist."

"A prodigious egotist—I dare to define you thus."

123

And that was, indeed, an improbable audacity, which made Dr. Hymen's hat leap up, and of which even things seemed to feel the repercussion, for the lights suddenly went out.

In the darkness, Choumaque thought that his last moment had arrived—but the sudden obscurity was only due to an omnial interruption necessitated by an external event. In fact, the sound of a bell rang out, and hearts remained in suspension, in the expectation of a phenomenon.

Soon, a segment of the wall illuminated. A fiery globe was depicted there, followed by a flamboyant tail of long sparks, which did not take long to disappear. Dr. Hymen's voice murmured: "It's nothing…it's a bolide…"

And the lighting reappeared, rendering every person and every object the precise animation that they had had prior to the eclipse.

Caresco had started laughing again. "You see, philosopher, how I'm able to protect myself. A bolide brushes my atmosphere, and I'm immediately alerted! What is a meteor, however: a pebble and gases! You understand that no attack from your old world has any possibility of making an impact here? God…yes, God, the other one…God is not better guarded than I am. But do you even believe in God?"

Before Choumaque had time either to affirm or deny his faith, however, Caresco went on: "Well, if you repudiate the Omnipotent, convince yourself of the existence of a Jehovah reigning here! That I affirm with all the liberty of my intelligence…for I'm not mad. No, I'm not mad!"

As he certified his reason, he stepped away from the table at which he had been sitting, came to Choumaque and parted his eyelids. He was searching for something, a sign, in the mysterious lair of life. In a low, voice, confidentially, he asked: "Have you never been mad? Has there never been madness in your family?" After which he seemed to forget his question.

The philosopher had time to remark in his interrogator the curious disposition of the black pupils, one of which was extraordinarily dilated.

"Let's see," the surgeon went on, "what are we going to do with you? As it's the rule here that every individual useless to the race..."

"But I'm still capable," Choumaque objected, with such a hesitation that the Thought-reader agitated again.

"No! I forbid you to create. You'd yield bad products, and I don't want that!"

"Are you going to make me a eunuch?" asked the philosopher, frightened.

"No, for we have what we need here to sterilize you. But as it's the rule here that an individual useless to the race must be useful to the community, I charge you, once a week, to reason philosophically before my assembled people. The theme of the dissertation will be: *Happy peoples have no history*."[16]

"That principle is contrary to my doctrine, for I deem, with Seneca, that the happy life is for the person whom reason has caused to understand the inappreciable benefits of desire and misfortune..."

"I have spoken!" cried the despot, violently, thumping the sonorous table.

Now Caresco addressed himself to Marcel.

After having listened to the information that Dr. Hymen transmitted to him in an unknown language, without dwelling too much on an interrogation that would have taken up time utilizable for other, more pressing, tasks, he designated the role that he intended him to play henceforth in Society:

---

[16] In spite of being rather sententious, this oft-quoted sentiment seems to have entered French proverbial parlance before being taken up by philosophers as a theme for discussion; one of its early British employers, Thomas Carlyle, credited the observation to Montesquieu, but the latter did not employ such a succinct formulation.

"You've been a naval officer, my friend," he said, without employing the informal mode of address that he had consented to apply to Choumaque—although that difference passed unperceived in the solemn emotion of the moment—"and we possess, moored in our waters, an ironclad, in truth very obsolete and quite useless, but which we conserve as an object of risible curiosity, for comparison to the ingenious machines that have guaranteed us the absolute conquest of the air. You will take command of it. That means that you will supervise its maintenance and its neatness, for it will never put to sea. Such will be your ceremonial title. But I intend you for better employment. Let's see what you can do for the race..."

Hymen passed him the notes that he had made. It was the report of the medical examination that Marcel had undergone, to which everyone who arrived in the realm was subjected.

The potentate continued, peaking to himself: "Well, this perfect! He's very well equilibrated, the mariner! No defect; his blood is rich in globules. He's of the blond type of the Celtic race, which we like. A place as a Sower is entirely indicated for him in our Palace of Reproduction..."

Then, turning to Hymen, who accepted the instruction without bothering to ask Marcel's opinion, he declared: "Inoculate him with my genetic serum number six, and confide him to the brunette women. You'll have the responsibility of classifying the products. It's an experiment..."

Marcel, embarrassed, looked at Miss Mary. His heart sank in the dread that the young woman might be scornful of the usage that the potentate wanted to make of his person. He feared that the strange destination in question might be an obstacle to the sharing of the love for her that had been engendered within him. But as he wanted to avoid his sentiments being betrayed by the Reader, whose attention he felt fixed upon him at that moment, by a kind of nervous envelopment, he hastened to repress them as far as possible, and slid along the natural slope of his mind, drawn away by facile diversions, toward the pleasant features of the island, the voluptuous bodies of the women whose superb flesh he had already admired, which were being reserved for him.

In any case, his attention was soon reclaimed by Caresco.

"Your turn, virgin," said the Superman. "We have made a unique exception in your favor. We have allowed you to penetrate our realm, with the promise of facilitating your departure as soon as it pleases you to leave. Never has such an irregularity been committed for anyone. It required, for me to decide upon it, my humanitarian weakness to impel me to help an unhappy child. It also required the incredible popularity with which you have troubled the old world, which has given me the desire to make your acquaintance. Do you know that you're almost as famous as I am, virgin?"

"A cruel celebrity, alas!" murmured Miss Mary.

"Well, let's see! What do you desire?"

The spectators of the scene had not failed to notice the extreme mildness, so contrary to his unusual abruptness, with which Caresco had begun the conversation. There were also obliged to remark the particular glint in his eyes, which had suddenly become gleaming, although an indefinable antiquity ordinarily tarnished its silvering.

Miss Mary had thrown herself to her knees. Arms extended, hands joined, with all the imploration of her lovely face turned toward the potentate, she declared the magnificent hope that was within her.

"Have pity, Superman! Pity for my poor homeland, which the coalition is strangling! Pity for the life and liberty of my brethren! You know their history, Superman, you know how I have dragged myself from country to country to obtain their help; how the egotism of governments responded to me by sending me away, by mocking me. Now, I have no further resource but you. For pity's sake, Superman, don't turn away from the frightful agony of a nation!"

"What do you want me to do, delightful virgin?" Caresco asked, lifting her up and retaining her hand in his, beginning to caress it softly.

"Only speak!" affirmed the young woman, more excited-ly. "Manifest your determination to see the arms fall, and the coalition will have no alternative but to flee! Do better: direct toward the Red Land an airplane equipped with just one of your explosive devices, and let everyone know that you are protecting us. Will that not be sufficient to disperse the blood-drinkers? Oh, do that, Superman, do that and God will not be better than you. God will not be so powerful!"

"Am I not God?" muttered the Superman, unintelligibly, shrugging his shoulders. And as she looked at him, astonished, he went on: "But are your people not destroyed? Your people are no longer counting on you. The inhabitants of the Red Land believe that you are dead."

"The English press has, indeed, spread that rumor, ag-gravating it with abominable insults—but my brother, General Harry Hardisson, knows where I am, and who I have come to implore."

"Your brother is dying," Caresco declared, coldly, with-out paying any heed to the dolor that contracted the young woman's features. Then, passing from tenderness to cruelty, the thrust away the hand that he was still holding, violently, and said: "I'll think about it. Go!"

They withdrew—but before they left the Temple of Sur-gery, Dr. Hymen took them, grumbling all the while, into a neighboring room, where he inoculated all three of them with a few drops of a serum, which, renewed every day, would pro-tect them from the attacks of all possible diseases and give them an incomparable vital force.

For Choumaque the sanitary precaution was even strict-er, for Caresco's instructions enabled him to benefit from an-other liquid destined to permit him to love fecund women without the integrity of the race being threatened in conse-quence.

# CHAPTER IX

*I'm sterile*, Choumaque said to himself, as soon as he returned, a trifle intoxicated by the various inoculations, to his apartment in the Caravanserai. *I'm sterile, but it isn't a blot on my character. In order to support the rigors of Stoicism more easily, I've never wanted to encumber myself with the joys of a family. I shall therefore await, with the constancy of a Sage, the results of this curious practice...*

Was it an effect of the serum? Was it not instead simply the action of benevolent nature continuing, in that new land, in the same fashion that she behaved everywhere? At any rate, when the philosopher had finished his reflections, strange frissons ran through his nerves, and after having made the tour, flowed into his brain in delightfully colored and tempting images.

The professor knew them well, those images, those burning visions that instinct caused to pass before his dazzled eyes. They had once haunted his poverty, when he brought back to his solitary room the cinematography of the amorous street, the memory of the couples who clung to one another as they walked, the shirts that delicate hands lifted up in rainy weather, uncovering the stocking of a muscular leg and allowing the suspicion, in their diabolical coquetry, of the hidden treasures of adorable Parisiennes.

Those visions, he always rejected, being neither rich nor sufficiently endowed by nature to convert them into an impetuous reality—and he consoled himself by shoring up his temperance with his compensatory philosophy. But this time, they took on an extraordinary intensity; they overflowed in processions of superb nudities, coming to offer themselves to him; and their seduction was all the sharper because he knew that he could content them more easily, simply by pushing one of the buttons on the utilities panel.

He looked at that panel intently. Was it not the moment to appreciate, out of simple curiosity, what it could furnish him, to respond to his desire? Among all the subscriptions that ornamented it, one—*amour*—even though it was engraved in the same fashion as all the rest, seemed to stand out more clearly, in five inviting letters magnified by fever.

*No*, he said to himself, *I ought to resist, for reason informs me that the joy in question will one day be equilibrated by a disappointment. I'll be no further forward, truly, when, after having yielded to the shock of the little epilepsy, I feel my back curved tomorrow and my marrow weary! Let me recall my last gallant enterprise, when, two months ago, I didn't want to disoblige a streetwalker who clutched at my arm desperately, O Venus! What a hard time she had earning her money, poor thing! Am I going to behave badly in this country too, and start with a fiasco? Let's wait for the effect of the rejuvenation that I owe to Caresco. Let's be virtuous! Virtue is something noble, sublime, invincible and indefatigable, Pleasure is something crawling, servile, enervated and tottering...*

In the course of this monologue however, he had almost involuntarily put his finger on the button. There was a click; a mechanism was engaged, and the pigeon-hole opened.

"It's not possible for a woman to come out of there!" said Choumaque, amazed by what he had done.

Indeed, all that he saw appear was a metal plate—from which, however, a voice emerged: "What do you want?"

"What you can give me," replied the philosopher, not daring to deny his action.

He had not finished his sentence when he heard a sound behind him. He turned round and saw a marvelous woman emerge from the rock beside the basin, which had just moved sideways. She came toward him, smiling and brunette, adorned with translucent veils characterized by the courtesans' red stripe. Pale flowers hung down with her hair as far as the marmoreal firmness of her breasts. It seemed to Choumaque that he had never seen any as magnificent.

Sighing with emotion and hitching up his belt, he listened to her.

"Philoxénie, the friend of strangers, comes to you! Philoxénie is yours! Appreciate her! Savor the camber of her bosom, feel the satin of her shoulders, breathe the perfume of her arms! You'll see that they are sweet!"

"I don't doubt it," said the philosopher, "but Mademoiselle, give me time to collect myself...I'm so surprised..."

"It's not necessary to suffocate yourself for so little, neophyte. Am I emotional?"

"Indeed, I can comprehend your calmness...you're obeying a service commanded..."

"Not at all. I've come here because I like your original head, red and black at the same time, because I have the habit of pleasing newcomers, and of pleasing myself with them; because love is good with everyone; because it's necessary to take advantage of every opportunity to give oneself voluptuousness...come on! One doesn't resist Philoxénie, the lover of strangers! No more procrastination...let's talk otherwise..."

Already she was enveloping him with a caress. The philosopher, however, determined to send her away, defended himself, weakly, against her hands. The contest was still going on in his mind between respect for his doctrine and Philoxénie's advances—but it was so unequal, so ill-armed on one side, so powerful on the other, that the result was virtually certain in advance.

His frightened mind murmured to him: "Beware! Don't imitate your master Seneca, who, while proclaiming the necessity of taming the flesh, had unfortunate penchants for women, most notably for Julie, to which he succumbed. Be stronger than your master, Choumaque! Can you even be sure of rising to the occasion...?"

But the courtesan's flesh, as odorous as a fruit swollen with sap, and the divine harmony of her loins, now undressed, replied: "What does Seneca matter? Isn't the delightful contentment of the senses preferable to anything? Go on! Let pleasure envelop you in its mesh, and don't think any further ahead..."

His eyes fluttered, when he sensed a breath as fresh as the azure breeze brush his beard, and the warm pulp of a kiss pose itself upon his mouth.

He stammered: "No, no! I don't want to! My doctrine forbids me! Lust is despicable!" At the same time he ardently twisted the mantle of scattered hair that he wanted to draw away.

He was impregnated by the effluvia he was resisting. He took hold of the feline body that he was trying to push away. He bit avidly into the fruit that reason told him to reject, and everything, alas—all his resolutions, his doctrine, his Stoicism, Seneca and Julie, everything—crumbled with Philoxénie on to the scarlet bed, leaving him astonished by the new force that he owed to Caresco.

When he had escorted her to the door, with a thousand confused thanks, the rock opened again. The Superman appeared. He was wearing a black costume, embroidered with silver vibrions, admirably outlining his elegant slimness. Irony was painted on his face.

"Ha ha! Already, philosopher! Already, I catch you in contradiction with yourself!"

"That's true; but on whom should the responsibility for that victory of instinct over my principles fall, Superman, if not on you, who have slipped mandrake into my veins?"

"Are you complaining?"

"Certainly. Already, in the old world, I deplored the fact that humans did not know happiness because they did not know beneficent suffering. What should I say in yours, great Gods? In yours, where, at the first step I take, you force me to taste a cup of intoxication for which I had no desire? Don't alter the life that mingles afflictions and benefits intelligently in the crucible of our sensibility, and then, Superman, your subjects will experience the joy to which dolor alone gives value."

"To have been able to dominate nature," Caresco exclaimed, "to the point at which she is a tributary of my thought; to have directed my citizens toward happiness with threads so tenuous that they do not even see the keyboard by means of which I move them—a keyboard so powerful that the forces of creation cannot paralyze its effect—to have remade the world as a magnanimous pastor...and then to be judged by a tavern orator! Go ask my people, then!"

"Your people? What importance do you want to attach to their opinion? I scarcely know them, but already I sense that they are so insignificant, so unworthy of the interest you take in them. They wallow in their pleasure and their insouciance. From the first day of their lives your subjects are marked with your seal, and it's not on them that you can base your claim to have beatified nature. It would be necessary, for your theory to be conclusive, for experiments to be carried out on a character in revolt.

"Is that how it is? The people you brought from the old world to constitute this island were individuals already enfeebled, worn down by tribulations, defeated by vicissitudes, entirely disposed to submit to your imprint. In them, nature was no longer manifest, with its beautiful expansion of resistance; in them, it was not longer able to baulk at the laws of fluctuation that I still consider to be ineluctable.

"The day on which you have dominated a truly strong and new soul; when you have reduced that soul by all your processes of seduction to the same softness as your other subjects; when you have convinced that soul of the idea that the existence to which you are leading it is the happiest existence; the day when you have suppressed therein ambition, hope, anger, love and hatred—all conditions that I, Choumaque, believe to be essential to happiness—on that day, Superman, I will declare that the great theoreticians of ideas, and even the creator of the doctrine of equilibria, are only valets be comparison with the master that you are, and I will erect a golden statue to you in my heart!"

At these words, Caresco began to laugh loudly. He seized the professor by a flap of his garment and drew him toward the bed, where he sat down. Then, still holding Choumaque, whose Stoicism he was disturbing, and tugging him with every convulsion of his laughter he exclaimed:

"You've said it, philosopher! That's precisely the experiment I shall attempt! And do you know on whom? Oh, not on you, to be sure, nor on your pupil Marcel..." He became grave in order to pronounce the words that followed, and new and vivid emotion was detectable in his voice. "...But on the Hardisson woman, the strong virgin. I was warned; I knew her character in advance, forged of pride and revolt, of which you demanded proof just now...

"Yes, she is a virgin pure in blood, race, muscle, nerve and thought! The most primitive virgin, the one closest to nature, that exists—the one whom circumstances have even exaggerated; who, instead of weakening beneath the solvent frictions of life, has been astonishingly exalted thereby, who has become in consequence a kind of sectarian of chastity and the ideal!

"She has, in brief, a temperament essentially different from that of my subjects. She is the Ultra-Virgin! And that's why the contest with her tempts me. That's why I want to see what results all my fluids and sortileges will produce, when I have thrown them into the crucible of her sensibility, as you put it.

"Well, philosopher, know this: she is the one who will be vanquished! Within two months, I want her to be trailing at my feet, caught by my enjoyments, a slave to my social triumph! I want her nerves to admit the happiness that the Epicureanism unanimous in Eucrasia provides. I want her to obey, like the others, the keyboard that I touch in secret, and no longer to think of returning to liberate the Red Land."

"And how will you know that she is in that mental disposition, and that she retains nothing of her initial ideal?"

"I have several means," the Superman replied, calmly. "For one thing, I have my Thought-reader, but that's an unreliable method. I made the mistake of leaving him too many cerebral pigeon-holes...I need to improve him. But here's something else..."

He slid his hand into his doublet and took out a little instrument made up of three parts: two contacts connected by wires to a central dial. He unrolled the wires and showed it to the astonished philosopher.

"This is my most recent invention. It's a psychometer, which infallibly reveals to me the degree of bliss in each of my creatures. In other words, it's sufficient for me to look at the needle on this dial, which can oscillate between zero and a hundred, to know exactly to what point the spirit of enjoyment has taken possession of my subject—and, in consequence, to exactly what point I have vanquished the nature that creates afflictions therein. The needle ought to indicate a hundred, the culminating point. A hundred: that's the designation of my omnipotence, the absolute of happiness. Yes, Miss Mary, who presently indicates zero, I shall raise to a hundred, and in a short period of time."

While speaking, he had placed the two contacts on Choumaque's temples, and, with his aged eyes, he followed the palpitations of the indicative steam.

"As for you, philosopher, I have good reason to think that you haven't been able to resist. This psychological compass indicates that you're already rising. You're at forty-five! But the fact of having told you has brought you back to twenty. Will you please refrain from recoiling? Imbecile! Since I've told you that happiness is a hundred!"

Involuntarily, Choumaque had started and pushed the apparatus away. Caresco calmly rewound the wires around the dial and replaced the device in his doublet. His flushed face radiated an immense contentment.

"That's marvelous," Choumaque admitted, "but Superman, what proof is there that your apparatus measures real happiness? For enjoyment, I repeat, is not being happy! To be happy is to feel good fortune by comparison with ill fortune."

That question obtained no response. The Superman had suddenly disappeared, with a pirouette.

The philosopher experienced some disquiet at such an abrupt retreat. Then, as the serum had not lost its influence, he thought about Philoxénie again.

# CHAPTER X

The next few days were employed, for the neophytes, in familiarizing themselves with the new life. Although they found themselves in a country where nothing lent itself to anxiety, where all exigencies and instincts were satisfied with the same simplicity as soon as one desired their realization, it was still necessary for them to adapt themselves to the use of those facilities and to lose the habit of complicating their existence, as they had become accustomed to doing in the Old World.

Choumaque and Marcel had to continue, for some time yet, to live in the sumptuous and deserted caravanserai into which they had been introduced on arrival. The law dictated that they would not live with the privileged indigenes until later, when their initiation was already well under way.

Marjah and Mirror-of-Smiles had been given the mission of edifying them. They accepted the responsibility with the kind of fatalistic complaisance that was the most curious characteristic of their gilded slavery. Every morning, they appeared successively in the apartments of the professor and his pupil. While the machines performed their functions, washing, combing, brushing and perfuming the neophytes, presenting them with their nourishment and collecting its modest superfluity, improved phonographs brought them news of the entire world; cinematographs, animated with a surprising reality, retraced before their eyes the scenes of contemporary history, detailing the scorned efforts of other countries.

A combination of the two devices even transported them to the Comédie or the Opéra, to watch the greatest actors of the epoch. Marjah was astonished that they delighted in that so much, for the rest of the people, concentrated in their particular tastes, were entirely uninterested in it. He told them that those futile curiosities would soon pass, having observed that people are only passionately interested in events susceptible of affecting them and causing upsets in their joy or sadness.

"Later, Messieurs," he said, "you'll no longer think of worrying about matters as trivial as a revolution in Kamchatka or the catastrophe caused by the opening of a crater in the heart of Peking"—the two principal news items of the day— "because you'll no longer have any need, knowing that the Superman wards off all dangers and that nothing bad can happen to you. Occupy yourselves, therefore, with taking pleasure, and nothing but pleasure!"

At these words, Mirror-of-Smiles, obedient to the prescriptions of his employment, ventured an inviting wink, but his offer remained futile. He was beginning to find that disdain surprising.

"But if you don't savor those curiosities," Choumaque objected to Marjah, "What do you admit? Yes, tell me, what do you like?"

"Everything! I like everything!"

"That's it. You like everything, so you like nothing," Choumaque concluded, faithful to his doctrine.

After dressing, in costumes of uniform hue—violet for Choumaque, orange for Marcel—of a remarkable luxury, richness and elegance, the neophytes absorbed their meal, consisting of a minuscule ball of complete aliment. That ingurgitation flattered their palettes with unprecedented tastes. Their stomachs experienced the pleasures of an easy digestion and copious sensation. Thus ballasted, they went out to visit to the four corners of the island. The pneumatic tubes transported them with lightning rapidity.

Always escorted by their guides, they went through magnificent halls disposed in the form of a lyre, in which the sweetest harmonies were produced on the most perfect instruments by the most beautiful performers. They ventured on foot along the four peninsulas, disposed like human limbs, which, projecting far out to sea, contained the palaces of families installed with the same luxury of commodities, the same fantastic richness of décor and the same superb gardens.

In the regions of the Thorax, the great Woods of Respiration, impregnated with vivifying scents, were animated every day by the games of the crowd. They found all the classes of society there, distinguishable only by their costumes, united in an edifying amorous fraternity. Sterile husbands, clad in red, wore long beards curling over the chest, and their muscles, perceptible under their leotards, had not been softened by maturity. They accompanied their virtual families: fecund mothers with pretty gilded torsades, whose blue tunics covered slender abdomens, emerged undamaged from frequent trials of maternity; joyful and healthy adolescent males in their emerald green doublets; adolescent virgins attractively curvaceous in their pale pink peplums, which they took off to wrestle. Small children were also frolicking in the open air, attempting their first flights with the aid of exceedingly light wings attached to an omnial apparatus.

All those people, all that variety, all that ostentation—the ostentation of Israel, Choumaque had observed, thinking about Caresco's Semitic origin—gentle on the eyes, iridescent and radiant, was animated, playing dancing, capering, placing rapid arrows in the taut string of bows, rolling balls along the flat ground, briskly catching knucklebones, or, calming down, allowing music to rise from the strings of harps, flutes and sistrums, mingled with pure voices, in order, later, to savor collations of candies, pastilles, fruits and sparkling wines.

Other members of the community sometimes mingled with their pleasures. There were gitons, clad in yellow tunics embroidered with the symbolic stripe, transformed into a cross by a second stripe when it ornamented the front of a slave. There were courtesans, languid in their mauve robes striped with red, which stripe was complicated by a perpendicular stripe for maidservants. There were also scientists, engineers and artists, freshly released from their labors, coming to add the serious note of their violet apparel to the polychromatic concert.

All of them, equals with regard to one another, fraternized and accorded themselves the trivial privacies of amour. Choumaque and Marcel saw the fathers of families drawing courtesans toward nearby arbors, under the complacent gazes of their wives. The latter did not repel the advances of young adolescents, and their husbands did not seem to want to punish that audacity.

When the neophytes expressed their astonishment, Marjah said: "What is more natural? Everyone's bodies are everyone's. The pleasures that each can offer belong to the generality. Are we not emanations of life, gifts of nature like air and light? Would you deprive someone of respiration, or bathing in the warmth of the sun?"

"It's a strange altruism, which must constitute very curious hearths," Choumaque objected, speaking aside.

They withdrew waiting until later to familiarize themselves entirely with that implausible social organization. Marjah promised them other surprises.

The next day, they visited the Heart. There, fluids were manufactured, automatically, almost without the aid of human labor. That excursion was prodigiously interesting for Marcel. He took pleasure in seeing the immense gears moved by wheels with a radius of two hundred meters, capturing the natural forces of the earth, the air, the sea and the stars and transforming them, by means of chemical reactions, into the unique substance named Omnium, the essence of all energies, able to become at will light, electricity, air, water, vapor, matter and fluids of every sort.

All of that was agitating silently, rhythmically, accomplishing formidable tasks within the shelter of high walls, in a paroxysm of labor. From an armored basin in which all the services were concentrated, enormous subterranean conduits departed, ramifying innately, to every diverticulum of the island, every branch of every individual house, distributing, on command, cold, heat, lighting, water, nourishment, perfumes, repose and activity. A single engineer sufficed to supervise these divisions; it was sufficient for him to press a button for the slightest arteries to be impregnated and saturated by them.

Then there were the palaces of the Stomach and the Liver, where the materials of subsistence were elaborated. In reality, people rarely ate, all hygienic nourishment being provided by the balls of complete aliment, but the most delicate pastries and confections were abundantly distributed. In addition, certain festivals were celebrated—those of the Brain, Omnium, Fecundity, Sterility, Eucrasia and Life—recurring on determined dates, during which there were bacchanals that permitted pleasures of the table in the fashion of the old world, but more refined and devoid of any animal substance.

These palaces, admirably organized and designed, obeyed mechanical genius with as much fidelity as the factories of the Heart. In the great kitchen-garden of the Liver, adjacent to the bagpipe of the Stomach, vegetables were cultivated intensively, from which organic juices were extracted in order to be mixed with the substances of the complete aliment.

All the detritus of the island, human ordure and liquid excreta and the wastes of machines were taken to the Renal and Intestinal regions, where, after being subjected to a chemical triage that conserved and dried the fractions still utilizable, they were dumped far out at sea, to be carried away by dirty currents. Thus Hygiene removed from the people all the harmful by-products of nature, as conclusively as the explosive devices protected them from human malevolence.

Marjah then took them to visit the Palace of Public Fortune, inhabited by the Chief Representative Zadochbach. They were able to go in as they liked, for, peculation being nonexistent, no special prohibition forbade entrance to it. They considered colossal fortunes there, in the form of papers that, if realized, would have been equal in value to the mountains of gold, which had no significance for the islanders. However, Zadochbach plunged his earthy face toward them gladly, and palpitated them lovingly.

The arena where Choumaque was soon to speak in public was adjacent to the Palace of Fortune, so they extended their stroll to it. The philosopher admired the open-air amphitheater, and the adorable panorama of verdant stages framing it. He promised himself beautiful phrases, in order to edify the women with the flavorsome flesh.

A little later, Marcel boarded the ironclad of which he had been given command. He recognized, not without astonishment, one of the units of the French mobile defense, which was said to have disappeared during a hurricane. The vessel was moored not far from the Mount of Venus, whose high summit was lost in the snows, enigmatic, wild and eternally icy.

What was to interest them even more than these various aspects of the island, however, was the region specially reserved for amour. Marjah promised them that they would not have to wait long to visit it.

# CHAPTER XI

From inside, Carabella drew aside the large curtain of red velvet, embroidered with gold, that closed her dwelling in the Courtesans' quarter. Her unfastened peplum, falling away from the globular splendor of her right breast, the scatter of her loosened brown hair extending to her waist, where geranium petals were mingled with it, and a residue of languorous ecstasy that continued to shiver in her dark eyes behind the silk of her long lashes, all revealed that she was emerging from pleasure. The three people to whom she granted passage, Golden-Gaze and his wife Veloutine, and Philoxénie, the lover of strangers, confirmed that she had not been partaking of it alone.

"Adieu, dear Carabella, tamer of our loins, hospitaller of our frenzies! We have spent moments with you that count among the most exquisite. Adieu!"

All three kissed her on the mouth before leaving. Then they drew away along the lawn delimiting the gem-like flower-beds, the brown-haired Philoxénie in the middle, slightly taller than the blonde Veloutine with cheeks as fresh as a peach, who was slightly shorter than Gilded-Gaze, with the blazing eyes, whose ample beard fell in curls over his chest. Soon, their three colors—red, mauve and pale blue—faded into the glory of the sunlit afternoon, and nothing remained visible except the scarlet of the sterile spouse, which finally disappeared as it went around the corner of the marble palace in which Philoxénie lived.

Then Carabella, excessively weary, decided to rest. She went back in, letting the curtain fall behind her. She went through one room with a gleaming mosaic floor, hollowed out by a basin in which fish as mauve as her tunic were swimming. A pet leopard came bounding toward her. She paused momentarily to caress its silky fur, and then crossed the threshold of another, darker room in which the windowless

143

walls, streaked with silver arabesques from floor to ceiling, enveloped a solitude propitious to meditation or religious voluptuousness.

There, a large unmade bed, still rumpled by the sojourn of her companions, occupied the center, raised up on an altar; around it were dressing-tables covered with bottles, ointments, creams and a thousand objects aiding the artifice of adornment: mirrors framed in precious metals, boxes full of jewelry, combs and diamante clasps, belts studded with gems, and various instruments, curious in form, with which she assisted pleasure in herself and others.

She felt a thrill of gratitude for that environment. Already she was stretching herself out on the warm bed, and her muscles, fatigued by recent vibrations, were about to relax into sleep when an order, simultaneously emitted by the microphone and luminously signaled by a screen, brought her to her feet again, hastily. It was the summons of the Almighty.

"Carabella, the Superman is waiting for you!"

She hurried. She tidied her hair with a few flicks of the wrist, and then went out, adjusting her girdle. A large airplane in the form of an eagle, decorated with the potentate's colors, was waiting for her in front of the atrium. Without it touching down, the four slaves who formed its crew skillfully collected the courtesan and laid her down on the cushions of the nacelle.

A rapid flight carried her away and soon deposited her inside the Palace of Surgery, in front of a small door of sculpted bronze, through which she went in order to go along a dark corridor. When she had traversed it, guided by a light emerging from a brightly lit room from which loud noises were emerging, she hesitated momentarily. Her presence had been detected, however, and a voice rose up on the other side of the wall.

"There you are, courtesan—come in!"

It was Caresco who had issued the invitation. She went in. The surgeon had just emerged from an operation, although he was not in the place where he had carried it out. There was nothing around him, in fact, but the apparatus and instruments of orthopedics.

Naked to the waist, his legs covered in a large imperme-able apron still streaming with blood, his hairy arms soiled with clots, he was delivering heavy blows of a hammer to a pedestal, in order to bolt the carapace of the half-man captain, whose breast he had opened a few moments before in order to resect a part of the malfunctioning heart. Satisfied with his work, he was expending his strength impetuously, raising the instrument and bringing it down, causing the anvil to ring. By his side was the thin, bizarre silhouette of Dr. Hymen, his as-sistant, who, similarly clad, was still sporting his furry top hat, fused with the shock of his hair, supporting the torso of the patient, who was still asleep.

"Do you think that's solid enough, Hymen? Take your fingers away, so that I can fix it more securely."

He struck again. A few incoherencies emerged from the half-man's pisciform mouth.

"He's waking up! He'll be content, the little fellow! Isn't that the thirtieth time I've worked on him? And it won't be the last!"

"No, no, it won't be the last! And I bless you, O Super-man!" trumpeted the captain's voice, with a shrill bleat, as he emerged from his artificial sleep. He went on: "O celestial bliss! O supreme recompense of my adoration! Blessed be the one who has once again brought me another step closer to perfection!"

"Take him away, and leave me alone with Carabella," Caresco ordered Dr. Hymen, who pirouetted and pushed the pedestal away.

When the machine-man had disappeared, Caresco sat down, and with the greatest mystery, beckoned to the courte-san to come closer. His exaltation had suddenly died away; an indefinable disgust tarnished his physiognomy. Thoughtfully, he bit his fingernails, without paying any heed to the blood that stained them. Then, interrupting with a curt gesture the manifestations of servility that Carabella was making, her moving hips splayed by prostration, he said: "Well, what about the stranger?"

"I don't have very much to tell you, Superman. She's very mysterious, and doesn't allow herself any effusion."

"Has she acquired a taste for adornment?"

"She disdains the jewelry that clutters her coffers."

"Does she eat?"

"Without pleasure."

"What does she say?"

"She only talks about her brother."

"And amour?"

"She remains insensible to it."

"The serum hasn't had any effect on her, then!" Caresco murmured, twisting his brown beard. Then he said: "Carabella, you're going to apply yourself to a delicate task."

"Speak! I submit myself to you as matter to Mind, as a creature to the Primal Being..."

"Well, it's a matter of planting in this Hardisson the seed of the joy that you respire so ardently. I want her to be intoxicated, like the others by the long delights that you cause to pant perpetually! I want her to feel, in the secrecy of her soul, the wonderment of our Beauty, and in the secrecy of her flesh, the impetuosity of our Voluptuousness! I want the obsolete memory of her homeland to vanish forever. That's what I want!"

"She has only to look around and let herself live."

"No, for in that virgin, nature, which I have tamed so thoroughly elsewhere, is still rearing up and rebelling. She is all nature, that daughter of the Red Land! And she complicates it with such purity, such temperance!"

Astonished, Carabella dared to raise her large dark eyes toward her interlocutor. He noticed the interrogation in them.

"But what need do I have to give you explanations? Content yourself with obeying. Attach yourself to her. Praise our way of life to her incessantly. Impregnate her with our transports. Impart to her the diapason with which you vibrated yourself when I possessed you with my Science! But above

146

all, let her remain virgin to men. You'll answer to me for her metempsychotic fortune..."

He threw her a box wrapped in golden cloth, which she picked up, kissing it piously.

"Take it. In the form of fruit confections, it's a variety of my Essence of Happiness. Those sweetmeats have already reckoned with a few strangers. Make her take two a day, until the end of the month, and tell me the result. Better than that—I'll monitor it personally."

"I shall obey, Almighty."

Dismissed, she departed in the same fashion that she had arrived. The airplane transported her to Miss Mary. The foreigner, who had not gone out that day, was sitting in a chaste indoor costume at a table in her room, occupied in writing a journal of her travels for her brother. She was telling dear Harry about her incredible adventures, how she had arrived in an extraordinary country where life was very different—magical and seductive, to be sure, but too facile for a soul like hers to delight in it. She added that nothing would be able to deflect her from the noble objective that she was determined to attain, of saving the fatherland. And her hand, as she wrote, trembled with a sublime fever.

"That's a strange occupation," said Carabella, as she came in, "describing little signs on paper."

"It's called writing," Miss Mary observed. "Don't you know how to write, courtesan?"

"I leave that concern to scholars. What use are the torments of the intellect to us? Have we not a thousand more ingenious ways to communicate?"

"Possibly. But that ignorance will always keep you apart from the beautiful legends of history and the pleasure of acquaintance with the thoughts of great writers."

"All that is of very mediocre interest. Happiness is found within oneself."

As she spoke, Carabella held out her box of confections to the neophyte. Miss Mary took one and put it in her mouth with an unthinking gesture, so absorbed was she in her dream, in flight toward the Red Land. After which she took up her pen, determined not to allow herself to be distracted any longer, and to enclose herself in her dolorous intimacy with the energetic Harry.

Almost immediately, however, a languor invaded her; entirely new images interposed themselves between the letter and the intelligence that was dictating its terms. Like a river alimented by the new water of glaciers, she expanded in a wave of spring-like descriptions.

Without abandoning her subject, she continued to relate the astonishments of the island, but in a different fashion. She cited the beauty of its people, the mildness of its climate, the magnificence of its monuments, the splendor of its incomparable locations. Iridescent colors, sunlight, the glinting of metals, all the pomp of flames, jewels, gold and harmonies of flesh flowed kaleidoscopically from her pen. She knew that she was not expressing the true thoughts of Miss Mary, because another woman had taken her place—but that other woman experienced a strange pleasure in being, and was delighted to feel that Carabella was behind her, sharing her intoxication. If she thought for a moment about Marcel, it was no longer to pose the problem of his expatriation, but to confide to Harry that the Frenchman was vigorously built, like the young men of the Red Land, and that he also had a native elegance and clarity of eye that rendered him entirely likeable and charming.

"You mustn't tire yourself out, divine neophyte," said Carabella, forcing her to stop work.

Then, putting her arm around her waist—which she permitted without resistance, Carabella took Miss Mary to lean on the balustrade of the terrace, before a prestigious panorama illuminated by the sunset. At the same time, she gave her the second fruit pastel prescribed by Caresco.

"Contemplate the day's end, divine one. All the jewels of the setting sun are accumulating on the horizon. And when they have disappeared, when the star is lying in its mantle of shadow, you'll see the delightful spectacle that the Superman is giving us to enjoy this evening."

Indeed, as soon as darkness had fallen, the moonless firmament lit up again. On the black screen of space there appeared, in a phantasmagoria of lights fixed at precise points in communication, a succession of pictures, each more extraordinary than the last. Unfolding in the auroras there were sumptuous processions; and then Pactoluses of fire, drawing, in waves of caresses, enfevered nudities; and then languid twilights in which human splendors were interlaced, embracing one another, shaking the spirals of their golden hair.

"It's the Passion!" murmured Carabella, intoxicated. "It's the Passion deploying. Look, Virgin! All of our amour is passing before your eyes! I recognize the guests at these divine feasts; I have savored with them the temptations of cleavages; I have drunk the philters of their breath! O sublime Beauty! O harmony of Forms! O divine architects of ecstasy! Do you understand them, Virgin; can you feel them? Is not that poetry worth more than the most beautiful epics of war?"

"I confess that I find it admirable," said the neophyte, who, gripped more tenderly by Carabella, felt the suggestion of the images invading her, impregnating her nerves.

But when Carabella wanted to test her fervor further; when, having drawn her into the room, barely lit by a rosy omnial glow, she tried to imitate the gestures that had been falling from the sky a few moments before, and approached the warm pulp of her lips to the virginal mouth, the latter suddenly turned away.

"What do you want with me? Go away! I don't understand! Go away!"

The foreigner stiffened. War, rifles, cannons, dying soldiers, Harry holding the lacerated flag—all of the other poem assailed her again. And those memories emitted such a perfume of health and the ideal that she felt disgust as she breathed the perfumed breath of the courtesan. She shoved her to the door.

149

The second attempt of Caresco's genius had failed. Nature remained the stronger, even though the strength of Miss Mary's modesty had been weakened in advance of the assault.

# CHAPTER XII

That morning, Marjah was alone when he came to collect the philosopher and his pupil. As soon as he came into their apartment he adopted an unaccustomed attitude of importance. After bringing them together he explained the gravity of his attitude.

"Today, Messieurs, I am going to acquaint you with the Sacred Region of the island. The Superman has put all his wisdom, all his science and all his bounty into it. There are no palaces there; there are temples, all of which are utilized for the religion of Life that we practice. I beg you to cross their thresholds with the same devotion that I experience myself in going into them."

Furnished with these holy recommendations, Choumaque and Marcel took their places in a rapid airplane, which Marjah guided with the greatest skill. The weather was exquisite, and skillfully distributed currents of fresh air contested without difficulty with the sun's heat to maintain a temperature of gentle warmth. Choumaque and Marcel had sat down at the front, vibrant with the light through which they were soaring.

"What a pity that Miss Hardisson isn't with us!" murmured Marcel. He had not seen her the previous day. On the few occasions when he had seen her approach, in the silence of the intermediate park, always under the equivocal surveillance of Carabella, she had seemed saddened by the uncertainty in which her appearance before Caresco had left her.

"It's probable," Choumaque observed, "that we're going to find ourselves in the presence of spectacles that a young woman whose initiation has not taken place cannot know..."

"Don't you think, Master, that she is being deliberately kept away from me?"

"That's an observation that manifests a great conceit, or a great suffering...and I hope that the latter reason is the true one."

Scarcely had Marcel expressed his anxiety, however, than he was given cause to change his mind. Cries departing from the ground attracted their attention, and on leaning over they saw Miss Mary and Carabella, who were making signs at them to stop.

"Superman's orders!" said the courtesan, when they had landed. "I am to inform you, Marjah, the neophyte is to accompany you to the sacred regions." She leaned over toward the High Priest and murmured a few mysterious words in his ear, as she slipped a little box into his hand. Doubtless she was passing on the orders imposed by Caresco, for the eunuch's face, as he listened, was infused with a sacerdotal gravity.

Marcel was delighted to see Miss Mary again. The excursion, undertaken with regret, was about to be converted into an intoxicating adventure. His hopes were dented, however, on observing that the foreign woman was listening to what he said in a reserved manner. He admired the pride of her attitude, her commanding presence, the freshness of her cheeks and the reflections of sunlight in her hair.

"Miss Mary!" he murmured. "Miss Mary! How sweet it is to pronounce your name! My heart recites it in secret, although my lips tremble to pronounce it aloud. Know what a disaster your departure will cast into one heart! Do you still intend to remove from this island the sole attraction that, for me, can exist here? Tell me, Miss Mary, are you still intending to leave?"

She did not reply. That music found no echo in her.

The sight of the panorama soon extracted them from those alternatives. They were approaching an enormous mountain of which the summit, having the circular form of an extinct crater, was lost in the eternal snows. Lower down there was red rock, carved in a picturesque fashion by sharp gashes, gigantic crevasses forming gulfs whose depths were invisible, plunging as far as the intersection of the island's two gigantic legs, lost in the blue sea that was enlivened by a silvery sparkle.

"That's the Mount of Venus," Marjah confirmed. "It's the sole reminder of the cataclysm that occurred thirty years ago. The Superman decided to retain all of its savage horror. It's well-known—but only mentioned in whispers—that in one of those fissures there's a cave into which only he goes. It's said that he works there, that he meditates these. Approaching it is forbidden, within a perimeter of two kilometers.

While they circled around the monstrous block, in order not to pass over the forbidden zone, Marjah, while maintaining control of the airplane, gave further explanations. He told them that the volcano, after several eruptions, had now become extinct and cooled. He had seen it still smoking twenty years before. Sometimes, one heard rumbles that revealed intimate convulsions, the muted work of the central fire continuing beneath its icy carcass—but since the Superman went there frequently, since he worked there in secret machines, the eunuch considered that there was no danger to the people.

Nevertheless, what Marjah also knew, but dared not recount, was a dark legend repeated clandestinely, reaching ears like the distant echo of an indistinct sound, so strange and so troubling that it had stirred his natural asexual apathy. Was it not said, in fact, that sometimes, individuals—especially young virgins—disappeared into that lair, abducted by Caresco, and never came back?

To be sure, the religious fatalism of the people, their absolute faith in the Superman, could not admit that they were subjected there to a dire fate. They even went so far as to believe that the virgins thus removed from the community were particularly favored, and that the Master had organized a different life for them inside the mountain, in which they enjoyed an even more fortunate destiny. But that was only a supposition, contradicted in reality by the appearance of lassitude, and even distress, the Caresco offered to the eyes of his faithful followers when he returned from the mysterious cavern alone.

153

The aerial craft was flying lower now, at a rapid speed. It soon came close to an agglomeration of buildings in the vicinity of a vast entrance on pink porphyry representing, with an incredible crudity of realism, the union of the two sexes. Choumaque and Marcel looked at that new symbol without overmuch offense; one might have thought that they were already impregnated with the morality of their new fatherland, accepting its licentious spectacles as well as the entirely natural manifestations of the religion of Life presiding over social organization. As for Miss Mary, her eyes did not turn away from it; she was following an internal reverie.

They became interested thereafter in a sequence of edifices that extended as far as the eye could see. They sensed that Caresco had lavished every luxury and wealth upon them. There were golden domes speckled with coral vibrions and ovules; towers of pink and green marble; gigantic campaniles in milky hues; then spacious gardens enameled with a prodigality of flowers forming, even at a distance, a harmonious polychromy; and, further on, shady parks with sinuous streams and blue lakes, shining in gaps in the verdure in which the iridescent foliage seemed fresher than anywhere else. All of it spoke of the unparalleled splendor of that area, delimited into two precise regions, following the straight lines of the terrestrial legs sinking into the sea.

The airplane touched down gently, and they got down, near two coupled organs, one of which—the male—was pierced with a central channel that constituted the entrance. As soon as they had passed through it, an immense room that Marjah called the Hall of Sensuality appeared before them. As it was dark in its center, they contented themselves with moving along the moderately illuminated walls, and eventually came out into a vast park filled with verdant arbors disposed like beds, or altars.

There, two paths were offered, the one to the right decked with pennants in pale blue and orange, the one on the left with yellow and mauve pennants, floating in the breeze. Two large avenues carved in the rock succeeded those decorations, indicative of fecundity to the right and sterility to the left. Strewn with extremely fine green gravel, they were being raked at that moment by automatic machines evenly propelled without the assistance of any human direction.

They hesitated over which route to take, but Marjah made the decision: "Let's visit Fecundity first."

Almost immediately, the found themselves in front of a group sculpted in onyx the color of flesh, with an incomparable artistic perfection. It represented, surging from the ground, a naked mother holding a baby in her arms to which she had just given birth, holding it out toward a man with a long curly beard, whose nudity indicated, by the presence of a nenuphar lily-pad over the location of the sex organ, a definite sterility. The play of an interior light made the head of the infant shine, even by day, expanding to reflect from the parents in an apotheosis. They admired the group, and circled around it, searching in vain for a signature.

"I thought that artists were only modest in France," observed Choumaque, with a sardonic smile.

"That is the symbol of the family," said a voice behind them. "The child, constitutive of the hearth, radiates joy and happiness upon the mother and the father—of whom, nevertheless, it is not the descendant."

Marcel and Choumaque turned round, thinking that they were dealing with a new individual. They could only see a small wheeled stele that had been following them for a few moments, seeming attached to their paces, moving back and forth and turning when they did. They could no longer be astonished by anything, and understood that they were dealing with an ambulant phonograph, which an unknown fluid, doubtless some new adaptation of the mysterious omnium, linked to their persons. Marcel's bright eyes smiled at his friend. All the same, it interested him; he admired the inventions of the marvelous empire.

The mechanical cicerone continued, in a quavering voice: "You have just traversed the Hall of Sensuality, which is only utilized on major feast days, when the license of sterility is extended to everyone. But you are now about to enter the Temples of Reproduction, where the eucrasic Sowers designated for Repopulation come religiously to accomplish the most sacred act of our religion, which consists of fecundating the blonde mothers.

"That will be your function," Marjah told Marcel.

"The husbands serve no purpose, then?" queried the young man. "That work wouldn't suit me..."

"Don't cast doubt on the wisdom of the benefactor," Marjah replied. "The fact is that for a man, being married does not imply the qualities of production that a valiant lineage requires. That's why the title of husband is purely gratuitous. Here, the family is constituted between two spouses by means of children almost always due to a strange Sower; at any rate, children are engendered in conditions of absolute security, while the isolation of the mother puts her beyond the reach of any sowing prejudicial to the race, as you shall see in a moment. There are women among those who have many children who no longer even remember from which men they obtained them.

"But what about the husbands?"

"The husbands are sterilized. The serum with which you have been inoculated, Monsieur Choumaque, removes their procreative virtues, but not their pleasure n amour. They have at their free disposition, additionally, the courtesans commanded by Madame Môme and the gitons of which I am the chief."

"And the mothers, between the periods of fecundation?"

"If you think about it, you'll understand that the mothers, outside of their times of production, can only have dealings with sterilized citizens."

"Those are improbable mores, but, in sum, more rational that one would be tempted to think at first glance," observed Choumaque. "Even supposing that practices as rigorous would not be honored in the old world. I would not be hostile to wanting to sterilize certain alcoholics, degenerates, litterateurs and politicians. Those inebriates generally engender offspring afflicted with disequilibrium."

As they were talking they drew away from the statue. Choumaque made a few more gracious remarks to his companions. He congratulated Marjah on having lived for so long in a country where cuckolds did not exist. To Marcel he predicted great joys in fulfilling the function of stallion in Caresco's stud-farm. Marcel did not want to agree because Miss Mary could hear.

The wheeled phonograph indicated their route. Under its direction they reached the first palace, named *Devirginicum*, of which a fresco decorated the frontispiece. The fresco represented, with a great richness of hues, a naked virgin lying on an operating table. Standing beside her was a man with the physiognomy of Dr. Hymen. In one hand he was brandishing a scalpel, while in the other he held a dandelion clock, which he was dispersing to the wind by blowing on it with inflated cheeks. The seeds thus dispersed by his breath were gradually transformed into chubby winged children. Beneath that allegory and inscription unfurled, which read: *Here the gates of eternity are opened!*

"What does that enigmatic symbol represent?" asked Choumaque, addressing himself to Marjah.

It was the phonograph that replied, as if it had understood the question. It recounted the fashion in which the virgins destined for maternity were brought to the palace before the approach of a man, in order that the virginity whose suppression renders the first instants of amour so painful could be surgically removed, under induced sleep. Thus, the young women could subsequently offer themselves to fecund caresses without experiencing the suffering that often discourages the attempts of lovers. Never to suffer, and scientifically to aid the pleasures that nature concedes for the expansion of life, such was the law on the island of Eucrasia.

With this explanation, the visitors penetrated into the Devirginicum. In a sumptuous oval room they found an image almost identical to the one they had seen outside, animated

157

this time. Dr. Hymen had just finished his practice on a superb blonde still lying there, divinely pale and pearly in her sleep, His right hand was holding a bloody scalpel, and although he was not blowing on a flower, at least he was looking with interest at a scrap of pink membrane, recently excised, which he was clutching between the thumb and forefinger of his left hand.

Doubtless that banal operation did not require great surgical rigor, for he had not put on his antiseptic smock. As on the first occasion that Choumaque had seen him, he was wearing his long frock-coat and green shirt, and his minuscule golden instruments, bizarre in form, were dangling over his protruding abdomen. His face was radiant; his long oblique and hooked nose, slanting toward his turned-up side-whisker—and from his shock of thick black hair, almost mingling with the nap of his flat-brimmed opera hat and dense eyebrows overhanging his glaucous eyes, a suggestion of frolicsome joy was emanating. He was gazing with compunction at eight virgins who were waiting their turn, laughing and chewing pralines.

He perceived the newcomers. "Caresco favors you, Messieurs!" he pronounced, extending his hands toward them, which they avoided taking in order not to touch either the scalpel or the membrane.

Without paying any heed to their hesitation, he immediately became gracious, particularly to Choumaque, to whom he offered a pinch of a sugary powder with which he had begun to fill his mouth.

"You see, my dear Choumaque, I'm accomplishing, in deflowering these virgins, one of the most fundamental rites of our religion. In the same way, certain practices of ancient cults were rules of hygiene. The imbecility of peoples deflected them from their origin and application, while we strive, on the contrary, to impose orthodoxy in all its naïve crudity, in order that our believers, knowing the objective, should conserve integrally usages useful to the species and favorable to Life."

158

He adopted a grave expression. His lips stretched toward his black side-whiskers, uncovering the unevenness of his sharp-toothed dentition. Everything about his person darkened, from his flat-brimmed opera hat to the pendants on his abdomen, which ceased dancing, in expectation of great truths.

Slapping his interlocutor on the shoulder, he continued: "And you've philosophized, my dear Choumaque! You've rambled on for hours about pleasure, dolor and the causes of social ills! You've even engendered a doctrine, called that of equilibria. And perhaps you've believed in the nonsensical ideas you've spouted! How much simpler life is! How easily one can force happiness with a little stroke of the scalpel! Get rid of that which causes suffering—the entire secret is there!

"Would you like to know, my dear Choumaque, who the happiest man in our realm is? It's the one who possesses the fewest organs, the half-man who commands the airplane that transported you from Paris to our island. And would you like to know who will be the citizen more favored still? It will be the human monad that our great Caresco is preparing at this moment, and from whom he will remove everything that is susceptible of being removed. No windows to the outside, no suffering within.

"And if people claim where you come from that physical happiness consists of the normal functioning of the organs; if they affirm there that living well is being endowed with a beneficent activity, that's hilarious stupidity: to live well is not to exist! And that's all there is to it!"

Choumaque made great efforts to follow this original argument. He was about to ask the fantastic philosopher why, in that case, he took so much care to ameliorate the health of his fellow citizens and favor fecundity—why he did not kill them all, and himself with them—when he saw the doctor's physiognomy change. Hymen smiled again; his facial hair and his opera hat were flamboyant with gaiety; the pendants on his abdomen clinked in a joyous frisson.

"It's not otherwise in amour, Monsieur Choumaque. As you see, I remove an average of five virginities a day. I open thereby, in five female loins, the gateway of generation! I am the concierge of eternity! And I have the honor of removing these little membranes, which, in your old world, three times in ten, are the cause of a woman's repulsion for men, and nine times out of ten—the statistics are there to affirm it—are forced in a detestably maladroit fashion..."

"You're making fun of me, Monsieur," Choumaque protested. "Nature has not put that little membrane there in order that it should be pierced by a scalpel. She has put it there, on the contrary, in order to make the woman remember—if not the man—that pleasure comes after pain. Voluptuousness is all the more welcome because it has long disputed with pain. And I see that as a further proof of my doctrine of equilibria, in which it is said that good compensates evil."

"Good and evil are merely hollow words for us. We do not know them; we do not want to know them. The citizen, in our realm, in subordinate to only one state: enjoyment."

Having spoken, Hymen turned his back and signaled to a virgin with a magnificent complexion, who advanced for the sacrifice, her hips swaying. Her blonde hair spilled over the pink silk of her tunic. She undressed and lay down on the central table. A current of fluid immediately put her to sleep. Dr. Hymen sniggered and seized his scalpel.

The neophytes and Marjah hastened to leave him to his delicate operation.

They emerged in front of a façade whose whiteness and cleanliness surprised them. Delimiting a vast park, it was bare of the ornamentation and excessive richness that embellished all the monuments in the vicinity; its architectural serenity was restful on the eye.

The soft shades of the allegory decorating the frontispiece were no less agreeable to see. They represented a radiant mother on the point of death scattering to the wind a cup whose liquid was transforming into little pink children; it was the symbol of the cup of Fecundity emptied by Ephemerality.

As soon as they had crossed the threshold, their ears were charmed by music that was harmoniously soft at times and passionately vibrant at others. They were glad to gaze at the cheerful sight of a landscape populated with beautiful trees, and to follow the lively course of nubile foam along streams bubbling over beds of yellow gravel. There were delicate little rustic houses covered in thatch, which the sun was caressing gently, and herds of cows grazing the tender grass; the sound of distant bells quivered in the purity of an atmosphere forcefully vivified with oxygen and embalmed with the fresh perfumes of lavender and heather—all of which reanimated in the eyes of two of the strangers the memory of old engravings representing the landscapes of Normandy a century ago: green, calm Normandy, of a pastoral beauty, when its décor had not yet be perverted by the abuses of tourism.

Only a few statues standing at intervals, all marvelously beautiful, disrupted that rural simplicity. They also saw young men and women, walking arm in arm. Some of them, sitting on the banks of streams, were playing reed pipes; others were dancing; others, leaning their elbows on massive tables, were drinking milk that was being served to them in earthenware ladles. The white foam, freshly emerged from the udder, splashed their lips, brightened by healthy, adding panache to their smiles. All of them were dressed with the utmost simplicity, with a few animal skins knotted round their loins.

As they went past the thatched cottages, they heard cries of amour coming from a few of them.

"You are now," the phonograph recited, "in the Eldorado of couplings. The Superman has determined that those of his subjects who are designated for creation should subsist here for some while in the state of primal nature. In his great wisdom, he esteems that children thus made are more soundly constituted. The statues you can see are designed to impregnate the passion of lovers with the spectacle of beauty, but they are superfluous, because these individuals, all beautiful, have only to admire one another. The music that you hear inspires the caresses whose frequency is sagely moderated, in order that the seed should be of the finest quality..."

"Rejoice, stallion in Caresco's stud! Behold the promise of beautiful days," Choumaque murmured to his companion.

But Marcel was staying in other visions. Without wanting to pause at what that animal regimentation of amour could offer him by way of tinkering, he told Miss Mary how he would have enjoyed that bucolic life in her company, and he was saddened to hear her reply that she had other things on her mind than relaxing in such infantile games. A pressure of the arm that he attempted had no more effect than if he had tried to move the indifference of a statue.

Thereafter, in the awakening of his desire, he allowed his thoughts to run over the delightful landscape and the people who animated it. Alas, it was always to mingle his companion therewith, in order that he might draw her into it, to see himself, like her, in a gleaming nudity, savoring the aroma of her bare skin, her hair loosened in luminous waves. He drew her to him in the shelter of those rustic roofs, laid her down on the ground softened with hay, searched the ecstasy of her eyes, palpated the resistance of her breasts...

These various curiosities led them—after a considerable time, for the garden extended for several leagues—to the entrance of another palace, which the phonograph identified as the Temple of Gestation. It was there that mothers, after the gift of insemination, spent the term of their pregnancy. They lived there in an atmosphere of calm and hygiene, severed from any masculine distraction, receiving intense corporeal care, gratified by a healthy alimentation, frequent baths, and incessantly admiring beautiful paintings and delightful sculptures. It was also the case that plastic living tableaux were performed for them by the best-formed subjects of the island, but always anaphrodisiac.

As the place appeared to visitors to be uninteresting and rather monotonous, given that no performance was being put on at the moment, they passed through it rapidly. Scarcely had they emerged than machines took hold of them and jets of pleasantly-perfumed vapor were directed over their bodies.

Immediately dried off, they saw that they were covered from head to foot by a layer of white dust.

Their amazement was calmed by the explanations of the wheeled cicerone. They were being antisepticised before being allowed to penetrate into the Temple of Childbirth. For the same reason, they put on impermeable garments, and thus frosted, they were able to witness the entire mechanism of delivery.

Choumaque and Marcel experienced a keen interest in the procedure, neither of them ever having witnessed a similar operation, but their emotion was considerably diminished, for sterilized apparatus stuck in the fashion of bell-jars over the sacred regions of parturition, which were not very translucent, and while assisting nature with pressures and tractions, hid the labor, so dramatic in its full spectacle.

In the same way, they did not hear any of those howls, like those of a wounded beast, to which the compassion of spectators usually gives rise. All the mothers were anesthetized by the same magnetism that had rendered Choumaque unconscious of his surgical metamorphosis.

They counted eight women laboring in that silence. Around the eighth a man was agitating. His dirty smock and his fury hat, both abundantly covered in antiseptic substance, allowed them to recognize Dr. Hymen. How did the scientist come to be there already? Did he have the gift of duplicating himself?

Choumaque approached him. "My dear Doctor. I bless this new encounter, and I see with pleasure that you're neglecting nothing in your function as the concierge of eternity, since, after opening the gates, you continue by pulling the cord..."

Had the joke been too strong? The strange individual did not reply. Arms bare, he was kneading a substance that resembled plaster, and when he judged it sufficiently manageable he used it to cover the belly of the woman who had just been relieved of both her child and the container that had facilitated the delivery. Choumaque deduced that, as a result of being

163

plastered, the abdomen avoided the deformation susceptible of subsequently discouraging masculine desire. They left Dr. Hymen to his task and his ill humor, definitively.

Marcel strove in vain to discover in the features of his companion what impression these spectacles were translating there. He was astonished to read nothing therein but indifference and scorn. The rude cohabitations of the Red Land, the overt life of the camps where the women came in search of the generous semen of warriors and sometimes to render them the fruits, had long ago revealed to the heroine the lacerations with which maternity is paid. She had seen the progress of those deeds in which nature demands tears, blood, suffering and screams from those who demand the joy of giving birth and of holding a child forcefully against their breast. By those contacts her character had been tempered even more, and she was genuinely disdainful of the comfortable mechanism of creation here.

A little further on, at the exit, a bath relaxed them as well as removing their microbicidal covering. They put on other costumes with joy. Choumaque put his on more hurriedly than the others, for he was in haste to hide the scars of his new beauty, even though they were scarcely apparent.

"The Temple of Puericulture!" growled the phonograph when, after a kilometer's march, they found themselves before an ornamentation a hundred meters high, representing, in a vermilion wake, clouds of chubby winged angels struggling as they hastened toward the distant radiation of a life-giving sun surging from a mountain licked by redness. The faithful instrument confirmed that it was the natural sequel to the creative events already revealed to them.

"Here children are brought up, rationally and intensively, from the hour of birth until the seventh year. You shall see, without me having to insist more particularly"—and these words, emitted by a machine, had something piquant about them—"with what care the Superman has organized the development of the individual who will become a citizen of his State. Here, nothing is left to the irreflection of nature. Science reclaims its rights and perfects being, in order to appropriate it to the exigencies of its destiny. A special nourishment, changing every six months, when measurements and weights have been scrupulously recorded, ensures the blossoming of all the organs, one after another.

"At the age of one year children can walk and have a full set of teeth; at two, they are taught to swim; at three, the art of flying in the air in no longer unknown to them; at six, they are nubile and acquainted with matters of amour. Finally, at seven, the supreme Master decides their fate anatomically: sterile or fecund. For a boy: giton and subsequently slave, or capable of fatherhood. In the latter case, he is returned to his hearth, sent back to his originating mother and his putative father."

"That's all very well," said Choumaque to his companions, when the phonograph paused, "but I perceive that the rights of the intellect are entirely neglected in that education."

"What purpose would it serve?" Marjah observed.

"But are great minds not necessary to plan, modify and maintain all your machinery? I've seen superb workshops in which young men are employed who are of a generation anterior to mine. When they have gone, what will become of all your discoveries?"

"I don't know," said Marjah, with a gesture of indifference. "It's probable that after them, things will progress of their own accord. Caresco protects us!"

*That eunuch is making use, without suspecting it, of the sad king Louis XV's "After me, the Deluge!"* Choumaque said to himself. *If the pleasures of philosophy could extract those cerebral cells from their somnolence, he would certainly be a partisan of the optimism of Leibniz.*[17]

---

[17] The quotation, which employs "*nous*" [we] rather than "*moi*" [me], was actually attributed to Louis XV's mistress, Madame de Pompadour, who was a good deal cleverer than the king and, as a sideline to her career as a courtesan, supported and sponsored the philosophers of the Enlightenment, including Voltaire. Choumaque's remark about Leibnizian

They were beginning to feel tired and hungry. Temporarily renouncing a visit to Puericulture, they called a halt and sat down next to a clean spring whose banks were carpeted with moss. A utility distributor fitted into the rock fortunately chanced to be within reach. They demanded alimentary pills, which relieved their hunger.

Marcel was sitting next to the young woman. He admired the curve of her muscular foot, imprisoned by a pink sandal. Miss Mary, perceiving the insistence of his gaze, calmly pulled her robe down over her ankles.

At that moment Marjah came over, holding out the box of fruits.

"Here's your dessert, neophyte. Carabella entrusted the care of making you the gift to me.

"Offer them to my companions, High Priest."

She was astonished that the eunuch did not obey her request, and only allowed her to select two fruits when she wanted three. Soon, however, she was no longer giving any thought to that observation. She had been illuminated by a sudden delight.

A great ardent dawn rose within her, and with its first rays, a sentiment of profound joy expanded her new soul. Soft spring-like effluvia liquefied the winter snows beneath which her soul had been shivering. She felt a consistent wonder, and her struggles and distresses, still so recent, melted in the universal warmth.

It seemed to her that she had begun to live again, and all her life attached itself to the person of Marcel, whose voice, in speaking to her, had just begun to murmur a delicious harmony. She would have liked to resist, to experience less charm in

---

optimism, understandable in the context of a work in which he is playing a role approximately parallel to that of Dr. Pangloss in *Candide*, is presumably not intended as an insult, as he has previously listed Leibniz among his favorite philosophers, and his own "solution" to the problem of evil is also a form of optimism.

contemplating the broadness of his shoulders, the luster of his beard, and suspecting the kind of frisson that their contact would cause to pass through her—but she could not.

What had Miss Mary become, then? Or, rather, what person other than the true Miss Mary had hatched out within her?

All that, the provocation of her brilliant pupils told the young man. She pulled up the robe that she had lowered shortly before, in order to show a little more of her ankle. Flushes of warmth rose to her cheeks, and she rejoiced in that as something that ought to render her more seductive. She laughed on hearing Choumaque, whose stomach was replete, belch agreeably. She approved his proposal to go directly to explore the regions of Sterility.

An intimate animation was pushing the philosopher toward that libertine excursion, for he was counting on encountering Madame Môme there. Indifferently, Marjah acquiesced, and took them toward their craft, which was waiting for them.

As they set off, they noticed that the phonograph, still attached to them by the fluid, had taken a place at the back. The machine continued talking, giving details about puericulture.

"Oh, no! It's boring us!" Choumaque admitted.

"Press it on the foot, my dear Choumaque, and it will leave us tranquil."

The philosopher pressed down on the pedal, as Marjah had prescribed. He felt a slight shake in his arm. It was the cicerone, freed from obligation, which was slipping into empty space, uttering a puppet's screech: the protest of its mechanical soul, broken down, perhaps dead.

They took off, flying over the palaces they had just passed through. In the distance, the sea was sweeping the shore of red porphyry with curt waves. Its hue, blue at the edge, was modified further from the shore, becoming green, with undulations, and a gray tint to its atmosphere that signified bad weather.

Choumaque, who had picked up a powerful pair of binoculars, observed a furious tempest. He expressed his fear to the High Priest, who reassured him.

167

"It's true that the weather is abominable out there at sea—wind and thunder, doubtless a cyclone—but our physicists deflect the atrocity away from our shores. If you want to be convinced, pick up that microphone hanging in the nacelle and put it to your ear, in such a way that the sensitive surface is directed toward the place where you want to hear sounds..."

Choumaque had scarcely raised the apparatus to his ear than he took it away again, going pale with terror. He had heard, dominating the whistling of the tempest and the roar of the waves, the desperate screams uttered by the passengers of a doomed ship that the waves were engulfing.

"The poor people! Is no one going to send help to them?"

"If one worried about the miseries of others, one would scarcely have time to enjoy life," the High Priest replied, with his customary indolence.

In spite of the mercy that was like a reliquary of her other personality, Miss Mary deemed herself infinitely pleased to be there, next to Marcel, sheltered from the wrath of the heavens. She possessed a new egotism in savoring safety in the face of danger.

All three of them were glad to hear the eunuch affirm that it was always thus. At midnight, the meteorological indications having advertised the storm, the scientists had launched reserves of omnial fluid into the atmosphere, which had kept away the mists accumulated on the horizon. The climate, always mild, was manufactured in the island's factories.

It was the first time that Choumaque had really congratulated himself for having accompanied his friend. To be sure, his Stoicism would have maintained his indifference to the engulfing waves, but why die? After all, life had agreeable equilibria. He admired himself, slim in his violet doublet. He passed his hand through his hair, and observed its gilded abundance proudly. His legs, although still a trifle twisted, were padded with solid flesh. He rejoiced in thinking that Madam Môme would not be insensible to their musculature, as well as the contrast between his russet hair and his black beard. He felt triumphant in his new youth.

168

They reached the regions of Sterility after having flown around the Palace of Sensuality and its dependencies. The airplane carrying them was part of a fleet responsible for transportation to that part of the island. It went, almost of its own accord, to deposit them under a hangar, in which a hundred similar craft, blue and prettily quilted were waiting, their wings folded and ever-ready to depart, attached to an immense central support where they were automatically accumulating the force necessary for aerial journeys. A few effeminate slaves with pretty beardless faces—former gitons who had passed the age of serving the pleasure of others—were cleaning them summarily, for nothing got dirty in this land. In addition, they were checking the stability of mechanisms that were always perfect. They were playing, making merry and singing as they carried out their tasks. Their symbolic crosses, like bloodstains on their yellow tunics, reminded Choumaque of the flags of field hospitals.

*After all, are they not amputees?* the philosopher said to himself.

The neophytes had got down from the airplane, their limbs rested by the aerial trip. An equivocal sentiment of curiosity urged them to hasten their visit to this mysterious corner of the island. Choumaque and Marcel, fashioned by the morality of a nation in which the consequence of modesty is libertinage, were perhaps the only people in this country to shiver at a naughty desire, rather than submitting indolently to the tranquil vice of others. Undoubtedly, numerous licentious spectacles had already blunted their sensibility, and they could foresee the moment when, blasé themselves in consequence of the abundance and facility of amours, they would no longer be able to appreciate immorality and would consider it as one of the essential vulgarities of the country. For the present, however, their long continence, Marcel's ardent youth and Choumaque's rejuvenation, imagined in advance the scenes that they were about to see. As for Miss Mary, she was floating in an inalterable contentment, à propos of nothing at all.

As soon as they were out of the hangar their astonishment was awakened. They found themselves in front of an adorably lush flower-bed ornamented by a group similar in its volume and subject-matter to the one they had admired that morning at the Fecundity. The resemblance ended with the size of the monument, however, for the subject glorifying sterile sensualities was quite different. A form in flesh-colored onyx, lying on the ground, was disposed in its nudity in such a way that one could have no doubt about its impotent androgyny. Above it stood a couple, a sterile husband and a fecund mother, bearing the same uniform visage common to the beauty of the race. The hermaphrodite was extending two fingers toward them, with a lovely gesture of amorous languor, holding a cantharid insect[18] whose wings, by virtue of a play of omnial light, formed a flamboyant torch in the daylight.

They went on, unimpressed by the grace of those frozen figures, expecting more realistic images. They did not take long to encounter them, on the frontispiece of the Temple of Sterile Lusts, whose fresco featured, with an unceremonious crudity, the science of voluptuous gestures. And when, after having parted the curtains of their archways similarly decorated with light paintings, they penetrated into an immense hall of unusual luxury, filled with perfumes, incense, music and light, they were obliged to stop, stunned and dazzled, hardly daring to look.

Precious metals, with droplets of precious stones rutilant on the walls, splashing the long ardent mauve silken awning, descended from the ceiling like the folds of a great cage of amour. All around, numerous beds stood out, erected on altars

---

[18] The reference is obviously to the "blister beetle" commonly known as "Spanish fly," from which the substance cantharidin is obtained. Cantharidin has a powerful effect on the ureter, generating a forceful but painful erection in males, which resulted in its acquisition of a much-inflated reputation as an aphrodisiac. The beetle is nowadays classified as *Lytta vesicatoria* and no longer attributed to the family Cantharidae.

170

spangled with red and gold; and young people, surrounding them, were studying voluptuousness there. There was an entire orgy of flesh, inclined rumps, radiant muscles, firm breasts, in ardent tones of life, which were mingling, palpitating and rubbing together there, savoring intoxication. On the floor, covered with a profound carpet ablaze with bright colors, naked bodies were writhing. Spirals of splendid hair were evaporating in fabrics and jewels, in a mist of incense. At intervals, gasps burst forth, as vibrant as the screams of beasts in revolt.

Marjah scanned the spectacle with his indifferent gaze. "You're working hard today," he said to a woman who, interrupting an entirely pedagogical surveillance, came swiftly toward them. He had just recognized Madame Môme.

She did not pause to listen to him. Shaking her amethyst peplum, braided with two stripes, which grated as they moved, she precipitated herself upon Choumaque, parted the hands with which he was veiling his face, and kissed him gluttonously on the mouth.

"Look at Zéphi! How nice and dainty he is! And bicolored too! Isn't that piquant? I knew that he had the makings of a handsome man in him. Your cloth has been recut, hasn't it, Zéphi? And I find you young and magnificent. You're thirty years younger and thirty times better looking! Turn round Zéphi, so that I can admire you!"

She made him pirouette. Dumbfounded, the philosopher hitched up his belt and let it happen, without, however, losing his critical sense, not neglecting to observe the casuistic debate that was unfolding within him.

He was astonished not to feel the thrust that he had expected propelling him toward his former mistress. The display of flesh automatically obedient to the custom of pleasure, the somewhat artificial fervor that reigned over those practices, the tranquil gaze with which Marjah contemplated that labor, Madame Môme's truly overexuberant welcome, and also the recent memory of what Caresco had said when the potentate had admitted to him that his subjects were merely puppets linked to a keyboard whose secret strings he pulled at will—in

171

brief, the regimentation and coordination of facile sensualities—rendered him perplexed, hesitating between his dogmas and the attractions of amour.

*Now or never*, he said to himself, *is the moment to prove to myself the supremacy of mind over matter. If I can resist the advances of this impetuous mistress, tomorrow, my joviality will not be diminished thereby, and my intellect, richly provided with phosphorus, will once again permit me subtle flights toward the pure conceptions of morality. If, on the contrary, I succumb, experimentation having proved to me a long time ago that one can't burn the candle at both ends, it will be the worst situation for me: that in which, an old, exhausted oarsman, I'll have expended all my strength in rowing my boat toward Cythera, so that none will remain to me for appropriate dissertation. But there's the rub: are the most beautiful theories of the soul worth as much as the possession of a sumptuous rump, I ask the creator of the doctrine of equilibria?*

As if she had divined that rude combat, the diabolical high priestess insisted more ardently, gluing herself to the irresolute individual, making suggestions to him with a skillful fluttering of her tongue.

"How happy we're going to be, Zéphi!"

"Evidently, But the happiness of the Sage does not reside in sensuality. On the contrary, it depends on a healthy chastity..."

He weakened. Effluvia ran through his marrow. He granted himself that he had become young again, and that his transports would doubtless be less dearly taxed than if he were still old. As his eyes blinked, and as uncertainty no longer made him carry out his customary gesture of hitching up his belt, Madame Môme understood his defeat. She agreed with Marjah that he would replace her in supervising the practical exercises.

And there was delirium. Having put her arm around Choumaque's waist, she drew him away impetuously, like a spirited mare. She seemed to be in haste to get it over with, hurrying the visit, scarcely stopping to give details, not insisting on any explanation, replying to Marcel's questions that he would have time to find out more later. In any case, she completely neglected the others, overly occupied as she was in pinching, tickling and needling her Zéphi, who felt a communicative warmth not devoid of an admixture of pride.

Thus, they virtually fled the Temple of Sterile Lusts, going past the habitations of the Palace of the Courtesans, which were as many marvels, like a gust of wind. There, superb creatures of the ardent brunette type special to prostitution were awaiting the pleasure of lovers, not very frequent at that hour. Some were yielding to the pleasures of bathing in a vast pool framed by a Byzantine colonnade in green stucco, rippling with solar rays. Their harmonious bodies could be seen cleaving the limpidity of the deep water. Their sparkling mouths, while they enjoyed themselves in the water, were more attractive, purer and more perfumed springs that the waves in which they were frolicking. Others were sitting or lying on carpets placed on the grass in front of the peristyles of their dwellings, occupied in the refinements of toilette. Holding mirrors in their hands, they were affirming their health and recreating the effects produced by various dispositions of their hair, retained by combs of gold, pearls and diamonds. Or they were making admirable fabrics sparkle, draping themselves therein, trying out hieratic gestures, modifying the harmony of their stances, always with the objective of beauty. Then, thus adorned with iridescence and color, they danced in groups, throwing flowers, waving bunches of flowers that linked their quadrilles. Others, finally, were coupling, twittering their pleasure.

But that was only a rapid visit for the High Priestess drew them, ever more hastily, toward the Palace of Gitons. And what they saw repeated, very nearly, the spectacle that they had just traversed. Alongside the dwellings ornamented with flowers wedded to the originality of the sculptures, on the freshness of green lawns, in the glitter of odorous water to which marble steps licked by moss led down, and in air of a marvelous limpidity, propitious to the deployment of wings, there were the same languorous distractions, the same concerns for adornment and feminine coquetry.

Now, Marcel and Choumaque contemplated those mores unfurling without experiencing anything but a slight astonishment. Miss Mary was only admiring Marcel.

"Does this interest you, my Zéphi?" said the High Priestess, driven to an extreme incandescence. "But if you knew how many surprises the tenderness of your Môme still has in store for you…!"

They had arrived at the terminal point of their excursion. Rocks rose up there that closed off the region of Sterility naturally. A small Ionian temple stood there, to which one gained access via a gentle slope bordered by myrtle and jasmine bushes. The High Priestess pointed to it with her finger.

"Come into Marjah's house," she said to Choumaque, pushing him into the path that climbed toward an incomplete phallus, which, standing on the frontispiece, constituted the emblem of the High Priest's command.

Marcel and Miss Mary remained alone. An equal intoxication inflamed them.

The young man took his companion's hand and took pleasure in squeezing the fingers of the huntress Diana. She responded by shivers that, after having run through all her nerves, communicated their vibration to the arms that guided them. Marcel felt his flesh, long deprived of amour, numbed by the succession of significant events that had occurred in the previous month, waking up under a breath of troubling impressions. His vigor palpitated at the memory of recent spectacles. He saw the courtesans again, mingling their young and beautiful bodies, playing on the grass, among the flowers, in the limpid waves, bruising the hardness of their rosy breasts. All those violent aspirations he now concentrated on the virgin whose hand was entwined with his own.

Miss Mary, her throat gripped by a spasm, her body simultaneously weary and exultant, her legs soft, abandoned herself delightedly to the new enlivening current, and cast herself without dread into the great dangerous furnace.

"Come! Come this way, my beloved! Let's rest upon the freshness of that moss, under the protection of those admirable cedars..."

She went with him. They paid no attention to a rustle of wings produced above their heads and which ceased where they sat down. So many curious and tame birds were fluttering around them!

"Finally!" he said, lying down on the ground in such a way that he formed a cradle with his arms, of which the young woman's pink tunic was the lining. "Finally, I have you to myself! But can I be sure of you? What enigma is hiding behind that incomparable beauty? Will your mouth confess this time what the eloquence of your hand and your eyes have declared to me? Tell me, oh, tell me, Miss Mary, that you're no longer thinking of fleeing this divine land, and that our days will go by here in an illumination that will never end!"

He put his arms around her. He caressed the blonde aureole of her swooning head. He drank from the source of her dark gaze all the juice of tenderness.

Softly she murmured: "Yes, it would be charming to live here...your companion forever..."

But scarcely had she expressed herself thus, affirming the desire for an eternal servitude, than she was suddenly shaken by a series of contractions. One might have thought that the amorous magnetism with which she was charged had fled, almost immediately. Her eyes lost their ecstatic fixity. Abruptly, she pulled away from the young man. However, she continued the conversation as if no transformation has taken place within her, with an appearance of logical succession.

"Yes, I'd like to remain, no longer to be forced by circumstances to go back home—but the war, alas, compels me to do so. Oh, why was it declared, that abominable war? Why are people everywhere not equal and satisfied, dormant in concord, calm and wellbeing, as they are here? That war! Do you know that admirable things are happening therein, Monsieur Marcel? For I haven't told you everything: Harry, my brother, whose death the Superman has announced to me, is

175

still alive! This morning, I saw him fighting on the screen in my room. He's alive! He's fighting! He's resisting! And I heard my compatriots' glorious cries! Oh, the brave people! The noble hearts! Defend yourselves, my brothers! Crush the coalition!"

With an entirely different enthusiasm, she had risen to her feet. Without taking the trouble to refasten her tunic, slightly loosened by Marcel's audacity, she extended a warrior bosom toward the distant battles, and eyes that were shining like flashing blades. All of the primal soul of the fatherland was exultant in her.

Marcel beheld that excessive turnabout without understanding it. He remained amazed by seeing her psychology modified instantaneously, like a chameleon changing color. When he advanced to put his arm around her waist, she looked at him with such scornful surprise that he dare not take his gesture any further.

A loud burst of laughter burst out above their heads. It came from Carabella, who was perched on a branch in the trees, and had been watching them.

# CHAPTER XIII

When the philosopher Zéphirin Choumaque woke up in Madame Môme's arms, after an hour of delicious lassitude, he was able to believe that he had gone back in time thirty years. Set aside the frame of his amorous escapade—the oval room in Marjah's dwelling, illuminated by a mystical half-light pouring from the curtains; the furniture of various forms, designed, one might have thought, to permit the strangest relaxations; and that great soft, unctuous bed, improbably mattressed and pillowed, in which he was lying, all of which formed an appreciable diversion from his room in the Latin quarter—and he could have sworn that he had beside him the same adorable mistress, and felt running through his own veins a youthful and amorous blood as vigorous as in the year 1920.

In fact, he almost extended his hand, with a gesture dear to his libertine prowess, toward the nearby table in order to pick up a pipe, fill it with tobacco, light it and enjoy the first blue-tinted swirls that accompanied the scattering of gilded sparks.

Madame Môme detected the signs of that privation. Slightly roguishly, contrary to the habits of her professional dignity, but rejoicing in a similar memory, she rubbed her nose with the back of her index finger, propped herself up on her pretty elbow, and looked at him with the old gaze of her young head.

"You're missing your puffer, eh? I can tell..."

"Indeed," said Choumaque, "I am missing it. I liked, after dalliance, to read the philosophers and plume my alcove. The mists of metaphysics and the fogs of tobacco hid me from the companion thanks to whom I had just accomplished an ever-disappointing act..."

"You're not very gallant, Zéphi!"

"I must admit," Choumaque went on, by way of restriction, "that I'm not demanding any compensation today.

You've just caused me to pass one of the most intoxicating hours of my life, my Little Panade. Oh, you've made progress, you slut."

He tickled her a little, while she defended herself, laughing, while slapping him on the buttocks, as of old.

Then he went on, more seriously: "Once, even on emerging from your caresses, I had an opinion of women that you've just caused to vary today. I told myself that man was, in all creation, the animal least favored with regard to the female of the species. It seemed evident to me that the bull with the cow, the gander with the goose, and the boar with the sow experienced more satisfactions in their natural relations than the human male with the daughters of Eve. What woman, once Venus was satisfied, gave you the pleasure of conversation? What lovers, as soon as their embraces were exchanged, did not become sulky and turn their backs? At least the bull and the cow, the gander and the goose, the boar and the sow, were not obliged to so much circumspection, and quit one another mutually satisfied, without any afterthought..."

"While this time?"

"This time, I don't experience that bitterness consecutive to amour, since I'm reduced to the mentality of the bull, the gander and the boar, and there's no point in thinking, in a country where the brain is becoming a superfluous organ."

"Render homage to the Superman!" said the High Priestess, putting her hands together devoutly.

"By Seneca, never!" Choumaque protested. "Me, a philosopher...me, the creator of a doctrine that I have intelligently founded on stoicism...me, render homage to that absurd genius who annihilates all evils, who forces us to float in a perpetual Epicureanism, and who has ensured that tomorrow, knowing that I can cherish you, my little Panade, as easily and as often as the whim takes me, I will no longer experience any but a relative pleasure, the mediocre contentment of a possession for which one does not even have to wish in order to obtain it...me, render homage to that leveler of accidents, who suppresses the joy of descent because he has suppressed the difficulty of the climb; to that dull shepherd who leads his flock straight to meadows ever full of fresh grass, without even imposing upon them the winding of the road—a flock whose members are, fundamentally, not even sheep; to that evil warrior of life, who takes away the intoxication of victory by preventing the battle! Get away! You don't know me any longer. No struggles, no triumphs! No unhappiness, no happiness! That's what my doctrine of equilibria says, at least..."

"Provided that he hasn't got the ear of a microphone turned on us at this moment! Provided that he doesn't hear you!" murmured the frightened High Priestess.

"You don't know, then, my Môme...I can confess it to you now...that I wasn't happy in our arms, thirty years ago, when I was conscious of the difficulty of tearing you away from other lovers! It was necessary for me to ensure your nourishment when you came to live with me; it was sometimes necessary for me to manifest my generosity with a silver coin. To procure them, I had to walk the streets of Paris for entire days, go to tap my friends' fob-pockets, always hermetically sealed, make up the most improbable stories...but when I held it in my fingers, that round coin, when I slipped it into your black stocking, what satisfaction! Your teeth had gaps in the front, you might say? Indeed—but know that I loved you more because of that imperfection, in imagining how beautiful you'd be on the day when I could buy you supplementary teeth..."

"You're exaggerating, Zéphi."

"Perhaps—but that's to make you understand that the pleasure of possession doesn't work without the desire. You've just spent an unforgettable hour yourself...do you know why? It's because I'm the new fruit of your old orchard, the early bloom of your festivals of amour; because I carry, in the flap of my undershirt, the spice of thirty years of separation. In a few days, when my lips have sated you, knowing that you can always taste them again, you'll only experience a relative pleasure in kissing me..."

"No, Zéphi, I love you!"

179

"That's understood. You love me, and you'll still love me tomorrow, neither more nor less than those who give you sensuality…as much as Marius, for example…"

"No less—what more do you want, my darling?" said a fine deep voice, suddenly speaking from the back of the rom.

The philosopher turned round abruptly. He thought that Marjah had come back without his having heard him—but the man who had just overheard their conversation and replied to it was not the High Priest. He was an individual who looked to be about thirty but whose gaze revealed that he was much older. Under long black hair, coiffed with a Rembrandt-style hat, he had a pleasant face with a pointed beard, a large flat nose, and thick, mocking lips. The rest of his figure was harmoniously elegant, in a violet costume similar in its cut to those that certain inveterate art-students in Montmartre still sported in the middle of the twentieth century, in spite of the caprices of fashion: a velvet waistcoat tightened at the waist and holding the neck in a ruff; bright check trousers broad at the waist and tapering in the legs, in such a way as to leave the ankles almost completely bare; and white deerskin boots on his feet.

"But I know that mug!" exclaimed the philosopher, slightly alarmed by the sudden apparition.

"He knows me, the pauper—he has reason to!" the newcomer replied, performing a few introductory somersaults. Then, winking as he approached the vast bed, he added: "And Môme has her reasons too! Do you remember, Zéphirin, your best friend, the one who cuckolded you? Marius from Marseilles…you earned me two months in prison when you threw my clothes out of the window. What if I were to do the same to you now that I've caught you in bed with my wife? Don't worry, old chap, it's not the sort of thing I do. And then, she must be very content, the darling, to have found her Zéphi again…"

Dumbfounded, the philosopher did not know how to respond. Fear still dominated him. He thought that the painter, after making fun of him, was about to pay him back for Madame Môme's infidelity. But the High Priestess smiled tenderly, in a familiar fashion; and Marius, with an entrechat, picked up a seat and came to sit down next to the bed.

"Adieu, eh!" he growled, amiably. "You're very comfortable there, the two of you, in Marjah's bed. A strange idea you've had, of taking refuge in a eunuch's sheets!"

"We didn't have another to hand," admitted Madame Môme.

"Yes, and you were in a hurry, I understand that. I'm not disturbing you, at least?"

"No, I've finished," said Choumaque, increasingly bewildered and not knowing what he was saying—but what he said had the effect of amused his interlocutors. The painter and the High Priestess started laughing, holding their sides.

Oh, that was a good one; they rarely had the opportunity to hear such eccentricities. And that echo of the past, that silliness emerging in the midst of their regular and monotonous enjoyment, was like a ray of sunshine parting the gray tints of a cloudy sky,

They stayed there for a long time, reviving baroque memories of the old Latin quarter: three friends, united, feeling entirely sheltered from all rivalry.

"Well, you hole in the air," said Marius, finally, rising to his feet, "since you're satisfied, get dressed, and let's go for a walk. I'll take you back to the Caravanserai. And then, you know, old chap, in future, don't hesitate…as often as you wish. Môme and I will be glad to be agreeable to you…"

"Thank you."

"Don't thank me. It's only natural, what! Our laws demand that meek sharing. Oh, if they only knew in other lands—in France, above all—how convenient the abandonment of the right to sole possession of a woman is, and how many complications of existence it avoids never to be shackled to a single individual…to get rid of jealousy…"

Choumaque hastened to get dressed. After having slipped on his violet tights, he put on a doublet with yellow topaz buttons, of an Oriental magnificence. It hugged his freshly-reduce figure marvelously. Marius had rendered him the service of pressing the tile in the floor permitting the walls to brighten and reflect images of the room infinitely.

On hearing the painter pass judgment thus on the theories recently applied by him to Madame Môme, he smiled slightly pityingly, but thought it futile to refute that doctrine of adorable communism. The High Priestess had retired, without bothering to bid farewell to either one of them.

"You've always been paradoxical, my friend," Choumaque said to Marius, "and I see that thirty years spent in this land has scarcely modified you. I recall anecdotes related about you—in particular, about an umbrella for which your poverty had been ambitious for ten years, and which you refused to open in order to protect yourself from a frightful downpour on the day that you took possession of it. If my memory serves me right, I believe that you even hid the umbrella under your clothes, in order that it wouldn't get wet..."

"I did that!" said Marius.

They laughed; they were inseparably united. They went out. Marius squeezed Choumaque's arm energetically, delighted to have found that companion of youthful exuberances so vibrant and so hilarious. And the philosopher experienced a joy no less vivid in hearing that thick southern accent resound once again, strewn with coarse exclamations, so indelibly inherent to his organism, of which the painter had not been able to rid himself in thirty years.

A flock of young women flew past at that moment in the air. They were courtesans coming back after bathing in the sea, racing one another. Still dripping with water beneath their veils, whose train, displayed by the race formed a gracious plume-like tail, they seemed, in the movements of their winged arms, to be admirable realizations of the dream of Valkyries.

"Look! What a beautiful flock!" Choumaque exclaimed, pointing at them.

"Oh, I no longer look. They're boring."

"That's true: they're boring," murmured the philosopher, swelling up, proud of the doctrinal confirmation that the abundance of goods is harmful, and that ugliness is therefore indispensable to beauty.

Then they exchanged confidences. Choumaque recounted his life, his past black times and good moments, and how he had finally decided to accompany his pupil Marcel to the marvelous island. "And you, what are you doing here?" he asked, when he had finished.

Then Marius related in his turn the providential hazard that had put him in Caresco's path when he came out of prison, and when, a painter of great talent, having rediscovered the method of ancient frescos, he was on the brink of dying of starvation. One day, in the street, he had been selling his last painting, hoping to get a cheap meal out of it, when a small man with a hooked nose had approached the exhibited work and inspected it for a long time, like a connoisseur. Then, after having bought the canvas for the asking price of twenty-eight sous, he had, in a sense—so mysterious was his voice— ordered Marius to follow him and had taken him to Caresco, introducing him with the words: "I've brought you a genius."

That introducer was none other than, Zadochbach, a genius himself of serendipity, an unearther of good opportunities. And that was what had happened: Marius had been parceled up, as a good opportunity, after having promised all his painting to the new venture. And for thirty years he had collaborated in the edification of the ideal state, part of the cohort of engineers, artists and creators who, living outside the people, added to the benefits from which everyone profited—the extraordinary maintenance of health and youth—the more real satisfactions of effort and endeavor.

"You're happy, then?" asked Choumaque.

"I'm not unhappy."

"Not being unhappy isn't being happy."

"Pardon me! I'm very happy, exceedingly happy," the artist protested, loudly, as if he feared that someone might have overheard the lukewarm quality of his first response.

Choumaque, however, was not duped by that explanation. Once again, he had just confirmed his opinion that the slaves of these benefits did not enjoy absolute felicity. Some—those who were born on the island—indolently abused enjoyments. Others—those who, before being adopted by Caresco, had known misery—were subject without attraction to the custom of no longer having anything to desire. Again, the personality of the surgeon, the creator of the social system, surged forth in the philosopher's mind. He discovered a great incoherence herein.

How could that man, who had given, throughout his life, the most prodigious example of labor, research and struggle, have imagined for others, and carried out, a project of perfect existence that as exempt from fatigues, difficulties and embarrassments? How had he been able to believe that his people were happy vegetating in that religion of pleasure, dissolving energy, paralyzing all pressure toward betterment?

Caresco, it is true, in order to palliate that constant bliss, to make a different flame shine within it nevertheless, had dictated the belief in metempsychosis, in a life always in movement, evolving toward perfection. But what obstacle held it back? Furthermore, once arrived at the goal of happiness, had he not said that the individual returned to the primal state, the cellular state, in order to recommence climbing all the steps of transformism? And was not that doctrine the very expression of incoherence?

No: another motive must have given birth to that nonsense—and Choumaque wondered whether Caresco had not imagined it in order better to enslave his people, in order not to be opposed in the frantic passion for omnipotence that, for three-quarters of a century, had been seething in the surgeon's tormented brain.

That problem, apparently insoluble, puzzled the philosopher of equilibria.

"And what do you think of Caresco?" he asked Marius.

"Caresco! What a genius! What a god!" the painter exclaimed. But immediately, all his old southern abandon got the upper hand, and he looked around to see whether anyone was nearby who might be spying. And, speaking in a very low voice—so low that Choumaque could hardly hear him, with a need for confidence as forceful as a natural secretion, he added: "Jut between us, darling—but keep it strictly to yourself—I think he exaggerates. He isn't the Superman; he ought to be called the surfeit. Let's hope that he's not listening to us right now. His genius is a joke—remember what I said, and not a word, eh?"

"Why do you think that?"

"Here," confided Marius, shivering gloriously at his courage, "there are a thousand scientists and artists who, like me, work anonymously..."

"I know. I've been through the Palace of the Brain."

"Well, darling, Caresco attributes all their inventions to himself. He wants to have the glory of them. Has he not claimed to me—me, the renovator of the fresco—that it's him who had conceived the method? It's the same for all the other discoveries…he pockets them, with the spirit of his race. He's simply an assimilator. Don't repeat that, eh? He has nothing of his own but his marvelous skill during his operations. That, old chap, is...."

He did not finish his sentence. He replaced the word that did not emerge with a mime expressive of terrified admiration, by a circulation of his arm designating the immensity.

"How do you know that? Are you, then, very close to him?"

Marius stopped walking and planted himself on his two long feet, emerging from his narrow trousers. Then, seizing Choumaque by the fat of his shoulders, looking into his eyes, he said: "Zéphirin, you're a brother eh? We've cuckolded one another. Have you got guts? Would you like to risk your life to see something unforgettable, at the same time as I'm risking mine to show it to you?"

He had put his hand over his heart, in a gesture of immense fraternal protestation—and Choumaque, who knew that such manifestations generally accompanied the most anodyne of proposals, immediately accepted.

"Well, I'm going take you to see Caresco operate."

"How are you going to do that?"

"By taking you with me into the room next door to the laboratory in which he operates. I'm doing a big painting at present, and the other day, while brushing a frieze, I put the paintbrush on an asperity that, when it's touched, renders the wall separating the two rooms transparent. Oh, darling, what I saw is tremendous!"

"Let's go," said Choumaque, whose curiosity was awakening, although he was still suspicious of his friend's imagination.

They went to an opening that plunged into the earth. The tube carried them away with the lightning rapidity of atmospheric pressure. They had to change vehicles once, which delayed they journey by two minutes. Marius manifested some impatience. He feared missing the bloody moment.

Finally, they reached the Palace of Surgery, and followed the secret passages that Marius knew well, and in which, fortunately, the gloom favored their audacity.

And for once, the Southerner had not exaggerated.

When, after having gone to the transparent wall, they perceived the operating theater next door, Choumaque was horrified to have to spend a quarter of an hour of his existence there. They arrived in the middle of the work. Around the table on which the philosopher had been lying a week before, two men were agitating, their arms bare, their torsos sheathed in smocks that were nothing but red rags.

One of them, Caresco, his face brown and ardent, his hooked nose curved over his shiny beard, his forehead streaked by a spray of blood, was holding his famous instrument in his hand and plunging it frightfully into violet-tinted living flesh. He crushed, he twisted, he tore away and he cut with a ferocious insouciance, without a muscle in his face quivering, his eyes perpetually dull.

Facing him on the other side of the table, Dr. Hymen, his eternal hat on his head, implausibly hirsute, was sweeping the operational area by means of large compresses, white at first, which became rutilant as soon as they were dipped in the human broth, and his slanting nose was palpitating with pleasure.

What gripped the spectators even more than those tragic attitudes, however, was the extraordinary aspect of the subject on whom the surgeons were working. It was reduced to a round ball that might have been a head, all the orifices of which save one—the mouth—had been filled in: a ball to which a kind of stump was attached, a morsel of trunk, in which the palpitating heart was at that moment laid bare, visible in the broad gap left by the excised ribs.

And, in fact, that was all that remained of a man, for on the ground, thrown down in a frightful pell-mell, lay the other parts of his body, in pieces, horrible shreds, sticky tatters: the legs, the arms, the abdominal viscera, almost the whole of the vertebral column and one lung.

"Hole in the air! He's working on his human monad!" exclaimed Marius, enthusiastically. "Isn't it marvelous? Look at that tranquil butchery! O great Caresco! O Superman! Realizing the admirable conception of an individual of whom nothing remains but a brain devoid of senses and almost devoid of organs! Reducing the head to one orifice that permits respiration and alimentation, and only conserving, in a section of trunk, one lung, a heart and a parcel of gut! O genius! Will you succeed, this time?"

Every fiber of Choumaque's being was shivering with fear. He scarcely remarked the real transport of his petrified friend, touched, like everyone else, by the fanaticism of the despot, even though his conversation of a little while ago had claimed the contrary. The only exclamation of which he took note was the last.

"What do you mean, will he succeed *this time*? This isn't his first attempt, then?"

"Personally, in the month that I've been working here, I've already seen the attempt fail seventeen times. When he'd finished, when all the organs had been sewn up again, enclosed in the flesh, and the skin had been coated with a varnish that protected the whole, at the moment when he wanted to extract what remained of his subject from the provoked sleep, the subject was no longer breathing, no longer moving, and the heart had cased to beat. The machine hadn't started working again, you see.

"He became furious then, foaming at the mouth...then he took the semblance of a cadaver and threw it at Hymen's head, accusing him of having spoiled his operation. That's why Hymen keeps his top hat on in all circumstances, in order to ward off the blows by lowering his head."

"And who does he take for these horrible experiments?"

"Slaves. There are too many. It's a means for Caresco to purge his island of them. It's a way for them—a much appreciated way—to disappear, while meriting a rapid progression along the scale of metempsychosis..."

"Do you believe all that?"

"Of course!"

They looked at one another, as individuals from different worlds, brains that were no longer vibrating at the same rhythm. Thirty years of mental poisoning had, therefore, reduced the friend whom Choumaque had once thought intelligent to stupidity. The philosopher was devastated by the thought that in his turn, he might perhaps allow himself to be infiltrated by the virus, and that his philosophy might be destroyed—but the interest of the spectacle gripped him again.

Caresco and his assistant had finished their operation. After having coated the human fragment, they were now leaning over the deformed matter, and were listening with anxious expectation for the sounds of the thorax; they were keeping watch, by means of little recording devices placed on the neck, for the manifestations of life in the remains of their subject.

Suddenly, they straightened up, their arms in the air, and a formidable cry escaped them:

"He's alive! He's alive!"

And then, while Caresco, having mastered himself, contemplated his masterpiece coldly, without a muscle in his face quivering, Hymen gave signs of the most inordinate joy. Perhaps for the first time, he was seen to take off his hat and throw it in the air. Then he accomplished a few fantastic somersaults, after which he threw himself at the Superman's feet, licking the hem of his smock in frantic adoration.

"Glory to you, Superman! Glory to you, God!"

With a gesture of disgust the Superman ordered him to go away.

Left alone, the surgeon was absorbed in thought momentarily. His eyes made a tour of the room. Their manifest tranquility proved that he did not know that he was being observed from behind the seemingly-opaque partition wall. His unconsciousness, or strange preoccupations, had caused him to forget that he had entrusted Marius with the duty of working nearby. He could not, in any case, imagine that the painter might have put sufficient pressure on the secret button that made the curtain imprisoned in the wall move aside, permitting the mysteries of his ferocious work to be discovered.

He got up and went to open a cupboard. An infinity of marvelous costumes was assembled within it. He chose one: a black velvet robe damascened with precious stones, so powerfully bright that the lighting was increased by a thousand new nuclei. He took off his blood-stained smock and washed his soiled hands and arms; he removed the red streak from his forehead. Then, after putting on make-up, he restored the gleam to his weary eyes with a vivifying lotion.

At that moment he was radiant with a new, strange, imperial beauty, completed by the posing on his head of a sumptuous golden crown. Thus adorned he closed the cupboard again and went to press a button controlling a trap-door. A woman lying on a divan emerged from the floor. She was admirably nude, also made up, but by the preparations of nature alone. Her brown skin was bright with all the nuances of a great flavorsome flower. Her firm breasts, with pink areolas, were caressed by the loose tresses of her ardent hair. The light, touching her teeth, made her smile flash like diamonds. No trace on her delicate abdomen revealed surgical profanation. She was a virgin.

Caresco knelt down beside her. He took her hand, breathed in its odor, choked by an anguished desire, He stammered words of admiration to which she listened with her eyelids closed and her hips writhing with lust. He implored her, but his gaze dominant her entirely. Vanquished, she extended the feverish pulp of her lips toward him. Then, triumphant, he took her in his arms and transported her to the operating table.

"What's going to happen now?" demanded Choumaque, alarmed by the spectacle.

"Good God, wait! You'll see! Not what you think."

The Superman handed the virgin the extremity of a mobile wire, which she applied to her own forehead. Immediately, her eyes fluttered; a few convulsions ran through her; her smile attested to the perfect bliss of her being. Palpitating with amour, she was asleep.

Then, veritably, the soul appeared in the Superman's face. His gaze, reanimated by the eye-lotion, was supplemented by an expression of mortal passion. His mouth quivered, palpitating in the stutters of his vice. With a profound plunge of his hand he kneaded the abdomen that sleep had delivered to him, and his touch caused sparks to crackle.

Then, disdaining his carescoclast, he seized a scalpel placed within reach on a movable table, and penetrated the lily-white skin with a superb sweep. Viscera sprang forth; blood spurted, which he caught in passage. His fingers, after having rummaged in soft red resistances, seized a harder mass,[19] which he brought violently to the level of the frightful gap. He twisted it in his athletic claw; he tore it out; and when,

---

[19] Considering the license adopted in the remainder of the text, this seems a trifle vague. Oblique comments made elsewhere, however, especially viewed in juxtaposition with the description of Professor Tornada's more limited surgical fetish in "Les Mémoires d'un immortel" (tr. as "Memoirs of an Immortal" in Volume II of *The Exploits of Professor Tornada*) strongly suggest that the operation that Caresco is performing is a hysterectomy.

the monstrous prey of his delirium, he had brought it to his lips, a great spasm ran through him.

"I no longer feel steady on my legs—support me!" Choumaque breathed, clutching his friend's arm, drops of cold sweat flooding his temples.

"What! He has a sensitive heart, poor fellow! Not used to it, probably..." said the painter, lying the philosopher—who had fainted—down on the ground.

Immediately, he closed the curtain; then, taking a little syringe from his pocket, he injected a drop of cordial into the arm of the over-sensitive spectator.

The effect was instantaneous. Choumaque recovered consciousness.

"Let's get out of here! Quickly!"

"Not a word about this to anyone," advised the painter, when they were outside. You wouldn't survive, nor me either, if anyone knew that we'd seen the Superman amorous. And I'm fond of my skin, for Metempsychosis..."

# CHAPTER XIV

After leaving Marius, Choumaque was hurrying his paces when he suddenly heard a strange voice calling to him.

"Hey! Where have you come from?"

The philosopher turned round, and was not overly surprised not to perceive any interlocutor, for the island was sufficiently tricked out for a phonograph to be hidden by a fold in the terrain, and for someone to adopt that surly tone in order to give him a scare. He was, therefore, about to continue on his way without replying, in order not to compromise himself, when a rustle of wings, followed by the appearance of the flyer from a clump of trees, suddenly immobilized him.

He was in the presence of a goose, and she repeated the question: "Where have you come from? What are you doing here?"

At first, Choumaque could only gaze at this new phenomenon dazedly. He had been greeted several times, with a few affectionate terms, by talking animals, but none had ever pronounced such a purposive sentence. Thinking, nevertheless, that the Superman's genius could not extend so far as to render a palmiped as notoriously stupid as a goose intelligent and loquacious, he smiled, and replied: "What are you doing here?"

"I guard the Brain, as my ancestors guarded the Capitol."

This time, Choumaque almost fell over.

The Jabotière,[20] perceiving his surprise, went on: "You must be as stupid as a human, Monsieur Choumaque, to be astonished to hear me conversing. Don't conclude from the fact that the animals in the other world express themselves in

---

[20] Jabotière is the name given in French to a particular bird species known in English as the swan goose (*Anser cygnoides*) but the word is also used in a more general sense, with a meaning roughly equivalent to the English "chatterbox."

an incomprehensible fashion that they're mute and stupid. It sufficed for the Superman to remove a little morsel of cerebral substance from the encephalum of a human and transplant it into my cranium for me to become more manifestly talkative than a windbag of your sort, and one commits a gross error when one measures intelligence by the abundance of words. Ask me questions about morality, and you'll see how I reply to them."

*This overturns all my ideas about the mental supremacy of humans*, Choumaque thought, still trembling with stupefaction, *and I've never regretted as much the good moments that I owe to* abatis aux navets.[21] *To think that I was eating philosophy!*

He approached the bird and stroked her, caressing her remarkably shiny feathers. Then, wanting to plumb the secrets of that unknown soul, he asked: "Just one question, little goose: are you happy?"

"I was. I'm less so since the Master's operation separated me from nature and brought me closer to humans. I now have concerns of diction and conduct that embarrass me. I no longer dare delouse myself in public, as I did before. I must, alas, befit my function and my status..."

Choumaque almost burst out laughing, but he contained himself, thinking that, in fact, the animal was to be pitied. Besides, an idea occurred to him that compounded his anxiety. Did not the goose's reply confirm Caresco's sentiment, in claiming to obtain the happiness of his subjects by making them stupid? Was the potentate not right, then? The greatest bliss of the soul consisted, therefore, in being retrenched in the cerebral activity of the brute, in getting rid of the intelligent

---

[21] A dish recorded in the *Almanach des gourmands* (1803) and many subsequent French cook-books, concocted with goose liver and other offal, mixed with vegetables in a sauce; it appears to be unknown outside France and has fallen into neglect there.

exchanges and amiable controversies of metaphysics and simple enjoying material pleasures!

That thought upset him, and he attempted to draw away from the bird that had suggested it—but the goose, in a confidential mood, did not want to stop. She continued talking, and followed him, waddling on her webbed feet. He was obliged to lengthen his stride to flee the unbelievable conversation.

He thus avoided the danger of the question that had been put to him at the beginning and giving an explanation of his presence in Caresco's palace. But while running, he reflected that the Jabotière had, indeed, become very human, because, for the sake of the pleasure of chatting, she had forgotten to guard the Capitol.

# CHAPTER XV

A large oblong room with coldly garish walls, painted in violet, heightened by a gold frame, and divided into two parts, one ascending in steps with tables and reading-desks, the other flattening out into a stage equipped with a vast blackboard covered with lines and symbols in white chalk, enclosed at that moment all the genius in the realm. It was the Academy of Eucrasia.

On the steps, two hundred violet-clad scientists were bent over books, papers and writing materials, and the artificially young heads had old gazes. On the stage was a porphyry throne where Caresco, seemingly tired and weary, was listening to a mathematician illustrating his speech with the calculations and lines traced on the shiny blackboard.

The man, a former professor from the British Museum in London, was explaining how a new mechanism of transportation due to his research would produce, thanks to an explosion of omnial gas, a force sufficiently considerable to launch a cabin-shell containing ten people from a monstrous cannon at a velocity of a hundred kilometers a second. The projectile in question would follow a trajectory so scrupulously calculated that it would infallibly, and precisely, fall into a receptive cage equipped with such powerful springs that the slightest shock to the passengers would be avoided.

The experiment had already been attempted a year earlier but, poorly planned, had not succeeded. The cabin-shell, occupied by an entire family, had missed its destination and had gone astray, no one knew where—into the sea, if not into the sky.

Caresco interrupted the inventor. "That's sufficient. I understand. I hope that our means of communication will eventually become more rapid. Get to work on it immediately. I'll inaugurate the new mode of locomotion by making the first voyage. Make arrangements in such a way as not to kill your Master."

Then, with a gesture he dismissed his flock of geniuses. The bowing violet backs were engulfed by an adjacent corridor. Soon, he remained alone in the silence of the enormous space. He got up and pressed a button. A metal dot opened, giving passage to a form.

"Come in, courtesan. Come here! Tell me what the result of my Quintessence of Happiness was on the foreign woman."

"It had none, Superman!" said Carabella, with fear in her voice, depositing flowers at the Master's feet.

"What! None?" the potentate growled, frowning.

"Alas, yes, Superman. On the first day, when I got Miss Mary to take the two fruits that you prescribed, I really thought that she was going to succumb to my tenderness. The images of the Passion enthused her. She almost fainted with pleasure, but the influence must have been too short in duration, and the virgin immediately pulled herself together. On the second day, it was Marcel, the young Sower, who nearly reckoned with her..."

"I instructed that she be kept away from contact with a man!"

"Have no fear, Lord; I was there, on watch. I would have stopped their audacity at the right moment, for I suspect that she's beginning to fall in love with that young man, but I didn't have to intervene. The neophyte snuffed out the flame of her own accord when it began to burn. Again, the reaction was too brief."

"And on the third day?"

"On the third day, it was impossible for me to get her to take the fruits. Miss Mary, her suspicions alerted, flatly refused them. Since then, she's even stopped demanding aliments from her personal utilities panel, she's so fearful that their composition might be modified. She obtains nourishment elsewhere—I don't know how."

At that declaration, the Superman stamped his foot. He would not succeed, then, in triumphing over the Redlander!

There existed, in nature, an energy that his science was impotent to overcome! He would not take possession of that virginal force, that heroism! He would not deflect them from their objective to make them love his land, his sky, his sensual delights, and all the creations of his genius!

What could he attempt to subdue the fibers of the foreigner, now that neither his serum nor his essence of happiness had succeeded? By what means could he tame the woman whose primitive constitution struggled so astonishingly against his magic?

But what precious flesh she would become when he had vanquished her, when he possessed her, when he threw her into everyone's arms—she, who did not want to be anyone's wife!

His brow furrowed, he continued to meditate and scheme for some time, Carabella, perceiving herself to be superfluous to his reflections, had made herself scarce.

# CHAPTER XVI

In the days that followed, Mirror-of-Smiles came several times, early in the morning, to look for Choumaque and Marcel, in order to take them to the games. They went without enthusiasm. In truth, the attraction of exploring the Inferior Limbs did not make up for the tedium of the exercise that they had to do beforehand.

A monitor, chosen from among the slaves, strove to teach them the somersaults that all the citizens of the realm were able to execute, and which constituted the formula of politeness, the hello and goodbye, that the indigenes accorded one another by way of graciousness.

It was necessary for Marcel to relearn the gymnastic exercises of his youth, to which his elegant and muscular slimness submitted easily. But it was also necessary for Choumaque, who had never been a gymnast, to apply himself to that task, scarcely in conformity with the flights of his metaphysical intellect. Although his body, renewed and stripped of adipose material, rendered supple by mechanical massages and toned up by fluids, had recovered an apparent youth of twenty years, the play of the muscles was still awkward, the creaky joints lacked elasticity and the perilous somersault completed by a considerable displacement generally left him refractory.

*Can one comprehend*, the philosopher asked himself, *what purpose these puerile manifestations of civility serve? Here's a Superman who desires the tranquility of his people, and begins by imposing the prowess of clowns! I'll surely break my bones!*

When Marius had explained to him, however, that these customs had entered into common practice in order that the Superman's subjects could accomplish, with the satisfaction of submitting to religious etiquette, to an exercise that was simply intended to maintain health, Choumaque conceded some

198

reason to the argument, and remembered that Greek and Roman orators had not disdained to enter the arena. From then on, he listened more benevolently to the advice piped by the soft voice of the good-looking slave:

"Bend your knees! Jump higher! Head down! Brace your back! Turn! Fall on your feet!"

He even took a certain pleasure in it, for the skillful athlete, with the aid of a net briskly deployed at ground level, prevented him from hurting himself when he miscalculated his thrust and botched his landing, which happened almost every time.

The only annoyance that he still retained was the presence of an audience always amused by his exercises. The games took place in the open air, in woods marvelously brightened by grassy lawns. There, a quantity of indigenes—fathers and mothers of families, adolescents, courtesans and gitons—for whom physical effort was simply a recreation of anatomical mechanisms, met up, arriving by tube, to amuse themselves.

The nearby sea, divinely blue, sent its spray through the gilded trees. Multicolored birds chirped and pronounced loving words in familiar language. Wild animals came to offer their fleeces to caresses. Forming improbable chains that wings could not sustain, adolescents swung in the trees, or mingled their harmonious young bodies in wrestling bouts. Then they took pleasure in forming a circle around Choumaque and his monitor, observing the neophyte's gaucheries, and not sparing him a little gentle mockery.

The games were accomplished in light costumes only protecting the hands and feet, with the result that the audience for the philosopher's inaptitude was able to observe, beneath their make-up, the still-fresh traces of his recent operations—which provided a further pretext for gibes. Perfect as he was in his new esthetics, Choumaque nevertheless felt that he was still the most counterfeit individual on the island. He was protected, however, firstly by the essential cordiality of the society, and also because people had learned that, although he was ill-equipped for gymnastics, he had considerable intelligence, and was due to speak in public about a subject of which they were all ignorant as yet, philosophy.

As for Marcel, he had immediately mastered that science of politeness. One day, he even executed a perilous double somersault, which won him universal applause. His superb complexion, his muscles, the force of his shoulders and hamstrings, were out of the ordinary, and as he had a new beauty, fecund mothers picked him out for the satisfaction of their ulterior concupiscence. He collected smiles. Several times, Veloutine, the wife of Gilded-Gaze, demanded his kiss when he passed by, his torso covered in sweat.

The newcomers, however, maintained secret causes for not enjoying themselves more completely. Choumaque still remained under the influence of the emotion that he had experienced watching the Superman's butchery. Although that anguish did not touch him personally, he was frightened of an autocracy such that, at a gesture from the surgeon, the humblest subjects might be submitted, on the operating table, to violations as ferocious as those that had been carried out on the human monad. Might not Marcel, his dear pupil, be dragged there? Might not the pure flesh of Miss Mary Hardisson tempt the Superman's dementia? For that philanthropist, infatuated with a seemingly-logical social renovation, that master whom a prostrate people adored in a servile fashion, that scientist whom the world pretended to ignore because to recognize him might attract his destructive lightning, was undoubtedly mad, with an insanity already long manifest in flashes of genius, and evident in any case to Choumaque, before whom that act of surgical eroticism had unfolded.

The same fears—less positive, it is true—troubled Marcel's amour, and he was reluctant to put them to the proof. He would gladly have allowed himself to be enveloped by the temptations of the island; the smiles at his ardent and pleasure-loving youth; they evoked in their splendor the libertinage that he had formerly practiced in a paltry fashion in Paris. Scarcely had he conceived the constant possibility, however, than his affection for Miss Mary returned to pierce his heart, like the stabbing of wounds that are not painful while at rest, but are awakened by the slightest movement.

He sensed instinctively that Caresco did not experience for the neophyte the same banal indifference as for his other subjects. He remembered the sudden transformation of the Superman, stripping away his attitude of lassitude and detachment in order to concentrate on Miss Mary on the day of their appearance. The covetous gleam that had spring forth in his eyes, and the procrastination of his pronunciation in response to the foreigner's supplication, when it would have been easy to content or reject the request, frightened him, without the motives for that fear being exactly definable.

What disturbed him more than anything else was the abrupt transformation that the young woman had manifested in her relationship with him, the fashion in which, after having been so tenderly amorous, she had resumed her previous proud mistrust almost instantaneously, as if she were pulling herself out of a dream or a second state. In those inexplicable changes of direction, Marcel divined the influence of the potentate.

Given that, what delights could he take in the marvels of the new life? What attraction was there in savoring the excursion that had been suggested for that morning: a trip to the sea-bed in order to visit the submarine defenses, the ingenious works thanks to which the mass of rocks defied any approach by submersible vessels?

Their exercises completed, they were about to leave. The white spume of waves was beating the sides of the motor-boat of which Marcel, heroically outlined in his leotard, was holding the tiller. People who had run to the shore were looking curiously at the unfamiliar means of locomotion. Sterile husbands, courtesans and children were pointing at the black hull of the distant ship swayed by the tranquil silvery sheet, to which the graceful launch was about to take them.

Suddenly, the appeals of new voices interrupted the mariner's gesture. Raising his eyes to the sandy slope, he saw the foreigner, in company with Carabella. A simple sheath of pink silk covered her from head to foot, over which she had thrown a light veil that allowed her splendor to show through. That simple apparel did not prevent her from advancing with the sovereign gait particular to her. Beneath her immodest garment, she had the supreme candor of her blonde beauty.

On seeing her, Marcel's heart leapt exultantly.

From a distance, she shouted: "Wait! I'm going with you. Carabella received the order this morning."

"I confide her to you," said the courtesan, with a hint of regret, when they came closer. Then she added: "You have fine weather, and an excursion beneath the waves will be particularly pleasant. In any case, the eddies are scarcely perceptible on the sea bed, even when the swell is heavy."

"Are we putting on our diving-suits right away?" asked Miss Mary, clapping her hands.

"We'll find them aboard the ironclad of which I have the command."

"Well then, let's go, Captain!"

Carabella kissed her mistress on the forehead, not having been permitted any other kiss. She obtained the promise of a seashell. Marcel, helping Miss Mary to get her footing, felt the divine and desired flesh lean delightfully on his shoulder.

The people applauded noisily when the white wake of the propellers striped the fluid immensity.

They had sat down, Choumaque in the bow. They breathed in the air, perfumed by spray; the water splashed; the waves were celestial. What poetry the excursion had in their radiant souls!

The little boat sped soundlessly. Miss Mary, collecting all the grave purity of the elements in her virginal being, lifted up her pink veils over her white sandals dotted with turquoises. One of her hands was supporting the adorable oval of her chin, and she was dreaming while Marcel admired her infinitely. Oh, if only the sweet moment might last! If only the cherished moment in which the splendor of the waves had thrown them into ecstasy might be prolonged!

For an imprint remained of those two assaults by Caresco on the entire character of the virgin, something like the trace left by the lick of a flame on the purest gem, in dissociating its elements and tarnishing its radiant gleam slightly. Everything denoted that imprint: the lighter costume she was wearing, her less serious bearing, and her joy at accepting an excursion that might, however, have another proof in store for her. In addition, under the influence of those poisonings, which had organized a kind of chronic breakdown, it had often happened that Miss Mary thought about Marcel, confusedly remembering the frissons that had run through her at the approach of his strong frame, his silky beard and the gleam in his gaze.

She had not forgotten the incidents consecutive to the effect of the quintessence of happiness; their unfolding had left a lacuna in her life; and yet, vague perfumes emanated from that dark hole, of nature and of amour, which it did not displease her to inhale. She reproached herself for it; she felt that she had lost her integral purity; she reanimated her patriotic ideal—but almost immediately, triumphant suggestion pierced the mists of Faith; Marcel took Harry's place; the senses surpassed sentiment; and it was perhaps the surest result of the Superman's enterprise to have led that exceedingly virginal virgin to suspect that human love existed.

Too greatly influenced by Caresco's alchemy to perceived her transformation clearly, she wondered, however, in short glimmers of reason that were quickly dissipated, what suggestion drove her to admire that mariner, whom her heart had not yet adopted. Yesterday still so pure, so sincere, so near to celestial lyricism, could she have changed so rapidly, and be impregnated already with the sensuality overflowing in all nations, but the unique motive force of the individuals here? Or was she now double; were there two souls in her body, one of them the valiant and heroic daughter of the Red Land, the other hatched in Eucrasia, the slave of Caresco and Marcel?

That reverie was of short duration. Soon, they were on the deck of the ironclad. The welcome they received astonished the former navy lieutenant. Far from the stiff attitudes imposed by the military discipline of his homeland, he found himself confronted by a crew of a dozen men at the most, six sailors and six cabin-boys, clad in the most frivolous and cheerful clothes, who saluted him while dancing and throwing flowers. Evidently, the uselessness of the vessel, considered more as a museum, the objective of excursions made by tourists to relax, and sometimes make love, rendered such license excusable. The island had other means of protection, which they were about to visit.

And yet, in carrying out an inspection of the ironclad, traversing the remotest corridors of the rubber-lined hull—a method employed in the middle of the twentieth century by maritime nations desirous of obtaining vertiginous speeds—and studying the watertight seals and the electric machinery that supplied motive force to the propellers, Marcel convinced himself of the efficient functioning and the remarkable maintenance of the vessel, which a turn of the wrist could have got under way. He contented himself with congratulating the crew of men and boys, and accepting from them a snack of tasty sea fish, boiled in exquisite sauces, washed down with particularly agreeable wine that resembled champagne, and was just as delicious.

That sparkling liquor disposed them to undertake their submarine excursion cheerfully. Marcel was amused to see Miss Mary putting on a diving suit, accompanying her movements with adorable laughter, displaying all the health of her young teeth. Choumaque remained perplexed, though, on observing that the diving suits had no tubes to conduct air.

"How are we going to breathe in them?" he asked a cabin-boy, whose physiognomy he had been contemplating with astonishment, remembering having seen him somewhere before but unable to say where.

The cabin-boy reassured him. Respiration was accomplished marvelously, thanks to a release of gas produced by composites of omnium, of which the mask contained several particles. At the same time as oxygen was produced, the toxicity of the expiration was annihilated: an invention of the

Superman that was both very simple and very ingenious. A week of submarine life was reserved for them, if they wanted to remain that long.

As he completed his explanation, a sailor abruptly dropped the cage over Choumaque's head, and he found it quite comfortable. A plate of glass placed before his eyes allowed him to see his companions, and a resonator placed at the level of the mouth even permitted him to speak and be understood by the others. It was thus that he heard that someone had just handed him a pick-ax, of which he was only to make use to defend himself from monsters, if they encountered any—for they were quite common in the region.

"I'm well-equipped, with that cane, to defend myself from the maw of an antediluvian..."

But a discovery suddenly amazed him. He had finally recognized the cabin-boy whose physiognomy had been haunting him for some time. There was no doubt about it; those dark ringed eyes, that palpitating hooked nose, those flavorsome lips and that wisp of black hair betraying the artifice of the blonde wig were those of Philoxénie, the friend of strangers. He had retained too precious and too embarrassing a memory of their seduction for him to be mistaken.

"Why is that slut…?"

A sudden maneuver on the part of the courtesan soon proved that he had not been mistaken to be suspicious of her. As she was holding out the mask that was to be fitted on to Miss Mary's diving suit he saw her swiftly remove the cupule of omnium and replace it with another that had been hidden in her hand. That substitution was accomplished in the blink of an eye, with such care that the neophyte did not observe it. Choumaque became anxious. He tried to protest, to prevent Philoxénie from doing it, but the heaviness of his apparatus immobilized him and the laughter of the sailors covered his voice.

Their gaiety increased further when, in order to complete the philosopher's equipment, they had shod him with little trampolines, fitted with springs so powerful that at the first step he took, he was precipitated into the sea. The cries that he uttered as he fell proved that the balance of his equilibria was tilting for the moment toward a rather painful quotient, and his Stoicism was subjected to a rude assault.

Marcel and Miss Mary, forewarned of what might happen, jumped in after him.

And there was a delightful excursion, utterly enchanted by unknown spectacles. They acquired the habit of making use of their trampolines, which did not cause them to rebound when they had taken the precaution of letting themselves flow without agitating their legs. The play of the springs was calculated in such a fashion that they could settle on the sea-bed at leisure or launch themselves up twenty meters with a simple thrust of the heel.

At first they traveled over large areas bristling with rocks and hollowed out by fissures, exposing an infinite number of abrupt, denuded environments, as far as the limit of the last recent volcanic convulsions. After that they came to a flat terrain strewn with the softest sand, where the submarine flora blossomed among long strips of sticky algae. They saw thousands of unfamiliar fish, which fled at their approach

They chatted joyfully, pointing out the views to one another; their respiration amplified, filling them with energy; they felt a delightful freshness. Then, as the masses of water overhead became more compact, when the light of the heavens, vanquished by the opacity of the marine surface, left nothing more beneath it than shadow, they perceived that their diving suits were radiant, and that they were as phosphorescent as the large fish that their passage disturbed.

Marcel had drawn closer to Miss Mary; he had taken her arm, and they both shivered beneath that immense unknown. He took pleasure in bounding with her, feeling the gentle waves brushing and caressing their carapaces at each of their upward movements, or afterwards, when they plunged vertically downwards. With interjections, brief comments lucidly transmitted by the resonator, he confided the delights of the adventure to her. Their masks permitted them to admire the animation of their faces.

Oh, the profound, absolute intoxication of those mysterious solitudes, those troubling depths into which so many unknown lives fled, so distant from their own, and so revealing of a constant creative amour! Oh, the infinity of the sea, where so many secrets lay dormant, where so many deaths and births were buried, where nature continued, more visibly than in the infinity of the heavens, her great rhythm of prodigious fecundity. And in his bounds, with a pressure of his hand, Marcel sealed his enthusiasm.

As for Miss Mary, for the third time since she had arrived on the island, she was subjected to an upheaval of her entire sensibility. The enchanting gas that she was breathing, another poison of the Superman emanating from the cupule slipped into her mask by Philoxénie, while leaving her a constant lucidity of mind, overwhelmed her with such an intoxication that she had never experienced anything like it. Although things conserved their appearance, the colors had not changed and the panoramas were curious, she considered them with an extraordinary intensity of magnification and seduction. Every phenomenon offered to her perception immediately became a element of a real joy, an incomparable bliss, in her mind.

Even Choumaque, wedged in his carapace, seemed to her as handsome as a young god, but less so than Marcel, the sight of whom transported her with a thousand acute admirations. She shivered unforgettably at feeing him beside her. When they held one another in order to jump, or slid toward the bottom, and he displaced water moved around their couple, she vibrated as if at a voluptuous touch. Soon, the only desire that persisted was that they might be nude, in order to feel the liquid embrace together.

A cry of alarm from Choumaque snatched her momentarily from her ravishment, however. A monstrous maw opened in front of them, ready to crush them. They perceived its gape, as wide as one of Hell's gates, in which white symmetrical and cruel asperities were aligned. At that moment

Marcel sensed his companion's entire soul taking refuge in his. With a sovereign self-control, he extended his pike in the direction of the danger. A globe of fire sprang from it, and the shark collapsed, thunderstruck. Still palpitating with surprise, they circled around it. The monster had settled on its side, no visible trace of a wound gaping among the iridescent gleam of its scales. Marcel blessed the day's unique event.

"That's a famous spear-thrust!" affirmed Choumaque, who had drawn nearer. "Oh, the fellow gave me quite a fright…for you, my children!"

"I owe you my life, Monsieur Marcel!" said Miss Mary, impetuously.

"Don't I owe you far more—love?" replied the young man, squeezing her arm gently.

They resumed their progress, the darkness having become more complete. Soon, they found themselves confronted by huge advertising hoardings, where, in luminous letters, the word BEWARE was repeated as far as the eye could see. They were approaching the danger zone, and had been instructed to proceed with caution.

What they saw a little further on seemed quite ordinary, not very complicated in its appearance. It was simply a network of metallic wires, its mesh about a meter wide, raised perpendicularly by a conductive masonry emerging from the bed. Behind it, however, there was an agglomeration of immense dead things forming a kind of second rampart.

As they came closer they recognized monsters similar to the one that Marcel had defeated a little while before—whales, sharks and enormous cephalopods in slow decomposition; then, at the same level, the carcasses of a dozen submarine torpedo-boats whose open flanks displayed their precious mechanisms crushed and reduced to shreds by a fantastic commotion.

Then, Marcel remembered a great event that had occurred ten years before, when an entire English fleet had disappeared, engulfed and swallowed up by the sea without the Admiralty wanting to admit to what region and on what mission it had been sent. The explanation was thus manifest before their eyes, and they admired the colossal organization of the island, that vast trap extended around its shores, abolishing natural ferocities and human determinations with a simple anonymous shock.

They were getting ready to return, retracing their route, when a bell extracted them from their reflections. Almost immediately, on approaching a luminous station, they heard several familiar voices. One might have thought that the incidents of the excursion were being followed from the interior of the earth.

"Adieu, eh! Are you well?" sang the deep baritone of Marius, vibrant with sympathy.

"Thanks to the Superman, we can see you perfectly," added Madame Môme. "We can see my Choumaque hitching up the belt of his damp trousers..."

"That's true!" admitted Choumaque, amazed.

"May Caresco operate on you, Mademoiselle and Messieurs!" exclaimed Mirror-of-Smiles.

The voices died away, and then the excursionists perceived that they had been replaced by luminous letters that appeared on the vast screen of the station, and which, lighting up and going out in their turn, signified rapidly-written sentences. It was a second means of security, the functioning of which they confirmed. They were able to take turns sitting down in front of a writing-machine situated at the foot of the luminous screen, disposed like a piano keyboard. They communicated by that means with their distant friends, joyfully, and arranged to meet them, in an hour's time, on the ship, where another snack and amusing games were being prepared in their honor by the crew.

They did, indeed, find them there. Night had fallen in the interim, and the crew had taken advantage of it to light up the ship marvelously. When they came aboard again, they thought they had been transported to an immense bed of magical flowers, whose brilliant corollas, harmoniously blooming, framed sumptuous beds next to tables covered with delicacies and exquisite beverages. They could not retain cries of admiration.

Miss Mary, very enervated, hastened to take off her diving suit. When she turned round to look for Marcel, she could no longer see him. In the distance, on the sea, a little boat was fleeing, carrying two people: Carabella and the one she desired.

"Is that my friend going away?" she asked a cabin-boy, who was none other than Philoxénie.

"It is, indeed, him. An order from the Superman has just summoned him to his duties as a Sower. But what does it matter? Does not love take hold with everyone?"

"Evidently," she replied, conceding entire truth to the statement, so far away had ravishment driven her reason.

The spectacle that she had had before her eyes soon made her forget the absentee. The entire sea had just lit up in its turn; the waves were no more than flames flowing immensely, as if the apotheosis of a setting sun had emanated from their depths to variegate the surface. That gave a diversity of admirable hues to the attitudes of a thousand dancers treading on the waves by means of rackets fitted to their feet, accomplishing gracious evolutions there. One might have thought them Neptunian spirits emerged from the dark depths, streaming with light, to dazzle the privileged humans.

Miss Mary, still under the influence of the enchanting gas, lay down on a bed beside Choumaque, and took an ineffable pleasure in seeing everything, in tasting the delicacies filling the precious vases, in wetting her lips in the sparkling glasses. Her eyes were shining more brightly with an interior reflection expressing all the new excitement of her sentiments, the piercing desire to melt into another flesh, to appease by strange contact the covetousness dilating every fiber of her being. When Philoxénie slipped a hand into the gap of her corsage, at the place where the neck extended delicately toward the shoulders, she uttered a cry stifled by a swoon. And as, in the gloom, she imagined that Chounaque was being audacious, no longer able to resist, she enlaced him with her muscular feet.

"Oh! What's happening? You're no longer seeing clearly, my child! I'm not Marcel. Don't persist, I beg you! Have you gone mad?"

"Yes, mad! Crazy for you! Crazy for your strange beauty."

Without having time to reflect on the improbability of that good fortune, the philosopher was obliged to defend himself. With an unhealthy avidity, she caressed his beard, demanded his lips and clutched his doublet. The efforts of Philoxénie, surprised to see the effects of passion whose joys she had been instructed to collect deflected in that fashion, only exasperated it.

The courtesan tried in vain to slide between them, used all her strength to try to separate them, and fought to distract the young woman's ardor to her own advantage; nothing could tear Miss Mary away from her bewildered philosopher. There was soon a melee of three bodies, pulling in opposite directions and rolling on the floor, to the great astonishment of the crew.

In the course of that struggle, though, the Redlander was exhausted. A liberating breath passed through her brain and sobered it up. Somewhat astonished to find herself on the floor, holding Choumaque tightly in her arms, she pulled away from him and stood up. Calmly, she took her place at the table and continued her meal. Then, wiping her drink-moistened mouth with a distinguished grace, she said: "What a charming soirée! But what's become of Monsieur Marcel?"

The philosopher abstained from interrogating her about the extraordinary act that she had just committed. Not without fear, he detected the power of the Superman therein, making use of all his occult forces to bend the heroically virginal complexion of the foreigner to his will.

# CHAPTER XVII

Although broad daylight had long ago taken possession of the room and returned their particularities, colors, projections and life to the things that darkness had confounded in a neutral equality, Miss Mary was still asleep. With her bare arm passed beneath her neck and entangled in her unruly hair, she was dreaming.

A smile, raising the corners of her red lips, confessed the pleasure of her thoughts. The same enchantment had pursued her throughout her slumber, and was still continuing at present to intoxicate her drowsiness. She saw herself on Marcel's arm, participating in pompous and sparkling processions, listening to music that their presence rendered divine, savoring with a tenfold intensity the marvels of the island of Eucrasia.

An importunate ray of sunlight woke her up, and the abrupt transition of her ideas caused her profound bitterness. She recalled her dream. She was astonished to find it so dissimilar to the obsessions that, since her earliest days had laid siege to all of her nights, torturing her with anxiety for the fatherland. She cursed the inconceivable seductions that, conquering her even in a waking state, now made her subject to the attraction of jewels and perfumes, filling her with an almost carnal voluptuousness when she touched precious fabrics, and then dressed on them, in order that Marcel should not find her displeasing. She resolved no longer to sacrifice anything of her virile ideal to them.

Alas, the oath was immediately betrayed, as soon as Carabella, arriving, said to her, after having scattered the petals of a large bouquet of wild violets on the floor: "Know, divine one, what I've just been told: your friends will be entering into their functions today. Monsieur Choumaque will talk about philosophy before the assembled people, and Monsieur Marcel will also employ himself for the public good."

"Will he be taking command of his ship, then?" she asked, hastily.

"It's not a matter of that. The position of commander is fictitious."

"Then I don't understand..."

"The nature of his functions? That's true, you're still so ignorant of our customs. Know that Monsieur Girard, having become a Sower, will be sent to the Temple of Fecundity, to make love there to blonde mothers and serve the repopulation. I prepared him for that important work yesterday by taking him away from the celebration, and making him go to bed early."

That confession had no sooner been made than anguish gripped the young woman. She had completely forgotten the transports that the gas respired the previous day had caused her to experience, but the word "love," pronounced by the courtesan, struck a dire blow to her feelings for the young man. Her heart palpitating, all her distress overflowing into action, she stood up swiftly, put on a peignoir, and strove to color with a pretext the urgency she felt in wanting to go and see Marcel.

"Quickly, help me get dressed! I don't want to miss Monsieur Choumaque's lecture."

The courtesan adorned her, delicately. After having made her put on a Greek head-dress, the crown of which was imprisoned by golden ribbons, she anointed her face and hands with semi-liquid mixtures of perfumed oils. With a stroke of a pencil she emphasized the pride of the eyes, and heightened the health of the cheeks with an imperceptible powder. The superb torso, the firm legs, the full arms and the gilded tufts of the armpits disappeared beneath the leotard that the tunic soon half-concealed. She declared her adorable and kissed her.

They were about to leave, intending to take the first transport that could take them to the philosopher's lecture, when a formidable rumble, like a roll of thunder, burst forth outside. At the same time, brass instruments blared, playing a triumphal march so loudly that the walls shook.

"Great God, what's that?" cried Miss Mary.

"The Superman! It's the Superman!" cried Carabella, prostrating herself face downwards.

The door opened and Cresco appeared. Behind him, in the vast gallery, his omnipotence was escorted by a numerous, scintillating, gaudy yellow retinue of slaves playing the role of lictors. He was discreetly clad in a black doublet sown with golden vibrions and ovules, thick in the sleeves and close-fitting at the waist, continued by tights of the same color. A circle of red velvet surmounted by a diamond spray wound around his young and weary head, and provided an admirable frame for his natural elegance.

Carabella wondered what surge of passion had made him go out in that accoutrement, surrounded by such a cohort. Except for public festivals, when he showed himself to the people in all his pomp, from the height of sumptuous stages, he was never seen like this. He contented himself with governing from the depths of his palace, skeptical and coldly jaded, thus maintaining his legend of power, mystery and benevolence.

He advanced toward Miss Mary and held out his hand to her. Only considering his silhouette, one would have admired his eternal youth. But his antique gaze fled; the smile on his broad lips was awkward, as if constrained to displayed itself there, and a strange equivocation emanated from the ensemble typical of old women who deceive age by means of artifice, without the certainty of their trickery being easy to affirm.

"Bonjour, my lovely friend," he said, as softly as possible. Then, addressing Carabella, in a tone that suddenly became imperious, he said: "Get up, courtesan, and get out!"

"Permit Carabella to stay, Superman," Miss Mary begged, fearfully. "I need her in order to go and listen to the eloquence of the philosopher Choumaque."

"I've come to find you precisely to take you there," Caresco said, seizing that pretext for his visit, "but before then, permit me to offer you this present, still unworthy of your beauty."

He made a sign, and two slaves came in, ceremoniously carrying a sumptuous robe whose weave, in dark pink, was

214

almost entirely covered by an embroidery of precious stones and metals, streaming like he droplets of a multicolored crystalline cascade. In the old world, that fantastic garment would have represented the fortune of a billionaire; here it was worth no more than the artistic distribution of the gems: topazes, turquoises, sapphires and amethysts, representing vibrions and ovules, while the train, falling in black pearls, depicted a chimera.

The Superman was excited. "I want to see you in this costume, neophyte. Put it on immediately!"

"In front of you?"

"In front of me."

She looked at him coldly. She found him seemingly abstracted; she distinguished something troubling and cruel in the laughter gurgling in his throat. She understood that there was no resisting him, and would have liked her character still have had the strength to do so. Assisted by Carabella, she took off her costume in order to put on the new one.

When she was adorned, more sumptuously than a queen in her sacred mantle, Caresco bounded toward her.

"Don't move!"

She thought that he was about to grab her, so violent was the desire transparent in the crease on his forehead. He did nothing of the sort. The Superman contented himself with applying the two poles of his psychometer to the young woman's forehead and interrogating the needles.

"Seventy-six!" he murmured. "Only seventy-six! She defends herself, that child! Have my prescriptions been neglected, then? Let's see, neophyte, confess: yesterday, did Philoxénie not tame you? What do you have in your soul, to resist thus?"

His furious eyes overwhelmed her. He was astonished to see that she did not lower her head, and that audacity, acting upon his mind, made him calm down almost immediately.

"Let's go! I'll take you. You're the mistress today, since I'm the master. Am I not all that I wish? I'm the Superman. If I wished, I could be the Other!"

Without further explanation, he put his arm around her waist, in front of two rows of prostrate lictors showing their symbolic crosses. Powerful harmonies burst forth again, and the artificial thunder exploded at the same time.

A magnificent airplane, entirely decorated with gems shining like as many suns was awaiting them on the third floor terrace. Behind it, hovering in mid-air with the slow movements of propellers, huge flyers that did not want to land, there was a pompous file of a hundred other craft, adopting the forms of the most various birds, ranging from the craziest fantasy to the most sincere reality: the potentate's retinue. All around, thousand of private balloons, smaller and infinite in hue, were coming and going, spreading their wings, filled with people cheering the Superman, delighted by the windfall that was showing them the Master in broad daylight. They were soon so numerous that the ground was darkened by them.

After taking his place facing Miss Mary in the vast gilded nacelle, Caresco soon paid no further attention to the Redlander. He tormented his brown beard and tugged the points of his moustache. Succeeding in pulling out a hair therefrom, he studied it for a long time, placing it in front of the luminous background of the sky, and then swallowed it with a kind of gluttonous joy. After that, he worked and made notes. His hand ran hastily over a writing-desk disposed on his knees.

The young woman noticed the eccentricity of his writing, whose lines always sloped upwards, and whose hieroglyphs, under the uncoordination of thought and gesture, were overladen with implausible flourishes. She was frightened by his strange attitude and searched around her for a powerful protectress. She saw no one but servants, greeting the presumably-customary mime without astonishment and murmuring, with compunction: "The Superman is working! Glory to the Superman!" That reassured her, and she turned her gaze toward the immensity, which an admirable sun was causing to vibrate with joy.

Almost at the same moment, Zéphirin Choumaque, with a scroll of papers in his hand, was walking back and forth at an even pace on a lawn whose verdure, circumscribed at the rear by a crown of marvelous cedars extended forwards to the steps of an amphitheater naturally carved in red porphyry.

The philosopher was awaiting events, the most imminent of which—one that he envisaged with a certain anxiety—was soon to be lecturing on the topic of "Happy peoples have no history." Thinking about his speech, he was worried. But was it only the contradiction of having to discuss a proposition totally opposed to his ideas that was importing a hint of dolor into his pensive blue gaze? Was it not because he was remembering the Superman's frightful butcheries, Miss Mary's unconscious actions, and the fact that all those symptoms revealed upheavals to come, that he was putting such scant urgency into throwing over his shoulder the gold-trimmed violet fabric of his Roman toga, which was trailing behind him, brushing the blades of grass?

*Why deck myself up like this?* he thought, grumpily. *Is it really useful to dress like a Roman of the Decadence in order to sustain bad arguments? Could the Superman not have spared me this masquerade? Will my unexperimented movements not end up leading me to ridicule, and is this really the means of earning the copious couch of Madame Môme again?*

Meanwhile, the amphitheater was filing up. A languorous wave of mauve-clad courtesans arrived, who sat down, sucking sugary confections. Small aircraft, light and gracious, were fluttering and landing, and were then parked under the cover of the woods by slaves. They were bringing the purple robes and curly beard of sterile husbands, the pale blue adornments and blonde faces of fecund mothers, the vigorous grace of adolescents in green doublets, sowers in orange tunics and robust virgins in pink peplums. A band of flying children soon landed and scattered.

All of them came and went, chatting and laughing, in an iridescence of rich fabrics, under the glory of a warm ten o'clock sunlight, of which light breezes provided by the tem-

217

perature service and perfumed with violet further accentuated the softness. In the distance, the green stages of the mountains were outlined, infinitely calm and restful, to fuse in a trail of pearly with the blue jot of infinity.

By the next tube, yet another society arrived: Mirror-of-Smiles pirouetting around Dr. Hymen, whose side-whiskers he was tickling with a cane, which he also used to brush the nap of his hat the wrong way; Gilded-Gaze and his wife Veloutine; Marjah, who sat down next to Philoxénie, patiently sculpting a piece of wood; and then more people—mostly women, for the men preferred the tricks of a conjuror whose amusing science was filling another corner of the mountain.

Marcel, under the gaze of fecund women admiring his stature and his perfect legs clad in orange silk, was running his gaze over the steps, trying to find Miss Mary, and saddened by not being able to discover her there.

Marius and Madame Môme appeared, arm in arm. The renovator of the fresco, his beard divided into three points to amuse everyone, his painter's costume tightly laced, knitted about his legs. A joyful murmur saluted his entrance, approving his longstanding liaison with the High Priestess.

A sack surmounted by a round, sealed head was brought; it was the Thought-reader, who was dropped like a packet behind Choumaque.

The half-man's pedestal silently backed up against a tree-trunk.

Dr. Hymen took his place in the front row and went to sleep.

The goose from the Brain had also come, and was jabbering noisily.

Madame Môme gratified the orator with a kiss blown from the tips of her pink-painted fingernails.

The latter, understanding that his eloquence was awaited, hitched up his belt and began.

"Mesdames, Messieurs..."

But a disapproving "Oh!" greeted his first words. At the same time, Marius, by means of a pantomime of his long arms, signified to him that it was necessary to salute before raising one's voice. Choumaque complied with good grace; he accomplished a perilous somersault, getting tangled up in his toga, which caused an outburst of jovial laughter and exclamations, with which the porphyry steps reverberated.

As soon as he was back on his feet, he resumed.

"Mesdames and Messieurs, I shall inflict punishments on those who do not respect the professor..." He was so confused that he thought he was once again in front of the dunces of the Pension Frontispice. As most members of the audience were unaware of the meaning of the word "punish," they thought it was a witty quip, and shut up.

Then he sat down on a mound and began to sustain the proposition that "happy peoples have no history."

With fine gestures emerging from his violet sleeves, before the polychromatic and silent assembly whose eyes widened, surprised by such language, he made his speech. He had recovered possession of his ideas and praised the new life, the one in which the people blessed by Caresco had only to be born, to enjoy living, without decrepitude, under a sky favored by the science of the master. Truly, the inspiration for the speech was furnished by the spectacle itself, but the satisfied and flourishing attitude of all those young, beautiful people on the steps satiated with substance and amour, whose indolence allowed them to be lulled by his voice.

Could a more perfect felicity reign? Could one worry for even a moment about obscure ethics when, without disturbances, without essential struggles, all the desires of the senses and a restricted mentality were profusely contented; when it was sufficient for any citizen to desire a beautiful body for it to be instantly offered to his lust; a good meal, for him to find it within arm's reach; good sleep, for him to draw tranquility from ever-open wells of fluids and to spend it beneath sumptuous shelters; hygienic garments—which were superfluous beneath that ideal sky—for him to see them laid out, as if by magic, at the foot of his bed in the morning? Dressing oneself, sleeping, eating and loving—the four primordial exigencies of existence—were delightfully easy to accomplish to one's fill on the clement island.

Elsewhere, to realize needs, peoples cut one another's throats, and citizens oppressed one another. Elsewhere, tears, blood and dolor flowed, and from their waves, rare parcels of happiness emerged. Weeping, bleeding, suffering: three words that the favored subjects of Eucrasia had the extraordinary good fortune not to know!

And Choumaque said all that, stunning himself with his words in order to persuade himself, for he had just perceived, almost behind him, but within his visual field, the leather sack surmounted by a round glabrous ball with only one orifice, the flaccid horror of the Thought-reader, the spy of his soul.

But the people believed his speech. Backed up against its tree, the captain's pedestal resounded with the applause struck by the back-scratcher that the half-man's single arm was waving. Courtesans clapped their hands without understanding very well. Mirror-of-Smiles, a pink and ender scamp, wrenched flowers from the bosom of a fecund mother in order to throw them to the orator, without yielding to the reproaches of Marjah, who was telling him to be quiet. Gilded-Gaze, Veloutine and Philoxénie approved vocally.

But Marcel was dreaming, and if Marius and Madame Môme applauded too, it was with less enthusiasm than everyone else, for, having known the other life, the one to which Choumaque had made allusion, they thought that their happiness was too regularly perfect. Meanwhile, Dr. Hymen's hat had just fallen off on to the pendants on his abdomen. The concierge of eternity was profoundly asleep. A tiger came to lick him, gently.

The orator was about to continue when there was a great stir, and clamors rose up, all the standing bodies stamping their feet, in response to a celestial apparition.

"The Superman! The Superman!"

The potentate's airplane circled magnificently and then landed. Caresco got down, holding Miss Mary, draped in her scintillating gems, by the hand. The slaves had had the time to

220

trace a path of violet petals for them. Around them, women emptied their perfume-sacs. Overhead, flying boys threw flowers, more of which tumbled from the aerial cohort. Polychromatic bodies were prostrated as they passed by, getting up again thereafter and celebrate their enthusiasm in awkward movements, confining their delirium.

The sunlight gilded the cortege, making gems scintillate and metals flash. Radiating over the spectators, it set the amphitheater, now full to capacity, ablaze.

"Continue!" order Caresco, sitting down, almost kneeling, at Miss Mary's feet, having not let go of her hand. On her part, neither reluctance nor repulsion was perceptible, although her gaze sought refuge in Marcel's direction.

Then, a great dolor was hollowed out amid all that exultant joy. The young man, struck in the heart, contemplated the new couple with black rage. His trembling hands seemed to be searching for an instrument of vengeance. The inert, as if unconsciously possessed, state that he divined in Miss Mary; the sentiment of his impotence to separate the despot from his prey; the docility with which that prey submitted to the empire of the Superman, while appearing to demand a protection from elsewhere—his, he understood—all those various demonstrations against him and in his favor, disconcerted him.

He could not succeed in clarifying the psychology of that floating soul, which seemed torn between two suggestions, which seemed, at least, no longer to be opposing resistance to Caresco, and at the same time reaching out to the companion with whom she had arrived on the island. Those multiple impressions tortured the young man with such a sentiment of jealousy that, unconsciously, he twisted the arm of Gilded-Gaze, who was sitting next to him. The sterile husband considered him in amazement; he had never seen an intimate storm translated with such brutality.

Choumaque sensed his friend's palpitating soul reaching out to him, and experienced a great compassion for him. Oh, how readily he would have given his own joys, the caresses of Madame Môme, and his philosophy, to soothe the hurt of his

221

cherished pupil! Immediately, however, he thought: *Evidently, he's suffering—but how much better appreciated the return of his happiness will be, when I have returned his beloved to him, when their two intoxications fuse! Every strong room has its weak point, every wall its crack, And have we not intelligences in the room, and stones in the wall? Will Môme and Marius not help us, in this circumstance?*

Divided by these ideas, contrary to the thesis that he was sustaining—which pursued him, involuntarily—when he resumed his speech, he soon altered the course of his argument. Certainly, happy people had no history, but those who had a history were even happier, for struggle, effort and energy were the conditions of true felicity, they alone set its value. To love, it was necessary to desire; to eat with a good appetite, to be hungry; and to suffer cold, to know the joy of being dressed.

To speak thus in front of the despot might have been an act of incredible audacity, which could have won the orator delicate operations with scant delay, taking him to the bloody table in order to be subjected to the resections of the human monad. Fortunately for Choumaque, no one was listening to him except for the Thought-reader, whose inertia at that moment affirmed that the philosopher really had unveiled the depths of his soul. But Caresco, holding hands with Miss Mary, was allowing his passion for victory to seethe; Dr. Hymen was asleep; Marius and Madame Môme were stimulating their imminent sensuality in hushed whispers; the half-man captain had deserted his tree to roll toward the airplanes; and the mischievous Mirror-of-Smiles was sticking dead leaves into the curly hair of Marjah, who was busy sculpting a piece of wood into phallus.

As for the rest of the amphitheater—Gilded-Gaze, Veloutine, Philoxénie, the sterile husbands, the fecund mothers, the languid courtesans and the impish gitons—they were chatting amiably, laughing singing, playing with fans, caressing tame animals, sucking pastilles, rolling knuckle-bones...with the result that, when Choumaque had finished, no one budged. Vexed, the philosopher was obliged to shout:

"I've finished!" and even to accomplish a few pirouettes to signify the conclusion of his lecture.

Immediately, the people rose to their feet and cheered Caresco. The latter had stood up too, drawing the foreign woman to his bosom.

"I'm going to leave you, virgin, but let me tell you, before I go, how much charm your presence has added to this lesson. What odor, more intoxicating than all my alchemies, expands from your bosom; and what mirages, more profound than the extent of the skies, shine in the purity of your somber eyes! Oh, be the queen of this land, the first woman, with me, the first man! Will you not you abandon, therefore, the desire to go away, to return to your Red Land, to your great fool of a brother and your stupid peasants? Native soil, fatherland—what inept concepts! Here, you see, I am the god. Listen to those cheers! They will acclaim you too, whenever you wish."

Troubled, she made no reply. But at the words *Red Land*, the evocation of the glorious past, a flash of anger, of shame and of revolt, the last spark of an almost-extinct ire, shot through her. And what drew her away from Caresco threw her toward Marcel. She darted such a tearful glance toward the young man that the potentate could not misinterpret it. He gasped.

*What? It's him? It's for the Sower that I'll have labored? It's to lead this Virgin to Nature that I'll have created my serum, and my Quintessence of Happiness, and my Enchanting Gas! Truly, it's too ridiculous... extraordinarily ridiculous...*

And he did indeed, laugh, ferociously. But soon, changing his expression, he shoved the young woman away, violently. With foam on his lips, he fled toward his airplane, knocking over the crowd, striking the backs of prostrated slaves, tearing the long beards of the men who adored him. The people, seized by astonishment, remained mute. The Superman had never been seen so out of control. Hostile gazes turned toward the foreign woman, and toward Marcel, who had just received her in his arms.

# CHAPTER XVIII

When Caresco entered the cavern into which no one but him ever came, he felt extremely weary, as if the enormous mass of rock accumulated above the lair—the two thousand meters of the Mount of Venus—were weighing on his back. He shook his shoulders in order to shrug off that oppression.

For thirty years, since the day when, on discovering that chasm, he had been seduced by its grim extent and had fitted it out in order to undertake mysterious labors there, every time he crossed the threshold, the same crushing sensation took possession of him, and the same gesture of pride caused him to raise his head, in defiance of all the forces of nature that he had overcome, and which still wanted to dominate him.

As he advanced toward the density of the shadow, he felt the ground becoming less steep beneath his feet. Soon, fine sand replaced the rock. A thick warmth, aggravated by electrical effluvia, revealed the proximity of the central fire. He headed toward a precise point, encountered a panel that he knew well, and without groping, in spite of the pitch darkness, turned the commutator controlling the lighting and ventilation.

Omnium revealed its effects; the lair lit up with a green glow; currents of fresh air dissipated the ambient heaviness. Then he looked, with a snigger of pride, at the natural room hollowed out but the cooling of the masses of lava, about fifty meters high and almost circular, with a radius of fifty feet. The last frissons of the liquid matter, as they died away, had described crazy anfractuosities, improbably balanced overhangs, stalactites with sharp ridges, some of which, reaching the ground, looked like columns designed to support the vault. In the middle of the vault, a monstrous chimney opened, the funnel of which was disposed as if to aspire the heart of the earth, disappearing into one of the flanks of the mountain in a sly, fleeting furrow.

In the side walls, crevasses yawned, allowing the filtration of limpid water, which channels hollowed out by the hands of engineers drained, in order to direct it meekly toward a nearby torrent, whose somersaults were inaudible. If the work of captation had not been completed, if the inferior orifice of the grotto had not been blocked, the cavern would doubtless have constituted a simple reservoir of water, which the ground would have heated up, and which would have escaped in a boiling stream from its sojourn in the location.

That was all that Caresco had permitted nature to leave. The rest had been modified, doctored by human genius. The burning floor—scarcely a hundred meters of masonry separated it from the central fire—had been covered with a refractory substance furrowed by refrigerant conduits. In order that the proximity of the volcano at that point would no longer be a danger, the Superman had warded it off, as he had chased away the darkness, by inundating the walls with omnial light, and the steam-bath heat was dissipated by bringing reserves of cold water into play.

The rest of the adaptation was consecrated to science. Display cases set against the walls of rock contained bizarre instruments and jars with strange contents: anatomical specimens; vague, hallucinatory forms; flesh stripped from life bathing in liquids favoring its conservation in spite of the temperature. There were even entire bodies—embryos, men and women—sacrificed to the surgeon's passion for operation. Stuck to glass walls, they exposed their incoherent cadaveric attitudes, their masks with frightful or risible rictuses, their open bellies, their projecting viscera, their butchered limbs.

In one corner, the silhouette of a child was outlined by the green backcloth; leaning her shoulder against the transparent wall, she seemed to be trying to escape. A smile was fixed upon her livid lips; her candid blue eyes, having conserved their mirage of life, were also smiling, while the rest of her features, shrunk by astringent substances, had shriveled, offering the paradoxical contrast of extreme youth fused with extreme decrepitude.

Beneath the central chimney, like a formidable sacrificial altar, stood a metallic table with complicated mechanical attachments, catching every gleam in its gears, animated at every corner and every curve by as many cold, cutting and cruel reflections.

In one fissure there was an enormous metal box, hermetically sealed, with a twenty-square-meter screen on the front, the ensemble mounted on a pedestal; and beneath it, a little to one side, a sumptuous bed, in mother-of-pearl, emerging from the ground like the two great parted lips of a shell, draped with rare fabrics in crimson and gold. Not far away, a small red panel shone, with an omnial contact button at its center. Next to it, a shiny circular steel band emerged from the rock, movable on a hinge sealed in the rock, just large enough, on being closed by a spring, to secure the neck of a man.

Caresco took a deep breath of that fearful atmosphere. Here, there were no delicate aromas due to the research of chemists, but the warm odor of rock, the antiseptic emanations of jars, and the indescribable reek of fixed flesh abandoned by life, but which death had not consumed. A viscous disgust oozed from the surroundings. Those exhalations, divine perfumes of destruction, he had breathed impetuously throughout his life before he set foot on the island, and throughout his new life too, since the time when he had set himself outside the law, outside society, becoming the sole master of twenty thousand human beings.

And in communicating with those funereal atoms, in allowing them to penetrate him, through the nose, through the mouth and through every pore of his being; in impregnating himself with them, espousing death in the green glow, he reanimated the precision of his octogenarian memories, reclaimed their fecund joys, the emotions of delicate and ferocious butcheries, of impetuous deeds and inventions, acts of violence, death-rattles, survivals and agonies.

Oh, the bloody epics, the magnificent contests with Nature, the macabre holocausts to science, and to glory, that those infinitesimal particles of death reawakened! As he inhaled them, his breathing accelerated; his rejuvenated heart beat more precipitately; his long-fingered hands seemed to want to draw toward his bosom so many dissected cadavers, so much still-throbbing debris, so much confused pulp...

He took a few steps toward the display-cases, without feeling the pain of a bump he had just sustained on the corner of the table. The rictuses and the masks were calling to him, inviting him to the other side of their glass. He recognized them all; he knew exactly when, and with what objectives, he had provoked their deaths.

He talked to them.

"Ah, there you are, Fabienne," he said to an open abdomen, of which a frightfully dislocated flap hung down toward the plump ivory of the buttocks, "there you are! How can you bear this long silence, O girl with the laughing mouth, scented by spring? I was still a surgeon in the other world then; I had a clinic for the poor. One day, you came to find me...I can still see your embarrassed smile, when you told me about your miseries, attributable to the impetuosity of one of your lovers. What was wrong with you? I don't remember...perhaps nothing...but it was necessary, you understand, to learn about the opening of the bile duct into the intestine, and I also wanted to know whether the conduits of the kidney could empty there without inconvenience. I opened you up...you died three days later, still smiling! You were born too soon! Now, I would have succeeded in that petty masterstroke!"

He took a few steps toward another case, about two meters high. An entire body, arms and legs apart, greeted him, with a grimace on his gaping mouth, while the rest of the face was almost covered with sticky red hair, abundantly developed after death. The torso was dangling, sunken in the pelvis.

"It's you, Druant! You, who had a cancer of the vertebral column! Was it really a cancer, in fact? At any rate, you begged me to rid you of an awkward tumor in that region. Oh, what a beautiful red orgy that was! Three hundred spectators were watching me. I broke your bones, I resected your sacrum and your coccyx! Didn't they weep with admiration around me, while you were weeping in your soul? You said *Aah!* and passed on. You were born too soon as well. Now, I would have removed the entire vertebral axis."

He continued his funereal review. After the immolated of the old world came those of the new continent, innumerable. They were, in general, better conserved; they retained slight traces of the happy life that they had led. To all of them he said a friendly word, calling them by their forenames, remembering some feature of their existence.

He also addressed himself to fragments of people still alive, speaking to them as if to entire beings. He recognized the pieces excised from the half-man, and saluted them. Bizarre subjects completely transformed or reduced, hermaphrodites and human monads, the results of recent attempts, completed the series. The evolution of his surgical conceptions was visible, all tending to bring an individual to the minimum of viscera and senses, after the suppression of the limbs.

Against those he got carried away, accusing them of being good for nothing, not even to operate on. His voice, magnified by the echo of the cavern, thundered, amplified by the growls that every anfractuosity repeated. But a hope exalted him. His latest human monad was not dead, and that idea filled him with an exultant joy.

"Reappear, my great deeds of glory!" he cried, going feverishly to put his finger on a button situated next to the nacreous bed, directly below the metal case—the phonographophone, whose screen immediately collected the intensity of an interior light.

He lay down on a fur made from the pelts of a hundred sables, among the gold-fringed crimson of cushions, his body slightly turned toward the spectacle he had just provoked. Immediately, individuals appeared in the transparency. One might have sworn that they were real, so evident were their color and movements, and so natural were the voices that the apparatus also repeated.

For a full hour, Caresco revisited his ardent communions, his violations of flesh, recorded on that surprising stage.

The spectacle was always the same: there was always the décor of a round white room, the gleam of metal and implements, red linen, hasty attitudes, curious heads, around an altar raised above pallors splashed with blood, on which a naked body was panting. He was at the center, his arms outstretched, his head sweating, magnifying the Feat; Death or life emerged from his hands.

The cries that he heard ended in outbursts of victory, gasps of agony. Whether the soul persisted, or flew away, he saw himself magnificently conserving his imperturbable indifference. Whether he was operating on kings, emperors or popes, his hand never trembled anymore; the orders that he gave profited equally from his formidable calm. He admired himself, for all those powerful clients, he could now have made into slaves, had he wished.

Then, the interest changed. A click of the phonographophone separated his two lives. He abandoned ancient France, organized his people. Discoveries had progressed; his carescoclast simplified everything; his feats no longer responded to anything but social indications. The two acts of castration and fecundation leveled human harmony. His sole curiosity, revealed subsequently, was that of reducing human being, of finding his monad-individual—a simple dilettantism whose modest interest he did not hide from himself. But he castrated, he castrated! All the courtesans had been his lovers; all of them, appeasing his surgical sadism, gave an increasing voluptuousness to his attitudes, animated his loins with shudders of keen lust. Oh, the captivating intoxications of blood!

He would spend days like this, gazing at the Past with his devouring eye; but at the end of his effort, the screen went dark. Then, in spite of the lighting, he found that everything fell back into the shadow. A great distress followed. He got up, went to lean against the operating table and wept, for a long time. His face, momentarily brightened by triumphal memories, darkened suddenly, and resumed its expression of bleak disillusionment and exhausted age.

What was the point of saluting all those phantoms of past hours? What was the point of continuing to hope for an energy prolonged beyond human limits? He had put an entire people to sleep in enjoyment, and postponed the moment of the tomb; for that people, dying was no more than a painless formality, a brief moment of transmission before the fortunate metempsychosis. Among those twenty thousand servile subjects, stupefied by their pleasures and his doctrine, Caresco had only to reach out his hand, and choose the elements of his surgical sensualities by the handful. All of them sacrificed themselves delightedly, all those virgins offering their sacred viscera to their Supreme Lover. So why did he judge, at present, the inanity of his work? Why was he weeping, with long sobs that the chasm repeated? Why did he see, beyond his present thoughts, a great void, a nothingness, into which he felt that his reason was about to sink?

Suddenly, lucidly, the reason surged from his mind. A phantasm, looming up in front of him, led him to it. A woman, emerging from a halo, came into the impregnable lair. Prostrate on the table, he watched her advance, divinely beautiful in her nudity, her arms folded over her bosom, her long-lashed eyelids adorably veiling the purity of her dark eyes.

What virgin had ever been more desirable? What breasts had ever translated more splendidly the vigor of a race? What flesh had ever possessed such solar reflections, beneath the tumble of golden hair? The perfection of nature had never been more sincerely expressed.

She was still advancing toward him, magnificently serene and chaste.

"O virgin among virgins!" he stammered. "Here you are, at last, then! Look! I was waiting for you. I'm trembling on seeing you appear—for no courtesan in my realm, no fecund mother, has your regal gait, nor your heavenly smile! Yes, you really are the foremost virgin in the world, as I am the foremost Pasteur. I have chosen you above all, as distant from Passion as any creature of heart could be, and I have impregnated you with my bewitching inspirations of Voluptuousness!

O magnificent enemy! In your flesh, rival nature triumphed over my magic; and I only ended up making you love a man, you whom I wanted unpolluted by a man but possessed by my courtesans, raised by them to the diapason of virginal erethism, which alone inspires my intoxication! Yes, nature rebelled in you. And now here you are, my slave, tamed by my science of Happiness, ready to surrender yourself to me!"

Gasping, his face filled with desire, he knelt down, and kissed the feet of the woman he had seen advancing, which he touched delightedly. Then, having stood up, with his two powerful arms disposed in arcs, he lifted her up and carried her like a trophy of love to his operating table.

He seized the hilt of a sharp scalpel, and he was about to plunge the steel into that divine pallor in order to deliver himself the supreme sensuality when an unknown force suddenly paralyzed his arm. At the same time, he heard a loud clamor made by a thousand distant voices, a thousand protests from beyond the grave, rise up behind him, in the enormous solitude of the lair...

Who, then, dared to infringe the law and cross the threshold of his cavern? Who, then, dared to protest?

Gripped by a vague anxiety he turned round, murmuring; "Me, Caresco! Me, the Superman! Me! Someone is permitting themselves..."

What he saw then nailed him to the spot with stupor. The cadavers contained in the jars had suddenly disengaged themselves from their flaccid immobility. They were advancing toward him, horrible and comical, causing their grimaces to move, their rictuses, their violet-tinted wounds, their caved-in skulls, their open bellies, their overflowing viscera, their dissected limbs. They were not walking; they seemed rather to be gliding, undulating, as if they had conserved, over the ground, the indecisive buoyancy of their submersion.

All of them were out, all those to whom he had been talking a few minutes ago, including Fabienne, a flap of whose abdomen fell back over the plump ivory of her buttocks, and Druant, whose gaping mouth was almost covered by sticky red hair. There were even portions of limbs and organs, detached shreds, hands and feet with jutting tendons, a toothless jaw, spongy spleens, polished and gleaming livers, extraordinarily interlaced and clicking bones, which were following the movement, also advancing, hopping along. One more adventurous heart, bouncing like a rubber ball, brushed the surgeon, whistling.

Stupefied, he gazed at that fantastic invasion, buzzing, grating and squeaking, whose circle was getting tighter and tighter, and swelling, piling up all the way to the vault, so many subjects were there, all the way to the shady flue of the central chimney.

"Indeed! Are you going mad?"

He laughed. But immediately, he shivered at the idea that perhaps he was sinking into madness. In any case, the interest of the macabre spectacle immediately gripped him again. Wanting to know whether these resuscitated individuals were enemies, or whether they were drawing closer in order to examine his magnificent rape at closer range, he winked at Fabienne to make her smile, for he had noticed the darkening of her expression.

But Fabienne, pointing at the virginal body lying on the sacrificial table, protested: "Do you dare to soil that abdomen too? You have no right to that foreigner! She is sacred to you! She is ennobled by the purest transports of the soul, by an ideal that you do not know, that your cruelty prevents you even from conceiving. She is Good, Honesty, Heroism, Purity—all splendors of which you are ignorant, which you did not think it necessary to impose on your people, which you, yourself, have trodden underfoot throughout your life. She is impregnable! She is holy! I forbid you to touch her, disemboweler!"

Caresco shrugged his shoulders. That dissected whore was truly grotesque, wanting to preach morality and breach the omnipotence of a man like him! Impatient at being delayed so long, therefore, he was about to plunge his scalpel when Druant spoke in his turn. The sounds escaped lugubriously from his mouth, the lips of which did not move.

"All, then? You want them all? But that one defies you! She is inviolable, and our desire—that of your victims—is that you respect her! You shall not profane that virginal flesh, which your maleficia have been unable to trouble, but which is too white to retain the trace of soiling. You shall not touch her: we forbid it!"

A little sputum came to flow from the surgeon's lips; their corners parted as the chops of a ferocious animal part to reveal the cruelty of pointed fangs prompt to rip. In sum, all those ridiculously resuscitated cadavers were annoying him. He pulled his head back between his shoulders, preparing to pounce on them and bowl them over. His propelled foot, aimed at Druant's flaccidity, encountered nothing but emptiness, and its momentum nearly caused him to fall to the ground, under the laughter of all the gaping mouths, all the wounds, of all that violet flesh.

"Damn! I'll kill! I'll kill!"

He started whirling round, brandishing his scalpel, all the horrors of dementia engraved on his face, his eyes exorbitant, the sinews and veins of his neck stretching as if to snap. But a sideways glance at the virgin caused him to go pale, and he rediscovered, running from head to toe, the same frisson of terror that he had felt once before, at the beginning of his career, when he saw a patient die during the deed: a frisson that his indifference had not allowed to recur thereafter.

The foreigner's body was still lying on the shiny table, but life had fled therefrom with a lightning rapidity, accomplishing in ten seconds the regression of ten months of withering.

First, it was the face that blanched; its adorable contours melted into a waxy thinness, the cheekbones appeared, the arcs of the jaw became more pronounces. Then the body followed that incredible decrepitude. The jutting of the clavicles described two dark holes; the torso shriveled, with the ribs traced in black. The breasts hung down, reduced to two limp pockets. The hips hollowed out into notches; the legs were no more than bones sheathed in tanned skin. At the same time, the coloration of the face was further modified, passing from yellow to livid. Soon, the eyes, revulsed in an abysmal agony, were not brightening anything but a skeleton.

Caresco roared! Death, then, was stronger than he was! Death was not obedient to his omnipotence, as life had obeyed him! And that marvelous flesh, which his sadism coveted, was evaporating thus, without him being able to enjoy it!

He gazed at the abdomen. It was no longer anything but a cavity held by a rigid and dull membrane. In a moment, decomposition would commence its work in its turn, putrefying that source of divine sensuality, introducing its abominable swarmings there, where temptation radiated. But he had to hurry, then! Let him hasten to extract what intoxication that he could still obtain!

With a cry of lust, he raised his scalpel furiously and brought it down on the lascivious region. His instrument, encountering the cold table, twisted. The metal uttered a plaint. Blood ran.

The sight of the blood astonished Caresco as if it were something impossible. Instinctively, he compressed the vessel that was yielding it, and convinced himself scientifically of the benignity of his wound.

And that bleeding was salutary. Freed from his hallucination, he breathed deeply. A weight had been removed with the red liquid. On raising his eyes, he saw that things had resumed their familiar aspect. In the display-cases, the cadavers, the anatomical specimens, were dangling hideously; Fabienne was still smiling; and Druant's mouth, frightfully open, was crowned with sticky red hair.

On the table, though, was the bent scalpel, and on his wrist, the trickle of blood.

What had he seen, then? What had he heard? Where had those images, and those voices, come from?

Panting, he raised his arms in the air. "I'm going mad! I'm going mad!"

He took a few steps toward the bed, and sank down on it, sobbing.

"I'm no longer the Superman!" his voice howled, immensely reverberated by the unruly echoes of the lair. "I'm a man…a madman!"

With the promptitude of transformation that was characteristic of his extraordinary brain, however, he immediately pulled himself together. Standing up, he shook himself. His neck retreated into his shoulders as he prepared to pounce. He thought hard. Figures, calculations and hieroglyphs seethed intensely in his skull. An enthusiasm illuminated him.

"The formula! O splendor of my genius! I've found the formula!"

A great enlightenment had suddenly revealed a new world. The formula for an aphrodisiac fluid, for which he had been searching for years, blazed forth on the blackboard of his dolor. Quickly! He had to realize it! He had to throw it as fodder to his scientists! All the crucibles in his empire had to be prepared, to recommence combining his omnium! And in a fortnight, the virgin, definitely defeated, a slave to lust, tormented by passion, would become his queen!

"Nature, O Nature! Three times you have held me at bay! Well, I defy you more than ever!"

# CHAPTER XIX

Choumaque hastened toward the Palace of the Heart, where Caresco had commanded a meeting. Assuming that the Superman did not like to wait, he ran, observing with joy now easily his articulations moved, how effortlessly his respiration supported the effort demanded of it. With one arm folded against the thorax, in conformity with the prescriptions of the gymnastics monitor, the other hitching up his belt to satisfy his inveterate mania, he was about to reach the great red façade when the muffled sound of wheels, which seemed to have attached themselves to his footsteps a few moments ago, caused him to look round.

If the object following him had not been placed on a pedestal he would never have recognized the mechanical man. The face of the half-man did not resemble the one he remembered at all. In fact, nothing could be distinguished now but a kind of aluminum cage vaguely adopting a human shape.

"Eh! But it's the captain!" he risked.

"Himself, Monsieur Choumaque. I see with pleasure that you've recognized me, even though a slight transformation has been carried out in my physiognomy by the Superman."

"To tell the truth, it does seem to me..."

"It ought not to *seem* to you. It's a certain thing. The divine Caresco has taken pity on me and has favored me with a marvelous operation. This cage that you see placed on my head replaces the various items of apparatus that were still juxtaposed there a fortnight ago. It is an integral part of my being; it multiplies my sight and hearing tenfold; it replaces both jaws, my tongue and my larynx. As for the sense of smell, let's not talk about it—it's superfluous. Have you noticed how powerful my voice is?"

"I confess that you're thundering, Reply to me sincerely, though, Captain: you must be horribly uncomfortable in there?"

"I've never been so much at ease."

"With the result that you still consider yourself the happiest man…forgive me, did I say man?...I mean the happiest individual in the realm?"

"I should think so! That's the twenty-fourth time he's opened me up."

"It seems to me," observed Choumaque, "that if your anatomy resembles a strong-box, your mind, on the contrary, is the very opposite of a financier's. The more that is stolen from you, the more satisfied you are."

"It's so good to allow someone one adores to take!" avowed the dwarf, introducing inside his mask the back-scratcher that he was holding in his only hand, in order to calm the itching of a scar.

On these reflections, they arrived at a large circular space occupied at the center by a vast recently-built chimney, the foundations of which penetrated to a depth of three hundred meters, which rose to some sixty feet above the ground, following the trajectory of a semicircular curve. From the open summit of that masonry, a metal tube with a radius of ten meters emerged, ablaze with the caress of the sun.

Before Choumaque had time to ask what this new invention was, the clamors uttered by the scientists assembled in the place welcomed the arrival of the Superman. The latter passed through the middle of two violet rows of prostrated bodies, his eyes proud, his expression smiling and his gestures astonishingly animated, with an attitude of exceptional satisfaction. As soon as he perceived Choumaque he beckoned to him to approach. Interrupting the pirouettes with which the philosopher was honoring him, he drew him closer to him and kissed him on the cheeks.

"I'm delighted that you've come, philosopher. During the month you've been in Eucrasia, I've scarcely seen you. However, you interest me, like every new puppet of the old world that I attach to my keyboard. Tell me, are you glad to be here?"

"I can let myself live here."

"That's the ticket. And your companion, the mariner?"

"Oh! Him..."

"And the foreigner, Miss Mary?"

"I dare not be as affirmative in that respect."

The Superman had taken Choumaque's arm, and, while chatting, drew him toward the entrance to the block of masonry. The philosopher, astonished by that graciousness, listened to the approving and slightly jealous murmurs with which the bearded violet-clad population was following them.

"I believe, in fact," the potentate continued, "that the young Redlander is less seduced than the two of you. My psychometer, placed on her temples yesterday by Carabella, revealed that after reaching seventy-six, she has now declined to fifty. Fifty is the figure that ordinary happiness gives—normal love, the love she experiences for the Sower, But wait a little, philosopher! Wait...I'll let her rest for the moment, while a little trick of my own is being prepared for her. Then you'll see! Just be patient..."

He concluded his confidences with a trenchant gesture that expressed the fate reserved for the foreigner. Choumaque shivered. The bloody doll came back to his mind's eye. The words he had just heard revealed the Superman's previous attempts, at least one of which had unfolded and gone awry before his eyes. They also confirmed his latent madness. Thus, the situation became clearer, and Caresco's projects were revealed in all their fantastic horror.

Once Miss Mary was reduced to the common mentality by the dissolving action of secret methods, vibrating at the same pitch of morality as all the other creatures on the island, the Superman would possess her, in the only fashion that permitted him to experience the joys of amour. He would sacrifice her with all the more intoxication because he would imagine that he was bringing a supreme tribute to his humanitarian dream, to his insensate conception of creating happiness by means of science trampling nature.

And that perspective, independently of the threat it posed to the young people, revolted Choumaque's doctrine.

It was under the empire of that emotion that he allowed himself to be led to the elevator set behind a heap of stones that no one had had time to clear away. It was dark, and damp air currents, coming from the recent construction, proved that the services, too pressed for time, had not yet regulated the lighting and the temperature. The neophyte became anxious.

"May I know where you're taking me, Superman?"

"I'm taking you on a rather interesting little voyage, and I beg to observe he honor that I'm doing you. You're going with me to visit the region of the Ankle, where my slaves live."

"The *cheville ouvrière*, then," said Choumaque, whose wit had not lost its rights.[22]

His quip flowed past the Superman's inattention; the latter continued: "Your philosophy will have reason for disquiet. You'll see how happy I've made individuals whose destiny elsewhere is to suffer."

"Are you sure that we're going the right way? I can no longer see clearly. I'm stumbling over stones. Don't you have a match?"

"A match, in the land of light!"

"In truth, I think that would be appropriate to the occasion."

"A match, when I'm going to take you on a journey at a hundred kilometers a second!"

"How many did you say?"

"I said a hundred, and I'm not joking. This morning, we're inaugurating my new means of transport. You're going

---

[22] "*Cheville ouvrière*," can be translated as "kingpin," but carries other implications that sustain Choumaque's pun; *ouvrière*, construed as a noun rather than an adjective, means "working girl"—a euphemism that carries the same implication of prostitution as it does in English—while *cheville* means "ankle," and in 1904, the display of a young woman's ankle was still considered daring, and marginally indecent.

to sit down comfortably in a cannonball, which my omnial force will propel at a hitherto-unknown velocity..."

"And it's an inauguration! Oh my God!"

"Don't invoke the Other!" the Superman objected, in the darkness. "The Other has never invented such a velocity. His bolides are tortoises compared with my bullet-cabin! God, that's me!"

As a chill invaded his forehead, Choumaque thought that he was sweating in fear. He had heard mention of the failure of a similar experiment attempted previously, and he would not have given ten centimes for the life of the creator of the doctrine of equilibria. His companion had introduced him into the elevator, which was engulfed in absolute obscurity. At the bottom of the abyss, a glimmer of light appeared, guiding them to a luxurious cage placed in the interior orifice of a large metal tube—the cannon.

Before going into it, the philosopher, veritably panicking, protested: "Do you really need me, Superman? Couldn't you make the voyage alone?"

"You're scared?"

"Scared? No, it's not so much that I'm scared, because courage is an entirely relative thing. To have courage is to dare to confront certain danger. The Greeks at Marathon, Henri IV under his white flag, Napoléon before the bridge at Arcole, had courage. Me, I have no need of it. Since I'm traveling in your company, no danger can exist. Of that I'm quite convinced. I add that for the sage, true courage consists, not in considering contrary events with an eye that doesn't blink, but in steeping one's soul constantly in the commerce of virtue..."

"Enough talk—let's go!" said the Superman, grabbing him by the neck and throwing him, chilled by fear, on to the soft cushions of the bullet-cabin.

What was happening was becoming so extraordinary and was accomplished with such rapidity that Choumaque scarcely had time to perceive it. A partition came down, blocking the cage. Calmly, Caresco pressed a button. A mighty explosion, like the shattering of a world, tore their eardrums. Then there was a flash, in which all the intensity of the firmament was concentrated. Finally, a scarcely-perceptible shock, felt in a new obscurity, indicated that the machine was at its destination.

"Well, what do you say to that, philosopher?" the potentate exulted, slapping Choumaque repeatedly, in order to bring him out of a faint.

"For the moment," stammered the philosopher, "I can no longer find anything to say."

After such a shock, the rest of the excursion could no longer present any real interest. Nevertheless, Caresco, without paying any heed to the neophyte's amazement, obligingly showed him the region of slaves.

The men there were former gitons who had aged internally, the women courtesans unusable as objects of lust. They lived in the atony particular to those deprived of reproductive qualities, very hygienically, in the midst of sumptuous palaces, their desires almost extinct, no longer even having the strength to make love to one another. Draped in yellow costumes embroidered with the symbolic cross, their flesh incomplete, under an appearance that make-up and tonic fluids rendered young, they dragged themselves around languidly all day long. They played knucklebones and feminine games, only disturbing themselves from time to time in response to a request for service, to which they devoted themselves indolently.

Caresco took the trouble to get them to talk, interrogating them about their sentiments, making them confess their hope in metempsychosis, extracting from them the confession of a happiness that Choumaque knew perfectly well to be non-existent, since it was the expression of a passionate neutrality—but the philosopher no longer had the energy to protest.

And already they were leaving, in order to return by means of the pneumatic tube.

They were following a little path framed by verdure when an unexpected encounter immobilized them. Collapsed on the edge of the path was the body of a slave, seemingly asleep. His arm, folded over his head, did not prevent them from perceiving a frightfully livid face, from which a greenish fluid was escaping.

At that spectacle, Caresco's physiognomy was struck by an indescribable stupefaction. "What? What's this? Can it be...it's impossible!"

He bent over the slave, and moved the arm relaxed by recent death—and the more he filled himself with the vision of that tumefied and pustulent face, the harder his alarmed faculties tried to resist the reality of a diagnosis.

"But it's...the plague! It's the plague!"

Horrified, Choumaque had taken a step back in order to escape. Seized by the shoulder, he was obliged to remain and witness the manifestations of the surprise and the fury that were throwing the mind of the potentate into confusion.

"The plague! It's unprecedented! Can you imagine that, philosopher? The plague, in my realm! Microbes in my giant State! The evils of nature in my supernatural country! It's stupid! It's not true! The plague! The plague!"

He drew him away, howling that formidably frightening word. His howls increased when, further on, they encountered the body of a second slave, and then a third, then ten, then twenty, and then a hundred, lined up among the path. The Superman's delirium increased with each discovery.

"The plague! The plague! Oh, Choumaque, can you believe it? Will nature be stronger than me? Will I be vanquished? Are you not God, then, Caresco? The Other is demolishing you, is breaking you, Caresco!"

His eyes haggard, he was fleeing now, muttering insults. However, his excitement suddenly died away when he had taken his place in the tube. After having completed the journey in an intense meditation, he took Choumaque to the Palace of Hygiene, and, having made him take off his garments while he undressed himself, he put him to sleep in order to pass him through a steam-bath and inoculate him with all sorts of serums. He submitted himself to the same treatments.

On the evening of that memorable day, however, the people, summoned to a hilltop, were able to witness an admirable spectacle. A colossal flame burst forth in the region of the Ankle, which had be isolated for several hours by a sanitary cordon. With choirs, music, and acts of grace, a universal intoxication celebrated the bounty of the Superman, who had thus enabled two thousand of his subjects to progress at a stroke toward the superior state of metempsychosis.

Those slaves who had not had the good fortune to be at the nucleus of the outbreak, and who had not been able to return there, lamented not being burned with their brothers and sisters in servitude. Their grief was the only shadow that tarnished the joy of the unexpected fête.

# CHAPTER XX

Choumaque spent all night battling insomnia. He had thought about going to apply his temples to the source of soporific fluid with which the utilities panel was equipped, but that artificial means of appeasing the inclemency of the natural was only half-pleasing; he preferred to get up, to drape himself in a handy peplum and go out on to the terrace outside his room, to await the dawn patiently.

The pure air did him good. The breeze, cooling his brow, dissipated the anxieties that had been agitating him dully all night. He leaned his elbows on the perforated balcony and watched the triumphal blossoming of the pre-dawn light. Beneath him, in the shadow, chaos still subsisted; nothing emerged therefrom—neither the distant Palace of the Face, nor the great specters of the crowns of the trees, nor the amorous block of interlaced rocks.

Above him, however, the firmament already formed a livid vault in which the last vacillations of the stars were struggling. One more resistant star exhausted itself attempting to continue its glow. One might have thought that the dawn, blowing on it, were reanimating its death-throes. Then, all of a sudden, it vanished, drowned in the sea of light that was visibly winning, and which soon swelled into immense mauve stripes, iridescent currents, like horizontal red ribbons knotting the two ends of the world. A golden dome burst forth, and all vegetable force was enthused.

In that celestial magnificence, a little airplane appeared. It had the form of a seabird holding the threads of a nacelle in its beak, in which two people were outlined. Choumaque recognized the beard of a sterile husband and the blue costume of a fecund mother. He hailed them as they passed overhead:

"Greetings, flyers! You're up early, worthy spouses."

"We haven't been to bed, philosopher. We've been up all night with Mirror-of-Smiles. We owe him that."

"Is Mirror-of-Smiles ill, then?"

But they did not reply; the airplane was already too far away. Choumaque assumed that they had been engaged in some legitimate debauchery, shrugged his shoulders and went in to get dressed.

An hour later he was pacing up and down under the peristyle of a small green sandstone temple. A gap between red porphyry columns brought an overt and immeasurably developed femininity to its frontispiece. Edified in the confines of the Sterility, set apart from any other kind of habitation, the temple was the residence of the High Priestess Môme. One reached it after traversing paths bordered with jasmine and rose bushes, delimiting transparent lakes where the calices and leaves of lotuses lay dormant.

Marius had spent the night there, and it was him for whom Choumaque was waiting. Since their encounter, the two old friends had become inseparable again. The object of their past dissent, Madame Môme, now formed the most solid link of their fraternity. They shared her.

Every second night it was Choumaque who climbed the steps of the little temple, assured of immediately finding the caress of odorous arms to welcome him. He had no wish to reproach his mistress for having granted Marius the same favor the previous night. Môme devoted all the minutes of the day to them when she was not absorbed by her apostolate and was able to go with them on long excursions, visits to forgotten corners of the island, sometimes accompanied by Marcel and Miss Mary. One might have thought that the mild communism had always existed, so easily had it become banal custom.

In the beginning, Choumaque had certainly found the unprecedented in the pleasures that the High Priestess lavished on him to the point of satiety. She had initiated him into all the mysteries of Venus. But after ten sessions, as instructive as they were ardent, he had begun to accept the accomplishment of those rites with a more moderate impulsion. He felt quite disorientated to observe that the great vital mechanism of the island extended its components all the way to the alcove. He experienced the feeling that his personality had been diminished, and sometimes, as he emerged from those comfortable intoxications, scratching his loins, he regretted the times when, in a situation of similar division, jealousy would have bitten his heart and exasperated the impetuosity of his kisses.

Every morning, however, the two friends met up. Marius, less discreet, generally went to surprise the lovers in bed. He enquired about their night, and permitted himself, while joking, a few petty liberties with Madame Môme's person. He pinched her in sensitive places, and administered joyful slaps on the buttocks. The High Priestess responded with a few delicate locutions, or playfully threw ampoules of odor at the painter's head, which burst in a salvo, prompting him to turn somersaults.

When they had calmed down, they chatted, while swallowing balls of complete aliment, washing them down with wine aromatized by exquisite and unfamiliar essences. Then, having completed the meal taken on the edge of the bed, the courtesan commenced her toilette. Both of them admired the constant youth of her body as she plunged into the perfumed basin, the natural transparency of her transplanted teeth, the abundance of her rich tresses enriched by new growth with gilded glints, and the serenity of her features, replastered by the fluid of beauty, without a wrinkle or a fissure.

If it had not been for the antiquity of their gazes, they would never have been able to believe that their combined ages were nearly a hundred and seventy years.

Choumaque more reserved, did not go into the lovers' dwelling in the morning. He waited at the door, in front of the charming panorama. He did not waste his time, though; he found material to content his curiosity. The courtesans' villas commenced their alignment not far away. Their style and their variety delighted him. The first rays of sunlight bathed them with a particular poetry in their frame of greenery and flowers. The great velvet curtains were lifted up in front of the atria, initially to give passage to domestic animals, and then to beau-

tiful young women, who stretched lazily, and kissed the noc-
turnal companions to whom they were bidding farewell voluptuously. They were alert gitons, or sterile spouses with long
curly beards, strong and powerful in their languid indolence,
or even fecund mothers, whose silky peplums opened slightly
to allow a glimpse of their blue tunics, unstigmatized by the
red stripes of the courtesans. Airplanes took away all those
lovers, mingling them with the aerial circulation that was very
active at that moment, steering them toward other pleasures—
or rather, other indifferences.

Finally, Marius appeared, finishing pinning the golden
clasp to his shoulder that maintained an unusual mantle.

"Hello there, Choumaque!"

He was clad, exceptionally, in a violet moiré toga, hiding
a doublet of the same color belted with white velvet and studded with gems He came down the steps of the peristyle in a
noble fashion and embraced the philosopher.

"I'm glad to see you."

Choumaque confessed an equal satisfaction, and enquired about their mistress. Was she still young and pretty?
Had she been, as usual, ardent in dalliance?

At those questions, Marius; expression darkened. "Well,
obviously—but between us, old chap, I confess that it wearies
me slightly. She's indefatigable, that tamer of my loins!"

"You're too happy, Marius. The heavens of your bed,
like the real heavens, are always too clement to your desires.
In Eucrasia, the women are too beautiful, awakenings too perfumed, the countryside too cheerful, health too perfect, and
everything too compliant."

"Don't say that, orator. Wait, before pronouncing judgment, until you're habituated to our ways. You'll see that we
are, in fact..."

"Too happy?"

"Even so..."

The philosopher shook his head. For the moment, however, he had at least one grave preoccupation that could, by
opposition, make him aware of the price of the real happiness

that would ensue if ever the threat suspended over Marcel and Miss Mary were dissipated. Having told Marius about the love of the two young people, and also the conversations he had had with the Superman, he had enquired about the possible outcomes. What would be the foreigner's fate? Might she not be taken to the table of immolation in spite of the promise of neutrality that should have protected her for the duration of her sojourn?

The frightful scene that Choumaque had witnessed, the flesh profaned, the blood shed, the insensate actions of the sacrificer, and the kind of perverted eroticism that the surgeon had given to the spectacle at the moment when he adored the extracted organ, all haunting the philosopher's unquiet mind like the fiction of a bad dream, had made him insist that Marius request the simple advice of their mistress. He had obtained the promise of a request made discreetly, in a whisper, for the walls, and even the furniture, in this ingenious country were so cleverly equipped with recording devices that it was almost necessary to speak in sign language—and one could not even be sure that confidence emitted by mime would not be captured by marvelous machines that would subsequently transmit them to Caresco.

So, that day, after a brief excursion, arm in arm, when the philosopher was firmly convinced that only the trees and the flowers could be witnesses to their intimacy, he leaned toward Marius' ear. "Well, what have you done about our young lovers? Have you asked our beautiful friend?"

"Shh!" murmured the painter. Don't speak so loudly! Do you have to shout? One interrogates more intelligently, damn it! Of course I've asked. I'm your brother, aren't I?"

"What did she say?"

"The divine Môme replied that there's only one means of putting the Superman off Miss Mary, and that's if she were no longer a virgin. That's up to Marcel to arrange."

"Virginity," Choumaque professed, "is a matter of elastic appreciation, if I might put it like that. How does one divine, from the mere silhouette of a demoiselle, whether she still possesses it? It's not as plain as the nose on her face, I imagine!"

Marius shrugged his shoulders. "That's an underestimation of our great man's resources of investigation, old chap, and to suppose that he has launched himself on a trail unworthy of his little foible..."

"Foible is an entirely appropriate term. So, how does the Superman know?"

The renovator of frescos leaned toward his friend far enough to brush his ear with his lips. "Know, my darling, that there are exceedingly well-organized archives in Eucrasia, in which the anatomical dossiers of every subject are catalogued, obtained by means of the omnial radiograph. When new subjects enter the realm, on the very first night, while they're asleep and without their suspecting it, photographs are taken, all the way the most intimate folds of their being, and immediately recorded. That experiment is repeated every week, for sanitary reasons."

"Bah!"

"Now, the Chief Radiographer, who is a great scientist and a friend of mine, confided to me yesterday evening the unfortunate continued innocence of Miss Mary."

Choumaque fixed his stare upon Marius' hairy head, which was ornamented by a violet beret from which a white silk tassel emerged. He would have liked to pierce those tresses, and then the skull, in order to search for the truth in the cerebral substance. To be sure, after so many marvelous surprises, the philosopher no longer had any reason to be astonished by a further eccentricity of social regimentation. On the other hand, Marius, a worthy child of the south, was endowed with such a fertile imagination that one had to wonder whether that declaration might not simply be the fruit of his fecund fantasy.

"In that case, let's await events," he concluded, letting go of his friend's arm, which the confidence had caused him to grip harder.

"Let's at least await today's event, of which you seem to have no suspicion, since your costume is the same as any other day. Haven't you noticed that all the men are wearing white belts over their tunics and that white also appears in their headgear? Today, similarly, the gitons who are the heroes of the celebration will be dressed entirely in white..."

"What celebration are you talking about?"

"Mirror-of-Smiles' funeral. If you need more ample information, ask that giton passing by. You'll understand the psychology of those people better than via my mouth."

An adorable adolescent was advancing through the flowers of the silky meadow. He was murmuring a gracious song that Choumaque had heard sung in chorus many times by groups of airborne musicians, and whose melody, compared with the stupid popular refrains of the country that the philosopher had just abandoned, was particularly captivating. His delicately vigorous torso was expanding in a white doublet, split from the neck to the heart, which came down to the knees in the fashion of a pleated tunic, decorated with a vertical red stripe, the symbol of asexualization. His wavy blond hair was crowned with a number of large lilies with a becoming pallor. He leaned over periodically toward the prettiest flowers and picked them in order to gather them into posies.

Choumaque went over to him. "Well, child, you're looking very handsome and joyful today!"

"Is it not a day of celebration for us, philosopher? We're celebrating the funeral of Mirror-of-Smiles, my brother before the Superman..."

"He's dead, then?"

"Yes. He's very happy. He's progressing toward the better life. Tomorrow, perhaps, his metempsychotic state will emerge from sleep, so that, reborn from the loins of a fecund mother, he will become a being superior to the one he was."

"But what has happened to Mirror-of-Smiles? I thought that no one died in this land, any more than anyone grows old?"

"Indeed, philosopher, one does not die. One disappears one day, without anyone knowing how, probably because it pleases the Superman that one disappears…but Mirror-of-Smiles has had the good fortune to fall out of his airplane and break his back. When the Superman reached him, he observed immediately, so badly broken was by brother, that there was no possibility of saving him, and he administered the *coup de grâce*."

"Did the child suffer?"

"Suffer?" The boy raised his wide eyes, full of astonished interrogation. He did not understand the meaning of the word. Choumaque remembered that all the people were equally ignorant. In any case, the drama had passed in the greatest mystery, the subjects having received the instruction, when such an event occurred, to flee the accident without rendering assistance. Only Caresco was to intervene."

"So, giton, you envy Mirror's fate?"

"Who would not envy it?"

"But you've never thought of assisting such a favorable event by letting yourself fall from an airplane, like him?"

"No, I've never thought of that."

"His mentality doesn't extend that far..." Choumaque murmured.

The adolescent passed by without even offering his candid vice, so intent was he on his flower-picking. Choumaque and Marius heard him resume his song.

*That*, the philosopher said to himself, *is the most admirable example of the sybaritic fatalism imposed by Caresco's malice on intelligent creatures. The idea of death that haunts the human soul with so much fear in other lands, which imposes so many discouragements or superb hopes, is welcomed here with the confident serenity with which the early Christians, Muslims, Buddhists and all peoples of primitive conceptions accepted, and still accept, paradisal superstition.*

*I believe I can divine Caresco's strategy. He would like to regress his creatures to the rudimentary sensibility of animals, vegetables, and perhaps even things, since it has been discovered that things also have their sensibility. Doubtless that's the motive that has driven him to attempt his human monad, and I can't refuse it an appearance of reason. It's evident that people suffer by virtue of their exasperated sensibility—but on the other hand, do they not benefit from a proportionate joy, as my doctrine of equilibria says?*

*Caresco has, therefore, had this madman's dream, consisting of returning humans to their state of original insensibility, to the state of indifference that must have been the lot of primitive humans. Because it will require several generations, he's imposed this faith in a future life—which is certainly a powerful means of domination, independently of the others he possesses.*

*What a strange paradox that man is, undoubtedly ferocious, who poses as a benefactor of his people to the point of wanting to reduce them to the mentality of brutes! Who can give me an explanation of that extravagance? Is it not better to believe that I'm simply dealing with a great mental imbalance, which has created and innovated a social theory with the sole motive of being able to satisfy at his leisure his mania for disemboweling?*

Suspended between all these suppositions, Choumaque was no longer listening to his friend, who was waxing lyrical in pompous descriptions of the spectacle that they were about to witness. Marius had to lead him to the pneumatic tube and help him to modify his costume. In a nearby house they found a white moiré scarf, with which the philosopher girdled his loins.

The ceremony was held on the Field of Truce near the Caravanserai. A mass movement of picturesque crowds was heading in that direction. They completed the journey in the company of twenty courtesans who declared that they were fond of funerals and praised the merits of Mirror-of-Smiles, whose caresses had been artful. Unselfconsciously, like excited animals, they recounted intimate details; they laughed as they activated the mechanisms of their perfume-sacs, while arranging their mourning coiffure, sown with irises and pow-dered with silver.

One of them, who had attended the philosopher's lecture, brazenly confessed the scant pleasure that she had obtained therefrom. Furthermore, she was not alone in that opinion, since all the attendees had promised that they would not come back to yawn at such nonsense. Perceiving that Choumaque had a mediocre appetite for frankness, however, the obliging girl strove to seduce him. She did not succeed, even though, for the sake of temptation, she loosened the fastenings of her tunic to uncover the rigidity of her breasts and the red line on her firm belly.

They headed for a bright patch among the immense ce-dars. It was a clearing in which, perched on a small mound, they were better able to see the cortege file past. The crowd was already massing along the entire route, and they quickly recognized, by the colors of the costumes, that all the classes of society were present. Their noses in the air and eyes wide open, chatting, laughing and larking about, the people waited, on the slope, for the gaudy procession to pass, enameled by dazzling decorations.

The irregulars—mauve-clad courtesans, white-clad gitons and slaves in yellow costumes decorated with snowy brain—had priority over families today. They were in the front rows, while the husbands and fecund mothers, virgins, adoles-cents and Sowers, held back. Marius, consulted, confirmed that it was the dictate of the law. Did not those creatures of pleasure and servitude have a right to the best places, since it was one of their own that the fête was honoring?

In any case, the harmony was perfect and universal. Bas-kets of glazed fruits and candied preserves were passed around and emptied. Canticles rose up, accompanied by musicians, languidly allowing their pink fingers to run over the strings of lyres and harps, waving sistrums and blowing with inflated cheeks into golden flutes. The long beards of sterile husbands shook gravely at every movement of the mouth, undulating over the red togas. Large white tuberoses were entwined in the silvered tresses of fecund mothers, and the breeze collected sweet perfumes therefrom. Courtesans, waving bunches of dahlias, sketched out a sacred dance. The delicate shape of their ankles, shod in bright sandals with mauve laces, was revealed at every step as light tulle took flight. Airplanes arrived, even more vibrant with music, hymns of praise to Caresco, pouring out of their sparkling polychromy.

One entire hillside was occupied by engineers, scientists and artists, disposed in accordance with the rectitude of a violet band. Less care in adornment was noticeable there; some of them, in pushing up their sleeves, revealed dirty hands. Like Marius and Choumaque, they were former inhabitants of the old world attracted by the Superman, and endowed by him with a usurpation of youth betrayed by the weariness of their gaze. The frivolity evident in the others was only apparent in them. However, they did not disdain all the favors of their new fatherland, for their illuminated eyes coveted the bodies of the dancers. One of them drew a courtesan behind a curtain of trees.

In the background, the monstrous group of rocks, the mountainous embrace in human form, was outlined in a warm mist, indicated by a deeper blue shade at the base, rapidly evaporating in the splendid sunlight.

Choumaque perceived Marcel and Miss Mary lost in the crowd. He waved to them, and as they did not notice his gestures, Marius, less inhibited, executed an expansive entrechat, which provoked the joy of the crowd. People liked the whimsy of the former dauber; the diversion of his humor thrown into the universal tranquility. The neophytes came over, holding hands.

The gracious couple—Marcel's bold gaze and Herculean torso, and Miss Mary's pride—imposed admiration. Their love was becoming common knowledge, and people were astonished by it. People moved aside before them, and flowers were thrown at them. People sensed a respectable force passing by. A sterile spouse caressed the foreigner's hip with a hand laden with rings. A mother thanked the mariner for having gratified her with his useful caresses the day before. A courtesan offered them pastilles and loudly deplored the chastity of the foreigner.

Once out of the crowd, as soon as they arrived on the mound, where Marius embraced them, the young people were able to talk. They had not seen one another for four days, and that separation, in spite of the diversions constantly offered to them, and in which they were beginning to take an interest, had seemed long to their hearts.

"Your eyes are clouded, I see, Miss Mary."

"I divine less chagrin in yours, Monsieur Marcel."

"Why do you say that? Don't you trust me?"

"Can I trust someone who has already surrendered himself to fecund mothers?"

"I have to carry out my social obligations, alas."

Privately, Marcel admitted that the duty had been easily accomplished. Introduced some days previously into the Temple of Fecundity, having put on animal skins and drunk fresh milk in thatched cottages, he had, without sacrificing anything of his heart to the fecund mothers, since he was retaining it integrally for the foreigner, given everything of his body with such a facility and abundance that the Superman's prescription that he be charged with genetic serum at the first sign of weakness had not had to be put into effect.

Informed of that lack of necessity, Caresco had been surprised by it, and even a trifle offended. He had almost reproached the young man for that natural generosity, when it was necessary, in order to obtain the same results from other Sowers, to deploy all the resources of the inspirational science of embraces.

Miss Mary, kept up to date by Carabella, had at first secretly deplored the young Frenchman's inconstancy. Nevertheless, when she learned with what extraordinary folly she had thrown herself upon Choumaque on the evening of the submarine excursion, she imagined that Marcel was the victim of influences similar to the one that had carried her away, and she no longer harbored any resentment toward him, while being unable to liberate herself from a great sadness.

Now, she feared as much as her friend the fatality that would separate them. The temporary respite in which the Superman was maintaining her, while waiting for his scientists to manufacture the new sortilege whose formula he had found—a respite that was, in the midst of so much madness, the sage thought of a physician leaving the body free of any medicament in order to be able to act more intensively afterwards by means of a new remedy—that regression to fifty degrees of the psychometer had had the effect of bringing the fanaticism back to the normal passionate level of the old world, and directing toward Marcel her pertinent feminine aspirations.

So, it was with a seductive joy that she heard him continue: "Oh, look! See how marvelous this country is, how sweet the air is here, and nature eternally adorned. See how the caressant sun envelops it in the blaze of spring! Have you ever seen water so limpid, soil more favorable to the health of flowers? All of creation here has a soul of tranquility, peace and grace. Every bud that opens declares its charm; every creature born here is ignorant of bitterness! Listen to those people singing; observe their perpetual gentleness. Do they seem to be maltreated by their lot? Oh, say the word that will unite us forever! Disown the past that has wounded you! Change your future!"

"The Superman has said the same thing to me, Monsieur Marcel."

They were interrupted by the arrival of the procession. On the route traced by a trail of white roses and lilies, a yellow compactness arrived first. It was a hundred and fifty slaves, blowing into golden trumpets, hieratically raised. Then came lictors brandishing, at the fan-like tips of their long pikes, as many suns, the omnial light of which, radiating like braziers in the light of day, symbolized the eternal work of Science, of the power from which harmonious Life flowed.

They were followed by a mixed group of all subjects, spouses and mothers of families, adolescents, slaves, sowers, gitons and courtesans, in a rich variegation of peplums, tunics and doublets, their white-flowered hair flowing loosely over their impeccable forms. They were singing a hymn to the Superman, the benefactor and master of their destinies. Closely accompanied by their domestic animals, they were carrying on the plane of their thousand shoulders a vast nacreous shell, that one might have taken for the carapace of some fantastic sea-creature, and whose funnel, pouring out powerful chords that regulated and accompanied the songs, was a sizzling hearth on to which ten Vestals, admirable in their nudity, scarcely covered by a white vapor of tulle, threw still-twitching human virilities that a golden trident extracted from a bloody bowl. At each gesture of the armed limb, a dove took flight, symbolic of life born from death.

Behind them came a pell-mell of five hundred adolescent perfume-bearers, swarming, ablaze with jewels and precious metals. They were swinging green onyx incense-burners, whose aromatic spirals snaked toward the crowns of the tall trees, and were confused with the vault of foliage—and then with the purity of the heavens, when they reached the clearing.

A procession of courtesans followed them. Devoid of belts around their robes, their sandals allowing the sight of the perfection of lascivious legs, they were sitting or lying on wisps of floating cloud that had no point of contact with the ground. Their long mauve veils melted admirable into the azured spume, unmistakably real, of their mobile décor. Seen from below, the make-up of their eyelids stood out, violet, ardent and voluptuous. They were plucking stringed instruments and singing, or throwing perfumes and flowers to the people.

Above their cohesion, in celestial flight, two of them, ardently embracing, their breasts and rumps juxtaposed, were engaging in sterile caresses; and the white cloud of gitons following them reproduced the same tableau, soon effaced by the appearance of a more natural couple in which, with cries of joy, a young Sower and a fecund mother were celebrating generative sensuality with equal immodesty—all of that flowing in the melodious tumult of lyres, harps, flutes, sistrums and horns, before the verdure of the hillsides, beneath the azure backcloth of a deliciously blue firmament.

However, the people were watching without manifest curiosity, and Marcel, fearful of the affront of the spectacle to his companion, had to recognize that she did not turn her eyes away from it.

Now the symbols made their appearance. In a cohort of scantily-clad dancers, waving their strong arms rhythmically and aching their heavy torsos, an erect phallus and a parted femininity were evoked, two pink axes around which thousands of vibrions and ovules were spinning and circling, joining and separating, maintained in the air by the magnetic play of fluid. The fecundation of the individual, resulting from the communion of seminal cells, successive embryonic transformations, to the birth of the child—the entire rigorously exact mechanism of generation—was thus developed before the eyes of the spectators, in a hundred different phases, in a hundred successive aspects.

The result was that an insensible death served as a pretext for a celebration of life and its voluptuous exasperation. But when the people applauded frenziedly was when the sumptuous effigy of the Superman appeared, on a golden throne constellated with diamonds, carried by five hundred violet-clad scientists, his hand holding his carescoclast. He was aureoled by a dazzling nimbus of omnial light.

Ten thousand voices acclaimed him.

"I assure you," said Choumaque to Marius, "that this spectacle only causes me an entirely relative intellectual emotion."

"Wait! You haven't seen the best yet."

After the procession of all the gitons in the colony—who, under the guidance of Marjah, clad in white and gold, their hair decorated with huge lilies, were waving garlands of pale flowers to delightful effect—the "best" predicted by the artist was the appearance of Mirror-of-Smiles. One might have sworn that he was still alive, not even asleep, on seeing him pass languidly by, lying on his side, on a couch of saffron-colored silk embroidered with crimson, which an invisible mechanism maintained in the air at head-height.

His charming mischievous face, eyes candid with vice, had been made up in such a way as to render the complete illusion of health and life. Surrounded by familiar objects, his zither, his knucklebones, his jewelry, with one arm supporting the head with its undulations of bright blond, he seemed to be lost in a reverie, awaiting the pleasure of a sterile spouse or a lust-provoked courtesan. His body, repaired after the fall, the wounds closed and the limbs reattached, was nude, allowing the divination, at the intersection of the joined legs, of the pink delineation of the incomplete sex.

"But he's not dead!" exclaimed Choumaque.

"Yes he is, old man. He's looking at you without seeing you; listening to you without hearing you. He's simply admirably embalmed. You'll know why shortly."

The rite dictated that the dearest companions should be around the cadaver, sending him incense and throwing flowers. There were more thurible-bearers swinging their perfumed spirals, waving pennants, running, jumping on top of one another, stamping their feet, standing aside to kiss the child's pink toenails, exposed by his open-toed sandals. And directly behind, framed by two rows of slaves raising trumpets fulgurant in the sunlight, was the crowd of those who had loved the boy's caresses, Carabella in the front rank, ardent in her flowing brown hair; and sterile husbands with long beards falling in ringlets over their crimson togas; and fecund mothers, sumptuously draped in their veils constellated with topazes; and courtesans clad in light azured fabrics striped with the characteristic embroidery; and then the entire anonymous, polychromatic, sparkling, singing, dancing crowd of twenty thousand people joyfully accompanying Mirror-of-Smiles, the giver of intoxication, toward his new stage of perfection.

And the cortege ended with the evolutions of splendid bayaderes, animated by Madame Môme's commands; while, in the last place. Adolescent flute-players, slaves striking cymbals, accompanied with a concordant tumult the melody issuing from a cart full of musicians and drawn by thirty pairs of lions. Behind the cart, the crowd flocked, jostling, noisy and picturesque.

"Let's run to the Field of Truce now, in order to get a place near the funerary crypt," Marius said to his companions, content to have caught a kiss blown by the High Priestess.

They detached themselves from the mass and took a short cut, leaping over steams invested by golden moss. Marcel had not let go of Miss Mary's hand, which he felt more warmly applied to his own. As they were about to go into a delightfully spick and span avenue that bordered the funerary habitations, however, the lovers perceived that they had lost track of Marius and Choumaque. Marcel took advantage of that to turn his companion away from the cortege, the immodest vision of which was renewed at the bend in the road, in a tumult of people, clamors, songs, harmonies, flowers and perfumes. Tranquil nature seemed more captivating still to them.

Marius stopped Choumaque, who was nearly out of breath. They had arrived near the mausoleum dressed for the mortal remains of Mirror-of-Smiles, in a location that was still deserted. In the vicinity, a quantity of similar monuments surged forth over blocks of red rock, beneath magnificent shade, framed by fresh lawns diversified in places by orgies of flowers, as if the entire vegetal soul of the soil were exhaled there. Little lakes cluttered with lotuses received flashes of sunlight there and reflected them into the infinite silence.

"Look, old chap!" said Marius, embracing the décor with an enthusiastic gesture. "What Elysian Fields, where you can discuss philosophy gravely with the Shades!" Then he added: "Anyway, I haven't brought you here to advise you to die here so much as to initiate you into a further surprise. Do you know why Caresco, who is as scornful of dead flesh as he is of living flesh, has instituted these pompous funerals around a made-up cadaver? Why, instead of omnially pulverizing the useless remains of Mirror-of-Smiles and extracting its chemical ingredients—as he does with the majority of those who disappear—he insists on magnifying the death of gitons and courtesans who provide sensual pleasure? Wait, my darling, and you'll see…it's diabolically ingenious!"

He drew the philosopher to a splendidly lighted crypt into which they both penetrated—and what Choumaque saw there did, indeed, fill him with astonishment. A magnificent naked female body was displayed there, lying on a nacreous marble slab, set ablaze by the ivory reflections of two long golden candlesticks. The dead woman bore, in her extinct splendor, the same artificial life at which Mirror-of-Smiles had caused them to marvel a little while before. At her feet, which three steps permitted the attainment, an adolescent had just knelt down, and he was speaking softly, melodiously, reciting the most delightful loving phrases.

He undoubtedly believed that she was replying to him, for after he had proposed an exchange of tendernesses, he stood up, ran his hand over the hardness of her frozen breasts, put his arm around her stiff waist, and placed his lips on her breathless mouth. His entire attitude, the frissons that ran through him, and the enthusiasm of which he was showing signs, proved that he was sensing the reality of an unreal intoxication.

"We can talk aloud," said Marius. "He won't hear us. That courtesan and that young man adored one another as much as one can adore one another in this land where the gifts of the flesh constitute the only fashion of loving. Now, it happened that one day, the courtesan was, like Mirror-of-Smiles, the victim of an unforeseen accident. She drowned, I think, stunned by erotic pleasure, while giving the benefit of it in a pool. She was immediately directed to this crypt, and as her lover felt severely deprived, the Superman decided that he should not be entirely deprived of her tenderness.

Every time that adolescent desires her, every time that a memory of the past reanimates his appetite for her, he comes here, places his hand on that lever you can see there, fixed in the rock, and extracts therefrom a fluid of illusion, which takes him back to the most beautiful hours of his amour. So you can see him embracing that mannequin as if it were still alive, and the fellow won't soon stop on such a fine route..."

"It's very well imagined," Choumaque admitted. "For isn't everything illusion? And what reality is worth as much as an illusion?"

"Admire, then, the wisdom of our Caresco, who knows how to adorn the chagrins that an abrupt separation can cause us. New fires, however, soon extinguish the old. At first, that lover came every day. Then he spaced his visits, after having savored the amity of a pretty girl. Now, it's been two months since he placed his hand on the lever, and it doubtless required the circumstance of that ceremony to bring him back here once again—perhaps for the last time."

The deluded individual accentuated the manifestations of his delirium. Choumaque looked at him with pity. "The unfortunate fellow, who has never suffered!" he said, shrugging his shoulders.

Outside, the crowd was gathering precipitately. A formidable cheer greeted the body of Mirror-of-Smiles, which slaves had just seized in order to introduce it into a crypt topped by a pink sandstone cross. They saw people who, after having followed the body directly, raced to seize the lever dispensing the fluid of illusion.

# CHAPTER XXI

The last trumpets and the last chants resounded, and the cortege scattered. Madame Môme, the High Priestess, followed her battalion of courtesans briefly with a satisfied gaze as their lovers took them away in airplanes. Then, protecting her eyes with her hands, placed as a shade, she looked for Marius and Choumaque. The latter, leaning against one of the columns of a mausoleum, saw her detach herself from the dazzling flow of colors and come toward them.

Her pastel peplum, floating about her body and fixed at the shoulder by claws of brilliant gemstones, was decorated with jewels representing in miniature the erotic instruments whose employment she taught her pupils. They greeted her young silhouette, and her languorously provocative gait, still swaying to musical rhythms, joyfully. She came to them, successively plastered on their lips the savor of her perfumed mouth; then, detaching two camellias from her hair, she planted one in Marius' brown mane and the other in Choumaque's red tresses. After which, taking their arms, she drew them away.

They felt united, brought close together by the communicative pressure.

"Oh, my boys, that ceremony has slid fire into my blood! Whose turn is it tonight? He won't have any cause to complain!"

"What, darling! You've already forgotten that I made love to you last night?" observed Marius' baritone voice.

"It is, indeed, me who will taste the supreme delight!" Choumaque admitted. He turned to his friend and proposed: "However, Marius, if your flesh is needling you excessively. I'll cede you my turn. Egotism is a vile sentiment, which is not acceptable in a country so favored by the benefits of Caresco..."

It was, in reality, a residue of egotism that caused Choumaque to abandon his rights so generously. The excessively easy joy wearied him, even though he had the resource of extracting from artificial forces the physical energy sufficient to respond to Madame Môme's ardent bounty. The mental energy that stimulated desire was already lacking. He looked back almost with regret to the distant hours when that same mistress, so beautiful now so imperfect then, arrived after an anxious wait with lies in her eyes and implausible excuses on her lips. With what a frenzy of belief he had accepted her explanations! With what burning desire he had taken her in his eager arms!

"Arrange things as you wish," conceded the High Priestess, ever accommodating. "Even if your desire, encouraged by the recent spectacle, has fixed upon one of my pupils, tell me and I'll send her to you. As for myself, I won't have any difficulty finding a substitute for you."

"I'll gladly substitute!" said a voice behind them.

They turned round, but their volte-face was not yet complete when, at the sight of the new interlocutor, they threw themselves face down on the ground in frantic prostration.

Caresco! He was before them, in disguise, pale and haggard, his arms folded. The yellow silk of his costume and the symbolic cross of slaves did not prevent them from recognizing his almightiness. He had coiffed himself with flowers that veiled his face.

"Glory to the Superman!" they cried, without daring to quit their position.

The potentate smiled with pride and satisfaction. His habitual humor seemed to be completely modified for the moment. His ordinarily dull, fugitive, somber, disillusioned gaze, traversed by brief flashes of imperious ferocity, was presently imprinted with a radiant cordiality, which did not exclude the stamp of his constant vanity.

"Come on, get up, my beloved subjects! Don't stand on ceremony! Leave these ridiculous affectations to others. Today, I want us to be four good comrades, chatting together as if we were freshly emerged from the old Latin quarter—or Montmartre, if you prefer, my dear Marius..."

They got to their feet, surprised by this declaration, Marius swelled up with pride at the flattering comment. Madame Môme blinked. She rediscovered the Caresco of the clinic, who had interrogated her gravely about her amours before opening her belly. Choumaque, more independent of observation and less directly petrified by the surgeon's autocracy, noticed that he was stammering as he spoke, and that he seemed to be having difficulty getting his words out, like a paralytic testing the ground before setting his foot down. He also wondered what trap the extraordinary amiability of the fake slave might conceal.

The Superman's physiognomy had just changed, however. His character, similar to those overheated countries where storms darken almost instantaneously, was manifestly excited. He seized a tree-branch that was overhanging he path and twisted it in his hands, making the improbable force of his muscles, naked to the shoulder, stand out.

"I tear everything apart! Everything! Will I not end up tearing myself apart, in order that my people can carry each of my shreds successively in triumph? What a magnificent funeral the funeral of Caresco-Superman, Caresco-God, would be! There would be a hundred days of mourning, I tell you! For the first time, my people would know tears, and I've calculate the hydrostatic pressure the torrent of flowing tears would produce in falling from one meter seventy, the medium height of my subjects' eyes, to the ground. Do you know that it would yield a force of twenty thousand horsepower for ten days—enough to power the factories for that lapse of time! What energies wasted! What elements of happiness annihilated! But now I think about it, isn't it better if I don't die? I'm only ninety years old! I've scarcely begun to live."

Bewildered and terrified, they looked at him, swollen with dementia; but a slight whistling in the air made him raise his head. It was an airplane carrying a family—a crimson sterile spouse, a blue fecund mother, and green adolescents—

265

passing overhead, returning from the ceremony toward the hearth. Joyful songs descended from it, supported by the chords of a huge harp employed by the gracious gestures of the mother.

"See them fly, the ugly brutes! Are they happy! To whom to they owe it? Answer me, Choumaque—to whom?"

"To their destiny..." But the philosopher caught the fearful glance that Marius darted at him, and continued: "To their destiny, which is you, Superman, obviously."

Caresco was not listening. He was following his own train of thought, without drawing any inspiration from the environment. Tears came into his eyes.

"Oh, my friends, my dear collaborators, what sadness can equal mine? What lamentations resonate in a heart like mine! I have beatified these people to the point of stupidity! I have gorged them on enjoyments to the point that the concept of unhappiness has become an idea impossible for their brains to entertain. On the other hand, do not humans suffer, most of all, from having given birth to speculative science? I have suppressed that education, and if I were able to discover in the human brain a region particular to that elaboration of ideas, I would open the skull of every one of my subjects in order to remove it...yes, I would accomplish that circumcision on every new-born mind!

"Alas, I have had to content myself with reducing my ideal creature to the animal level, which is to enjoy by satisfying the instincts. Who would dare to claim that I have not succeeded completely? These brutes eat as I wish, and reproduce when I wish, selectively...I am, therefore, more powerful than Nature, am I not? Since Nature nourishes creatures with substances that are always identical, and permits the generation of flawed individuals! Am I not the creator? Am I not the Other? Admit it, my beloved philosopher! And you, Môme—what do you think?"

Without waiting for the replies, he burst into sobs, increasingly stumbling over his words.

"Those poor people—what will become of them when I'm dead? Who will take charge of regulating their lives, as I have done? Who will operate on them? Who will discover the human monad? That doubt causes me abominable anguish! When I think about it, I'm tempted to blow up the island with myself, in a frightful cataclysm, like the one that swallowed up a corner of the world in order to permit this one to spring forth thirty years ago! Can you see that, my beloved subjects! What a melee of bodies and matter, and me! What an admirable sterilization I'd achieve by that colossal fire! And it would be so easy to provoke...so easy! A simple button to press...my masonries disintegrate...the volcano roars, everything explodes...for we're dancing on a volcano, my dear friends! Ha ha ha!"

Immediately, livid, terrible and drooling, he started dancing. His laughter screeched. As if he were fearful of having allowed too much to be heard, however, he came back to them, and put a finger over his mouth, while accentuating, with a frown, the pleats of his eyebrows, traced in kohl. With an unusual mobility, his face became somber again.

"Don't say anything!" he commanded. "For if I did that, I'd like to die with the virgin of my choice. There's one I find infinitely seductive. Do you know her? Her hair is the sun, her cheeks are flowers, her laughter crystal! She's my queen—she's your queen! What do you think she'll think of me? Will she love me?"

He had resumed his expression of amorous fatuity, all his features relaxed by the certainty of soon being adored by the young woman. He picked a dahlia and tore it to pieces with staccato gestures. Then silence fell, no one daring to reply to him and he no longer speaking. The embarrassment was beginning to become strained when a group of men came toward them. By the negligent fashion in which they wore their long violet togas they could be distinguished as scientists at a distance. That apparition seemed to render Caresco a glimmer of reason. He went toward them, while they, after having recognized him in his borrowed costume, prostrated themselves.

"Well, Messieurs you aren't at work? Is not happiness, which is idleness for others, work for you? I asked you for a report on the meteorological conditions of our island ten years ago; where is it? And you, Monsieur, what's become of your new valve? And you, your cultures of myxomycetes? You're slacking, Messieurs; I'm very discontented with that!"

He accompanied them, intoxicating himself with his commandments, having become practical and positive again, in the service of science, the benefactress of his people. He soon disappeared, leaving the three interlocutors where they were.

"I don't believe I'm being too adventurous in affirming that he's mad," Choumaque declared.

"Mad—do you think so?" said Marius, dubiously. "For thirty years we've seen him like this. In thirty years, a madness has finished evolving, old chap, if I can believe what I read..."

"That's possible," concluded the wisdom of Madame Môme, "but me, I agree with Zéphi; it's incontestable that the Superman is soft in the head."

# CHAPTER XXII

Marcel had fallen asleep during a play at the Athenée, a theater in Paris, of which the ingenious combination of the cinematograph and the phonograph had offered him the spectacle.

After the emotions of the funerary day, with the memory of the pleasant walk he had taken in the company of Miss Mary, and the sweet promises that had been exchanged between them when they had lost sight of their friends—an entirely chaste walk and entirely pure promises, provoked by the threat they sensed hanging over them—he had he had come home, confused by the young woman's new change of mind, and had gone to bed. Then, as he had been unable to sleep, as his excitement, whipped up by the visions that he had had before his eyes, kept him agitated between the sheets, making him search for places there that did not burn like contact with overheated flesh, at the limit of his resistance, he had gone to demand a little appeasement from the utilities panel. For a moment, he had placed his temples on the conductive wires of dreams, and the whole night had gone by in delightful transports in which imagination played the sole role, and brought him the presence, in unsuspected attitudes, of Miss Mary, the courtesan Carabella and even Madame Môme.

So, when, on awakening, Marjah had told him that it was time to go to the Temple of Fecundity, where the blonde mothers were waiting, the young man, by virtue of an entirely natural transition of fiction to reality, had seen reappear with the sentiment of his dignity the proud, chaste and serene silhouette of Miss Mary. Then, he envisaged in all its deplorable consequences the critical problem that the pirouette of the slave, now departed, had left behind him. He told himself that he was already weary of the pleasures of the Temple. He would rather conserve in the young woman's heart the place that he had already acquired, attracting if he must the anger of the Superman.

He resolved to submit that casuistic anguish to the resolution of his kindly master's common sense. As soon as he was dressed, he went into the corridor to press the button advertising his presence, and to confide his name to the mouth of a resonator, which, in its turn, would transmit it to the philosopher's ears.

When Marcel had been announced, there was a tumultuous stir in Choumaque's room. Madame Môme had spent the night there, in obedience to the invariable pact of amorous alternation, and the barked name surprised her just as she was trying to give her second lover a further proof of her valiant tenderness and professional *savoir faire*. The philosopher shoved her away.

"Get out, quickly! Go, quickly! I don't want my pupil to catch us!"

"Why? He's seen many others!"

"Let's go! Out!"

He threw garments at her pell-mell, and made her run around the room, disheveled and bewildered. And as there was no door, he ended up engulfing her behind the artificial rock framing the basin of the bath. He lay down again, and waited for her to finish panting, hurling a few insults at her. Then he shouted "Come in!"

"What! You're not up yet?" Marcel demanded, going to dart a glance at the sun and observing that its height indicated approximately nine o'clock.

"I slept late," Choumaque replied, yawning and stretching in order to put on an act. Then, sniffing the perfumed air that the ventilators, he added, with feigned indifference: "We've woken up to opopanax today! Is that really opopanax? Tell me—your sense of smell is more discriminating than mine."

"No, it's *Peau de France*," Marcel estimated, "but forget such trivia, my friend. Oh, if you only knew what's happening in my heart…!"

"I have a slight suspicion..."

In a heart-rending tone, the young man related the extent to which he was supersaturated by the pleasures of the island, how, in a country where everyone was able to believe that everyone else was at their beck and call, he had to go and serve as a stallion in the Superman's stud. Certainly, at the start, he had done full honor to his musculature; he had not even had to have recourse to the genetic serum—but now he had had enough! Did not that exigency surpass the most arbitrary military service and taxation of other lands? They were burdening him with a duty of insemination! And what if the blonde mothers didn't please him, after all? And what if he had reasons for not satisfying their caprices?

While he listed his reasons for not obeying: his love for Miss Mary, and the certain sadness that child would experience in believing him detached from her—the loquacious Carabella had told her everything—exposing his distress with a exaggeration that belied the infidelities of previous days, Choumaque listened gravely, caressing his bicolored beard and hair with a golden comb and polishing the pink varnish he had just put on his nails with an ermine fur.

"So, what do you think, my dear Choumaque?"

"I think, my friend, that you're damnably lucky to encounter obstacles before your desires. If my theory of equilibria is no lie..."

"Oh, I beg you, Choumaque, don't lead us astray in your philosophy! I'm asking you for practical advice. Is it necessary to continue to betray the woman I love? Is it necessary for me to rebel against Caresco? What will come of it?"

"Nothing good, certainly, in one solution or the other. My personal sentiment is that. if the love of one woman is already something cumbersome, that's all the more reason for the love of a colony ought to tire you out! It's up to you to decide whether your loins are solid enough...or whether your fear of the Superman is less than your affection for Miss Mary. Furthermore, as I know you, the two sentiments are bound to predominate by turns."

"I beg your pardon, Master, but you're mistaken! I love Miss Mary far more than I fear Caresco! And I'd gladly overthrow the latter!"

"No, he can't be overthrown. And then, don't speak so loud!"

Deep down, Choumaque rejoiced to see the spirit of revolt lighting up in his pupil's eye. He had feared that the solvent mores of Eucrasia might already have completely perverted his character—worthy, to be sure, and full of generous impulses, but which continual depressions had weakened fatally and led to the concessions of egotism. Go on! There were resources there!

And to convince himself of it more fully, he told him about the operation that he had witnessed surreptitiously in the company of Marius. He did not spare any realistic detail in depicting the sadistic madness that was translated in the surgeon by visceral ablations.

"And these people tolerate such horrors! These stupid people don't rebel, don't break their chains?"

"What chains?" Choumaque observed. "They don't believe there are any; they don't feel them—or, at least, they're so sugar-coated that they're content to lick them. They have faith in their Superman, in his metempsychosis, and that's sufficient for him to tie their hands, to cloud their minds, to drive those magnificent creatures all the way to the operating table in delight! Faith has always led to the most improbable immolations, as witness the Christians, as well as to the most abominable atrocities, as witness the Inquisitors. In the name of faith, certain negroes at the beginning of the century roasted their relatives on a spit and ate their tongues with pious delectation. In the name of faith, the people of the Red Land allow themselves to be slaughtered by the English. In the name of faith, Miss Mary herself has come here, toward a mystery, and will stay here, corrupted and castrated.

"In sum, faith is encrusted stupidity, and Caresco, with his new religious system, only had to bring back and exploit ideas as old as human stupidity—which is to say, immemorial.

272

And you, my poor friend, who are uttering such a cry of protest at this moment, I wouldn't give you a year living among these women, these flowers, this music, these perfumes, these serums and these fluids—and that's a generous estimate—without arriving at the same cacothymy as the people surrounding us, without accepting to lick the sugar of your chains, in the company of Miss Mary, dispossessed of a pound of flesh and a pint of her blood. Don't be astonished—you're already following that downward path. I've acquired the conviction from certain little signs that escape you. Anyway, it's inevitable. It's human."

"Never! Never!" Marcel shouted, more violently. His whole frame was vibrating. To affirm his determination, he punched a malassite motif decorating one of the bedposts, and broke it.

A cry of anguish responded to his vigorous action. Madame Môme had just emerged from her hiding place, showing herself immodestly nude and ruffled, the symbolic trace on her abdomen displayed on the polished ivory of flesh like a sign approving the words that had just been pronounced.

"It's not necessary to smash the furniture, my boy!" she said, going to nestle in the arms of the confused philosopher. Addressing her lover, she added: "And that's why you got rid of me, Zéphi? Am I, then, incapable of giving salutary advice?"

She darted an anxious glance around the room, suspicious of the perfume vent, the artificial rock, the utilities panel and an enigmatic little container yawning in a corner.

"Let's hope that Caresco isn't in communication with us at this moment, and doesn't have his ear to the microphone! Let's hope that the graphophones aren't working! I pity the two of you! Something similar happened one day before my very eyes. A young man freshly disembarked, like you, my little Marcel, gave Dr. Hymen a beating when he was trying to remove, painlessly, a growth that was dishonoring his occiput. Oh, he didn't last long! The next day he was dissected, displayed in a jar. Caresco had tried to make him into his human

273

monad, as he calls it. He was a prince related to the Russian imperial family—a very handsome fellow, believe me—who had had bad luck gambling and decided to solicit the favor of repopulating our realm. He'd warmed Philoxénie's couch as soon as he arrived..."

While speaking she had got dressed, and Choumaque had done likewise. Then, sitting on the philosopher's knee, becoming more serious in the face of the gravity of events, she went on: "Listen, both of you...come closer, so I can speak quietly...very quietly!"

Marcel leaned toward the couple. She brought their heads together is a single attentive bundle. An airplane was audible outside, whose flight projected a shadow ion the mosaic tiles as it passed by.

"What I say to you, my little Marcel...blood of ovaries!...just as long as Caresco doesn't overhear me!...come closer..." She hesitated momentarily, rejected with a gesture an idea that had occurred to her, and then said: "I have two means of getting you out of this, but for the moment, because of the surveillance exercised over you, one is impracticable. It's therefore necessary to flee."

"Flee!" whispered Marcel. "But how do you expect us to flee? Everything is guarded. Within a radius of two kilometers from the coast, our slightest actions and gestures would be denounced. My ship could carry us away, to be sure, and I know enough about navigation to steer her on my own, if necessary...but the very water on which I'd be sailing would betray my heading, and a few meters further on we'd be destroyed by the omnial net..."

"You're talking too loudly, my boy! How passionate men are! Let me speak. Know this, then. Zadochbach the Inexhaustible is leaving this evening for Paris aboard the airplane that brought you here, under the control of Captain Tronc-de-Jatte. Persuade Miss Mary to go with you, then, and at eleven o'clock exactly, be at the entrance to the tube next to the landing-stage. No one will be there at that time. I'll take charge of the rest."

"But what about Zadochbach? And the captain?"

"One's stupefied by his calculations and the pleasures of Venus. As for the other, I'll make sure to distract his attention during the time it will take for the young folk to go across the deck and get into the hold. I'm on very good terms with him."

"But I thought it was impossible for that man to be on *good terms* with a woman?" Choumaque objected again.

"Oh, don't worry Zéphi, you don't have to be jealous— it's completely platonic." So saying, she teased the philosopher intimately, in order to prove to him that it was not the same for them. He pushed her away, reminding her about her professional duties.

Marcel immediately made himself scarce, after having given Choumaque a poignant farewell hug. He ran toward the park in search of Miss Mary. He had to see her before the evening, but nothing was more problematic; entire days often passed without them running into one another. For some time, Carabella seemed to have been keeping a closer watch on the virgin and avoiding any meeting with him. Was she acting of her own accord, or following some superior order? Both explanations were plausible.

Thinking about that, Marcel realized all the peril of his audacious action. At the same time, though, he found pretexts for hesitating to carry it out. Why had Madame Môme omitted to facilitate their meeting? Why had she not informed Miss Mary herself? He thought about going back to the High Priestess and asking her to alert the young woman. But where should he look for her? How could he get into the Temple of Sterility? And even supposing that he reached Choumaque's mistress, would she consent to neglect her functions?

He raised all these objections in order not to be in too much haste to make a decision. And time passed; hours went by without him overcoming his uncertainty. His surge of revolt had lost all impetus. He took pleasure, as usual, in the delights of enchanting location extended before him: the sunlit verdure, the gracious booming of the flowers, the murmur of streams licking the rocks, the libertine images that all those things described, and the huge mountainous couple in the distance.

He told himself that by running away, he would lose the sight of those delightful panoramas forever. Similarly, would he not have to renounce the admirable and hygienic orange costume that was so becoming to his build, which facilitated the circulation of air, in order to return to the grotesque and narrow fashions of the other world, the tight trousers and pleated frock-coat?

It was, however, necessary that they leave. If they did not take advantage of the opportunity that Madame Môme was offering them, a month might pass before it was renewed—and a lot could happen in a month! He imagined the surgeon's action profaning the object of his adoration; he saw himself overtaxed by the demands of fecund months. He stimulated his despair, but with more reason than real sentiment, because, deep down, the work of creation seemed to him less frightening than his mind was striving to make him envisage it.

Fortunately, an event made up his mind for him. The sudden appeal of a siren, coming from an airplane, made him lift his head. At the same time, these words came down: "Sanitary visit! Everyone to the Heart!"

The monstrous voice repeated the order several times, designed to be audible even through the also of dwellings, to extract sleepers from their slumber and the amorous from their transports; then it drew away.

Marcel knew that no one escaped that inquisition of a particular order, extended by Caresco over all his subjects. He concluded that he was certain to encounter Miss Mary soon. But would he be able to speak to her in secret? Not daring to hope for that, he resolved to alert her by means of a note, which he wrote with his blood on a piece of white cloth, for he had neither ink nor paper. He clutched the message in his hand, ready to seize the first opportunity to pass it surreptitiously.

His precaution did not seem to have been needless. When the foreigner appeared, she was accompanied by

Carabella, who surrounded her with ardent attention. Delightfully draped in radiant silk, as usual, she took pleasure in making the fabric rustle as she walked. Her hands were overladen with jewels since she had started accepting those the courtesan offered her.

As soon as she saw Marcel, she signified to him with her gaze all the annoyance she felt at not being able to meet him on her own. She held out her hand him, and was very surprised to find the piece of cloth in the young man's hand. She concealed her astonishment, however, understanding that she had to hide whatever it was that he was giving her in secret. All three of them took the pneumatic tube to the Palace of the Heart.

The immense symbolic façade, in red stucco that seemed to be bleeding, with orifices similar to sectioned and gaping vessels, loomed up before a bare plain paved with mosaics, where a considerable crowd had already gathered. One might have thought it the rendezvous for another fête, so cheerful was the animation, and so many songs were emerging excitedly from so many mouths. Rhythmic dances, quadrilles of pretty young women, the gitons' feats of skill and strength, the sound of flutes, harps, sistrums, the sparkling of colors, jewels and metals, the placid comings and goings of spouses, animated children's games, perfumes—a chaos, a tumult of varied sensations—greeted them. They passed through. Mischievous children threw flowers at them. Courtesans, surprised kissing one another on the mouth, offered to do the same for them.

Carabella had to guide them through the dense crowd to reach a kind of wicket-gate at the entrance to a vessel. There they were recognized and their presence recorded in the columns of a huge book. They went through a circular arch into a gray infrastructure similar to the interior walls of an artery. As they were a trifle cramped for room and the temperature was somewhat elevated, a sterile spouse in a long purple toga demanded fresh air, and his plea was rapidly granted.

Immediately, Carabella shouted to him: "Gilded-Gaze! I haven't seen you for a long time. Don't you and Veloutine love me anymore?"

"Veloutine's at the Fecundity at present," the spouse replied, causing the gold of his eyes to shine toward the courtesan.

"What are you doing here, then?"

"I've come for the visit, and to be sterilized."

"With courtesans, Gilded-Gaze, the latter measure isn't necessary, as you know..."

"Thank you for the offer, Carabella, but at the moment, I'm very smitten by a fecund mother..."

"Whenever you wish, charming spouse," said Carabella, complaisantly.

They continued chatting. Gilded-Gaze told her about the happiness of his household and the three boys who filed his dwelling with laughter. One of them, however, had been designated for castration. The other two would be scientists, after having been reproducers. Then, his turn having arrived, he hastened to go and offer himself to the serum that rendered him refractory.

Carabella, becoming serious again, explained to her companions that that was how Caresco preserved the purity of the race.

After five minutes of kicking their heels, Marcel and Miss Mary were pushed into a little oblong room resembling a laboratory, where people were getting undressed while others were putting their clothes back on. Slaves were indifferently assisting all those temptations of beauty. Their torsos, tight in the yellow sheath of their doublets, marked with the characteristic cross, were leaning emotionlessly toward adorable nudities, aiding the gestures that unveiled or covered up the splendid flesh.

In one corner, Dr. Hymen, wedged into his long frock-coat with the green short-front, with his gold trinkets dangling over his abdomen and his shock of black hair fusing with the tufted fur of his top hat, was bending over the bodies, palpating, ausculating, tapping, measuring, making his scrutinizing instruments clink and their mechanisms click. He too, busy as he was, did not allow himself to be troubled by any special sensibility. When he concluded an examination, he bustled the person who had been its object, propelling them to another corner of the room, where attentive aides listened to the only words he pronounced—"One milligram!" or "Two milligrams!"—before applying the treatment. And the docile people obeyed, going to offer their arms to the injection of the serum preventing all maladies, distributed by a hollow needle fitted to a tube equipped with a little automatic counter.

All ambient life was then extinguished in the religious solemnity of that vaccinatory practice; and the beautiful human harmonies, the blonde flesh of fecund mothers, the warmer complexions of courtesans, the nacreous grace of virgins, the powerful anatomy of sowers, the sleekness of gitons and adolescents, all communed with health, without any lubricity. Then, immediately after the inoculation, the noise began again, the movement, the animation, the collisions and the kisses resuming under the influence of the recovered vital force.

"Undress!" a slave instructed the two hesitant young people.

Fortunately for them, the flood of people, poorly contained by slaves, who were insufficient in number since the majority of them had been burned, threw them into a corner of the room before they could be undressed and subjected to the application of the serum. Carabella, fully occupied with Gilded-Gaze, had lost sight of them, and they found themselves isolated in the swarming and jostling mass of nude bodies that were getting dressed again, their faces so close that their breath was almost confused, and they shivered. But time was pressing, and Marcel had no thought other than to explain the contents of his note verbally.

"Let's hide, Miss Mary! Let's avoid the injection, since we've been lucky enough to escape the solicitude of the slaves. And listen: a danger threatens you—yes, a danger such as you have never known, you who have made war, breathed in the acridity of gunpowder, heard the whistle of bullets!"

She considered him with her large dark velvet eyes, which the pale brown wave of her hair rendered more energetic. He saw reappear therein, reanimated by the evocation of peril and he fatherland, all the primal virtues of the valorous soil that the two drops of the avoided serum would doubtless have annihilated.

He went on: "I believe you have faith in my word. It is that of a devoted lover. Caresco, I tell you, no longer wants to let you leave his realm. In order to force you to remain, he will employ an abominable practice. It's necessary to flee, Miss Mary. It's necessary that this evening..."

Crystalline laughter cascaded beside them. It was Carabella and Philoxénie who, finally discovering them, were making fun of their gravity. Both of them, their cheeks animated by the recent inoculation, were astonished that the vital force was not more apparent in the neophytes' attitude. They drew closer,

"Read my note; it will inform you," Marcel just had time to whisper to his companion, as he moved away from Philoxénie's hand, which was venturing toward his waist.

# CHAPTER XXIII

The moon appeared more triumphantly than ever that evening. Miss Mary, having returned to the Caravanserai, stayed in her aerial garden for a long time, contemplating the enormous fluidity descending from the infinite. How good one felt, so close to the sky, and how one entered into communion with the splendor of the firmament! An exaltation as vibrant as the rays of the star dilated her heart.

Was that because she was nearing the moment that was about to liberate her from this country—where she had, however, only found disappointments for her dream of revenge—or because that same country had particular beauties and she wanted to fill her eyes with them, profoundly, one last time, drinking in the spaces where her heart had opened to love? She could not have said—but she felt the magnificence of the night divinely; she was excited by a desire to fly away into that lunar shimmer, to glide, a magical form, though that silvery expanse, to melt into the sovereign tranquility of the firmament.

She knew the Marcel would follow her there. With him, both rendered immaterial, she would swim in the soul of nature, and that psychic embrace would calm the suspense that was lacerating her nerves.

Eleven o'clock, he had written!

The microphone inside her room announced a visitor whose name she could not make out. Palpitating, she got up swiftly in order to run to the visitor, imagining, implausibly, that it must be Marcel—but it was only Carabella. The courtesan was wearing a long evening veil over her tunic, symbolically embroidered, which she put down as she came in.

"You're not in bed yet, my divine one? I was hoping so much to find you in bed..."

"Why have you come at this hour, Carabella? You know that I don't need you when I'm asleep."

"So it's not to let you sleep."

"What do you want with me, then?"

Carabella dared not admit that she had been sent by the Master, with the mission to discover whether the foreigner still had the same degree of resistance—fifty on the psychometer—that had led to his cessation for some time of the alchemical methods designed to impregnate her with Passion. She was to strive, by attempting the power of caresses, to ascertain that nature was still predominant in the young woman, and convince the potentate that the long fast in question would result in a more decisive influence for the aphrodisiac fluid whose formula the violet scientists were synthesizing.

"Carabella! You're looking at me as a drunken man might look at me! Why is that? Are you a masculine soul clad in the body of a woman? In that case, know that I'm not free. Know that my heart is fixed..."

"On the handsome sower!"

"It doesn't matter on whom. Leave me alone I want to rest."

"Virgin! O virgin who has no wish to try Passion!"

She placed her burning lips on the young woman's shoulder. But she could not have been more untimely, and her offer had never been welcomed with more disdain. To convince herself of that resistance, she parted Miss Mary's corsage and plunged her hand within, delighting in feeling the firmness of the breasts within. Immediately pushed away, violently, she was astonished to retain between her fingers a scrap of silk which she mistook at first, in the dim light, for a handkerchief or some sort of sachet, and which she did not return, in order to conserve the perfume of her grim adversary, whose voice repeated: "Get out! Go away! I don't understand your persistence! I don't want to understand it!"

When Carabella had gone, Miss Mary listened to her footsteps for some time. She heard the atrium that was carrying the courtesan away slide downwards. She did not know exactly what time it was but the decline of the moon had been prescribed as prior to the meeting with Marcel, and the star

282

was already retiring toward the emergence of the great trees populating the park.

She waited a little longer. A little talking bird came in through the open bay and chirped a few words, after which it flew away, seeing that she was paying no attention to it. It was one of the things that always surprised her, that amity of animals for people. She discovered therein the proof of a meek humanity. Now, she was about to return to the lands where humans were still submissive to their destructive instincts, where the animals fled from them—and that observation weakened her determination to go. Where was happiness to be found?

She felt hungry, and contented herself with a nugget of complete aliment. Sated, she found herself more valiant, and as the moon had sunk, she seized the veil that Carabella had forgotten and put it on, taking care to display the distinctive embroidery clearly, in such a way that she could, if the need arose, be mistaken for someone else. Then she made the door rotate and went into the corridor. In the silence, she could hear her own excited heartbeat. She preferred to go down the thirty floors on foot, wand that seemed interminable, so enormous was the emptiness around her, so much did her bravery decline as the porphyry rattled beneath her steps.

At the bottom, the great luminous sandstone columns of the atrium extended enigmatically. When she went outside, two slow springs singing in the darkness guided her.

"Miss Mary! Bless you for coming!" said Marcel's melodious voice, as his elegant silhouette detached itself from the trunk of a cedar.

She was glad that he had recognized her under her borrowed mantle. Without saying any more, he guided her to a light airplane that was waiting a hundred meters away, hidden in a clump of trees. The young man knew how to fly it, the controls being very simple. He helped her to take her place on the soft cushions of the only banquette. He cast off the mooring-rope, seized the tiller, pressed a few buttons, which animate the vehicle's flanks, and the craft took off, like a fantastic bird stealing a treasure, its wing-beats precipitate at first, and then less hasty. For greater security, Marcel had put out the lights.

Then Miss Mary realized, briefly, the dream that she had had a little while before. The craft, heading upwards, brought her back to the caress of the astral light, and in the immense fluidity, she was inundated by the warm serenity of the night, melting into the languorous radiation of the silvery heart. What magnificent peace! What sweet tranquility, before the events that might soon become as many upheavals!

She breathed in a pure fiction. She herself was a gentle and vibrant ray of light, floating in the brightness.

She would gladly have laid her hair upon the shoulder of the companion who was taking her away from this world of vice and indolence; she would have nestled against the broad, strong chest in which a noble heart was beating for her. Not daring to do it, however, she contented herself with collecting the warmth of his hand, and feeling pass through it the ingenuousness of their reciprocal disturbance.

They divined one another thus for a full hour. At intervals, omnial radiations burst forth. Marcel, his eyes fixed on the immensity of the ground, unfurling confused panoramas, explained why he had chosen this mode of locomotion. The tube would have exposed them to meeting people, while the airplane isolated them completely. He approved the precaution she had taken in covering herself with Carabella's mantle.

In fact, two craft crossed their path and their searchlights, directed toward them, engendered the idea of a courtesan's escapade. The people laughed and joked, the veil instigating libertine desires. When Miss Mary, fearing that they might be pursued, became frightened, Marcel reassured her with warm protestations. Was he not taking her to liberty, toward a more tranquil love? She only had to let herself be guided, and soon a virile sky would be resplendent.

To each of these observations, the young woman, intoxicated by his voice, either replied with a few words: "I believe you; I love you; you're strong and I'll obey you..." or contented herself with squeezing her hero's hand a little harder.

Suddenly, the breeze brought them a saline perfume and the sound of waves. An incandescence appeared a few kilometers away, and the perspective of an immense red airplane decorated with golden vibrions was outlined, with the bulges of the elytra attached to its sides. On leaning over, they made out the animation of the deck, where cranes, silently distributing their effort, were embarking packages. A few brisk sailors sufficed for the maneuver. A little black dot glimpsed at that distance, like a moving picket, was moving back and forth, and rotating; they recognized the captain's pedestal.

"Is that the vessel that will take us away?"

"Indeed. We've arrived. Keep quiet. We have to stay out of sight."

Marcel circled, made a turn, and organized the descent in the shelter of the portico indicating the entrance to the pneumatic tube. They had no sooner set foot on the ground than a shadow detached itself from the side wall and came toward them.

"Here you are, at last!" said Madame Môme. "I thought you'd abandoned the plan. Perhaps that would have been wiser. What are you going to do at the other end? Do you think, once arrived in Paris, you can deceive the surveillance of Zadochbach and the captain? You're not counting on getting rid of them violently, I assume? The Superman wouldn't have much difficulty find you and making you feel his vengeance. Children! Aren't they sweet? You're still intent on leaving, yes? Idiots, who can't take happiness where they find it! For isn't that what Caresco demands, in sum? If you knew how frequently inconvenient that which he removes from us can be!"

While chattering, she unwrapped a parcel filled with clothes. Silencing Marcel, who was coughing to cover the sound of her bad reasons, she went on: "Here's what you need to put on. They're sailors' costumes. I thought at first of dressing you as courtesans and passing you off as members of the

285

group of my pupils who are on service during the voyage, but Marcel's beard was an obstacle, and the captain has a keen eye. He checks each entrant, but pays less attention to his crew. So, you go across the deck quickly, while I distract the dwarf. I'm conducting a flirtation with that demi-siphon, who's as curious as he's impotent. He composes verses, which he trumpets to me through the aluminum of his mask! The other day, he tried to kiss me! It was exquisite!

"Once inside, go and lie low in cabin number sixteen— that of a sailor that I'm retaining unduly in the arms of one of my priestesses, gorging him on a soporific. Stay there until you reach Paris. That will take three days. There, you'll be able to love one another deeply. It's necessary that when you reach the end of your voyage Miss Mary will no longer be entitled to orange-blossom. You hear, Marcel? You wouldn't believe how important that is to your ulterior security. Is it so very difficult to take a maidenhead, or allow one to be taken? Oh, look—here's some pastilles of complete aliment. You haven't thought of that, no doubt? Young lovers! They never think of anything!"

She continued to pour out further floods of spicy remarks while they each put on the short trousers and jerseys, leaving their arms and lower legs bare, and decorating their chests with ruffs of precious lace. Miss Mary, her hair tucked up into a beret, thus took on the appearance of a charming adolescent, and when she was in the light, her eyes, collecting sparks obliquely, filled with silver. Before setting foot on the gang-plank, the High Priestess gave them some final instructions.

"One never knows what might happen. It won't be at all astonishing if you're recaptured. In that case, don't betray me. I'm being stupid in facilitating your flight...but I love Zéphi so much!" Taking Marcel aside, she added: "You hear, my boy—if you want to avoid big trouble, violate her! It's very serious. Make sure you do."

They waited a little longer, watching for a moment when the captain and the crew were busy at the rear. Then, certain of not being seen, they ventured on to the deck. At the same time,

Madame Môme's ruse protected their perilous passage. She performed a series of pirouettes and uttered cries of joy that deflected attention. Before disappearing below decks, the young people saw her surround the pedestal with her arms and flatter the half-man with a few voluptuous slaps on the back of the neck.

Although the cabin in which the two runaways had taken refuge was that of a simple sailor, it was large, sumptuous and endowed with all the comforts for which one could wish after a sojourn on the island of Eucrasia. A vast bed with rich curtains occupied one corner, with there was a large utilities panel within arm's reach, checkered by a multitude of pigeon-holes, similar to those of which the young people had already made use. In another corner, the metallic plate of an ingenious device transcribed the captain's orders in luminous letters, at the same time as it pronounced them in a loud voice. Little ventilators with active wings distributed warm air, perfumed with delicate essences, renewed without even needing to be touched. A screen occupying the whole of one aluminum sidewall recounted delightful stories at will, and reproduced scenes of the invariably happy events that had taken place in the land favored by the Superman.

On a table, there were a thousand other elements of distraction, uncomplicated games in which one could test one's skill—knucklebones, dice—and images, pastilles and perfumes. A long pair of pink wings, equipped with the receiver of their motive force, hung from a peg, just brushing the abundant pile of the rich carpet. Finally, in a special item of furniture, various utensils proved that amour had what was necessary to obtain patience, and that the on-board seraglio served the crew as well as the passengers.

It was the first time that Marcel and Miss Mary had found themselves truly isolated, and they felt an infinite disturbance in consequence. A young couple departing on a honeymoon voyage could not have been favored by a solitude more complete than theirs. They made that reflection privately, and their gazes, meeting at the same instant, divined the solemnity that they were according to the moments that were about to follow.

Marcel, in particular, saw the moment advancing, with increasing hesitation, to accomplish the act of violence recommended by the High Priestess. In vain, he racked his brains trying to understand the necessity of hastening such a solution. The virgin, trembling with emotion, seemed to be thinking about something else, and he scarcely had any desire to brutalize her. To begin with, they waited, not knowing what to do with themselves, for there was nowhere to sit down except for the bed.

"How long it's taking," murmured Miss Mary. "Aren't we ever going to set off?"

They listened to the movements overhead, the appeals of the siren, the voice of the captain barking orders. Attentively, with their ears glued to the wall, they tried to catch the slightest noises. They recognized that Madame Môme had retired after bidding farewell to her pupils. Rhythmic footsteps, the chords of zithers, indicated to them that the courtesans were dancing. They overheard the late arrival of the Chief Representative, muttering incomprehensible phrases. Then there was a final clamor of a hundred throats intoning a farewell hymn to the blessed land and to the Superman—and the muffled throb of the propellers was heard, revealing the action of the great mechanical heart, and the beating of gigantic wings, whose movement eventually regularized. The porthole through which they darted a glance betrayed a dark blue immensity, from which the infinite gazes of the stars looked down.

They were on their way.

Oh, the lovely scene of amour and purity that unfurled thereafter in the cabin of the sailor who was asleep in the arms of courtesans! Words could not describe the emotion, nor the delightful gravity. Marcel and Miss Mary, weary of standing, had ended up sitting on the edge of the bed, and it was a spectacle of unexpected fantasy that of the two beautiful bodies of the bold mariner and the proud heroine presented, scarcely clad in light comic opera costumes, chastely enlaced, stammering in intoxicated voices, the profoundest oaths of tenderness. He, especially, found divine echoes in his heart to lull him, and it was a music so poignant in which she was trembling that tears originating from the most distant roots of her being came to the brim of her pretty velvet eyes.

At those simple harmonies of the soul, however, the violation extolled by the High Priestess stopped. For when, perceiving the superb line of the legs held in the tights, and respiring the young woman's odorous cleavage, Marcel, more adventurous and more nervous, remembered Madame Môme's recommendations and attempted an embrace that led them to the threshold of the saving act, he read such virginal supplication in his companion's eyes, and sensed now, by contrast with the scornful expressions with which she had previously rejected his tenderness, such a frisson of distress and bewildered protest, that he was softened by it. He did not dare go further, and retreated to mild stammerings of love, audacities limited to compressions of the hand and the tenderness of heads upon shoulders. And those simple familiarities were sufficiently fatiguing for them eventually, exhausted by so much emotion and action, to lie down on the bed and go to sleep chastely in one another's rms.

That night, Marcel dreamed about the good Dr. Hymen gazing before the celestial light at the transparency of a little pink membrane, freshly excised.

Confused noises woke them up. The omnial lighting was extinguished, and an abundantly sunlit daylight was streaming through the porthole. Extraordinarily surprised, they smiled at first—but the noises they could hear quickly converted their joy into poignant presentiments. Hasty footfalls, obedient to the thunderous voice of the captain, were running over the deck. Above their heads, the muffled explosions of slammed doors propagated along the hull of the vessel.

The resonator transmitted the half-man's words to them: "Imagine that! They're hidden here and I didn't see them. I'm doomed! The Superman won't operate on me again! Come on, lads, search—overturn everything! Dig, dig! Turn over every flap of curtain, stove in every plank of wood, pierce every aluminum plate! Destroy the vessel, if you must, but I want them brought to me in ten minutes, tied up like birds for the spit!"

"We've been betrayed!" Marcel murmured, putting his arms around his dazed companion, whom he strove to render sufficiently docile not have to give any further thought to Madame Môme's prescription.

Alas, the captain's voice, much nearer, paralyzed him. The inexhaustible Zadochbach, attracted by the racket, was demanding explanations, and the conversation of the two chiefs, although conducted in low voices, reached them distinctly.

"Can you imagine that, Representative? I went back to my cabin to look for my back-scratcher when three rings of the bell made me quiver on my pedestal. Those repeated appeals generally signify grave events. I put my microphone to my auricular cage, and what do I hear? The voice of the Superman! I'd have preferred a clap of thunder, my inexhaustible friend! And this is what the Master told me: two of the passengers we brought here a month ago had disappeared. Where to? No one knew. Caresco had assembled his council, consulted his engineers, his scientists, his thought-reader, set all his tracking devices in motion, but nothing and no one could discover the neophytes' hiding place.

"A general order went out through the island; the people joined the hunt; the least redoubts of amour were searched, the smallest arbors, ditches and rocky spurs. Nothing, still nothing! The Superman fulminated; he threatened to abandon his subjects! All was about to be lost when, by the most blessed of hazards, the courtesan Carabella, sweating after so much running, took a piece of cloth from her cleavage in order to wipe her brow. See what luck the Superman has, my dear Representative! The piece of white silk contained letters written in red. Caresco, who was there, leaps upon it.

"'Who gave you this rag, courtesan?' he asks.

"'I took it from the Redlander,' she replies.

290

"'When?'

"'Yesterday evening.'

"O power of destiny! Do you know what that writing contained? Quite simply a rendezvous—a rendezvous at the landing-platform arranged by Girard with Hardisson for the time of my departure! So, according to all the evidence, the fugitives have hidden here. And I didn't see anything! Oh, kill me, Inexhaustible! Crush me! I'm doomed! Caresco won't operate on me anymore!"

A long wail of grief terminated that explanation. Then the pedestal rolled on; the encouragements to the pack were repeated.

Marcel stood up, furious.

"We'll see!" he said, searching for something that he might use as a weapon.

He circled the room in vain. There was nothing to aid his anger but a pair of pink wings, the games of dice and knuckle-bones, the bottles of pastilles and perfumes, and all the paraphernalia of amour. He brushed those derisory objects aside. Then, roaring, he tried to dislodge the porthole. His strength multiplied a hundredfold, he was about to succeed when the door of the cabin opened and the pedestal, surmounted by the half-man, appeared.

"Here they are!" the phenomenon howled. "I've caught them! The little ones were making love in my sailor's bed! Don't disturb yourselves, my lambs! The pleasures of the island didn't satisfy you, then, and you were trying to run away! Let's go! We'll try to do better henceforth. The Superman will take charge of that with more solicitude. He's waiting for you, the Superman! And I truly wonder what pleasant surprises he has in store for you!"

He turned to Marcel. "For you, a place in a jar, no doubt." Then, accentuating the stereotyped smile on his cheeks, visible behind the mask, for Miss Mary's benefit, he went on: "And for you..."

291

He did not finish—but his backscratcher cut through the air with an incisive downward gesture, signifying the operation he had in mind.

Then Marcel could control himself no longer. He leapt upon the machine-man in order to crush him, to batter to an atrocious pulp his metallic frame, his leather sheath and what remained of his flesh. His plan was simple. Once the commandant was exterminated, he counted on easily terrorizing the apathetic crew of a few men and twenty boys. If necessary, he would kill them all; he would throw Zadochbach and the sailors overboard, into space, then remain alone, master of the airplane; he would steer at the hazard of the winds, and end up landing somewhere. He would prefer a mortal plunge into the vast ocean, in the company of Miss Mary, to a return to the island.

But just as he launched himself forward, his fingers splayed, to grab and wring the neck of the half-man, a terrible force suddenly knocked down the arms he had raised so magnificently and threw him back, paralyzed, on the floor. At the same time, his adversary's voice clucked: "Imbecile! Naïve child! He thinks one can touch the Captain like that! He doesn't know all our secret forces. Caresco alone has the right to cut into me, child. Let's go! Tie them up!"

A few sailors came into the cabin, tied up the lovers with silk cords and carried them up to the deck with an ease that disconcerted, while proving to him that he had presumed too much of his strength. While the crewmen supervised the maneuver, now steering the airplane toward the return, pretty cabin-boys came to distract them. They performed a thousand graceful somersaults in front of them, threw them flowers, pulverized perfumes; and as the cold, in spite of the distributions of warmth, was intense at that altitude, they covered them with ermine mantles in which omnial heat maintained a mild warmth. Then, after having checked that their bonds, while immobilizing them, were not too tight, they left them alone.

"Monsieur Marcel," said Miss Mary then, "I've been very disappointed by my peregrinations through the world. I've knocked on all hearts, but none has truly opened to my pleas. But at least, when I wanted to go away, the people formed a cortege for me and let me go. Governments even assisted my departure. Alas, here I've been subjected to the greatest injustice, don't you think, since Caresco, after having promised me freedom of action, has taken me prisoner?"

"If only that were your sole destiny!" Marcel murmured.

"Well, know that I don't regret this new misfortune," Miss Mary continued, "for it has finally been given to me to admire a man...and that man was you! Your revolt was superb, Monsieur Marcel! But it was futile, as you can see. It's therefore necessary to resolve ourselves...at last, I'm becoming fatalistic...to support what we cannot prevent."

"They're going to separate us. Will you resolve to forget me?"

"I don't know what will become of me; I don't know whether, now that I'm going back a captive forever, I'll be able to struggle eternally against the new seductions that will tempt me...for moral resistance, alas, is exhausted like any other.... But remember this, Monsieur Marcel: my heart is entirely yours. Whether I live splendidly or die miserably, no one other than you will ever cross its threshold!"

Sunlight irradiated her hair, and her proud profile, emerging from the large mantle that covered her, was outlined very purely against the clarity of the blue spaces. Marcel was content with that declaration. He felt that he had run out of energy. He hoped that their fate might be less cruel than the captain had made them envisage. However, one last time, when the clouds traversed by the descending airplane covered his companion with their mist, he was gripped by one last surge of rage. Were not the light wisps that were now surrounding Miss Mary, seemingly rendering her more distant, a presage of the future, indicating that she was irremediably lost to him?

At that thought, he writhed in his bonds. Oh, if only he could free himself from the silken cords, in the denser cloud, pick up his fried, traverse the ten meters of deck that separated them from a liferaft-balloon, cut the mooring-rope and flee, flee again, with her, toward the unknown toward oblivion!

But his shackles were inextricable, and, in trying to rid himself of them, he sensed that he was only rendering them tighter.

The celestial blur cleared and returned them to their thoughtful and impotent contemplation. The temperature became exquisitely warm. The sailors reappeared, relieved them of their mantles and restored the liberty of their movements. It must have been about ten o'clock in the morning when they perceived the distant murmur of waves. Winged children came to alight on the metallic ringing. Songs and perfumes saluted them.

When they were taken to the bulwark to contemplate the enchantment of the landing, a unanimity of cries acclaimed them; the entire population of the island was there to receive them. They saw forty thousand arms extended toward them, in a swarming, picturesque, variegated disorder. Around them were verdure and flowers; in the distance, there were the gilded pegs of shiny monuments, red, silvery and pompously multicolored domes. The seductions of the panoramas took hold of them again. They were no longer thinking about escaping.

They landed.

Then, an enormous, inextinguishable laughter, from all the mouths and all the bellies, greeted them. The hilarious contagion had even gained Choumaque, Marius, Carabella and Madame Môme, all four of whom were placed in the first rank of the crowd. Courtesans, gitons, fecund mothers covered them with rose petals and inundated them with perfumes. A spouse with a long twisted beard tickled Miss Mary. At any other time Marcel would have reacted violently—but without knowing how, he was overwhelmed by that gaiety, and he began laughing invincibly, as the Redlander was laughing herself. Marjah took him away, while Carabella took possession of the young woman, after having planted the two bloody swellings of her mouth on her lips.

There was, in the crowd welcoming the captives so comically, only one man who was not laughing. Hidden behind the others, in the third rank of spectators, he resembled a sterile husband in the abundance of his large beard. But if that fake ornament, rendered apparently real by artifice, had been removed; if the frightful intensity of his gaze, fixed upon Miss Mary, had been observed; if the few words of madness that emerged from his contracted throat had been overheard, the joyful people would undoubtedly have ceased laughing for a moment. That man was Caresco.

After the scattering of the crowd, left alone on the shore, he watched the sea coming and going. Then he began to howl.

# CHAPTER XXIV

His forehead taut and his eyes cruel, with a weary gesture, Caresco pushed away the crucible in which he was attempting, by means of chemical combinations, to give birth to the cell, the first manifestation of Existence.

Disappointing labor! For twenty years, after many calculations engendered by his overheated mind, after many formulae, he had applied himself in vain. The infinitesimal particles of Omnium, alloyed and triturated, only ever produced Forces or Matter, but had never at any moment resulted in Life, that animate protoplasm whose combinations would have ensured the synthesis of Being.

Weary of his ardent research, the potentate was obliged to struggle with long mental effort to distinguish the place where he was. He finally recognized the sumptuous room in the palace, the walls streaming with precious metals and the most sumptuous fabrics sheltering his futile laboratory.

He shivered on finding himself alone—but the presence of Dr. Hymen, somnolent on a nearby stool, reassured him almost immediately. He considered the risible thinness, draped in the long frock-coat and the trinket-dangling waistcoat, coiffed in the furry top hat. That company was a benefit to him. It lulled his increasing anxieties and his ever-more-tormented humor with a sovereign calm.

"Hymen! Wake up, Hymen! Come here. You were asleep; and me, I'm so tired! Examine me! Something's happening in my organism that frightens me. Do you think I have a fever?"

"I don't think so," said the doctor, coming to take his pulse.

"Look at my eyes—are they normal?"

"They're such as I've always seen them, with unequally dilated pupils."

"And my reflexes, Hymen? Look for my reflexes!"

"What's the point? They don't exist…but they've never existed, for as long as I've known you."

"So?"

"So, undoubtedly, in another country people would say that your brain was that of a madman—but here, I can only observe your genius."

"Yes, my genius!" proclaimed the Superman, suddenly straightening up. "My genius! And think, Hymen, in what cause I've employed it! In struggling against nature, in creating happiness!"

"For thirty years now, every day, you've repeated the same words to me. I know them. You'd have done better to let me go on sleeping. You tire me out; I need sleep."

"Not at all!" protested Caresco. "You have no more time to rest than I have. Are there not a thousand things for us still to plan? Do you not have to watch over a thousand details? Have you thought about the foreigner? Do you know that I've subjected that daughter of the Red Land to my aphrodisiac fluid, and that she now measures eight-six on the psychometer? She'll be my triumph, Hymen!"

He calmed down. He stood up; then, palpating the oblique face of his collaborator, he said: "Why do you keep that ridiculous nose? Would you like me to put it straight, right now? You'll never be able to serve as a witness at my marriage like that!"

"Your marriage?"

"Yes, I shall marry the purest of the pure, the virgin of Virgins, Miss Mary Hardisson in a week's time, when my aphrodisiac superfluid—the Superman's superfluid, is that felicitous?—will have ten times the ordinary power that it exerts at present, and will have revealed he culminating point, the hundredth degree, of my scale! Know that! My scientists are working on it…ardent brains concentrating my new formula…violet backs bent, day and night, over crucibles, over needles, over mechanisms. Oh, the brave servants, the good subjects! And in a week, the evening of the Festival of Life, everything will be ready; the virgin will have blossomed in

Passion...and I shall possess the Nature in her! Let's go! Un-freeze yourself, Hymen—we'll see where we've got to!"

Bustling the doctor, he shoved him toward a cabin in which they both shut themselves up. Immediately following the pressing of a switch, a window opened on Miss Mary's room. Although a hundred kilometers separated them, they were able to see what was happening in her apartment, hear the voices that rose up there, contemplate the individuals who were there, exactly as if they had been in the next room.

The young woman, recently impregnated with the fluid, was at grips with Carabella. With a gesture of supreme inde-cency, the courtesan, employing ardent protestations, had just unveiled her body, swollen with amour like a fruit full of sap. The virgin, a prey already subjugated by the delirium of Pas-sion, was on the brink of no longer resisting. Their unfastened tunics confused their pink and mauve fluttering.

"There's no need to see any more—the rest is banal," said the Superman, closing the window. "She's already suc-cumbing! What will become of her when my intensive fluid takes effect? Prepare yourself, Hymen; I want to give a splen-did fête to celebrate that definitive triumph of my genius over Nature. Caresco-King, Caresco-God, will espouse the Virgin of Virgins, Nature tamed by him!"

# CHAPTER XXV

Choumaque and Marcel paused momentarily outside the entrance to the Temple of Fecundity, which the philosopher was not authorized to enter. He admired the cheerful perspective of the green hill pierced in certain places by white cascades allowing glimpses of their beds of red rock. A group of parasol pines delimited the crest. Nearer, three little lakes were alimented by the foam of torrents, and fish as blue as sapphires were zigzagging therein. The quotidian fête of the elements was renewed, adorably languid.

A fecund mother, her toga loose, with scarlet shoes studded with gems, emerged from a sandy pathway and passed close by. Her delightful blonde complexion was animated by a rush of blood when she recognized Marcel.

"I'll wait for you, handsome Sower!" she said, as she went by, with a provocative undulation of the hips. "I'm your privileged, today!"

"That's an admirable rump," Choumaque observed, "and I congratulate you, my friend, on being its beneficiary."

Marcel did not reply, occupied as he was in smiling at another fecund mother whose tunic he had untied the day before, and who was emerging from the same pathway, which ended at the bright façade of the gynaeceum.

"That one too!" exclaimed Choumaque, laughing. "My God, my friend, you have solid muscles. Madame Môme tamed mine more easily. How do you satisfy them?"

"Every morning I'm charged with a provision of genetic serum, which, as soon as it spreads through my veins, gives me the valor of Hercules with regard to the Amazons."

"August deeds of the Sower, you're losing your magnificence," Choumaque murmured; then, aloud, he added: "You definitely seem to be getting a taste for your new functions."

"Why not? One gets used to everything. That amorous diversity is easily supportable."

"So I see. O great Seneca, forgive them!"

Automatically, Choumaque hitched up his belt. In the six days since the fugitives had been returned to the island, as they had been separated, definitively affected to different social roles, the philosopher had observed the evident victory of his pupil's new mores. Marcel, having become a "Sower" for the constant repopulation of the island, had experienced a recrudescence of pleasure in going into the Temple of Creative Sensualities, where the quotidian labor awaited him. He no longer hid his appetite for it. He offered himself to the genetic serum as a drinker of other lands returned to his glass of alcohol, the morphine addict to his Pravaz syringe, the opium smoker to the blue spirals of his pipe, by virtue of a need for intoxication.

Yes, it was certainly the sybaritic poison of the island that had taken possession of the young man, which had dissolved his character so rapidly, had so promptly reduced him to the restricted mental level of the other subjects. Soon, undoubtedly, he would acclaim the autocracy of the Superman, and recognize in him the beneficence admitted by everyone.

The philosopher was only astonished by the rapidity with which that transformation had been accomplished. It gave him an even more wretched idea of humanity. He wondered what had become, in that collapse of character, of the keen passion that the young man had felt for Miss Mary, which seemed almost extinct. He knew, however, that during the first three days, the separation had been dolorous. For Marcel, no longer encountering the foreigner, remaining in horrible ignorance of the fate reserved for her, obliged to give to others the tenderness that he would have like to keep preciously for her, had constituted an ensemble of sacrifices whose affliction the sensual diversions of the temple had had difficulty overcoming.

At that time, Choumaque had kept silent, not wanting to torment a wound that was still raw, all the more so because revolt would have been futile, and he had made no attempt to disengage that soul from the inextricable seductive net that was enveloping it. Alas, that dolor had only lasted three days, so quickly did the phenomena of the soul, like those of the body, evolve on the island. Since then, the initial suffering had gradually dissipated. But if Marcel avoided interesting himself in the young woman's destiny, was it because of a taste for his new functions, or out of a cowardly desire no longer to torment himself? On hearing his pupil's declarations, the philosopher wanted to clarify the matter.

"My friend, what would you say if you learned that Miss Mary, for her part, remains no more hostile than you to the distractions offered to her?"

At the name of his beloved, Marcel was obliged to put his hand over his heart to quell its protestations. Choumaque approved of his initiative. Come on! There were still warm ashes in the hearth, since a little breath could reanimate the flame!"

"That's true—what has become of Miss Mary?" the young man said.

"I'm glad to be able to tell you that nothing has become of her yet. However, it's quite possible that that status quo will cease any day now. After your failed flight, Madame Môme, Marius and I thought that Caresco would definitely take possession of the child…you know in what fashion…the status of courtesan would then have been reserved for her, and you would have had the leisure to take advantage of it, like everyone else…"

Marcel could not repress a quiver of anger. The philosopher observed, however, that the surge was rapidly attenuated by a shrug of the shoulders translating the thought: *Why not, after all? Since there's no means of not submitting…*

Saddened by that mute restriction, he continued: "No, nothing has happened yet. The Superman seems to be disinterested in the Virgin. He's left her in the guard of Carabella, and appears not to be occupied with her any longer. I'm certain, anyway, that Caresco has other preoccupations…if preoccupations can grip a man to the point that he spends entire days meditating, his face stuck to a wall that his fingernails scrape, his mouth pronouncing incomprehensible words…

"At other times he summons his council of engineers and scientists, and, suddenly becoming amiable, submits projects of an insane conception to them. Has he not proposed to them, seriously, to take possession of the sun and the moon, attracting them by means of omnial forces, and founding another realm there? He supported it with positive calculations...it was even discussed. Evidently, people around him are becoming anxious...it's said that he's always been strange, but that this time it might really be the onset of madness. And note that, in addition, he passes through periods of remarkable practical sense; he succeeds marvelously in the most delicate operations...three human monads have been manufactured in one night!"

"Have you seen her often since our return?" asked Marcel, cutting those details short, seemingly in a hurry.

"Yes, sometimes."

"Does she talk to you about me?"

"Perhaps she thinks about you; she doesn't talk about you."

"Tell her, my dear Choumaque, that her memory is imperishable in me. Come on! I have to leave you...the mothers with many children are waiting for me..."

He shook the philosopher's hand, and then moved away with a light tread. The grace of his stature, the high stance of his head, the perfect elegance of his orange doublet with crystal buttons and his harmoniously tailored legs—the whole ensemble of strength and charm that made him one of the most sought-after sowers—disappeared round a corner of the portico open in the façade of the Temple of Fecundity.

On seeing him stride away so rapidly, so insouciantly, Choumaque felt filled with melancholy. *It's time to act,* he said to himself, *but how? What can I do? Now that he's declining toward the neutral state, I feel less ambition to get him out of his rabbit-hutch. And then again, truly, what can I do...?*

Prey to lamentable ideas, but more confident than ever in his theory of equilibria, the principles of which he ruminated,

Choumaque took the road to the Caravanserai, where he in-tended to pursue his enquiry. Miss Mary was still living there, and the park was her favorite place to walk.

Every time he had encountered her there, dreading that he might reawaken her dolor, he had not dared evoke the memory of the companion torn away from her tenderness, nor that of the persecuted fatherland from which Caresco's tyran-ny had separated her forever. Every time, too, he had to admit that he had found her less sad. Carabella, her faithful guardian, by virtue of personal attachment as much as the despot's or-ders, no longer left her side. She was gradually initiating her into the pleasures of the island, which Miss Mary no longer seemed to be disdaining, and for which she even seemed to be acquiring a taste.

The neophyte's conversation, instead of concerning, as before, memories of the past, now revealed the advent of her senses of life. She spoke about the frivolities of the land, the tranquility of mind that the indigenes experienced there, ex-tolled the beauty of bodies, of places, of monuments, fêtes and games. On several occasions, she had spoken without fear about the marvelous operations with which the Superman fa-vored the health and happiness of his subjects.

She still remained faithful to her brother's efforts; she made daily pilgrimages to the reportage screen, which showed him to her, ever valiant, with his handful of brave followers, offering desperate resistance to the collation, but Choumaque thought he divined a habit rather than a real concern. Was that defection only apparent? Was Miss Mary feigning indifference in order to deceive her companion's surveillance? Or was she really, by virtue of a moral decline, showing that she was less well-tempered than she had seemed, sufficiently submissive to the deliquescent influence of new mores for the sacred images of General Hardisson and Marcel, her two heroes, to have been burned already by the sun of seductions?

In his present discouragement, the philosopher would willingly have leaned toward that second supposition. Howev-er, in this case, as in Marcel's, he would not have dared to swear to anything, for his usual skill in diagnosing psychological states had been disrupted by the fact that on the island, people's personalities were so extensively modified by stupefying and stimulating fluids, and also by the medical and sanitary practices, that he had to wonder whether those physical agents did not constitute an entirely artificial mentality, incomprehensible for a philosopher whose mind had remained sane, and whether their suppression might not bring his friends back to the pure conceptions of normal life.

Having arrived outside the foreigner's apartment, he hesitated momentarily. Access to the room was forbidden to him, but, more than that prohibition, he feared the friction that his irruption into such a sacred refuge was about to cause. After confiding his name to the announcer, he was, therefore, very surprised to observe the enthusiasm with which he was received.

"There you are, my dear Choumaque! Come in! Sit down as comfortably as possible, on that divan."

Miss Mary was to longer afraid to show a part of her body naked beneath the rich brocaded surah fabric that ornamented her bed. Her hair, gathered up in a torsade, leaving the pure slenderness of her nape uncovered, still had the same delightful blondeness, iridescent in the sunlight, but her face was enlivened by warmer and more youthful colorations, as if, in order to spice it, she had had recourse to the fluids and ointments with which the courtesans rendered their seductions more evident. Dark violet-tinted rings around her orbits suggested a hint of lassitude, and Choumaque wondered what the nature of that fatigue might be, for the large bed was in a state of disorder, and the trace of another body persisted beside her, hollowed out in the feathery softness.

"You're not alone? I'm disturbing you..."

"Not at all. Carabella, who spent the night with me, has just left."

That confession made her blush. She felt the visitor's gaze settle on her shoulder, where there was still an ecchymosis, the trace of an excessively ardent kiss. Understanding that

304

that signature might have betrayed the impetuosity of her companion, she hastened to cover it with a large sachet embroidered with golden arabesques, on which she was lying. Then, to deflect the philosopher's perspicacity, she asked: "To what do I owe the joy of such an early visit, my dear Choumaque?"

"Nothing in particular. I simply wanted to enquire as to your health, to learn from your own mouth whether your reintegration to the island is not saddening you excessively."

"No, not excessively. I won't hide from you that I'm rather enjoying it. Carabella is an exquisite friend, who has made me understand that one can live agreeably here."

"Evidently...but you ambition was not, at the beginning, to attach yourself to this soil. Your brother, your compatriots...."

"Truly, one thinks oneself too indispensable to everyone. They are maintaining the resistance very valiantly without me. Will they be victorious? Perhaps. I imagine that my presence might even be an obstacle. Carabella has assured me of it."

"And the Superman?"

"I no longer hear mention of him. He wishes me well..."

"It's doubtless for that reason," Choumaque persisted, "that I've caught sight of him on several occasions prowling in the gardens perfumed by the odors of the night, once disguised as a slave, once as a feline and a third time covered in foliage, like an ambulant tree..."

"Don't you think that you might have been led astray by your imagination, my dear Zéphi? Carabella has told me what the Superman wants of me...doubtless you know that? Confess that it's very little, in compensation for the happiness that an entire lifetime will have in reserve for me?"

"And Marcel?" Choumaque finally risked, anxiously hitching up his belt.

At that name she stated slightly. All the aspects of her valiant past and present decline were more imperatively specified by that question than the preceding ones. She lowered her eyelids over the confusion of her eyes.

"Yes, Marcel…he's the sole cloud that persists of my dissipated tempests. I dream about him every night, even though Carabella informs me as to his occupations elsewhere. I hope that we'll be reunited in the future. If Caresco is good, we'll make a household later, as Madame Môme and Marius have made one. I hope so…and why not? I envisage a pleasant enough liaison thus…have you seen him? Does he still think about me? Have you talked to him about me?"

"I was talking to him about you this morning. He has not forgotten you, either."

"So you see, my dear Zéphi, that everything is for the best!" the young woman concluded, becoming joyful again, and offering the philosopher a box of pink pastilles, with which she began to fill her mouth.

Choumaque thanked her and fled. It was high time that things took a different turn in order that those two cherished children could retain one another, before Caresco, with a sweep of his scalpel, cut the last fibers that linked them together. But what could he do?

Then, in his confusion, he resolved to consult Madame Môme. The High Priestess alone was capable of giving him good advice, given that her functions had familiarized her with the secret mechanisms of the island, and that she had not hesitated to assist the young people's flight the first time. At least she would tell him positively whether there was anything that could still be attempted in order to save them.

Against the façade of the Palace of Sensualities there was a kind of large translucent cage reminiscent of a leech attached to the wall, level with the frescos swarming like a colossal Sabbath of erethism and recounting in violent colors all the practices of amour. Silhouettes were agitating inside the bell. After having admired the erotic sculptures that descended from there in cascades of gestures all the way to the base of the monument, Choumaque paused momentarily to listen to a song, celebrated on the island, emitted by a familiar deep voice; then, omitting to applaud the singer, he hailed him.

The same voice replied: "What! It's you, pauper! Come up, then."

"I'd like nothing better, but how?"

"That's true, unless..."

Sliding along the wall, the cage descended, stopping at the level of the portal. Choumaque stepped over the two pink marble breasts of a recumbent nymph, set foot on the red porphyry loins of a faun lying next to the woman, trod on the shoulders of a blue sandstone satyr who was sitting watching them, and then, after having climbed a ladder of attitudes no less equivocal with the aid of his hands, finally reached the cage, which opened to let him in.

When he was inside, Marius pressed a switch that took the apparatus back to the level of the frescos that he was re-gilding.

"As you see, darling, I'm retouching my masterpieces. I'm patching up the façade for the festival the day after tomorrow. What do you think? Will posterity celebrate my talent?"

Choumaque did not reply. He said bonjour to the paint-er's companions: Madame Môme, who was lying languidly on a sofa, mixing essences in her pulverizer; and a radiantly formed adolescent clad in a long green smock, who was Mari-us' apprentice. He sat down, curiously inspecting the painter's airborne laboratory, which could easily have been mistaken for a boudoir if a display of brushes and polychromatic recep-tacles had not affirmed its laborious utility. In one corner, on a glass-topped table, there was an ingenious device animate by omnial force, a kind of miniature pile-driver, crushing colors and combining them with solid materials that ought to render their brightness imperishable. At intervals, the adolescent left his brushes and went to regulate the machine, or pour into the elements of the compound into a funnel: sparkling substances with ardent reflections, liquid silicates, powdered rock and chemical ingredients.

"Anyway, do you see this installation? It's not in Paris that the members of the Institut can decorate a monument with as much comfort as if they were working in their studio, is it?

This cage is my studio, which moves every time I inaugurate a new endeavor. Madame Môme knows it well, too. She's spent exciting hours here, eh?"

The High Priestess responded with an affectionate grimace. Then, in order that her other lover should not feel unequally favored, she came to sit next to him, taking his hand. She was astonished to find it limp and discouraged.

"So, my dear Zéphi, it's not going well?"

"Not at all."

"Tell, then."

"Not here. The walls are talkative, the ears remember..."
He pointed at the adolescent.

Marius protested. "For once, old chap, the judgment you're making is false. Here, I'm at home. No exterior purchase is possible on our thoughts or our words. This cage, which I ordered in crystal, in order that light could illuminate my work naturally within it, isolates us. In the same way, the substances in my paint are insulating. As for the adolescent, don't worry any more about him than my pots—he's as deaf as they are."

"Deaf?"

"Totally, because his function in the State will be that of painter. Caresco, deeming that the perfectibility of one sense is improved by the abolition of competing senses, destroyed the child's hearing—look at the scar behind his ear. He renders sculptors deaf in the same way, and musicians blind..."

"But that's absurd!" exclaimed Choumaque. "To paint, to sculpt, to find rich harmonies is to create—and it's necessary, in order to create, to have the assistance of all the senses, which complement one another!"

"That's just it!" objected Marius. "You don't know that, according to Caresco and the cohort of scientists and artists he brought with him, the people, once definitively installed in their happiness, will no longer have any need to create! After us, science and art will be definitive. The apprentices we instruct, like this adolescent, will no longer have to produce. They will maintain the good condition of our discoveries and our ideal, repeating their ingenuities or copying their esthetic, but they won't contribute anything themselves. They'll be remarkable workmen, no more. Progress is at its apogee."

"Absurd! Vanity!" proclaimed Choumaque. "It's a recipe for collapse, with brief delay. In a hundred years, other people will have overtaken you…the circle of machines that protects you will be destroyed by a new discovery. Your manifestations of art will be out of date; your monuments, already ridiculous, will be odious; your people, separated from nature by chemistry, will fall into decadence; and the rest will follow logically. You don't understand, then, that happiness requires progress, and progress effort, and that perfection doesn't exist! To dare to say that one has achieved it is the pretention of cracked brains!

"And that's why I'm stifling in your indolence, why I'm fed up to the back teeth with your dream! For Caresco's dream is a golden chimera seated on a bolster of ennui, and his island of Eucrasia is a paradise of flesh that makes my soul howl! Yes, to save myself! To save myself, taking my two friends with me!"

In despair he buried his bicolored head in his hands.

The High Priestess felt deeply moved. "That's what's making you sad, Zéphi, I can see. Well, know that there's no longer any possibility of flight. You're stuck here in perpetuity—all the more so as Caresco, if my knowledge of men isn't mistaken, is utterly infatuated with the Virgin. Yes, she's got under his skin. Take it from me, old men falling into senility are the silliest of lovers!"

"How do you know?"

"I know because he's charged me with a certain task…"

"Oh! Tell me!"

Madame Môme's physiognomy, until then so glad of these few moments of intimacy, so delighted to be able to manifest abandon by a return to her old expressions of mischief, suddenly resumed all its gravity. Making several movements with the back of her fingers sliding them over the soft underside of her slightly fleshy chin, she refused.

"Impossible, Zéphi."

"I beg you, Môme!"

"Will you keep your trap shut, if I tell you?"

"On our love!"

Then, at that invocation, she yielded her secret, explaining that the Superman had given her the mission of charging the foreigner with an aphrodisiac superfluid of new invention, which would vanquish the virgin's last resistance. The means was not new, since Môme herself, when she had still been conducting herself like the daughter of a superior officer, had been the victim of an honorable old man who had seduced her by offering her cantharidated bonbons. Blood of ovaries! What a broadside, for a first time! But here the method changed. It was necessary to march with Science—with the result that he had to guide Miss Mary to a special contact on the evening of the fête of Life—in two days time, that is...

"And then?" asked Choumaque, choking.

"Then, when she's done to a turn, he'll take her away."

"Where? To do what?"

Marius, ceasing to paint, had turned round. He was the one who finished: "You know very well!"

"What do you expect?" concluded Madame Môme. "It's his way. All tastes are in nature...and after that, there'll be the great repose..."

"The true repose is only found in the study of wisdom," Choumaque observed. In spite of the affirmation of that precept, however, such sadness invaded him that Madame Môme thought it her duty to console him. With her bejeweled hand she caressed the cherished face of her old lover. At the same time, she became indignant.

"Why didn't that Joseph Marcel pop her cherry? I told him to do it! I said to him: violate her! That was the only means to make the Superman lose interest in the child! He couldn't do it. So much the worse for him!"

"We still have two days and one night," Choumaque objected, timidly. "Couldn't we, between now and then...?"

"They're being kept apart; it's impossible. Unless..."

She meditated. A great breath of devotion suddenly illuminated her. She sensed the soul of a New Earth. Choumaque leaned toward her anxiously, hoping that deliverance might yet emerge from her indecision. And as she still remained hesitant, he had recourse to the sole means of persuasion capable of acting upon her. He took hold of one of her breasts, bursting forth beneath her loose tunic, and squeezed it forcefully.

"Unless," the High Priestess continued, won over by that testament of sympathy, "on the evening of the fête that they have to attend, in the general disorder, in the noise and the crowd, I can..."

"Oh! Yes, my little Môme!"

"I'd be taking a big risk, Zéphi!"

She did not have time to give more ample explanations. A sound of thunder shook the glass walls of the cage. The Superman descended from his red airplane sown with golden vibrions and ovules, which was accompanied by a numerous entourage, and came into the cage. His costume, a vast butcher's apron, left the violent musculature of his hairy torso and arms bare, stained with the blood of recent operations. His haggard eyes and clenched jaws, making his teeth grate, were terrible. Without paying any attention to the other people present, he was only interested in the High Priestess, whom he took into his nacelle, in order to give her orders.

# CHAPTER XXVI

The night was magnificently extended. Airplanes appeared in the dark blue serenity. First their two headlights became visible, shining like double stars, and then, gradually, they were constellated by red, blue, yellow and green scintillations: an entire display of celestial jewels, whose gleam rendered visible the palpitations of wings, which did not take long to fold up. They landed, crammed with people, rutilant in splendid fabrics, dazzling with the light reflected by sashes studded with gems and precious metals Couples disentwined; adolescents, their legs outside the nacelle, waited to jump. Music, soprano and contralto voices, supported by masculine counterpoints, the chords of lyres, citharas, harps, flutes and sistrums, mingled and intersected, coming together in the same diapason. Arms raised hieratically toward the sky acclaimed the night of joy: universal joy, unanimously radiated. Everything melted, intersected, palpitated, prayed, sang for the Festival of Light, moving toward the Temple of Sensualities.

"Glory to the Superman! Glory to Life! Night of ecstasy, blessed voluptuousness! Sublime heavens!"

On the ground, along the hillside, at the feet of the giant trees, yet more people gathered, all rutilant. Fragments of processions, poured out by the tubes, brightened the roads fantastically, and the spreading branches formed vaults of gleaming chlorophyll. Cascades, growling at the passage of the happy crowd, caught their flamboyance, and their foam prolonged the memory of the magical vision in the shadow of their subterranean flight.

Children, covered in flowers and bearers of luminous torches, walking at a brisk pace, ran ahead of processions of courtesans, whose light veils, scarcely posed on their naked bodies, seemed ready to evaporate. In the air, gitons were buzzing, fluttering like butterflies of delightful and infinite hue. A pell-mell of a thousand family groups, surging around a bend, waved great luminous palm-fronds, which enthused the firmament. By contrast, their shadows, on the ground sonorous with their footfalls, were dancing as far as the eye could see, and their superb silhouettes echoed the cadence of a song of joy.

The long beards of sterile spouses slicing through the brightness of scarlet togas; the breasts of fecund mothers jutting beneath vaporous vestments; blonde hair mingled with flowers; the solid figures of laughing, agile children—everything filed up with the redness shed by the torches. Courtesans searched the area for their lovers, or consulted light mirrors suspended from their belts in order to smile at their beauty. More airplanes landed, going to place themselves, still lit up, in two scarlet ranks that were two stripes of fire from which, at intervals, multicolored fireworks soared, setting the velvet sky ablaze and embalming it with intoxicating essences.

Soon, the fragments of the cortege joined up, the colors combined; the fête was disciplined into a perfect order before the façade of the Palace of Sensuality, the stone gestures of which were magnificently fulgurant. Then the splendor moved, the songs resumed, and the host began to snake piously, like an enormous luminous stream coming from some celestial spring, whose dissolved individualities no longer existed.

Choumaque and Marcel had placed themselves at the last column of the peristyle in front of which the procession passed. Sculptural enlacements hanging over them kept them isolated in relative shadow. They were thus able to distinguish all of the physiognomies that were filing along the colonnade in ranks of ten to go into the temple. They marveled at the nudities splendidly apparent beneath the transparency of polychromatic veils; at the faces enlivened by the glare of the brandished torches; at the torsos, gracious in the gitons, broad in the spouses; at breasts, hard in the courtesans, delicate in the virgins; at rumps, firm in the fecund mothers, undulant in the nubile; at the shoulders, powerful in the Sowers, gracious in the adolescent; at the Form, in sum, radiant in all of them, even the slaves, two ranks of whose yellow tunics framed the flow diversified by the distinctive hues of the castes.

Harmonious bodies, desirable bodies, bodies evocative of fecund Life or sterile Sensuality passed by in thousands upon thousands, all as impeccable as one another, all as vibrant with the same unanimous adoration. Between the compact groups, gaps appeared, occupied by flamboyant allegories surrounded by dancers. Thus, in the tumult of footsteps and songs, they saw the symbols of creation file by: the Mysteries of Life that the funeral of Mirror-of-Smiles had already showed them, but appearing this time in a dazzling phantasmagoria.

In the distance, all the way to the sides of the hill reddened by the lights, the procession formed a sumptuous trail of flames, a wave of gold, from which departed, toward the depths of the immensity, dusts of light, which came together to reproduce in the sky the images on the ground. In consequence, there were two spectacles, one on the real ground, the other in the enigma of space.

Then, a final apotheosis irradiated. It was the coronation of Life: two naked bodies celebrating the fecund act, on a cart drawn by twenty lions, whose manes were stroked by naked virgins. To honor them, the voices and the instruments swelled, more enthusiastic still. Thuribles swung by nubile young woman, to whom luminous flowers were thrown, immediately extinguished, sent delightful scents toward the couple, whose nostrils filled with them voluptuously.

Miss Mary, drunk with exaltation, appeared amid that delirium. Her body, beneath the diaphanous vapor of a floating pink peplum florid with white lilies, was writhing in the same undulations as her companions. Her hair, raised in a headdress and crystallized with diamonds, had glints of coppery yellow and mat gold. Behind her, ten paces away, the High Priestess was conducting a battalion of dancers by means of gestures, in the first rank of which, Carabella, never taking her eyes off the neophyte, was matching the rhythm of her arms and legs to the perfect movements of star-like bayaderes.

"There she is!" Marcel murmured, suddenly breathless.

She passed very close to them, brushing them. Choumaque, with a rapid movement that Carabella could not see, her eyes being momentarily hypnotized by a celestial apparition, grabbed her abruptly by the wrist and drew her into the shadow. Then the wave flowed on, dominated by the enormity of domesticated elephants and airplanes in the form of gigantic birds, crested by an orgy of women and flowers, human and vegetal corollas fusing in the light. A thousand dancers of both sexes, a hundred musicians playing fulgurant trumpets and tambourines, sistrums, flutes and cymbals, the tail of the cortege, soon separated them from the High Priestess, who had had time to give them a sign, and from Carabella, who had not seen anything.

"Oh, Miss Mary! Miss Mary!" stammered the young man, clutching her to his heart.

"Marcel! I've finally found you again!" she replied, scarcely defending herself from further caresses."

"Let's go in!" said Choumaque, pushing them toward the august threshold of the temple, with the end of the cortege was now invading. "We need to find Môme again now."

After twenty marble steps, the immense hall appeared, paved with a brilliant mosaic, garnished with a circular gallery sustaining the crimson ceiling speckled with golden vibrions and ovules, with huge alabaster pilasters from which scarlet flags studded with precious stones flew. At the back there was a blaze of omnial light displaying an immense stage, with four sets of violet-carpeted steps, at the top of which a single black-clad man, standing on a gold entablement, was officiating: the Superman!

Six smoky pylons, rising to his height, threw him swirls of blue-tinted perfumes, which lit him up as he passed through them, causing him to scintillate. Twenty thousand faces were looking toward him, their expressions full of ecstasy, their eyes completely fascinated, and frenzy in their flesh.

As they penetrated into that furnace of light and adoration, they felt that no terrestrial or divine dementia, no royal coronation, no elevation of the papal tiara, had ever equaled that moment of frantic devotion. The man in black had just made a gesture, which the people followed. All attention was fixed on an immense screen supported by two ivory columns, on which images succeeded one another, animated with such artistry that one might have sworn that they were real.

And it was Life that the people then adored: Life in all is phases, from the moment when the male and female seeds, having agitated separately for a moment, came together in impregnation, and then fertilization, to form the human egg, to which being succeeded. One could follow their evolution, see the affirmation of sex, see the man and the woman grow, see them unite in sexual intercourse. At each transformation, music fell from the ceiling, translating the particular sensibility of each mode, from the soft melancholy twilight of conception to the impetuous intensity of creative caresses.

At times, the people fell silent, and only the murmur of emotions rose up and dissolved into one agonizing voiced of passion. At others, when the harmonies became sharper, bosoms incapable of moderation exhaled their delirium in cries; then, a long frisson of amour passed through the assembled flesh.

What charmed the three neophytes most of all, however, was to feel themselves in the same perfect unison of intoxication, and to celebrate Life like the others. It seemed to them that the colored perfumes escaping from the enormous pylons in blue, green and red swirls changed their sentimentality as they breathed them in, enabling them to enter into a communion of profound sensuality with the soul of the crowd. Their faces were inundated by tears. Their breath was amplified, as if at the summit of a mountain of delights. Without having learned any of the words, they sang the melody that everyone was singing. Their voices had soft and sweet vibrations; their hands joined; their features filled with a magnificent joy.

Marcel and Miss Mary had no time to reflect on the intoxication that took hold of them, to wonder how they were submitting to it. They were traversed by the tremors of an in-

vincible passion; and they knew that the frissons were imper-
sonal, that they would not have been able to extend the sentiment to their companion. The seed evolving before the
Redlander's eyes, and which ultimately became a man, really
was *The Man*; the predominant ovule whose changes Marcel
was following, which was transformed into a woman, was,
from the very beginning, *The Woman*. And if they appropriat-
ed a designation, if they paid homage to anyone, it was to the
black-clad dominator in the bright light. Caresco alone absorbed their frenzy; on him alone was their overexcited adoration concentrated. He was God.

Suddenly, that magnetism dissipated, and silence fell.
The evolution of Life had just been completed. The omnial
glimmers went out; everything fell back into darkness. They
grasped the verity again and were able to look at one another.
One place in the Temple was still resplendent, like a hole in
the light, but infinitely distant, where the vault faded away.
Something that could not be distinguished was happening at
that point. A mass movement was produced in the crowd, carrying them in the direction of the stage.

Standing there, draped in a black velvet mantle fringed in
gold and sown with diamond vibrions, the Superman, extending his carescoclast like a scepter above still-quivering viscera,
was officiating. They had difficulty making him out because
the perfumes that filled the atmosphere formed a mist interposed before him. But in that pageantry he seemed taller, his
features more sharply sculpted with violent domination—
which did not prevent them, under the suggestion of the intoxication, from finding him divinely handsome and superbly
young. His every movement, brought out the golden luster of
his costume and caused the diamond vibrions to glitter. All the
light was concentrated on him, creating an aureole about his
monstrous presence, while obscurity filled the rest of the
Temple. Zigzagging sparks ran over his brown beard, over the
curved ridge of his nose, over the jewels of his diadem. Only
his eyes remained insensible to such an orgy of clarity; they

did not catch the rays; an emptiness as unfathomable as his thoughts subsisted there, in the orifices of the orbits.

He extended his golden instrument hieratically above the bowl containing the viscera, and proclaimed: "I am the Superman! I celebrate Life!"

An ocean of acclamations unfurled in response to his voice; forty thousand arms reached out toward him.

"Glory to Caresco! Gratitude to the benefactor!" howled the crowd, its members falling to their knees.

Then the Superman made a sign toward the inferior stage. Choumaque, hoisting himself up on tiptoe, saw the troop of geniuses—artists, engineers and scientists—in their violet togas, crowned with flowers. He recognized some physiognomies that he had seen before in the Palace of the Brain when he went through it on his way to undergo the operation that had rejuvenated him. They were all imprinted with the universal exaltation. In the first row, Zadochbach's lips and Hymen's shock of hair were displayed, confounded in adoration.

Behind them, along the steps, there was a brilliant cascade of prostrated backs, descending as far as the third stage, where the sterile spouses, fecund mothers and the most notorious gitons and courtesans were similarly prostrated, bowing their heads to the floor, carpeted with red velvet. The fourth plane formed a vaster oval reserved for sacrifices, where the symbols guarded by nudities had been deposited. After that, there was the anonymous and operable crowd.

At an order from the potentate, six nubile young women stood up, abandoning the pylons where, as magnificent vestals, they had maintained the fire into which, at intervals, they had thrown the substances of perfumes expanding amid showers of sparks. The first three were swinging fuming gold incense-burners; the other three were armed with tridents, which they were brandishing in the air. They headed, passionately, toward the Superman. At intervals, their rhythmic strides parted the mantle of their hair, allowing the sight, as they went up the steps and came into the light, of their nacreous flesh, the curve of their hips and the proud emergence of their pink-tipped breasts. They were six incomparable masterpieces of creation, as similar as art-works cast from the same mold, endowed with the same simultaneously powerful and delicate type common to the entire race.

Having reached the Sovereign Officiant, they bowed down and kissed the hem of his mantle, then got up again and advanced toward the sacred vessel. The polished arms of some plunged in the tridents, spearing the viscera, while the others presented their incense-burners. The human fodder, oozing crimson liquid, emerged, traversed the gap, reached the flame and sizzled with a troubled swirl, from which three doves escaped.

The crowd howled: "Life is not extinct! Nothing dies! Fire purifies life!"

Caresco had taken hold of the vessel, now dispossessed of its organs but still filled with blood. He raised it to his lips and drank a mouthful, and then, with a circular gesture, scattered the rest. The crowd converged upon that rutilant rain in order to collected the manna. Hands extended. Bodies convulsed, mouths grabbed. Miss Mary received a drop on her cheek and uttered a vibrant cry, which was a cry of joy.

Then, horrible things supported on delightful shoulders filed along a winding path traced along the steps and concluding at the Superman's feet. Through a tumult of flesh and perfumes, a riot of light and music, passed the monstrous fruits of the imagination, science and genius of Caresco. They were deformed beings fitted with apparatus juxtaposed with their shreds, all the attempts made to reduce the normal, complicated and suffering individual to the primal individual, simple and devoid of dolorous organs: a demented conception of a state bordering perfection.

First, the half-man captain, planted on his pedestal, presented himself. The surgeon had rid him of his remaining arm, with the result that the machine-man now presided over all the functions of his life with simple thrusts of the head delivered as required to a panel placed behind his occiput. Each pressure activated an ingenious omnial mechanism in the service of his rare needs. Beneath his aluminum mask and his leather carapace, one sensed that he was radiant with joy.

An enthusiasm saluted him, and its joy mingled with the shrill stridency of his reformed larynx.

Then, no less acclaimed, came the hermaphrodites, men changed into women and vice versa, displaying their sexual organs; the Thought-reader; the talking animals; an elephant whose trunk had been replaced by the tentacle of an octopus; then the guardian goose of the Brain; then deformities without number, tumors adapted to healthy locations, hollows and lumps, heads without skulls, skulls without brains, and even parts of individuals sustained by an artificial life. Finally, the supreme tableau was the appearance of the last surviving human monad: a fragment of trunk that could be seen to be breathing, with difficulty, and a quarter of a head without a skull, almost devoid of cerebral matter, devoid of eyes, ears and nostrils—all replaced by pieces of flaccid skin—with a single orifice, which was the mouth. In any case, when it arrived in front of the Superman, it burst like a punctured balloon, collapsed and died.

"Glory to the Superman! Glory to Caresco!" the delirious crowd was still howling.

"Isn't it admirable, Marcel?" murmured Miss Mary, her hands extended toward the man in black. "Into what Heaven have we been transported?"

"Yes, we're in Heaven!"

*It is, however, necessary for us to return to earth*, Choumaque observed to himself, regaining a slight grip on positive verity, like one of those drinkers in whom the sentiment of reality reappears in the midst of their drunkenness, reanimating a gleam of reason in their mental confusion.

He made a heroic effort to maintain his ideas in that state of normal equilibrium. He understood that if he allowed himself to be impregnated for much longer, he would share the fate of his friends, and that the folly was reaching them from the troubled perfumes emitted by the smoking pylons. New,

320

more compact swirls were escaping at that moment; the vestals were reanimating the fires of Passion.

He grabbed the hands of the young people and dragged them toward the exit. He ran, crushing their wrists. Purer air suddenly inundated them, as soon as they had patted the heavy curtains at the entrance.

They breathed in delightedly, feeling their brains relieved of an enormous weight. Now the lights were setting the Temple ablaze again; the fête was resuming. Harmonies rose up tempestuously; dances were deployed, causing all the flames to sway, exulting twenty thousand radiant, almost naked bodies caressing one another.

Emerged from their fever, they gazed at the spectacle through a veil of transparent smoke, like a distant, remote fairyland that was foreign to them.

"We were in there!" said Marcel. "And we were joining in with their actions, their songs, their hypnotism! What power drew us away, then? What power has now disengaged us?"

"And how admirable it still is," remarked the young woman, with a hint of regret.

"Breathe deeply of the air that the night sends you!" Choumaque was content to order. "Breathe the air of salvation!"

Madame Môme appeared. Her garments were in disorder, her jewels were missing and her peplum was ripped. It seemed that she had been obliged to make a violent effort to get out of the crowd in which her profession retained her. At intervals, she raised to her nostrils a little gold flask incrusted with emeralds; at each dose of essence that she breathed in, her eyes became more lucid, and the fever left her cheeks. She had to draw the energy necessary to her courageous act from that receptacle.

"Follow me, quickly!" she said, finally.

They obeyed. She opened a bronze door in the wall, hidden by a thick silk curtain. They went into an ill-lit corridor in which the sounds of the fête no longer reached them. Even their footfalls were silent. Then, at a turning, there was a dazzling light. It was a sumptuous crypt, a glare of gold, green and red, which suffocated them with its vacillations of gems and rare metals, and the cascades of riches springing from the walls, as if all the brilliant treasures of the earth were accumulated there. One a pedestal of precious stones, at waist height, a pink marble group was radiant: a man and woman, naked, marvelously beautiful, engaged in sexual intercourse.

"Come closer!" the High Priestess ordered. "Look! Touch these divine bodies, while holding hands! Impregnate yourselves with Passion!"

Immediately, Miss Mary found herself projected toward the sublime Inspirers. Her wrist encountered Marcel's, and pressed against it. A spark sprang from the couple, which traversed them both. The fluid was in them. They shivered.

"Now, my children," said Choumaque's mistress, "get away from here, in order that no contrary force can oppose the aphrodisiac benefits. Get out! Avoid Caresco! Stay away from Carabella! Both of them are searching for you. You, Zéphi, watch over them. I'm going back to my post, to die there if anyone has seen me! Oh, Zéphi, how I must love you, to have turned his own weapons against Caresco!"

She dropped her flask and fled.

An unknown ravishment had taken possession of the two young people. They put their arms around one another's waist as they left the crypt. They seemed to be walking in Heaven, so light were their footsteps; in Hell, so much lust was coursing through their veins. They went out, no longer interested in the gigantic festival that was now displayed, prodigious, tumultuous and lascivious, in a fury of embracing bodies.

Immediately, the night took hold of them by the splendor of the moon at its apogee. They had never seen it as magnificent. Going around two rows of flamboyant airplanes, they went toward a wood of immense parasol pines, which the celestial fluidity plastered with blue tints among the shade of its branches. Underfoot, fresh grass sloped upwards to a rock beside the sea. They could hear the soft and solemn waves caressing the emergence of the island; and through a gap excavated in the caprice of the shoreline, they saw the brief spasms of waves glinting in the distance, running and dying away, in a languor of amorous achievement. The frissons and incense of nature were prowling around.

"Look, Miss Mary—Passion is singing and shining universally! Everything is telling us to love one another!"

He hugged her to his torso; he could feel her heart beating more precipitately, her breath gasping. He led her toward one of the tall trees, whose foliage extended its giant protection.

"O Mary! O virgin! Let's imitate Creation! Let's imitate those who fill intoxication with kisses! Everything is caressing! Everything is swooning! The slightest murmurs of the warm night bring us the testimony of a unanimous sensuality!"

She did not reply. She listened to that grave voice like a delicious music, as passionately enveloping as the perfumed air, as the light of the heavens, as the cadence of the waves and the scattered harmonies. She allowed her admirable head coiffed with large white lilies, which the radiance filtering from infinite space illuminated divinely, to tilt backwards.

Thus inclined, the velvet of her large eyes, the most pulp of her mouth, and the delicate nacre of her cleavage appeared, touched with celestial cosmetics. At the same time, two tears of tenderness confessed that her soul was similarly vanquished, offering itself.

"You're weeping! You're weeping! If I were only able to translate that which is also weeping in me! For you, indescribable songs are rising up there. Listen to them, understand them! My heart is broken for you, O whiteness emerging from the night, which I would like to drink!"

Then, she huddled more closely against him. She raised two hands hot with fever to his bold forehead, and caressed his silky hair; she caressed his ardent face, and it seemed that the touch of his beard released a thousand delights, which shook her to the deepest roots of her being. Their mouths approached, breathing in one another's breath; their lips communed recklessly.

She said: "The earth is large, the sea profound, the heaven infinite, but all that is nothing compared to my desire for you, Marcel. Close to you, I forget everything; I renounce everything. I forget my fatherland, which is bleeding, my brothers, who are falling, my countrymen, who are dying. O desire to love, which fills me, which is killing me, where are you taking me? What will you make me do? In what pincers will you crush me? With what frissons will you torture me? What does it matter! O Marcel, my lover, take me! I give you my flesh! Open your arms, that they may become for me a gulf like the sea, an immensity like the heavens, that I might bury myself therein forever!"

She had cast aside her veils, and her nudity, bathed in the astral light, burst forth like the most sublime vision in the universe. O splendor!

Deliriously, they lay down on the ground.

But suddenly, just at the moment when their exasperated senses were about to lead them to embraces akin to death, a deadly air expanded, engulfing them, paralyzing their movements, freezing them in the magnificent posture in which, sealed against one another, they were preparing to unite themselves.

# CHAPTER XXVII

Placing before his mouth the small omnial apparatus, as pretty as a precious box, that permitted him to breathe pure air when all his people had been put to sleep by the dispersion of soporific gases, Caresco threw off his ostentatious and resplendent mantle, a black silhouette decorated with brilliant jewels, and looked down on the pompous polychromy of his numbed subjects. The beneficent inhalations did not calm his domineering transports.

Sniggering, he came slowly down the onyx steps, which red stripes streaked like trickles of blood over flesh. The smoking pylons were exhausting the last of their combustible materials, and their blue swirls, increasingly sparse, were evaporating idly. The lights had gone out. All that remained to give relief to the apparent corpses were two powerful jets of omnial radiation departing from the ceiling, which cut two vast golden cones through the darkness, in which little solid particles danced, which might have been taken for vibrions of matter.

Having traversed the violet ranks of his scientists, engineers and artists, surprised in their attitudes of spectators, he stopped at the last step and contemplated the frozen mass of the people. What power was his, which instantaneously, by pressing a switch, suspended the animation of twenty thousand individuals!

Traversed by a frisson of immense pride, he murmured: "O life! O succession of partial deaths! I am stronger than you!"

All his creation, his lot of splendid flesh, was there, within a radius of one square kilometer. The background formed a seed-bed of heads and arms drowned in the variegation of garments: red, blue, yellow, mauve, and green veils held by hands stopped in mid-dance, but closer at hand the gestures stood out, and conserved their light, undulant, rhythmic grace.

He noticed, in particular, the admirable profile of an adolescent and a courtesan surprised at the moment when, the one having seized the other's waist, their attitudes offered an astonishing indication of the intoxication thy felt in enlacing. He recognized them. It was Philoxénie, with a giton.

The woman, with her head tilted backwards, her brown hair crowned with red geraniums deployed over her floating mauve veils, would have collapsed if the child's arm had not been supporting her thus, in a swoon. The contours of her arched back, her lascivious loins, her red-striped abdomen, developed magnificently, bearing forward the challenge of her heavy, pointed marmoreal breasts. Her right arm raised, parting with a grandiosely impure gesture the veils of gauze, seemed to be opening a jewel-case to display the gem that she was. The adolescent, bending toward her, his torso going toward the naked flesh without yet touching it, had stopped at the moment when their two inclined heads were about to meet. They were smiling, the pallor of their teeth uncovered, and the ecstasy of their wide-open eyes catching sparks.

Caresco swelled up with pride at the thought that he could immobilize them thus until death, until desiccation.

He passed on.

Further away, it was Carabella toward whom a circle of sterile spouses and fecund mothers were blowing kisses. She had been caught at the moment when, executing a step of the sacred dance, her body, inclined toward the floor, silhouetted the vision of the future. One of her delicate hands, the little finger raised, was held perpendicularly to the forehead, seemingly permitting her sight to plumb the depths of distant spaces. The other stiff arm was extended backward toward the firm rump. The surfaces of fabric stretched over her hips scarcely hid their perfection. Beside her, two children lying on the ground were maintaining her ankles; the ensemble symbolized the idea that if one could foresee the future, the present, more certain would attach you back to life.

And elsewhere, around, in the distance, higher up, all the way to the ivory of the giant columns and the streaming crimson of the draperies, there was the same adoration, transparent in the gestures and the postures of the cataleptic bodies, in the hypnotized fixation of masks impregnated with sensuality: bodies offering themselves and taking one another with candid immodesty; other collecting caresses; others fleeing certain touches to go in search of those preferred, gliding over the floor, scarcely placing the soles of the feet; others, finally, tipped on the ground, coupling frantically, in an insensate lust, in which the sexes were not always distinct.

And all of that was still aflame, a furnace of life and enjoyment alimented by the pulp of vibrant flesh. The two great cones of light falling from the vault overlapped in the middle to give their relief of apotheosis and supreme conflagration to twenty thousand passions suddenly suspended there.

Caresco passed on, stepping over bodies. He was looking for Miss Mary, whom he had not perceived in the darkness. His obstinate desire was alarmed at not being able to find her right away. He did not think that she might be in Marcel's arms; he had forgotten the young man completely.

On the other hand, a strange memory was reanimated in his mind. He remembered, forty years before, having been represented in an English wax museum, after a famous night of operations in which his carescoclast had triumphed. Later, he had gone to join the crowd that could admire his incredible feat for three pence. He had seen himself there, faithfully reproduced, his body leaning toward his patients, surrounded by an elite of scientists watching him work, plunging his ardent hands into a massacre of flesh. He had listened to the horrified and enthusiastic reflections of spectators. What glory he already had then! But what power he had now! He suppressed the memory of another age. He searched for Miss Mary.

"The virgin! Where is she?"

His inability to find her filled him with rage. Momentarily, he hoped to discover her in a group of dancers of which Madame Môme and Marius occupied the center, paralyzed at the moment when they were repeating the fantastic waddling of a naturalistic quadrille. He remembered confusedly that the

High Priestess had had the mission of charging the young woman with the new fluid. He interrogated her, asked her what had become of his treasure, and when she did not reply, he extended his hands to obtain her confession at the same time as she exhaled her last breath—but already he was turning his head in another direction.

"Miss Mary! Miss Mary!"

Let her emerge from that stupid mass, then! Let her come toward him, arms open, to appease the devouring fury of his heart.

He called to her again. He listened to the echo of his voice make a circuit of the Temple, pass behind the draperies of the pilasters and come back to him, almost extinct. Then he launched himself forward and ran, the only animate being amid that vast slumber, jostling bodies, knocking them over, leaning over insensible physiognomies, tearing away veils, disentangling embraces, twisting hair, trying to recognize the woman for whom he was searching. The silhouettes collapsed with a flaccid thud, and he dived into a litter of bodies.

"O virgin, are you alive? Are you only asleep? If you're asleep, show yourself, and I'll wake you up! If you're dead, let yourself be recognized, and I'll bring you back to life, my queen! My queen!"

Now he was making prodigious bounds, howling. His feet trampled soft flesh. He tripped over a couple lying down to couple. Hindered by the tangle of garments that held him back, he ripped them, and then, in a rage, he stamped his heel on the face of a fecund mother, pretty and blonde, whose punctured eye stuck to his sandal and caused him to slip again.

He breathed in; he sniffed, with the ferocity of a hungry wild beast tracking its prey. His broad sensual lips were slack, flecked with foam. And as a slight vertigo also gripped him, indicating that he provision of fresh air was running out, he still had sufficient presence of mind to run outside in order to escape the somniferous effect, Going up toward a height that he knew to be above the layer of spreading gas, he ran into two individuals, and recognized Marcel and Miss Mary, asleep.

The worthy philosopher Choumaque, sitting at the foot of a parasol pine, was awaiting events. To impregnate himself more easily with the admirable spectacle of the night, and in order not to disturb the decisive intimacy of his two friends, he had gone up on to a mound, from which the panorama was splendidly deployed, in the enchanted calm of nature, beneath the twinkling of the stars.

A delight filled his heart. Ah, the lovely return of equilibria! In an instant, Miss Mary would no longer be desirable to Caresco. The energy magically drawn from the source of love unveiled by the High Priestess would soon make Marcel the sole master of the foreigner. No longer to be astonished by anything...*nil mirari!* To remain stoical, even in the face of happiness! He departed from that sage maxim in order to address himself congruently to agreeable dissertations in which was mingled the joy of having seen the entwined lovers disappear toward the nearby clump of trees, and hearing, he thought, the pleasant music of their kisses.

He was wondering how to extract from that immoral scene an edifying application in favor of his doctrine—and finding that the heavens were replete with admirable glimmers, and that the earth itself, so drowned in blue moonlight, was their element, infinitely—when, all of a sudden, he shivered.

That bounding body, which the successions of shadow and light hid and revealed by turns, was it not Caresco?

An incommensurable emotion seized him. Was the battle, then, already lost, at the moment when it was scarcely engaged? Had they been betrayed?

The Superman had just stopped, suffocating, and he folded his arms.

"Is that you, philosopher? Why aren't you asleep like the rest? I've thrown twenty cubic meters of somniferous gas over my people, for two kilometers around...how have you managed to escape it? Can't you ever do as you're told? Aren't you my plaything, my property, like all my other subjects, like your friends, whom I've just tripped over, there, in passing?"

Choumaque did not reply. He could see exaltation blazing in the madman's eyes. He wondered what part of truth his words contained. He listened to the punctuated monologue.

"Yes, they're there...why were they together at the moment when the fluid took effect, at the moment when the virgin ought to be marking a hundred on my psychometer? Tomorrow, I'm going to kill Madame Môme...but it's time to hasten my marriage. I'm God, certainly...but the Other? The God on high, my rival...has he not taken sides with that Sower? For he knows that I want her virginal...yes, virginal...!"

Then, turning to Choumaque, whom he was mingling with the chaos of his ideas, he said: "Give me your advice: do you think I should wait? To remove her might be dangerous at this point...come on, speak!"

"You should wait," Choumaque replied, at hazard, hoping to delay the peril.

"Joker! Are you advising me to do the opposite of what you think? For think on this: if I don't take her now, will there be time tomorrow? Everything's asleep, that's true; but how do you know that everything will still exist tomorrow? Come on—you're going to help me, philosopher..."

Choumaque wondered what it was to which he was about to lend his assistance. He admitted that if it were to help the potentate of this world disappear, he would not hesitate to intervene. Never had murder seemed to him such a simple act, so rational and so practical, to get out of a situation. He suddenly discovered within himself the energetic measure of a dispenser of justice.

Caresco took him to an airplane, not far away, whose gray mass was level with the crowns of giant trees fringed by the moonlight. He forced him to sit beside him. Then, having switched on the searchlights and directed their glare toward the ground he mumbled: "Remember this, philosopher: when you see me lean over the side of the nacelle, you lean over too.

330

When you see me draw back, you draw back. But above all, don't breathe in while we're in the zone that puts everything to sleep. You understand, don't you?"

"I understand perfectly," Choumaque affirmed, knowing that one should never contradict a madman, and not thinking that the words were sane.

The Superman operated the controls and the vehicle, extending its wings, came to hover momentarily above the place where the two young people were lying. The precision of the movement, placing the machine between the layer of dangerous atmosphere and the vault of the trees, demonstrated the extent to which the Superman had momentarily recovered his practical lucidity.

Choumaque looked over the edge and perceived his two friends, confusedly, lying twenty meters beneath him.

"Above all, don't breathe in!"

It was as rapid as thought. The airplane dropped abruptly to the ground while its wings made an upward movement. Gripped by anguish, the philosopher saw Caresco take advantage of the second's respite that the machine's bound left him to lean over swiftly toward Miss Marry and draw her violently toward him. But the lovers, stiffened by the slumber, were no tightly enlaced that Marcel was grabbed at the same time as his companion. Instinctively, Choumaque aided the abduction. The couple, lifted into the air by the airplane, which resumed its flight, remained suspended in the void momentarily. Finally, secured by one last traction, they sung toward the nacelle and fell on to the floor.

"I've got her!" Caresco howled, brutally tearing the confused bodies apart.

He seized his prey in his arms and carried her effortlessly to a seat near the tiller. He was careful to direct the airplane toward one of the crests of the Mount of Venus, who snow-spangled summit was on the edge of the horizon, bathed in light. The surprising logic that edged his dementia, and had enabled him to accomplish the capture with so much precision, did not abandon him when he wanted to ascertain the young woman's condition—when, with an expert hand slid beneath her veils, he had diagnosed that she was such as he desired.

"Virgin!" he cried, triumphantly.

Immediately, he applied the two poles of his psychometer to the sleeping woman's forehead, and leaned over the needle on the dial.

"Glory to me, philosopher—it marks a hundred! Look! Observe the triumph of my science over nature! It's definitive—absolute! I am God!"

"Is it not rather due to nature—the good, sane and generous nature that has pushed these two young people to love one another—that you've arrived at your objective?" Choumaque suggested, timidly.

The Superman was no longer listening. All his nerves vibrant with an immeasurable pride, forgetting his companions, he fell back into his delirium, and let incoherent words spill out: invocations to his queen, his power and his empire, and threats against the Other. Beneath the fabric, his hands palpated the young woman, whose delicate head, leaning on his shoulder, swayed at the slightest movement.

Frightened, Choumaque felt Marcel's face. He found that it was still warm; he made out the slow rhythm of respiration, the pulsation of the heart. He rejoiced, for the moment.

But where were they going? This abduction was the most extraordinary thing he had yet witnessed. There was no more doubt now about the intentions of the Superman, whose actions were coherently concurrent with the accomplishment of an insane action. Caresco must be taking all three of them to the cavern from which no one ever returned.

In truth, Choumaque genuinely did not care much about continuing to live. He estimated that he had compensated his dolors with enough joys, and that the term of his equilibrium, although premature, could arrive: he expected it. But them— the dear children! Had they not still days to travel, united in love? And certainly, if they ever managed to quit this neutralizing island, they would have to shed tears, they would have to pay dearly for their partial happiness; but was that not preferable to this nonexistence? And who could tell what there was after the death toward which Caresco appeared to be conducting them?

While philosophizing, in the splendid serenity of that aerial journey, while savoring bitterly the contrast between the magical sky and the menacing madman, he studied Caresco's actions, listened to his incoherent voice. He was waiting for the moment when the surgeon, perhaps discouraged by the young woman's immobility, would weary of talking to her about love and release her from his arms. Then he would hurl himself upon him, grab hold of him and bundle him overboard; he would launch him into the void, in order to annihilate his monstrous genius, hostile to suffering and, in consequence, hostile to happiness.

But the Superman did not abandon his prey. He hugged her, warming her up against his torso, with infantile babble. And when the mass of the mountain appeared, when the craft, skimming over the asperities of the rocks, glided under terrifying projections that overhung bottomless gulfs, he scarcely turned away from his adoration to give the direction control the few flicks of his thumb that narrowly avoided catastrophe.

Finally, the airplane's velocity relented; the wings were folded away into their elytra. They had arrived.

"Come with us, philosopher!" said the Superman, lifting Miss Mary in his arms with the facility he would have had in carrying the lightest of burdens.

That order left Choumaque perplexed. There was certainly no lack of temptation to follow the madman. As well as obeying a duty of protection toward the young woman, he would discover the secrets of the mysterious location about which it was said that the Superman never let anyone leave. Nor, moreover, had he abandoned the plan to liberate the people from their monstrous despot, and the opportunity might yet present itself. But to abandon Marcel, his pupil, his friend, to leave him alone at that moment, when the effects of the somniferous gas had not yet dissipated—how could he?

Finally, he made the decision. Having made sure that the balloon's moorings were solid and that the young man's breathing was regular, he set off in Caresco's footsteps, along a steep narrow path carved into the rock, to the entrance of a cavern, enigmatically open, like the mouth a bandit's den.

As soon as all three of them were inside, the Superman was transformed. He suddenly seemed to shed his cloak of madness. His gait was no longer jerky. His hands did not hesitate when he turned to commutator of the omnial light in order to illuminate the lair. One might have thought that he was preparing to carry out the most routine act of his daily occupation.

He went to place the young woman on the central metallic bed and brought within arm's reach a wheeled table covered with surgical instruments. He began to make the preparations for the operation, taking off his victim's clothes, placing wads of cloth around the radiantly pure abdomen, bursting with fecund splendor. His eyes adored the divine head with parted lips and tangled golden hair, coldly. Then he absorbed himself calmly in readjusting the mechanism of a long curved needle fixed in the supportive notch of his carescoclast. His movements had resumed their mathematical certainty.

Choumaque thought he was no longer living on earth. The horrible aspect of the cavern, the shadowy corners full of display-cases; the enigmatic fragments of bodies gleaming or floating in their liquid; the empty gazes of cadavers, their grimaces, the frightful holes, the contortions that some of them exposed to the proximity of jars; the precise, methodical gestures of the sacrificer; and that beautiful body lying on the metal of the table where a thousand gleams blazed, like metallic eyes: all of that bewildered him even more than it frightened him. He wondered whether the Superman's dementia had not flowed into his own brain, infecting it.

But what bothered him most of all was a piquant odor of sulfur floating in the heaviness of the air, to the point of provoking an irritation in his eyes, and he was no less surprised to hear dull and distant explosions rumbling beneath his feet, like the muffled repercussion of the central boiling. He was suffo-cating. He had to pull himself together to remind himself that he had to prevent an abominable profanation.

Putting down his instrument, Caresco said: "Well, phi-losopher, what do you think of my installation? Have you ever seen anything like it? Are they not charming, the patients on whom I've operated, whom you can see there? Understand that I enjoy their company. Appreciate with what grateful eyes, what smiles, they salute my presence! In a little while, they'll acclaim my wedding! For I'm going to marry before them, philosopher, and I intend them to be my witnesses. Just think—I owe them that! Philosopher, you're going to witness the greatest event of all the centuries: the marriage of Caresco-Superman, or Caresco-God! Ha ha ha!"

He prolonged his laughter terribly. Then, striking the rumbling ground with his foot, he continued: "And you see how nature intends to come to the party! Can you hear that cracking? One might think them gigantic salvos. It's for me that the volcano is exalting! But perhaps you don't know that I'm getting married on a volcano, philosopher! Do you doubt it? Come and see..."

He advanced toward Choumaque without the latter, para-lyzed by fear, thinking of resisting. He took him by the arm and led him graciously toward the table where the young woman was asleep. Then he pointed at the vault.

"Take note, I beg you, of that enormous chimney. It loses itself in the mountain by way of a furrow that I alone have followed. Thirty years ago, it was still giving issue to fumes, ash and fire! Yes, philosopher, here, where we stand, their fire passed through! And it's here that I'm going to espouse her, the virgin of Virgins, on an altar that is a volcano! Isn't it sub-lime, to marry in a crater? And yet, if I wished, how easy it would be for me to render its violence to it! Yes, my genius has foreseen everything. I could, if I wished, reanimate the fumes, the ash and the fire almost instantaneously, a colossal upheaval! It would be sufficient for me...come and see, phi-losopher, what it would be sufficient for me to do..."

He pushed Choumaque toward one of the walls. He pointed with his finger at the red plate sealed into the rock, alongside which there was a kind of iron collar, moving on a hinge, just large enough to be able to encircle a human neck, when its catch was closed.

"It would be sufficient for me to press that button, the size of a pea, to unleash the volcano! In ten minutes, my omnial force, activated, would provoke ten consecutive explosions of dynamite, and create a conduit giving passage to the fumes, the ash and the fire! In ten minutes, this corner of my empire would explode, and all my people asleep in the Palace of Sensualities would burn. Do you see that, philosopher. What power! What a cataclysm—which my rival, the God of other worlds, could never equal! Me, I can...me, I can, by doing this..."

Hallucinated by the idea of an orgiastic crime, he extended his hand, and Choumaque had to hold him back.

"Oh, indeed, I've thought about it long and hard! Of ending it thus, on the day when I'm tired of it all: of sterilizing my realm in the blink of an eye, of making it new again, virginal, like Miss Mary! Virginal, as it was when I took possession of it! I've deflowered everything...can I not, once, restore everything to virginity? And that moment will come! And when I've decided it, I'll imprison myself in this collar that I've sealed into the wall, in order that nothing can make me go back on my resolution. Then, I'll only have to reach out my arm, press that button, and give myself voluptuously to the entrails of the earth, to the purifying fire of life! O life! O nature! How I dominate you! And you, the Other, God of the old worlds, can you do as much? What a dwarf you are alongside the giant! Gigas is me! Satan is me! I am. I am the Force benevolent to the point of destruction. I am God! Look, philosopher: God is about to espouse the dove!"

He undressed. His garments, lacerated by his eager hands, fell to the floor. He revealed the violent musculature of his torso, its youth conserved, of his hairy legs, his erect penis.

His bulging eyes with the strange unequal pupils shone. Foam appeared on his lips.

Returning to the operating table, he made his dilated flesh shiver on contact with the cold metal, the touch of the splendid body.

In the meantime, Choumaque, behind him, moved on tiptoe in order to get nearer to the table, to grab a knife and plunge it between his shoulders. Yes, kill him, kill him…!

Alas, the madman seemed to have divined his thought; he turned his head just as the philosopher's hand descended upon the hilt of the instrument—and he was the one who took possession of it, and raised it voluptuously into the air.

But just as he was about to plunge it down, Miss Mary woke up, and raised herself up on one arm.

"Run, my child!" Choumaque shouted, with an anguished gesture. "Quickly, this way!"

Then, there was a palpitating chase. The young woman, terrified by the horrible threat that greeted her awakening, had thrown herself off the table, and her divine form scrambled desperately away from the brandished knife. She circled the cavern, which her screams filled with terror. Her gaze sought in vain for a gulf into which she could throw herself and disappear. Caresco followed her, roaring, with blood on his lips and in his eyes.

Twice she slipped through his fingers like an eel. Finally, he grabbed her by the hair at the moment when she grabbed hold of the rock, and tore her away from it with the violence of a predatory carnivore. Their two nude bodies came together, interlaced, and became confused. But when, having lifted her up, he tried to bring her back to the table, suddenly, a steel grip strangled him and stuck him to the wall, paralyzing him.

Taking advantage of the moment when the struggle had been prolonged in the vicinity of the collar, Choumaque had abruptly shoved the madman into the trap. The click of the catch acclaimed the capture. When Caresco's raised blade came down, Miss Mary was free, and it was the philosopher who felt the cold blade plunge into his arm.

"There," said Choumaque, aloud, sustaining the young woman, who had fainted, "is the most evident, albeit extraordinary, compensation that could ever be given to the creator of the doctrine of equilibria to observe. The joy that I feel at this moment only equals the thousand tortures that my soul suffered during the previous ten minutes. If you weren't screaming so loudly, Superman, I would prove to you, by one equals one, that my philosophy is superior to yours, and that it wasn't worth the trouble of accumulating so many dreams of grandeur to end up in an iron collar. But you're wailing too much. Then again, I have better things to do than occupy myself with your education. I have to transport this virgin, as decently as possible, to the arms of her lover. How he cries! How he kicks! Have you finished, loudmouth? By Leibniz, it's insupportable! You don't want to shut up, eh? Hang on! I'll make a tampon and stick it in your gob! For the sight of blood upsets me...especially when it's mine!"

He looked at his arm. He could not feel the wound, but he could see the blood running down his sleeve, coming to stain his numb hand crimson.

"Just like Seneca! Caresco has opened my vein!"[23]

He started to laugh noisily. His joy almost covered the howls of the madman, and there was a strange collision of echoes in the cavern. Soon, however, the howls and the laughter died away at the same time. The captive was no longer moving. His eyes, which had become calm again, indicated that he was reflecting.

"What is he planning now?" said the philosopher, following that transformation anxiously.

---

[23] Seneca was ordered by the emperor Nero, to commit suicide after being caught up in the aftermath of an assassination plot; he used the traditional method of opening his veins in order to bleed to death. According to Tacitus, it took a long time, and he was finally placed in a hot bath intended to speed the process and ease his agony, where he suffocated in the steam.

He was right to be alarmed, for the madman's features suddenly expressed an abominable silent intoxication, while his hand, reaching out to the metal plate next to the collar, pressed the red button.

Then Choumaque panicked. "The volcano! I'd forgotten about that! The volcano! Everything's going to explode! Oh, if only I'd killed him!"

Carrying the body of the young woman, he launched himself toward the exit.

Dawn was breaking. The freshness of the air, whipping him, increased his strength beyond human limits, and he continued to maintain his precious burden in one arm. He ran down the steep path, nearly losing his footing twenty times over, but he could see no other death, could feel no other threat, than that of the explosion.

Exhausted, he finally arrived at the nacelle and threw the body of the young woman into the arms of the recently-awakened Marcel. An initial tremor of the earth, subjected to the repercussion of a deep explosion, told him that one minute had already elapsed.

"To the boat! Quickly, to the boat! Don't ask questions. We need to be on board in nine minutes, or we're doomed!"

Automatically, Marcel obeyed. He seized the tiller, lifted the airplane, and orientated it. A second, louder noise had just exploded. The craft hesitated momentarily, then launched forth at top speed, fleeing through the immensity. A third detonation, and then a fourth, were bellowed by the rocks.

More coolly, Choumaque murmured: "Hurry, my boy. Use full power! The volcano will open up in six minutes. Our only hope of salvation is to be aboard before then."

Marcel quintupled the energy without understanding anything except that there was a terrifying threat. The great wings beat ardently; the entire mechanical carcass vibrated, creaking in unison with their hearts. Three more detonations jolted them. Again, the imperious fear of the philosopher resounded, gasping: "Three minutes, my boy! We only have three minutes left. The mountain is going to blow up, the fire will burn us, the fumes will asphyxiate us. We're not going fast enough. Hurry, I beg you! Listen! There's the eighth explosion! We only have two minutes!"

"I can see the sea!" Marcel shouted, wildly, tearing off his doublet. "I can see the ironclad! Clothes off!"

One last and intense swerve filled the ninth minute. The airplane went down at lightning speed and plunged into the waves sixty meters from the ship. They dived. The water seethed in their ears, gurgled in their throats.

Marcel grabbed the young woman's hair. Stunned, he nevertheless conserved the consciousness of what he had to do to save her. He struggled. A desperate effort brought him to the ladder to the deck, on to which he hoisted himself. On turning round, he still had time to grab Choumaque's foot as he sank.

Streaming, glorious, dragging two bodies, one by the hair and the other by the heel, he climbed the few steps that led to the deck. Exhausted, he noticed that the sea was still calm, that the carcass of the airplane was sinking slowly, that Miss Mary, woken up by the coldness of the water, had opened her eyes again, and that Choumaque was vomiting. He exulted at those spectacles.

Then, what they saw and what they heard was terrible. The tenth shock burst forth, mightily. A mountain of fumes, gases and fire sprang from the Mount of Venus, propelling worlds. The land tore; its immense abdomen yawned, in a monstrous and superb quartering. The sea, lifted up by that revolt, swelled up, reaching for the heavens. The ship was carried away by the formidable blister of the element.

Everything went black. A colossal jet of glaucous water, which they saw agglomerating frightfully in the air for fifteen seconds, finally crashed down on to their shoulders, and flattened them against a mast, to which the instinct of conservation made them cling.

# CHAPTER XXVIII

"My dear children," said Choumaque, interrupting the clergyman—who, with his hand on the Bible, was about to pronounce the sacramental words of union—and stopping him with a gesture, "my dear Miss Mary, my dear Marcel, before accomplishing the marriage of which this worthy servant of one of the gods of the old world is about to celebrate, permit me to confide some of my hesitations to you.

"I am, in sum, the artisan of your present resolution. If fortune aided us to survive the cataclysm, by placing our ship precisely at the summit of a waterspout that carried it over the island's redoubtable circle of submarine protection; if, after two days of drifting, hazard, which is a great benefactor, brought us, dying of cold and hunger and as naked as Verities, within sight of this hospitable steamer, whose obliging passengers picked us up, warmed us up, dressed us and nourished us; if, finally, chance dictated that a saintly clergyman declared himself to be fanatically disposed to exercise his profession in your honor, for twenty shillings; you will, on the other hand concede that without me, Miss Mary, you would at this moment be part of the Superman's anatomical collection, and that you, Marcel, would be continuing your employment, as in the past, with the sensualities of the fecund mothers and repopulating the island of Eucrasia. I therefore pride myself on the important role I have played in your destinies sufficiently to ask you to submit, for a moment, to the exposure of my scruples."

The two young people, holding hands, gravely approved this preamble. The glance that they cast over their own accoutrement and the philosopher's—risible heliotrope costumes extracted opportunistically from the wardrobes of passengers, did not lessen their compunction at all.

Choumaque continued: "My children, I am struggling in a strange casuistry. Certainly, with regard to myself, my seat

341

has been taken for a long time, since the day when I became the creator and sole adept of the doctrine of equilibria—don't try to understand, honorable clergyman; your commerce closes you off entirely to my theories—but you, my dears, do you know that you're giving a diabolical twist to my philosophy? I'll tell you why. I'll skip over as delicately as possible the memory of the six extraordinary weeks that we've just spent."

With his habitual customary gesture, he hitched up the belt of his borrowed trousers, which, if they imprisoned his calves rather parsimoniously, were, by contrast, generous at the level of his renovated waist. Then he went on.

"When, on the thirty-first of December 1950, last year, urged by various motives, we arrived in the unknown land, it was easy for me to distinguish the secret attraction that became, for my pupil, the result of your first meeting. Anyway, could it have been otherwise? You both possess the divine gifts of seduction, you were two opposed electricities from which a spark spring—and the spark did not take long to shine, for Miss Mary, in her turn, and after many hesitations, became smitten with Marcel. However, that sympathy did not seem to me to augur well, since the Redlander was only to make a short sojourn on the island, while the Frenchman was formally fixed there. And, indeed, that uncertainty increased further, and caused the two of you—initially, at least—cruel sadnesses as soon as you had recognized, like me, the impossibility of satisfying your love.

"Oh, my friends, to what magnetism were people subjected on that island, in order that within a fortnight, your passion—very sincere at the start, I'm convinced—was already eroded, in order that you should become so lightly amenable, one to the perverse influence of the courtesan and the other to the demands of the fecund mothers? Don't blush, don't be confused; my knowledge of the human soul permits me to affirm that you could not have done otherwise. So, you resolved yourselves, without too much despair, to your separation; and it's me who united you again. That's why, before you engage yourselves forever, I want to tell you my scruples.

"A little while ago, the wireless telegraph informed us that the cataclysm organized by Caresco, with a view to the disappearance of his people, was incomplete in its effects. Although we saw the Mount of Venus crumble into the sea, we now know that the convulsion of the ground was limited to engulfing that region alone, and allowing the rest to subsist. There is, therefore, within four days of navigation, a land that you know, where you have the right of election, and which, under the government of the Superman's two disciples, Zadochbach and Hymen, subsists with all of its organization of facile, joyful, magical—if not happy—life.

"Nourishment there is obtained by means of exquisite capsules of complete aliment, which give the satisfaction of the most succulent repasts without ever provoking indigestion. One is clothed magnificently there, without cost. It is never cold, since a radiantly warm sun shines there incessantly. The most sumptuous dwellings protect sleep there; the most de-lightful landscapes welcome the idleness that it the rule there. Everyone there is rich, and all needs are satisfied, thanks to an organization of machines and marvelous fluids. The most ab-solute security has annihilated the fear of war. Effort is un-known there; the uncertainties of metaphysics have no pur-chase on indolent minds. Love itself—yes, love—which brings so many dolors, heroisms and cowardices in its wake elsewhere, is offered there to the point of satiation, with all its refinements and—let's not say too much in front of the cler-gyman!—all its vices; and everyone can, when weary, extract new inspiration from the aphrodisiac reserves. Ugliness does not exist there; beauty is the rule; and I am the most convinc-ing specimen of what renovative science can achieve with a worn-out body. The creation and birth of individuals are orga-nized there in the fashion closest to perfection, in such a way that atavistic flaws do not develop, and mothers do not even feel the pain of childbirth. One can live for two hundred years in that Eden, without seeing the advent of old age, without sensing the torturing approach of death.

343

"To sum up, honest clergyman who is listening to me, the genius of Caresco has built an earthly paradise there, a marvelous Elysium, with its houris, its décor and its sensualities, as I imagine that, without admitting it, you conceive Paradise, a worthy recompense for your life of integrity and your prudent fidelity to a unique companion, who is—I've seen her, and you will agree yourself—dried-up, shrewish and only responds to your sentiment of esthetics with an overly red nose and excessively long teeth.

"Well, my children, reflect on the land of misfortune to which your marriage will return you. That old world is narrow, cluttered and dolorous. Calm enjoyment is not possible there; one is too bustled and jostled. One eats indigestible foodstuffs acquired with difficulty. One freezes in winter, and roasts in summer. The right to sleep in unspacious dwellings is only obtained when the brain and limbs are weary of toil. One scarcely has time to contemplate nature, which is, in any case, generally ingrate. Garments are expensive, and wear out quickly. The most fortunate sense the rumbling of the envy of the poor, and when individuals are not tearing one another apart, it is peoples who are massacring one another. The most diverse philosophies torment the mind without ever contenting it. The good are forced to become ferocious to protect the bad. One sees celebrities and honors acquired at a monetary price, litterateurs become famous by spending a hundred thousand francs, and merchants of transparent cards receiving the most envied decorations. And love...oh, let's talk about love! For every pair of young lovers who, like you, are disposed to make their hearths radiant, how many household disunited by interest, by hatred, by revolt; how many ridiculous cuckolds, how many girls seduced and abandoned by ferocious Don Juans; how many children raised at hazard, clad in nothing but their misery and their flaws?

"That is the world, my children, that you are about to re-enter. I know, on the other hand, that the meal long desired is eaten with the heartiest appetite; that an overcoat is donned with more pleasure when the weather is colder; that a room seems more cheerful when it welcomes you after a day of fatigue; that the bare countryside is embalmed with a delicious air when one rarely breathes it; that the unfortunate squeeze a hundred sou coin in their hand with more joy that the rich obtain from their sacks of gold; that after the horror of war there are the consolations of peace; that metaphysics provides comforting illusions; that ill-acquired celebrity makes one smile; that the good rejoice in not being bad, and the bad in doing harm to the good; and that in love, finally, the cuckolds always end up believing in the fidelity of their spouses, the deceived by contenting themselves elsewhere, seduced girls by knowing the bitter joys of vengeance, and mothers by hugging their child to their breast with all the more intoxication because their loins have been ripped apart...and those compensations summarize my theory, and permit me to affirm that happiness is made of dolor...

"But you, my friends, you who can avoid those struggles and miseries, you who can return tomorrow to countries where they do not exist, are you going to subject yourselves to the pressure of an old fool of a philosopher, who is perhaps blinded by his theory of equilibria? Are you going to persist in your intention to return to the Land of Effort, when the Land of Enjoyment is still so close, within four days of navigation? Answer me."

Marcel let go of Miss Mary's hand, and, fixing his eyes on the distant horizon, as if seeking inspiration for his words therein, he spoke.

"When I arrived on the island, I fell in love with Miss Mary. My only memory of happiness stops at the moment when I saw her smile at me. The rest—the mildness of the climate, the facilities of existence, the sumptuous palaces, the fêtes, the sensualities, the favors of the fecund mothers and the frissons of sterile amours—although they numbed my personality and contented my indolence, never offered me real joy. I was subjected to an inexplicable traction, a kind of hypnotic entrapment that never allowed me to blossom. I only truly recovered joy, Choumaque, at the moment when I was able to hope once again to share it with my bride, even at the price of the harshest sacrifices. I want to return with her to the Lands of Effort."

"That's the most beautiful triumph of my theory of equilibria!" said Choumaque. "And you, Miss Mary—answer!"

The young woman took a solemn step toward the clergyman. She placed her hand on the Bible. Although she was clad in a peignoir that was two tight, in an unspeakable hue, she was radiant with all her vivid beauty, and collected Marcel's adoration even so.

"For myself," she said, "I must agree that I look back on the weeks that have just gone by with a stupefied gaze. How could it happen that I became so miserably forgetful of the veritable objective of my voyage, that I no longer thought about Marcel's charms, to allow myself to be enveloped by Carabella's? I don't know, and I'm confounded by shame. But, returned to the clarity of my soul, I swear before the priest that the most captivating realizations of pleasure never caused me a joy as sincere as those of hoping to save my fatherland and being loved by Marcel. I am therefore returning to my initial ambitions: to this bold mariner, whose children I want to have; to my country, which, although now delivered from the coalition and the possessor of its autonomy, offers ruins to be rebuilt, miseries to be alleviated. Choumaque, you are a benefactor! Take me back, in my husband's arms, to the Land of Effort. I shall suffer there again, but my happiness will compensate me fully for my pains!"

"I am, decidedly, a great philosopher," said Choumaque, "and the harmonious combination of stoicism and my doctrine will make that Redlander a happy woman. However, my friends, let us address to the Superman one last grateful thought, for it is to his practices, contrary to nature, that you, Miss Mary, owe the ability to cherish my pupil. You were too much a virgin; you are becoming less so; try no longer to be one at all this evening. Now, clergyman, do your work, quickly. Happiness flies, it's necessary to seize it on the wing. Unite these young people!"

"But what about you, my poor Choumaque," asked Miss Mary, emotionally. "What will become of you?"

"The man who has not got drunk on the cup of happiness is not consternated by any sudden reversal," the philosopher dogmatized, wagging his finger. "Nevertheless, if, in your country, General Hardisson can procure me a professorial appointment..."

"I promise you that, Choumaque!"

That night, a little migratory bird, fatigued by a long journey through the air, came to rest on the deck of the ship, next to the window of a cabin from which the sound of kisses and promises was emerging. It listened to them, while the stars palpitated delightfully on the pure tranquility of waves that were scarcely stirring. Oh, what exquisite things it heard! But two words recurred incessantly in that conversation interrupted by embraces, in the midst of the sighs and delighted cries that the lovers uttered. Those two words were "joy" and "sadness."

Joy and sadness! Those were the same sentiments that the little bird experienced alternately in its primitive soul. It thought that although it was unhappy, at that moment, to be traveling alone in the immensity, it might soon be able, after a long struggle against the wind and the cold, to rejoice in having reached the liberating land, warm, calm and propitious for love. Then, having pecked a few fallen crumbs, with a new effort sustained by Hope, it resumed its flight in the blue-tinted firmament.

Thus lives pass, with alternations of peace and action, shadow and brightness, misfortune and bounty, ugliness and beauty, torment and enjoyment, the ones made to give the others their value. Thus, Evil is necessary to Good.

# *Afterword*

There is a good deal of evidence in the text of *Caresco, surhomme* that the author made up the story as he went along, although he probably always intended to follow the conventional story-arc leading to the escape of his three protagonists following the eruption of the volcano. Such episodes as the talking goose and the slave-slaughtering plague, which do not fit into any coherent overarching scheme, were probably the product of momentary whimsy, and it seems likely that the non-destruction of the island by the eruption was probably an afterthought.

Afterthought or not, however, that merciful whim does raise the interesting question of what might happen to Eucrasia once deprived of its dictatorial Superman and aspirant God. Would there be a contest among the surviving subordinates to take over his position, whose violent competition would inevitably lead to the ruination of the island's utopian credentials, even before the eventual successor began to introduce his own modifications to its program? Or would the mantle simply pass to Dr. Hymen, unopposed by the contentedly apathetic hedonists, who would maintain his predecessor's social design with religious fanaticism?

The question is difficult to answer without knowing more about Dr. Hymen, the one major character in the plot who has no vestige of a back-story, and who remains a very puzzling individual. It seems likely that he is, like Caresco, a surgical fetishist who obtains orgasmic satisfaction from wielding a scalpel rather than a penis—albeit one who is satisfied with excising hymens rather than uteri—and might, therefore be the ideal maniac to take over the maintenance of the social system. He would not, of course, be able to maintain Caresco's more ambitious quests, but that is probably no bad thing, given the consistent failure of the Superman's human monad project, and Hymen would surely be able to handle the simpler surgeries, even if he never mastered the use of the iconic carescoclast.

The main problem with the island's continued existence, however, is that—as Choumaque points out to Caresco—its lead in the matter of technological invention is bound to be eroded as its scientific discoveries are duplicated elsewhere. It cannot maintain its isolation forever, and once the envy of the ugly and the sex-starved is able take full effect on its beauty and lotus-eating satiation... well, the result is too horrible to contemplate. That would not prove, of course, that Choumaque's criticisms of it are valid, and that his theory of equilibria really does provide an adequate proof of the necessity of evil.

The basic argument of the theory of equilibria has something to recommend it, in that it really is the case that the occasional experience of unhappiness gives us a better appreciation of the value of happiness, and that if we were entirely insulated from all evils it might not make much sense to refer to the resultant invariance as "happiness." Friedrich Nietzsche's response to Choumaque would, of course, be that insulation from evil is merely a first step on the way to a positive reconceptualizaton of good; Nietzsche would have agreed with Choumaque that the vast majority of contemporary humans, freed from the spur of evils, would simply vegetate and stagnate rather than aspiring to become overmen, but he would have disagreed with him strongly that the answer to that problem was carefully to maintain, and stoically to tolerate, the empire of the evils.

Nietzsche, apparently being more familiar than Choumaque with the work of another philosopher very much in vogue with the French writers of the Symbolist and Decadent movement, Arthur Schopenhauer—cited in the text by Caresco, but not by Choumaque—would have had no difficulty in pointing out that the flaw in Choumaque's theory of equilibria is not in the notion that happiness is only meaningful in compensation for unhappiness but in the unproven and frankly ridiculous notion that the two are bound in the long run to enter into equivalence. As Schopenhauer points out, anyone idiot enough to believe that the account books of pleasure and pain must ultimately balance only has to ask whether the momentary pleasure of the owl in devouring a mouse—one of hundreds the bird will have to consume in order to live—can possibly be held to be equivalent in value to the pain of the mouse, whose existence is cancelled at a brutal stroke…and then to multiply that non-equation infinitely.

The simple fact is that happiness and unhappiness, pleasure and pain, life and death and good and evil do not balance out in the world; in every case, the scales are tipped very heavily in favor of the latter—and inventing a posthumous paradise as a balancing fudge factor is lazy and cowardly as well as blatantly false accounting. As Schopenhauer argues forcefully in *Die Welt als Wille und Vorstellung* (1818; rev. 1844; tr. as *The World as Will and Idea*), no rational calculation of the probability of reward and suffering can make the gamble of life seem worthwhile, and what sustains it in spite of that reality is the blind "will to survive," whose only motive force is the perpetuation of the species, and which is utterly uncaring about the quality of life. His disciple Eduard von Hartmann suggested in *Philosophie des Unbewussfen* (1869; tr. as *The Philosophy of the Unconscious*) that the only logical response to that rational realization is for everyone to commit suicide, but failed to do so himself. Despite being nicknamed "the great pessimist," Schopenhauer was not so negative; he thought that the answer was to make a stern psychological effort to substitute the conscious force of an enlightened Idea for the dark urges of the Will and to manufacture a heroic reason for living in terms of artistic creativity—i.e., in Nietszchean terminology, to become an *übermensch*.

Oddly enough, in spite of his idiotic optimism, Choumaque seems to agree with that prescription, and would probably follow it himself if he had adequate mental equipment—which, alas, he does not. Perhaps, though, even a lousy idea is better than no idea at all; that would hold for Caresco too. As for André Couvreur the literary physician, where

Caresco left off, Professor Tornada eventually took over, absorbing not merely the key elements of Caresco's skill and inventive genius, but also the key elements of a philosophy considerably less optimistic than Choumaque's, and far more scathing in its contempt for the woeful inability of the vast human majority to transcend the irrationally dire and vicious effects of the Will in order to get the slightest intellectual purchase on an Idea. That made Professor Tornada as disquieting a presence in the literary firmament as Caresco, and every bit as valuable as an enlightening idea.

# SF & FANTASY

Adolphe Alhaiza. *Cybele*
Alphonse Allais. *The Adventures of Captain Cap*
Henri Allorge. *The Great Cataclysm*
Guy d'Armen. *Doc Ardan: The City of Gold and Lepers*
G.-J. Arnaud. *The Ice Company*
Charles Asselineau. *The Double Life*
Cyprien Bérard. *The Vampire Lord Ruthwen*
S. Henry Berthoud. *Martyrs of Science*
Aloysius Bertrand. *Gaspard de la Nuit*
Richard Bessière. *The Gardens of the Apocalypse*
Albert Bleunard. *Ever Smaller*
Félix Bodin. *The Novel of the Future*
Louis Boussenard. *Monsieur Synthesis*
Alphonse Brown. *City of Glass; The Conquest of the Air*
Emile Calvet. *In a Thousand Years*
André Caroff. *The Terror of Madame Atomos; Miss Atomos; The Return of Madame Atomos; The Mistake of Madame Atomos; The Monsters of Madame Atomos; The Revenge of Madame Atomos; The Resurrection of Madame Atomos; The Mark of Madame Atomos; The Spheres of Madame Atomos*
Félicien Champsaur. *The Human Arrow; Ouha, King of the Apes; Pharaoh's Wife*
Didier de Chousy. *Ignis*
Jules Clarétie. *Obsession*
Michel Corday. *The Eternal Flame*
Captain Danrit. *Undersea Odyssey*
C. I. Defontenay. *Star (Psi Cassiopeia)*
Charles Derennes. *The People of the Pole*
Georges Dodds (anthologist). *The Missing Link*
Harry Dickson. *The Heir of Dracula*
Jules Dornay. *Lord Ruthven Begins*
Alfred Driou. *The Adventures of a Parisian Aeronaut*
Sâr Dubnotal *vs. Jack the Ripper*
Alexandre Dumas. *The Return of Lord Ruthven*
Renée Dunan. *Baal*
J.-C. Dunyach. *The Night Orchid; The Thieves of Silence*
Henri Duvernois. *The Man Who Found Himself*
Achille Eyraud. *Voyage to Venus*

Henri Falk. *The Age of Lead*

Paul Féval. *Anne of the Isles; Knightshade; Revenants; Vampire City; The Vampire Countess; The Wandering Jew's Daughter*

Paul Féval, *fils*. *Felifax, the Tiger-Man*

Charles de Fieux. *Lamékis*

Louis Forest. *Someone is Stealing Children in Paris*

Arnould Galopin. *Doctor Omega*; *Doctor Omega and the Shadowmen* (anthology)

Judith Gautier. *Isoline and the Serpent-Flower*

H. Gayar. *The Marvelous Adventures of Serge Myrandhal on Mars*

Léon Gozlan. *The Vampire of the Val-de-Grâce*

G.L. Gick. *Harry Dickson and the Werewolf of Rutherford Grange*

Edmond Haraucourt. *Illusions of Immortality*

Nathalie Henneberg. *The Green Gods*

V. Hugo, P. Foucher & P. Meurice. *The Hunchback of Notre-Dame*

Romain d'Huissier. *Hexagon: Dark Matter*

Jules Janin. *The Magnetized Corpse*

Michel Jeury. *Chronolysis*

Gustave Kahn. *The Tale of Gold and Silence*

Gérard Klein. *The Mote in Time's Eye*

Fernand Kolney. *Love in 5000 Years*

Paul Lacroix. *Danse Macabre*

Louis-Guillaume de La Follie. *The Unpretentious Philosopher*

Jean de La Hire. *Enter the Nyctalope; The Nyctalope on Mars; The Nyctalope vs. Lucifer; The Nyctalope Steps In; Night of the Nyctalope; Return of the Nyctalope; The Fiery Wheel*

Etienne-Léon de Lamothe-Langon. *The Virgin Vampire*

André Laurie. *Spiridon*

Gabriel de Lautrec. *The Vengeance of the Oval Portrait*

Alain le Drimeur. *The Future City*

Georges Le Faure & Henri de Graffigny. *The Extraordinary Adventures of a Russian Scientist Across the Solar System* (2 vols.)

Gustave Le Rouge. *The Mysterious Doctor Cornelius* (3 vols.); *The Vampires of Mars; The Dominion of the World* (w/Gustave Guitton) (4 vols.)

Jules Lermina. *Mysteryville; Panic in Paris; To-Ho and the Gold Destroyers; The Secret of Zippelius*

André Lichtenberger. *The Centaurs; The Children of the Crab*

Jean-Marc & Randy Lofficier. *Edgar Allan Poe on Mars; The Katrina Protocol; Pacifica; Robonocchio; Return of the Nyctalope;* (anthologists) *Tales of the Shadowmen 1-10*

Xavier Mauméjean. *The League of Heroes*
Joseph Méry. *The Tower of Destiny*
Hippolyte Mettais. *The Year 5865*
Louise Michel. *The Human Microbes; The New World*
Tony Moilin. *Paris in the Year 2000*
José Moselli. *Illa's End*
John-Antoine Nau. *Enemy Force*
Marie Nizet. *Captain Vampire*
C. Nodier, A. Beraud & Toussaint-Merle. *Frankenstein*
Henri de Parville. *An Inhabitant of the Planet Mars*
Gaston de Pawlowski. *Journey to the Land of the 4th Dimension*
Georges Pellerin. *The World in 2000 Years*
Ernest Pérochon. *The Frenetic People*
Pierre Pelot. *The Child Who Walked on the Sky*
J. Polidori, C. Nodier, E. Scribe. *Lord Ruthven the Vampire*
P.-A. Ponson du Terrail. *The Vampire and the Devil's Son; The Immortal Woman*
Edgar Quinet. *Ahasuerus*
Henri de Régnier. *A Surfeit of Mirrors*
Maurice Renard. *The Blue Peril; Doctor Lerne; The Doctored Man; A Man Among the Microbes; The Master of Light*
Jean Richepin. *The Wing; The Crazy Corner*
Albert Robida. *The Adventures of Saturnin Farandoul; The Clock of the Centuries; Chalet in the Sky; The Electric Life*
J.-H. Rosny Aîné. *Helgvor of the Blue River; The Givreuse Enigma; The Mysterious Force; The Navigators of Space; Vamireh; The World of the Variants; The Young Vampire*
Marcel Rouff. *Journey to the Inverted World*
Han Ryner. *The Superhumans*
Angelo de Sorr. *The Vampires of London*
Brian Stableford. *The New Faust at the Tragicomique;The Empire of the Necromancers (The Shadow of Frankenstein; Frankenstein and the Vampire Countess; Frankenstein in London); Sherlock Holmes & The Vampires of Eternity; The Stones of Camelot; The Wayward Muse.* (anthologist) *News from the Moon; The Germans on Venus; The Supreme Progress; The World Above the World; Nemoville; Investigations of the Future; The Conqueror of Death*
Jacques Spitz. *The Eye of Purgatory*
Kurt Steiner. *Ortog*
Eugène Thébault. *Radio-Terror*
C.-F. Tiphaigne de La Roche. *Amilec*

Louis Ulbach. *Prince Bonifacio*

Théo Varlet. *The Golden Rock. The Xenobiotic Invasion; The Casta-ways of Eros; Timeslip Troopers* (w/André Blandin); *The Martian Epic* (w/Octave Joncquel)

Paul Vibert. *The Mysterious Fluid*

Villiers de l'Isle-Adam. *The Scaffold; The Vampire Soul*

Philippe Ward. *Artahe*

Philippe Ward & Sylvie Miller. *The Song of Montségur*

## MYSTERIES & THRILLERS

M. Allain & P. Souvestre. *The Daughter of Fantômas*

A. Anicet-Bourgeois, Lucien Dabril. *Rocambole*

A. Bernède. *Belphegor; Judex* (w/Louis Feuillade); *The Return of Judex* (w/Louis Feuillade); *The Shadow of Judex*

A. Bisson & G. Livet. *Nick Carter vs. Fantômas*

V. Darlay & H. de Gorsse. *Arsène Lupin vs. Sherlock Holmes: The Stage Play*

Séamas Duffy. *Sherlock Holmes in Paris*

Paul Féval. *Gentlemen of the Night; John Devil; The Black Coats ('Salem Street; The Invisible Weapon; The Parisian Jungle; The Companions of the Treasure; Heart of Steel; The Cadet Gang; The Sword-Swallower)*

Emile Gaboriau. *Monsieur Lecoq*

Goron & Emile Gautier. *Spawn of the Penitentiary*

Rick Lai. *Shadows of the Opera: Retribution in Blood; Sisters of the Shadows: The Curse of Cagliostro*

Steve Leadley. *Sherlock Holmes: The Circle of Blood*

Maurice Leblanc. *Arsène Lupin vs. Countess Cagliostro; Arsène Lupin vs. Sherlock Holmes (The Blonde Phantom; The Hollow Nee-dle); The Many Faces of Arsène Lupin*

Gaston Leroux. *Chéri-Bibi; The Phantom of the Opera; Rouletabille & the Mystery of the Yellow Room; Rouletabille at Krupp's*

Richard Marsh. *The Complete Adventures of Judith Lee*

William Patrick Maynard. *The Terror of Fu Manchu; The Destiny of Fu Manchu*

Frank J. Morlock. *Sherlock Holmes: The Grand Horizontals; Sher-lock Holmes vs Jack the Ripper*

Jean Petithuguenin. *The Adventures of Ethel King*

Antonin Reschal. *The Adventures of Miss Boston*

P. de Wattyne & Y. Walter. *Sherlock Holmes vs. Fantômas*

David White. *Fantômas in America*
Pierre Yrondy. *The Adventures of Thérèse Arnaud*

## SCREENPLAYS

Mike Baron. *The Iron Triangle*
Emma Bull & Will Shetterly. *Nightspeeder; War for the Oaks*
Gerry Conway & Roy Thomas. *Doc Dynamo*
Steve Englehart. *Majorca*
James Hudnall. *The Devastator*
Jean-Marc & Randy Lofficier. *Royal Flush*
J.-M. & R. Lofficier & Marc Agapit. *Despair*
J.-M. & R. Lofficier & Joël Houssin. *City*
Andrew Paquette. *Peripheral Vision*
Robert L. Robinson, Jr. *Judex*
R. Thomas, J. Hendler & L. Sprague de Camp. *Rivers of Time*

## NON-FICTION

Stephen R. Bissette. *Blur 1-5. Green Mountain Cinema 1; Teen Angels*
Win Scott Eckert. *Crossovers* (2 vols.)
Jean-Marc & Randy Lofficier. *Shadowmen* (2 vols.)
Randy Lofficier. *Over Here*

## ART BOOKS

J.-M. Lofficier & D. Taylor. *Tongue\*Lash*
Jean-Pierre Normand. *Science Fiction Illustrations*
Raven Okeefe. *Raven's L'il Critters; Rave's Faves*
Randy Lofficier & Raven Okeefe. *If Your Possum Go Daylight...*
Daniele Serra. *Illusions*

## HEXAGON COMICS

Franco Frescura & Luciano Bernasconi. *Wampus*
Franco Frescura & Giorgio Trevisan. *CLASH*
L. Bernasconi, J.-M. Lofficier & Juan Roncagliolo Berger. *Phenix*
Claude Legrand, J.-M. Lofficier & L. Bernasconi. *Kabur*
Franco Oneta. *Zembla*

L. Buffolente, Lofficier & J.-J. Dzialowski. *Strangers: Homicron*
Danilo Grossi. *Strangers: Jaydee*
Claude Legrand & Luciano Bernasconi. *Strangers: Starlock*